THE NISSELINKA CLAIMS

Book 1
Private Ventures

Book 2
Public Company

by Robert Longe

Suite 300 - 990 Fort St
Victoria, BC, Canada, V8V 3K2
www.friesenpress.com

Copyright © 2015 by Robert Longe
First Edition — 2015

Edited by Michael Kenyon

Cover designed by and maps prepared by Alan Davidson of
    Current Creative Group

Portrait on cover page courtesy of Kamloops Museum & Archives
    (photograph 370)

Scene of Coast Range mountains on cover page by permission of Donna Balfanz

Map inside front cover from Annual Report of the British Columbia Minister
    of Mines for 1914, page K192

Access to libraries and archives provided by:
    Vancouver Public Library
    The Royal BC Museum, BC Archives
    Land Title & Survey Authority of British Columbia

Catalogue data available from Library and Archives Canada

All rights reserved. No part of this publication may be reproduced
in any form, or by any means, electronic or mechanical, including
photocopying, recording, or any information browsing, storage, or
retrieval system, without permission in writing from the publisher.

This is a work of fiction. Except for certain actual persons who
lived in the historical times described, no character in the story is
intended to resemble any actual person, living or deceased.

ISBN
978-1-4602-5294-9 (Hardcover)
978-1-4602-5295-6 (Paperback)
978-1-4602-5296-3 (eBook)

1. FIC014000   FICTION / *Historical*
2. HIS006020   HISTORY / *Canada / Post-Confederation (1867 To Present)*
3. TEC026000   TECHNOLOGY & ENGINEERING / *Mining*

Distributed to the trade by The Ingram Book Company

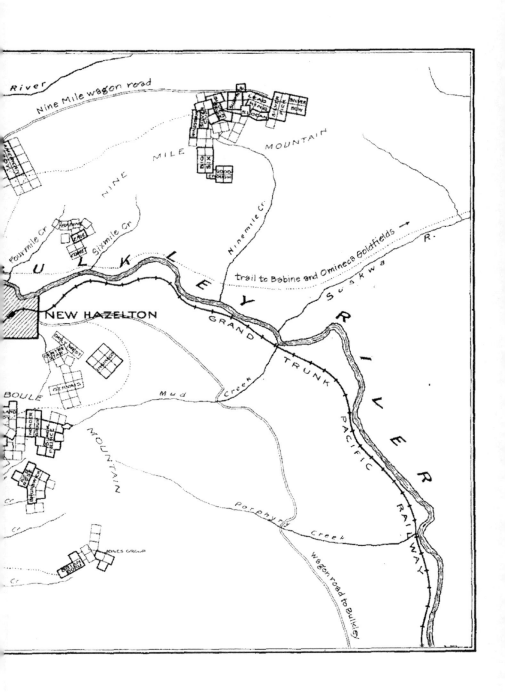

Acknowledgements

I wish to thank all those who have given their time to comment, advise and correct earlier versions of this book. I am particularly indebted to: Jack Marr (author of "A Gem of a Town") for early encouragement and to Colleen Miller, Rick Conte, John Kalmet and Byron Richards. Their comments and contributions have ranged from matters of historical fact to style and content, and have led to a much improved story. Among family members, my son Robin helped with initial editing and with legal aspects of the story, and his brother, Jonathan, provided invaluable technical support. My daughters-in-law, Natalie and Becky both made useful suggestions. Information on specific topics, including amateur hockey, and the history of Smithers and Old Hazelton was provided by Brian Abraham and Tom Schroeter. Colin Thomas, following an initial review, made editorial suggestions. Alan Davidson of Current Creative prepared the illustrations with patience and skill. Michael Kenyon's detailed and expert editing made major improvements to the final text.

Book 1 required research into historical events and cultural practices in the early and middle nineteenth century. For this work, the B.C. Archives, the Vancouver Public Library, and the knowledgeable and helpful staff in both of these institutions were invaluable. At the Land Title and Survey Authority of B.C., Calvin Woelke's diligence and knowledge of the archives led to the original, nineteenth century plat on which one of the illustrations is based.

The museums, tourist centres, and archive repositories to be found in Smithers, Hazelton, Terrace and Prince Rupert provided numerous nuggets of information which would have been hard or impossible to find without a visit. Some of these are typescripts of journals and memoirs which are unlikely to have been distributed beyond their town of origin.

Author's Note

This is a story about settlers, prospectors, and junior mining, an extraordinary, multi-faceted industry in which I have had the privilege of working for many years. The industry is populated by a diverse network of prospectors, financiers, promoters, scoundrels, geologists, technicians and lawyers, driven by their chosen mix of adventure, treasure hunting, greed, fame, scientific curiosity, camaraderie and commitment.

The story follows three generations of a family working as settlers, prospectors and citizen soldiers, as they experience the dreams, disappointments and rewards of owning mineral claims in a remote part of British Columbia.

Book 1, "Private Ventures" covers the lives of the first two generations, starting in the early years of the twentieth century and ending in the 1980s. Book 2. "Public Company" describes an adversarial relationship between the third generation to own the claims and the combative promoter of a junior public company.

This is a work of fiction. Neither the Nisselinka mountains, nor the geographic sites within them, exist, but other places mentioned are real, as are the historical events and the persons associated with them. None of the fictional characters in the book is intended to resemble any real person, living or deceased.

Illustrations

Inside front cover
Mineral Claims in the Vicinity of Hazelton, British Columbia, from Annual Report of Minister of Mines, 1914, with minor adjustments to improve legibility

Chapter 7
Prospector's sketch

Chapter 9
Surveyor's plat 1895

A Glimpse Ahead

to July, 1986

Unless you were to count an owl disturbed during what should have been his period of rest, there was no one to see a man, axe in hand, striding, scrambling and running through a forest on the south slope of the Nisselinka mountains in central British Columbia. Like a competitor in a long-distance race, the man knew he was physically incapable of moving faster without jeopardizing his ability to sustain his pace over several miles. Every fifteen or twenty feet, he raised his axe and with a short glancing blow removed a thin layer of bark from one of the jack pines that made up most of the vegetation. Where the forest was more open, with patches of grass between the trees, he pulled orange plastic tape from one of his pockets, tore off some eighteen inches, and tied it to a shrub or low-hanging branch. Periodically, he used his left hand to flip open the case of a small compass suspended from a cord around his neck and held it horizontal for a moment. The most audible sounds were the ringing of his axe against a tree, the scraping and snapping of undergrowth being pushed aside and, if you could have been close enough, the man's panting. During one of those two-second pauses, when he stopped to read his compass, the man heard a distant rhythmic thudding, which would have spurred him, if that had been possible, to greater exertion. Two minutes later, all sounds were swamped by the noise of a helicopter moving slowly from behind until it was directly overhead. The man stopped, stood absolutely still, and cursed. As he heard the sound of the helicopter moving away, the man started again on his urgent passage through the undergrowth.

His path, dead straight to the north, took him into a gully where trees yielded to a thicket of tag alder and its ground-hugging branches. The man's right boot landed on one of these lying on the sloping ground and concealed by leaves. Without any traction the boot slipped rapidly downhill to the left, pitching its owner to the

A Glimpse Ahead

right. He took the fall with his shoulder while keeping his axe off the ground. Winded, he picked himself up, swore again, and continued, conscious of a twig which had fallen between his neck and collar and was now digging into his spine. The forest of tag alder ended against a large rock which the man climbed on his way out of the gully. As he emerged into woodland, he heard the helicopter land a couple of hundred yards to his front and right and, a minute later, take off again.

The man's purpose was to acquire the legal rights to the minerals below the ground before these rights were claimed by others. He was there because the mineral claims had been in his family for three generations. First staked by his grandfather, who had discovered copper on the ground seventy-five years earlier, the ground had been maintained by his father, and then passed on to him. He was determined not to be the first in his family to lose the ground to a gang of claim jumpers. But he had a fight on his hands and he knew it was just beginning. His competitor was well organized, well equipped and apparently unconstrained by the rules of decent business conduct.

That was in 1986. The story begins with those who staked the claims at the beginning of the century and then struggled to develop them.

Book 1
Private Ventures

Chapter 1

Edward

Raised in Victoria in the 1880s, Edward Wickford grew up with a determination to put a significant distance between himself and anything that resembled poverty. By the time he left home, he was well aware that western Canada had provided opportunities for men who started with little and accumulated fortunes. He followed the progress of the CPR as it joined British Columbia to the rest of Canada. He knew about the wealth being generated in the forests and the mines, the latter in particular. At the age of eighteen he volunteered, in return for a token wage, to help take a flock of sheep from the Gulf Islands to the miners in the Klondike. But by that time the gold fields around Dawson were well staked and the opportunities limited. Heading south on his own, he arrived in Atlin towards the end of the summer of 1899. Through a combination of cash from his Klondike adventure, luck, and a certain shrewdness, he gained ownership of a small but rich placer claim, which he and others exploited and then sold. In 1900 he returned to Victoria with enough money to impress the local bank manager, with self confidence earned in the bush and bars of the north, and with dreams of making a fortune. Above average height but not enough to stand out in a crowd, Edward Wickford appeared as yet another confident young man about to secure his place in a bountiful and exciting world.

After working on a number of construction sites, Edward bid on a job himself and succeeded in completing the project to his own satisfaction and to that of his client. The team he formed became permanent and led to a business which provided him with a reasonable income. He demanded a lot of his workers, some of whom found him too harsh. But, by looking after the interests of those who remained in his employ, Edward earned a loyalty which would serve him well.

Chapter 1 — Edward

While in Vancouver with a contract to build three houses, Edward met Florence, one of four sisters from a family headed by a well-established timber merchant. "Flo", as she was known in the family, was an attractive brunette with an easy self confidence, which sometimes extended to mischievous challenges to accepted social norms.

Over the objections of the merchant's wife, anticipating the decision of his eldest daughter, and recognizing some of his own attributes in the young man, the *pater familias* offered Edward a job in his own organization. But Edward was a man with a mission and the mission came first. After negotiations with the man Edward hoped would become his father-in-law, he arranged to postpone his involvement with the timber company. Then, after Florence had accepted a secret betrothal, he headed north in the spring of 1906. He had come to believe that there was a future in the Bulkley Valley. Arable land was available, timber licenses were being sold along the Skeena River, the mining potential was reported to be high and there was talk of another railway to the coast. Edward's plans were taking shape as he journeyed north by sea, paddle steamer and then by stagecoach along the wagon road. Over the summer he would select promising land and purchase a sufficient quantity to ensure a reasonable living, while prospecting the surrounding country and watching the land appreciate in value.

His mission accomplished, he returned to Vancouver at the beginning of October. Although Florence had kept her secret, the rest of the family had placed their bets, most of them on an engagement before year-end. And so it was. Over the cautions and mutterings of Florence's mother, the couple became formally engaged and, amidst a volatile mix of their parents' divergent opinions and their own envy, Florence's sisters agreed that Edward was a "very rough diamond". They were married in New Westminster on December 15, 1907.

Within a year of their marriage, Florence and Edward, or "Ned" as he was known, had spent their first summer on the land Edward had purchased, Florence returning to New Westminster for the winter. Like most settlers, they found the work hard and the living uncomfortable. But they were not alone and they shared with other settlers a confidence in their own abilities and their future.

Chapter 2

An Incident

After arriving in the Bulkley Valley in 1906, Edward had acquired some land by "pre-emption," a process which was available to settlers and promoted by the government as part of its policy of settling the north. A year later he bought an adjacent patch of uncleared land, much of which was available because many would-be settlers found that clearing acres of aspen and poplar was too arduous and the winters too severe. Now, after over three years of toil, and with over three hundred acres adjacent to the wagon road from Hazelton to Aldermere, he made a reasonable living selling hay, milk and sometimes a steer or two. Hay was the main source of revenue as it was usually in demand for the horses and mules taking supplies and goods from Hazelton to the settlements along the valley. Like the other settlers, he anticipated the completion of the Grand Trunk Pacific Railway with mixed feelings. Goods from the rest of the dominion would become more available and cheaper, but less of his hay would be required for the pack trains. On the other hand the expected influx of additional settlers should make his land more valuable.

Edward's wife joined him in 1908, bringing with her their first child. Brought up in New Westminster, Florence had no experience of pioneering or of the north. Several of her friends had advised against going. But she had married Edward and the north was to be their life and that was that. She was comfortable with their decision and her commitment. The first summer had been exciting and she remained comfortable with the challenges until the reality of the first winter caused her to wonder what she had undertaken. But she remained committed and came to think of herself as a capable and resourceful settler's wife. Numerous other settlers were working their land between Moricetown and Aldermere and most were within half a day's ride. In any emergency a settler could count on neighbours to help and now, with a

Chapter 2 — An Incident

general store in Aldermere, there were opportunities to meet and talk with other wives and mothers.

During her second summer in the north, after a severe winter, there was an incident which Florence found both disturbing and reassuring. This was a year when a short supply of hay had escalated prices along the wagon roads between Hazelton and Fort George. Edward and two Indians were removing stumps of aspen and poplar while Harry Wiggin, the fifteen-year-old son of neighbours, was employed selling hay from a temporary stall where Edward's land joined the wagon road. First thing each morning the men would toss a score of bales down from the loft and load them onto a stone boat. Harry would hitch up the draft horse and escort the bales up to the wagon road. He'd stay there and sell hay to passing teamsters at the price of $7.50 a bale, about three times the normal price, but the going rate at that time. The wagon trains heading south were unlikely to pay such a price as they were only two days out of Hazelton and were usually well supplied. On the other hand, many of those heading west from Quesnel or Fort George counted on hay being available en route. "Hay for sale" was a welcome sign, but the price, when they heard it, was not. On most occasions the buyer bought fewer bales than he needed. When someone grumbled about the price, Harry would always say he didn't set the price and that other people paid it because hay was hard to find.

It was about midday when Edward and his workers stopped for a break after making slow progress with three very large stumps. The sky was clear and the winter's cover of snow had been reduced to a few inches on the open ground. Working conditions were good and the stumps were easily towed away by the single horse with them that day. A frost overnight had turned yesterday's melt into a thin crust of ice, which was why sound travelled well, and they could hear voices raised from the wagon trail where Harry was selling.

"What the hell's that all about?"

"Sounds like an argument."

Edward got up, grabbed the rest of the bread and ham which made his lunch. "I'd better go and see. Carry on with that next stump when you've eaten."

There was only a quarter of a mile, most of it slightly uphill, to the wagon road. Edward started off with the long, loping stride of a farmer. He had not gone far when he saw Harry heading downhill towards him at a run. Edward quickened his pace and it was not long before the two met in the middle of the field, both out of breath.

Edward, seeing no need to prompt an explanation, waited for Harry to get his wind back.

"Wouldn't pay the price! Said it was too much. Took four bales, paid $5.00 each. I said he couldn't do that and I started to take them back. Then he pointed a gun at me. Told me to go back home."

Edward's concern turned to anger. "Damn thief!" Then, putting his anger aside, he made sure that Harry was listening attentively. "You know the riverside trail that leads from my barn towards Moricetown?"

"Yeah."

"Get yourself down there where it crosses Stony creek. I'll get my horse and meet you there. We'll go through Marlow's land and intercept the bandit before the wagon road hits the river."

They each turned downhill and went their separate ways at a gentle run. Some twenty minutes later, Edward, riding his horse at a canter, saw Harry waiting at the appointed place. "You're not too heavy. Can you get up behind me?"

"Yeah. I used to do that with my brother."

After fifteen minutes at a steady trot the riders came to the intersection of the narrow trail with the wagon road and dismounted. Edward tied up the horse, slid his gun from its saddle holster, and explained what he wanted. "We're going to get the money or the hay but I don't want to put you in danger. Your father would never forgive me. All I want from you is to know we have the right wagon train. You have to identify the bandit. They should be here in a few minutes. Unless they stopped to feed the horses."

"I know the horses were hungry. They were trying to get at the hay."

"Then we may have more time. Let's find a branch or log we can pull across the road."

The available branches were lighter than what Edward wanted, but without an axe the heavier logs would have taken too long to move. After they had dragged enough vegetation onto the road to cause any horse or mule to stop, they took up a position from which they could look south along the road for some two hundred yards.

Harry made no attempt to conceal his excitement at the prospect of action. "Will they come soon?"

Chapter 2 — An Incident

"Perhaps, but if the horses are really hungry, he might have a hard time getting them moving again until they've had some of the hay they were smelling."

"Are you going to shoot?"

"Not if I can help it. Remember, I don't want you in the action. Just stay here in the trees and—"

"They're coming!"

"Are you sure it's the one who took the hay?"

Harry didn't answer as he strained to get a better view. It was not more than a minute before all eight horses came into view. The four rear horses were carrying bales of hay. "That's him. That's him."

Edward put a hand on Harry's shoulder. "Wait till they have to stop."

After another minute, the lead horse reached the blockage and came to a halt. A man in a newish hat and a frayed coat came forward and started pulling branches to the side.

At this point Edward whispered to Harry: "Stay here." Experience in the bush camps had taught him the value of bluff, that it could be a useful tool if performed with perfect timing and utter confidence.

He stepped out of the trees onto the road, gun in hand. "You are surrounded. There are three guns pointed at you and your horses. You owe me ten for the hay you bought. Pay now or we'll take your goods for payment."

"I'll have the law on you!" shouted the teamster.

"The law doesn't like thieves. You paid twenty. The price of four was thirty. If you don't pay, we will take enough from your horses to make up the difference."

Muttering an oath, the man fumbled in a leather bag, took out a handful of change and moved as if to hand it to Edward.

"Don't come near me," Edward barked. "Put it on that log there, the one with no snow, so I can see."

The man did so. Without another word, with his gun in his left hand, Edward pulled a branch from the road and signalled to his adversary to remove the rest. These were quickly cleared and the wagon train moved on, Edward watching until they were out of sight around the next corner a hundred and fifty yards away.

"Let's go," he called as he beckoned to Harry who had remained hidden among the trees.

Harry emerged grinning. "That was good. But next time I don't want to stay in the trees."

"Thank you, Harry. You did just what I wanted. Time to go home. And I need to talk to your father."

It was not long after that incident that all of Aldermere and most of the travellers who stopped there had heard the story. The reaction of Harry's father was predictable. As the family were warming themselves by the kitchen stove that evening, Archie Wiggin, looking at his wife, explained yet again his reaction to the day's event: "That's good! Good for Ned and good for Harry." Putting an arm on his son's shoulder, he continued: "I'm not sure I could have done that myself with Harry watching. I would have wanted him out of the way." Then, after a pause, he changed to the broader consequences. "You know, that's the second hay grab I've heard of. Maybe that'll stop them."

Edward wasn't sure how Florence would respond so he opened with a casual mention. "A little incident selling hay today. But we sold most of the bales we took to the road."

Florence looked up from the kitchen table but continued kneading the bread.

"What sort of incident?"

"Someone tried to steal hay from Harry by paying less than the price. The teamster pointed a gun at him."

Florence glanced back from her work at the stove and asked: "Pointed a gun at a child?"

"Well, at fifteen he's hardly a child, almost a man. But I agree it was outrageous."

"So what happened?"

Edward sat down and leaned back in his chair. "Harry and I rode along the river trail and intercepted them on the road beyond the Marlow farm."

"They paid up?"

"Yes. I had a gun. I made sure Harry was in the trees, out of the action."

"You threatened the man?"

"Well, the gun was pointed at the ground, but towards him. He could see I was serious. I told him there were two other guns pointed at him. Not true of course."

"So he paid?"

"Yes. Then we let him continue."

"But you held him up at gunpoint?" Florence turned to face her husband with her hands on her hips: "You could go to jail."

Chapter 2 — An Incident

"I don't think so. He's not going to lodge a complaint. In any case, I was just taking back what he had stolen."

"I don't like it. This is not the wild west."

"I know. But we are on a transportation route. Anyone coming from Fort George or anywhere else in the interior comes along our road. So we get a lot of strangers."

The following morning, Florence, grateful to a neighbour for offering to mind her toddler and baby, rode to a neighbouring farm a mile east of the wagon road to collect a bag of flour and other staples from her friend Jill Milford.

The two women often saved time by taking turns with their grocery runs to town. It was efficient and gave them a chance to visit. For Jill, who was approaching middle age and had been in the valley for several years, the friendship was a opportunity to pass on some of the knowledge and experience she had acquired.

Florence started the conversation with the topic on her mind. "Did you hear what my Edward was up to yesterday?"

"Sure did. And young Harry, too."

"The valley used to be so peaceful."

Jill expressed her sense of outrage by standing back with her hands on her hips. "Just think what that teamster did. "Pulling a gun over some bales of hay!"

"Yeah. And Edward staging a holdup on the wagon road. I don't like it."

"Well. You can't blame Edward. All he was doing is taking back what someone had stolen."

"That's what he says, too."

"You wouldn't want a husband who just said 'That's too bad.' There will always be some people who will walk all over others."

Florence was quick to respond. "But to hold up a man at gunpoint for just ten dollars? That's less than a week's wage for a farm hand!"

"Some men are like that and maybe Edward's one of them. Stolen is stolen, whether it's one dollar or a hundred."

"That's my Edward all over. There are not many shades between black and white for him. It's either right or wrong."

Florence fell silent.

Jill continued: "You know, it makes us all safer. The word gets out. Travellers get to know that you don't mess around with the people living here. You're probably proud of him."

Florence smiled and took a while to reply. "Yes. I suppose so. But I try not to think like that."

Jill had to ask the obvious question. "What would your family think?"

"Oh. I'm not sure I want to be asked that." She paused then continued. "Well, my father. He would laugh, puff out his chest and tell all his friends!"

Jill laughed. "Oh, my father is the same."

Both women were enjoying their conversation as it began to look into deeper layers of their pasts.

"But then his friends would tell their wives," said Florence, "and that's how my mother would hear about it."

Jill was not going to let it stop there. "And?"

"That would become a problem. Perhaps it really will. But that's New Westminster, not here!"

They both laughed.

Chapter 3

Opportunity
July 1910

Edward Wickford was walking home from the seven-acre meadow he had been clearing for the last three years. He had more to do, but that would have to wait for fall. The first crop of hay was already in the barn, and the second was growing well. The incline he had been climbing for ten minutes made him breathe deeply. There were three hours of daylight left, but the sun was already casting long shadows from aspen and pine that formed the sparse woodland through which he was walking. He turned at the crest of the hill to look at a view he always enjoyed. To the west the meadow spread below him, with the Bulkley River beyond. After pulling a much-treasured pocket watch from his vest, he smiled, turned again, and with breath to spare for this easy downhill trail, found himself whistling a tune from his childhood. He had plenty of time. Ten minutes on the trail, half an hour for a bath in the outside shed where he had arranged a stove and system of pipes, while Florence finished preparing the meal.

As he came down the trail, he looked with satisfaction at the house he had built, rough though it was. The walls and pillars were made from local logs, peeled by axe. The floors were planks he and a neighbour had whipsawed two years ago. The roof was of cedar shakes he had split himself. Above the basement and crawl space, which served for storage, was a main floor and veranda. The upper floor was a single attic room. The main appliance was a kitchen stove hauled in pieces from the Hudson Bay store. And inside the house he would find Florence and their children.

As he approached the house a child's face appeared at one of the windows and immediately disappeared. But not for long. Jeffrey came running out to meet him, followed by Annabel.

Edward bent down, picked up one, and then the other, and continued to the back of the house.

"Down you go so I can take my boots off."

"There's a man here!" said Jeffrey.

"Do you know his name?"

"I don't know. He just said he wanted to see you."

Florence appeared, wearing an apron, and smiling at her brood and her husband. "There's an Indian who wants to see you. He's waiting for you on the veranda. Supper will be ready in about an hour. And the children are expecting their turn."

Instead of going through the house, Edward walked around and approached the veranda from the outside. He was pleased to find as he walked up the steps that he recognized the man who greeted him. He'd hired Charley Raven some four years ago for a spell of fencing: miles and miles of tripod uprights and cross beams, all of pine logs, each of which had to be felled and limbed. Hard work at the best of times, it had been particularly tough during the hot August of 1906. Charley had been a very good worker, strong, reliable and possessed of a good sense of humour. Then, after ten days on the job, he just announced he had to go home. Edward found others to assist him, but none as good as Charley.

Edward, took the veranda steps in few strides, and extended his hand: "How are you, Charley?"

"I'm well, Mr. Wickford. Thank you. Your place is looking good."

"Thank you, Charley. And so it should. I've put a quite a bit of time into it, as you know. What about you? Where've you been?"

"I went back to the reservation. Then I needed some money so I went on a fish boat, but I got restless and went hunting." Charley paused.

Edward motioned him to sit down and pulled up another rough wooden chair for himself.

"Hunting?"

"I hunted some of the time but mostly I just walked. When I was a young man, my uncle took me on a long trip up the mountains."

"The Nisselinka Range?"

"I think so, but we never called it that."

"Go on, Charley."

"This time I went by myself."

"Just living off the land?"

"Yes. There were plenty of fish, and spruce hen. In the mountains I could snare marmots and squirrels."

Chapter 3 — Opportunity

"It's three years since you were here," said Edward who remained puzzled as to the purpose of Charley's visit. "You must have been gone for months."

"Yes. I was in those mountains for nine weeks. I remember how you showed me some minerals and said that you would like to know if I found any myself."

"That's right. So what did you find?"

Charley reached down beside him to a leather shoulder bag and pulled out three lumps of rock about the size of large potatoes. Parts of them were rusty, parts a shiny yellow with small patches of green.

Edward held out his hand and, as they were passed to him, examined each rock closely.

"Looks like the real stuff: chalcopyrite! And, I think, a bit of silver glance. Is there much of it around, Charley?"

"All these rocks are from the same pile at the foot of a hill. I don't know where they come from, but they're easy to find and there are lots of them."

"Well it's your find, what are you going to do with it?"

"I can't do very much. I don't know about minerals at all. And Indians can't own mineral land."

Edward responded with an impassive expression concealing any embarrassment he might have had. "Well, here is a suggestion. You and I could go to see it. How long would it take?"

"If we can get horses it would take six or seven weeks to get there and back to the town."

Edward leaned forward, his interest evident. "Starting from Aldermere? Telkwa?"

"We have to go through Hazelton, so it would be best to start there."

Edward nodded. "Good. That would be the place to put together the pack train. We could get just about everything we needed at the store there." By now pacing the veranda, he was thinking aloud: "We would need to get the right people. People we know from around here. How many? You, me, a couple of helpers good with axe and shovel, cook, wrangler, a prospector. That sound about right?"

"That's about right. The wrangler might need a helper."

"How many horses? Mules?"

"We'll have to make our own trail. Horses would be better."

Edward, now sitting down, was still thinking aloud. "So two, no, three weeks to get in, three to get out, one on site. That would take the month of September, and more." He shifted in his chair then, looked directly at Charley. "After I have seen what you have found, and if I think something could be done with it, we could become partners."

Charley's expression displayed a hesitant satisfaction. "That would be good."

Edward was feeling almost apologetic: "You know, your name wouldn't show on the ownership. It just wouldn't be allowed. You would just have to trust me."

"I will trust you, Mr. Wickford."

"Then if we had to raise money to dig a tunnel, we would both have to give up most of the ownership to the people putting up the money."

"Whatever you say, Mr. Wickford."

"I'll be back in a moment." Edward got out of his chair and walked round the house to the kitchen window. Florence opened the window to talk to him. He could tell from her expression that he was already out of favour for being late and that his request was not going to be well received.

"Sorry to get tied up like this, but can we handle another for supper? I'd like to have mine on the deck with Charley."

She looked less than delighted. "It's not the best day. We don't have a lot as tomorrow is my day in the village, but I half expected you to ask. We'll stretch the portions."

Edward could see irritation in her eyes. Then it changed to just a hint of a smile. He blew her a kiss and left with a wave. "You're marvellous."

"Ten minutes. You'll have to make your peace with Jeffrey. He was expecting the story you promised him."

Back on the veranda, Edward sat down again opposite Charley. "How about some stew? We'll have it here."

Chapter 4

Family Discussion
July 1910

"I don't like ham!" said Jeffrey, emphasizing his point by pushing his plate to the middle of the table.

Florence turned from the stove and looked at her son. "You liked smoked ham when we had it a month ago."

"But that was before you sold Pog."

Florence glanced at her husband, as if to say she expected him to carry the argument for the next stage.

Edward picked up the ball: "I bought this in Aldermere six days ago at the butcher's shop. I didn't sell Pog and the other pig until four days ago. So don't worry. You're not going to eat Pog. Next time I'm buying meat what would you like me to get?"

"Do all pigs get eaten?"

"Most do. If they're lucky they lead happy lives and then it's all over."

"I'd rather be a cow—no, a bull."

"Lot's of them get eaten too. People have to eat. People can't just eat vegetables," said Edward before changing the subject and addressing Florence as well as Jeffrey. "Much more important, I want to tell you about the prospecting trip I'm going on. I'm going to look for minerals. You remember Charley who came to see me a few days ago?"

Jeffrey was evidently interested. "The Indian?"

"That's right. A good man. He has offered to show me where he found some copper. I think I should go and see it. It will take us a bit more than a month. Do you all think you can manage while I'm away?"

"Can I come?" said Jeffrey.

"Not this time. I'd like to have you but you will have to be a bit older."

"Copper? Eat it?" asked Annabel with her mouth full of potato.

Edward watched his wife grimace, then smile, but she said nothing. It was up to him to answer Annabel's question. "No, copper's not for eating. But, if there is enough of it, we could get rich."

Annabel looked puzzled so Edward continued: "And, if we get rich, we could buy whatever food you like."

"Then we could get a motor car," said Jeffrey, "and I could drive it."

"Yes, if we had lots of money we could, but the road to town would have to be better or we'd get stuck all the time. I hear they're not as reliable as horses."

After Jeffrey and Annabel had been read their stories and put to bed, Edward and Florence sat on the veranda, each holding a large mug of tea. Edward was aware that he had some persuading to do. "I can hire someone to look after the farm. Roland said he would lend me one of his men. Says he's very reliable."

"You're talking of going how many miles?"

"Must be at least seventy, could be more."

"And there is no trail?"

"It starts with an old grease trail, the one to the Omenica gold fields. Then we'd be off the beaten track."

"Rivers to cross?"

"Charley said there are two. They don't sound too difficult."

Florence looked unconvinced. "I'm just wondering if it's really worth it. What if you come back with a broken leg, or what if you don't come back at all? We're just beginning to make this farm work."

Realizing that this was one of those moments when a husband and wife had different priorities, Edward took a few seconds before he replied. "The farm will probably provide us with a reasonable living for as long as we are young and healthy. But if we had to sell it now, we would not get much for it. If I found a good mineral showing there would be lots of possible buyers. I admit I like prospecting and would like to make a big find. In this case I also think it would be good for the family."

"Do you think it's really a good idea to risk the whole thing just for the possibility of some mineral?"

Edward tensed slightly in his chair and looked directly at his wife. "You know I've always been a prospector. In fact, I've made quite a bit of money at it. I told you about Atlin. If I hadn't done that we wouldn't have this farm now or, if we did, we'd be struggling

Chapter 4 — Family Discussion

without enough land or the ability to buy another horse or cow when we need it. We've got one of the best houses around here. Look at that place north of here, just before the river. They've still got a dirt floor and sod roof. Not many families have the sort of stove we got for the kitchen. My prospecting has to take a lot of the credit."

"But that was when you were a single man. Now it's different. We've been toiling for almost four years here. This farm's coming along because we made a commitment. Without that it won't work."

"We'll hire whatever help we need while I am away."

Long before she uttered a word Florence's growing discomfort with the plan was broadcast by the expression on her face. "You mean I can hire them, direct them and supervise them, all with the children to look after, and you away for two months? That wasn't what I agreed to. When you asked me to marry you, you talked about my helping on the farm. You never said you would leave me doing it all, with you away for months at a time!"

"Look. We're trying to make a living for ourselves, trying to be independent. Would you want me working as an employee somewhere? Dependent on others for the bread on our table? Men who work for others can get laid off anytime. Look at the situation your sister is in with a husband without a job."

"That's not fair. He'll get another job. And he won't leave his wife on her own for months at a time."

Edward winced, took a breath and spoke slowly. "I'm the breadwinner. You have to trust me. We can't afford to pass up opportunities. All that country beyond the Babine Range. It's wide open. No one knows what will be discovered there."

Florence stood up and faced her still-seated husband. "I can't stand this. I'm going to bed."

Watching his wife depart, Edward felt he should say something. He managed a "Good night." It didn't feel right and his wife's reply, if there was one, was inaudible. With a frown and pursed lips he slumped into his chair and looked at the thunderclouds hanging over the western mountains. After staring at them for a few minutes, he stood up, walked into the kitchen, poured some rye whiskey into a small brown mug and went back to his chair on the veranda.

Chapter 5

First Expedition
August, 1910

Among the itinerants, drifters and fortune seekers to be seen in the Bulkley Valley during the summer months there were always young men looking for opportunities to earn a few dollars. Most farmers took on one or two when they could afford the extra cost, but Edward's enquiries of his neighbours as to whether they knew of any men suitable for his expedition had yielded only one name. Although men in search of work could always be found in Hazelton, he wanted those who came with recommendations from people he knew. Reluctantly, he put out the word about an expedition to follow up a new mineral find, and men started appearing at the farm, while others left messages or letters at the general store in Aldermere.

By the end of August Edward had three men selected. The first to come to the farm in search of a place on the expedition was Peter Cooper who, presenting himself as a miner from Vancouver Island, had Edward's immediate attention. "I've read about the coal mines in Cumberland. Are they as dangerous as we've heard?"

"That's why I came north. I've seen three men killed right close to me. Nearly was myself a couple of times."

"Explosions?"

"Yeah, and rock falls."

"Looking for something safer?"

"That's what I want. Met a girl but she wouldn't marry me unless I quit the coal mines."

"So you could drive a tunnel?"

Peter nodded. "Hand drilling, blasting, mucking out, all that."

Edward felt he should challenge his first impression by thinking of reasons why this miner might not be exactly the man he was

Chapter 5 — First Expedition

looking for. "The rock we have will be much harder than in the coal mines."

"That just takes longer."

"And your girl. Where is she?"

"Waiting for me. She's in Comox."

Rus and Frank were among others who turned up at the farm. They'd had plenty of experience in the bush, were very keen and came with recommendations from farmers farther down the valley. After Edward had described his prospect and the skills he was seeking, he offered the three men a period of trial employment: a week's work on his farm at $2.50 a day with two meals and accommodation in the barn included. Peter Cooper was glad to accept, as were Rus and Frank. More applicants showed up during the trial week but Edward was pleased with his selections and had to disappoint them. At the end of the week the three were told what equipment to bring and to be at Hazelton for the trial pack scheduled for noon on the day before departure.

On a cold afternoon in the late summer of 1910, Edward Wickford was in Hazelton looking over the six packhorses fully loaded for a dry run. The horses and seven men were due to set off at dawn the following day. All the supplies had been assembled in the yard behind the Inlander hotel. Four of the six animals had matched pairs of wooden boxes strapped across their backs. One of the others carried a smaller pair of metal boxes, each with iron hasps to hold the straps. Another had a balanced pair of larger, softer loads, mostly of tentage. Each box and contents had been weighed before being placed on the back of a horse. Weights were written on each box, together with the name of the horse destined to carry it.

The transportation of supplies was in the hands of two wranglers, each utterly different from his partner, but together forming a team with an enviable reputation. These were the men on whom Edward was going to depend for moving the team's goods and supplies for the next six to eight weeks. Syd Dods was a jack-of-all trades. Daniel O'Toole, called "Danno" by anyone who had worked with him, was a slight and wiry man normally seen with a wispy beard. Danno was well known in the valley for his abilities and his habit of saying more to horses than to people. His replies to questions were short, usually no more than one or two words: "Yes," "No," "Not there," or "Too much." He was by no means inarticulate. Danno just said very little, except to horses. To horses he was always saying something; to men nothing, until he had something important to communicate. And if anyone were to strike one of his horses, the act would trigger him into releasing a stream of eloquent invective the offender was unlikely to forget. Not as famous as Caux, who handled pack trains on established routes, such as between Hazelton and Fort George, Danno was known for taking his animals along lesser routes. He was paid by the number of horses and the time travelled, not by weight and distance as Caux was.

Edward looked at his watch and turned towards a group of men. "Morning Rus, morning Peter. Hullo Charley. Fred, I didn't expect to see you. I hope I made it clear that we have everyone we need."

"Yes, Mr. Wickford, but I came just in case you need another one."

"I would like to take you on but it isn't possible. All those horses and all those bundles are just right for the men we have. No more."

Edward scanned the people who were assembling to watch the trial pack, then turned back to the men he had been talking to. "Where's Frank?"

The replies gave him the answer he didn't want to hear. "Haven't seen him." "Not here yet."

He opened his watch again. "I said noon. He's got five minutes."

By that time both wranglers were standing at his elbow, evidently wanting to talk. He chose to address Syd, not the taciturn Danno. "Is everything on? Are we at the limit?"

Syd looked at the patiently waiting horses and then at the man who knew them so well. On receipt of a nod, Syd pointed at two sturdy looking beasts at the left of the line "Those could take another fifty pounds each but best to leave them as they are. They'll be fine until we leave the grease trail. If it gets rough after that, we may need to change the loads."

Edward then pulled a folded piece of paper from his pocket and proceeded to read aloud what he had written. "Staples: enough for more than a month. Tents, beds, cooking equipment, ammunition." Beneath the heading *Mining* he had listed: *mattocks, hammers, moils, drill steel, powder*. After turning three pages, he folded his notes and addressed those around him. "I think we have it all. If

Chapter 5 — First Expedition

not, we'll have to do without. We each have a gun, so meat should be there when we need it. Fish too, perhaps."

He pocketed his list. He knew that if Charley's find was any good he would need to raise money to investigate it further. For this he would have to collect outstanding samples and ship them to Nelson, possibly New York or London. Collecting samples might require blasting, which would require hand steeling. Good samples would be the key. He hoped the loads on return would be as heavy as those he was looking at. He caught Syd's eye. "Shall we unload?"

"Yes, let's do that," replied Syd. "Six o'clock in the morning, did you say?"

"Yes. We will saddle up at six-thirty and be off by seven o'clock. I'll get the hotel to have a mug of tea ready for everyone and something to eat."

With the start time settled, Edward walked over to Peter and Rus who were still at the edge of the crowd. "Frank not here?"

The answers left him in no doubt. Rus was the first to respond. "Not yet."

"He could be here any time," said Peter.

"That's no good. I said noon." Edward then turned to Fred: "You want to do it?"

"Yes, sir. I do."

"You have the right equipment with you?"

"Yes, sir."

"Boots are good?"

"Very good."

"Then you're on. Be here at six am tomorrow."

"Yes, sir. I'll be here."

Edward went over to Charley. "Everything look fine to you, Charley?"

At that moment a young man carrying a heavy pack and breathing heavily came striding up and threw his pack on the ground. "I'm sorry to be late, Mr. Wickford."

Edward faced the panting man, glanced at the pack, and said, "You're too late. I said noon, so the job's gone to someone else."

"But…"

"There is no room for 'buts'. I have to rely on people to follow my instructions. And that's the end of it. The job is filled."

The young man bent down to pick up his pack, then stood up, evidently ready to speak again, but by then Edward had turned

21

and was walking over to the horses, most of which had been freed of their loads.

The next morning Edward Wickford and six others set off walking alongside the horses, four of them well laden, the other two with lighter loads. They took only one dog, Danno's Klip. Part sheep dog, part everything else, Klip was familiar with the horses and they with him. If one got loose and strayed away from camp, Klip could be counted on to round it up.

A day later the seven men and their horses were heading east along the old grease trail along the Suskwa river valley. For the first five days the route lay along established trails and progress was rapid, covering as much as eight miles on one particularly easy day. On most days they maintained a steady pace between one and two miles per hour, but diversions for tributaries or rocky bluffs always slowed progress. Then one morning Charley increased his pace to take himself ahead of the horses. When they caught up with him, he pointed to a narrow trail leading off the well-used path they had been following. "Now we go in the forest."

The deer trail started well enough. Animal trails were useful, but whenever they traversed a north-facing slope, the stops became frequent. Several times each day they had to cut deadfall before the horses could pass. Progress sometimes slowed to less than one mile a day. The all-enclosing forest, the damp, the frequent stops and poor camp sites all contributed to frayed nerves.

One morning, Fred and Rus, bringing up the rear with two horses, took advantage of being out of hearing of the rest of the party. Fred started on a topic of interest to both of them. "I keep thinking about Frank."

"Me too."

"That was harsh. I've been wondering what I've let myself in for."

"Yeah. Can we trust him?"

"I never know what to call him. Syd calls him Edward or Ned. I stick to Mr. or sir. But, yes, I think we can trust him. We just have to perform."

"Or else."

"That's it. Just do what we're told to do."

The first river took them an entire day to cross. Syd waded and swam to the other side with a thin rope, then used it to pull over a heavier rope. Attached to trees on either side of the river, the

Chapter 5 — First Expedition

heavy rope was used to support packages attached to pulleys. It was then lowered to water level and each packhorse, now free of any load, was secured to a sliding loop and sent across the stream. One of them lost its footing but, held by the rope from being swept away, managed to right itself and reach the far bank. An hour before sundown all the men, animals and equipment were on the far side, and the horses were enjoying the lush grass growing at the water's edge. The packages were stacked on a bench of the river some ten feet above water level. One tent was slung beneath a ridgepole supported by a small fir and two squaw poles, the other between two large trees. Fred opened a crate and was whistling as he distributed dry biscuits and beef jerky. A small patch of fading sky was framed by the tops of hemlocks and pine. Charley, having started a small fire with cedar twigs that had been drying on the trunk for years, now added green branches to smoke away the mosquitoes.

Syd folded himself against a log he had just hauled into the clearing around the fire and addressed Charley through the smoke. "You said one of the crossings would be difficult. I suppose this was the easy one?"

Before Charley could answer Edward, still standing, biscuit and jerky in hand, intervened with more than just humour in his tone. "If that was the easy one, you had better go on ahead of us and build a bridge!"

Charley replied, laughing: "That was difficult. Next one easy."

"Wonderful news! Who's cooking?"

Their route through the forest—miles of hemlock, cedar in the lower ground, pine on the ridges—offered little fodder for the horses except when they came to clearings, usually swamps. In many such places they stopped for two or three hours, not knowing how long it might be before the horses would find food again. Where fodder was absent, the horses were given oats, but these had to be carefully rationed.

One evening, when supper was corn-beef from a large can and dough crusted on the open fire, Charley produced a vegetable he had collected, one which neither Edward nor anyone else recognized. At this stage any variation on the dreary fare of bacon, beans and bannock was welcomed.

"Tastes like spinach," commented Syd.

Charley, amused at his companions' apprehension, provided encouragement. "Soon, we reach the mountains, plenty of animals. Fresh meat."

Wrapped in blankets and lying on a bed of fir boughs, which he usually found remarkably comfortable, Edward's thoughts turned to home. He thought of the many tasks he had left behind. Florence, though she did not like his absence and liked even less the risk of this journey into the unknown, had eventually provided encouragement for him to go. Ranching in a new and frontier land was a wonderful way of life, but they both realized they could run into problems, even disasters, at any time. They might be able to build up their herd to sell for a useful sum, but they had watched others struggling with limited success to do the same. On the other hand, mineral finds could generate extraordinary wealth, and this country was almost unexplored.

The new venture, Florence had admitted, might be worth the loss of Edward's time on the farm. The real risk to life and limb was something they did not talk about. And she had acknowledged his interest in minerals since he was at school. She knew that, in addition to standard texts on minerals and geology, he had a collection of papers on discoveries in the province, and he always bought a copy of the Annual Report to the Minister of Mines. She also knew he dreamed of finding an orebody, and playing a role in bringing it to production. And Florence had told him she did not want to be known as a wife who shackled her husband's dreams. Edward rolled over and went to sleep.

One morning in the middle of the second week, Fred and Charley were in the lead, each with his axe. It was hard work. As soon as they had cleared a stretch of trail, the rest of the team and the horses would catch up while the next obstacle was tackled. At times there would be four or five men opening up the trail. After the two of them had pulled a particularly difficult log out of the way, Charley caught Fred's attention and pointed upwards. "More sky. Forest is going."

Fred glanced up. "About time too. I've had enough of this."

"Three more days."

Fred swung his axe into the log, sat down and lit a cigarette. "Three more to what?"

"Open country," said Charley, "grass for horses, no big trees."

Everyone knew the plan was to reach the high ground as soon as possible even if it meant leaving the trail Charley knew.

Chapter 5 — First Expedition

Once above the tree line they would be able to see for miles, and Charley would be able to locate himself again.

Two days later, the team of men and horses was winding its way north in single file through open grassland where the largest of the trees, most of them squat and scrubby, were outsized by the boulders. And the boulders themselves were dwarfed by the craggy cliffs from which they had fallen. Men and horses seemed to share a delight in the open country. No longer were they working their way slowly through the skyless forest with obstacles at every turn. The sky was open; their route could be seen for miles; patches of wild flowers added colour, and their destination, Charley announced, was only two days away.

Chapter 6

Charlie's Find

Edward was apprehensive as they neared their objective. The expedition had been expensive. In the original plan he was to have paid for half the cost of supplies. A friend had talked about participating, but had then decided against it. Syd's and Danno's offer to provide the animals and services for fifteen percent of the find had been withdrawn when they began to understand the magnitude of the task and the risk that they would end up with a percentage of nothing. That left Edward paying one hundred percent, ten percent of which was carried for Charley. What if it turned out to be a disappointment? He had asked Charley many questions about the place where he had found the copper and what the rocks looked like, but still remained anxious as to what he would find. The Inspector of Mines had attended one of his meetings with Charley and had lent his support to the expedition. As described by Charley, it sounded really promising, but much could change in the finding.

After about two hours travel on the morning of the eighteenth day, Charley dropped back from walking the lead horse to talk to Edward who was bringing up the rear. Charley pointed to a cliff and line of boulders about half a mile away. "See those rocks over there?"

Edward nodded.

"That's where the mineral is."

"Is it going to be good, Charley?"

Charley shrugged, laughed, and pointed to a patch of flat ground forward and to the left of the trail: "Good place to camp."

After another mile of easy travel, Charley turned off the trail towards the site he had selected. When they had unloaded and tethered the horses, Syd made an announcement everyone was glad to hear: "Danno and I can do the camp." Looking at Edward with a wry smile, he continued, "Then we will wait for your report

Chapter 6 — Charlie's Find

on whether it was worth coming all this way. Take a gun in case you see a marmot."

Edward needed no further encouragement. He and Charley were soon scrambling over a pile of boulders, most of them grey, some rusty. The boulder field was some hundred yards across and extended to a small cliff. In the distance could be seen other cliffs leading like a staircase to a mountain ridge several miles away. Near the middle of the boulder field, as Charley slowed the pace and began looking around, Edward saw what he had hoped to see, a line of rusty boulders, some with patches of bright green. After the first blow with his eight-pound sledge had shattered a rock the size of a coal scuttle, he felt the journey had not been in vain. The fragments were of a yellow mineral: the copper sulphide, the mineral which could make a mine, together with the common minerals, quartz and some calcite. Charley, appearing very satisfied, looked at Edward for confirmation.

"Good work, Charley! Now we have to see where it comes from."

Just then both men heard a shrill whistle lasting two or three seconds. For a moment Edward thought it might have been a call from the camp, but then he realized it was a marmot's alarm signal. Charley, gun in hand, was already moving rapidly over the boulders in the direction of the whistle. Leaving him to his quest for meat, Edward moved up the hill towards the cliff. Before he reached it, he came to a six-foot ledge which looked like a half-buried version of the cliff ahead of him. In the ledge he could see a streak of rust and the bright green he knew to be an oxide of copper. The vein was about two feet wide where he first saw it. After he had moved a pile of small rocks from the ledge, he could see the exposed vein for seven feet. Where it disappeared under more substantial rocks it had widened to over forty inches. Would it continue to widen, narrow, or disappear? The smooth and level surface of the ledge would make obtaining samples a long, slow process with sledge or moil. Just as he was thinking that blasting should be effective for sampling the vein, he heard a shot ring out. Within a couple of minutes he saw Charley returning across the boulders, gun in one hand, a large marmot hanging from the other.

The next day, while the wranglers and the horses remained in the camp, the others cleared the vein for a further three feet. It maintained most of its width and at the point of disappearance measured thirty-seven inches. The next step would be blasting, but for blasting one had to drill, and drilling the blast holes would be a slow and laborious process.

Just after the sun appeared over the eastern hills the following morning, and with the smell of wood smoke and bacon greeting the men as they came out of their tents, Edward went looking for Fred. He found him sitting on a boulder, sharpening an axe.

"Fred, I'd like you to give Pete a hand today. He'll be drilling the first two blast holes into the vein. He's an old hand, so you may pick up a few tricks."

Fred was always ready to take on a new task and, once he had been told how to do it, could be relied on to do it well. Never quite sure how to address his boss, and in the absence of instructions, he continued with the formal response which Syd and others had dropped.

"Yes, Mr. Wickford."

"Good. I'll be prospecting, but will come by this afternoon to see how you're getting on."

An hour later, Pete and Fred were getting set up on the vein close to its disappearance beneath rubble and boulders. Among the equipment for sampling were three drill steels, one a foot long, the others three. A cold wind was blowing down the valley as Pete looked at the sky. "I think we'll have a dry day. Otherwise we'd have to use water, which would take longer."

Fred needed to make sure Pete understood that his assistant was unskilled. "I've never done this before."

"You'll know all about it by the end of the day. Main thing is to avoid getting hurt."

After they had selected the place for the first blast hole and cleared away rocks, grit, and sand, Pete pointed to the steels lying a few feet away. "Let's start with one of those."

Fred picked up one of the longer rods. "This one do?"

"No, the short one."

Kneeling on one knee next to a crevice in the vein, Pete held the rod in his left hand and used his right to strike the top with a heavy hammer. Then he rotated the rod and struck it again. Fred, watching the procedure produce smidgens of dust at the end of the steel, saw an opportunity to help. "I could hold and turn it while you hit."

"Never! Too damn dangerous. I've seen a guy with his wrists smashed. Another one with a piece of hot metal in his eye. In any

Chapter 6 — Charlie's Find

case the boss said no double jacking. It's a long way to go if you get hurt. I'll let you do it soon."

"The boss, d'you trust him?" asked Fred as Peter put down the hammer.

"Bosses? I've seen so many. Good, bad, and very bad. Some in the mines didn't care a pinch of coal dust for anyone except themselves. What if a man got killed? We'll get another one tomorrow. There's plenty more where he came from. Other bosses seemed to care. Just luck who you get. This one, Mr. Wickford, he's good. You've got to perform or you're out. When there's danger, bosses have to be strong. A weak one's no good, even if he cares about you. Enough of that! Let's get this hole going."

After half an hour the steel was three inches into the rock and Fred had the hang of it. Pete went back to his pile of equipment and returned with what looked like a spoon with a very long handle. "We'll need this when we are down a few more inches to get out the rock dust."

Fred looked up at the spoon and shook his head. "Ought to be machines for doing this."

"Sure," said Pete. "There are steam machines in some of the mines, but they weigh a few tons so we won't see them here. Also compressed air, but we have to use the old way."

By mid-morning the next day, they had reached thirteen inches on the second hole. By the end of the third day the two holes were each over thirty inches deep—sufficient, in Edward's opinion, for the next step.

As with drilling, so with explosives: the old methods had yielded to the new at the more advanced mines and construction sites and, although Edward could have obtained dynamite and the blasting caps to detonate it, he preferred the black powder and safety fuses which he had used many times on the farm for stump removal.

The following day, with the rest of his team at a safe distance, Edward poured a bag and a half of black powder down the holes, attached a fuse consisting of a thin line of powder wrapped in paper. He inserted a wooden plug, which he had shaped to fit the hole, with a slot for the fuse. He gave himself four feet of fuse—enough time, he thought, for an unhurried retreat over the boulder field. He lit it and spent forty of the available hundred-and-eighty seconds reaching the safe point now occupied by Pete and Fred a hundred yards away. As he crouched with them he counted aloud until the charge went off at a hundred and eighty-six. He smiled with satisfaction at the sound, loud and sharp enough, he thought, to have served its purpose. They had been waiting for a minute, when Fred, evidently impressed by his boss and the process said: "Let's go and see."

Edward's reply was instant. "No one goes until I say. We'll wait a full five minutes." And, looking directly at Fred, "I knew a farmer who was stumping and was maimed by a second explosion, a minute or two after the first."

When the three men approached the site, they saw that the vein had been exposed by a hole about two feet deep, eighteen inches wide and two feet long. A large fragment of the vein had been driven sideways towards neighbouring boulders and had remained intact. This would provide the samples he would send to Nelson and perhaps, who knows, to London.

At the end of the long summer day, with the evening meal finished and mosquitoes held at bay by an early frost, seven men were sitting around the fire for a few minutes of relaxation before turning in for the night. Edward, who had been listening to the animated conversation about Charley's discovery, gold and future riches, liked to use the evening to talk about the tasks for the morrow. At an appropriate moment, he took the opportunity to introduce his own topic. "You're right. This has to count as a discovery. No one knows what value it has, but it certainly needs more work. So we have to stake some claims. Have any of you done that?"

There was no reply, except for a few shaking heads.

"Nor have I. I staked some placer claims a few years ago but never any for lode minerals. But I know what we have to do. I'll explain it." He turned away from the fire, picked up a straight stick about six inches long, and pushed one end into the ground so that the stick remained upright. "We start with a Discovery Post. This will be near the vein, near Charley's discovery. It has to be at least four feet long and squared off at the top. We have to write 'Discovery Post' and the name of the claim on it."

By now those who had been sitting on the other side of the fire had come round, bringing their seats, logs or stones, with them. Pete, anticipating the next step, handed his boss another small stick.

"Thank you, Pete. That's what we need, another post. We call this one The Initial Post. We need to know roughly the direction

Chapter 6 — Charlie's Find

the vein is going. The initial post should be on the trend of the vein about seven hundred feet from the discovery."

Rus asked, "Why seven hundred feet?"

"Each claim has to be no more than fifteen hundred feet in length, so we need to start the claim about half that distance from the discovery." Edward stopped talking when a puff of breeze brought smoke from the fire towards them. Once it had cleared, he thrust the second stick into the ground a couple of feet from the first. "So we'll put the Initial Post here."

By now Pete had supplied him with more sticks. With one of them he scratched a line between the two vertical sticks. "And we have to mark the line between these two posts by blazing the trees. Where there are no trees, we will have to put in more posts. Then we put in the Final Post fifteen hundred feet from the Initial Post." He continued his explanation as he pointed to each of the outlying sticks. "And the two sides have to be no more than fifteen hundred apart."

"So that makes a square. It looks simple enough," was Peter's comment.

"It is. But we also have to write on the Initial Post the direction and distance we are claiming to the right and left of the centre line."

Rus, who was beginning to wonder what it would be like to take up prospecting, started asking questions. "Then you have to give that information to the Gold Commissioner?"

"That's right. I have to fill out a form and pay two dollars and fifty cents for each of the claims."

Rus wanted to know more, "How long will the staking take us?"

"Two days should be enough for two or three claims. But we have to do some prospecting first to see where it goes. We can all see where the vein is pointing. I hope we will find another place where it surfaces. Then we'll be ready to stake. I'll take one of you with me tomorrow and we'll see how much we can get done."

By noon the next day Edward, prospecting with Rus, had found a patch of similar boulders some two thousand feet to the northwest. He pulled the compass from his pocket. "I'll take a back bearing to the camp and then we can use that direction for the claims. We're going back to camp now. We'll collect a couple of axes and the hundred-foot rope. We should be able to get one claim done today."

In fact, the country was so open and the staking so easy that it took them little over two hours to measure and mark a line fifteen hundred feet long, with an Initial Post and Final Post at each end and the Discovery Post between them at the site of the tunnel. By dusk, when it was time to head for camp, they had completed the first two claims.

The claim names had been decided by Edward many days before the staking. With Charley's approval, the first was always to be named "Raven." For the second, Edward had thought back to significant events of the previous year and decided on "GTP," for the railway on which so many people were pinning their hopes. Danno's request that the third claim be named after his dog had been accepted.

Sitting round the campfire that night, they all had reason to feel satisfied. Edward let them know that the task they had set themselves had been completed. The mineral specimens they were about to take home were every bit as spectacular as he had hoped. The meal they had just consumed had been equally excellent: roast leg of caribou. Charley had spotted the animal two days earlier on a rocky ridge a couple of miles away. It had been easy to stalk. The beast had been more curious than frightened of this unfamiliar biped. He had made the kill late in the afternoon, and the next day Pete and Charley had carried to camp enough meat to last the team for several days and buried it in a patch of snow nearby.

Danno seemed to enjoy the meat as much as the others, but afterward he took Edward aside and said more than he would usually say in an entire day. "We should get going tomorrow."

Edward shook his head. "I've still got prospecting to do. Another three days, I think. We're in good shape for food."

Danno was clearly agitated, which prompted Syd to join the conversation and take over from his partner. "It's that meat. Once a grizzly discovers it, we've got real problems."

"But it's under two feet of snow."

"I know it's under the snow, but grizzlies can smell blood for miles and we butchered the carcass not far from here. Danno's right."

Edward was unconvinced, so Syd continued. "Do you know what will happen if a bear comes close? Have you seen what horses will do when they see or smell one?"

Edward said nothing, waiting for him to go on.

Chapter 6 — Charlie's Find

"We won't be able to hold them down. They'll break their tethers and be gone. Then where will we be? We'll have to leave everything here, including your rocks, and walk out. Empty handed."

Edward liked to be in control. In fact lack of control usually made him uncomfortable, but he wasn't about to take unnecessary risks, and he recognized the force of the wranglers' argument. "Can you manage the horses for one more day? Then we'll leave the following morning. I'll cut back on what I was planning to do. And we won't stake that timber claim. It can wait."

Danno looked uncomfortable, but then he relaxed: "We can do that. I'll keep watch tomorrow."

Satisfied with the compromise, Edward thanked them both.

Danno and Syd spent the next day in camp, rifles to hand, all the horses tethered. Much of the time was spent organising packages for each horse. They packed about three day's supply of meat in salt and placed it in cooking pots wrapped in cloth to keep out flies. Some two hundred pounds of prize specimens of chalcopyrite were distributed among the horses. The following morning, just as the sun was appearing over the hills, the line of men and horses headed south. All that remained of the camp were poles that had been holding up the tents, and circles of stones around charred wood and burned cans. Three days and about twenty downhill miles after the camp had been struck, the team rested for a day for the horses to enjoy the last grassland before descending into the forest.

The only serious incident on the return journey happened on the easier of the two river crossings. One of the horses had to be destroyed after it had broken its leg in mid-stream. With a minimum of words the man whose life was horses made it quite clear that the party should move on and leave him to deal with the injured animal. Ten minutes down the road they heard the shot. After waiting in a clearing for half an hour, they watched Danno walk up to them carrying his rifle. He looked distraught, but predictably said nothing, just motioned them to continue.

The expedition party walked into Hazelton on a cold day in late September, having been away for almost seven weeks. The seven men and the five returning horses were in good health. The return of the expedition and the specimens brought back were the talk of the town for a week. A ten-pound sample of sulphide was on display at the Taku Inn and another at the bank. Several groups indicated they were thinking of mounting similar expeditions, but the advancing season, the cost, and the reality that, unlike Edward's, another expedition would not be guided to a showing, cooled enthusiasm. One group raised most of the money required but, influenced by reports in the newspapers that "Wickford had it all staked," decided against the commitment.

Edward often sought the advice of a retired Inspector of Mines, George Carthorpe, or "Sir George" as he was sometimes known because of his imperious manner. Mr. Carthorpe, now living in Fort George, but often seen in Hazelton when he was standing in for the incumbent, had a reputation as a difficult person to get on with. But Edward had persisted and George Carthorpe had become a constant source of encouragement.

Anticipating that the assays would be good, Mr Carthorpe used his experience and connections to provide Edward the names of people in Nelson, Vancouver, and Toronto who might be interested in financing further work. The next stage would almost certainly require driving a tunnel for several tens of feet into the mountain to determine whether the vein could maintain the widths and grades seen at surface. Such work would require a larger, better-equipped expedition to remain on site for at least three months. The cost would be a lot more than Edward and any partners he might find would be likely to raise themselves.

The assay results, when they came in the mail from Nelson, were every bit as good as Edward had hoped for, and better than the Inspector's deliberately conservative estimate.

"At four-and-a-half percent copper with four ounces of silver, that's better than what they were mining at the Silver King," said George Carthorpe, leaning back in his chair on Edward's veranda one evening. "But you have to find sufficient size, and you've got transportation problems they don't have, so you would need the extra grade. You might get something for gold, but so far the only people who would benefit from the tenth of an ounce detected by the assayer would be the smelter."

Edward knew that the Silver King, a mine which had been in great measure responsible for the growth of Nelson, had in its heyday mined three percent copper with three ounces of silver. He also knew they had mined a vein eight feet wide. Anyone putting up money for his venture would be betting on the grade being above three percent and the width being more than the thirty or

Chapter 6 — Charlie's Find

forty inches indicated so far. The inspector's professional interest in the venture was obvious: "What interests me is the possibility that you might be onto a new copper camp. Did you have much chance to look around?"

"I had a couple of days. Once on my own. Once with Syd when we took a horse each. Two of his packhorses were trained to take a saddle. We covered quite a lot of country, but not in detail."

The inspector evidently regarded two days as inadequate. "Two days isn't much. If you get an expedition funded for next year, you should have a man full time on prospecting while the rest of you are driving the tunnel."

"I might even prefer to do that myself," said Edward, who did not relish spending day after day on hand steeling and blasting.

Chapter 7

Securing the Claims
October, 1910

Edward kept the rock samples collected in August in a walled-off part of the barn next to the tool shed. Of the two hundred pounds of rocks brought back, many were single, fist-sized samples, but several represented diligent attempts to obtain a representative sample from one side of the copper vein to the other.

Since returning, his time had been taken up with necessary and urgent tasks on the farm. His mine-finding had to take second place. But most visitors to the farm, being members of the local community, knew something about the discovery and, if Edward happened to be around, the conversation rarely omitted "your find." Any kind of real interest on the part of the visitor always led to an offer by Edward to show the samples, and the offer was nearly always accepted. Among the visitors, mostly farmers or men connected with agriculture, there were some who knew enough about minerals to pass comments, which only served to reinforce Edward's perception that his and Charley's find was likely to be valuable.

By early October, with the first falls of snow expected to remain until spring, Edward had completed the paper work for recording his claims, principally "Form S" which, along with a "solemn declaration," and the payment of two-and-a-half dollars, would secure the ground. He also prepared a sketch map showing the Discovery Post, claim boundaries and distances. Later that month, he saddled up his mare and left to record his claims with the government agent in Aldermere, less than an hour's journey from his farm. In a satchel in his saddle bag were two completed copies of the registration forms for each mineral claim, with sketch maps showing the locations of his claims, their corner posts and their boundaries, in relation to local geographic features.

Chapter 7 — Securing the Claims

As he rode across his field to the wagon road, he was acutely aware of the consequences of his two-month absence from the farm. Florence had done the best she could and the men she had employed had worked well, but it was all too evident that the farm would be better prepared for the winter had he not been away for so long. He was also aware that Florence, despite her expressions of support, still regarded his prospecting as an unfortunate and expensive distraction. Knowing this was a problem that further thought was unlikely to solve, he set it aside and enjoyed his ride through the fall colours. The woodlands around the field were alive with the shimmering yellows and vibrant orange of poplars, aspens and birch. Although most such trees were destined for removal in the constant drive to improve productivity of his farm, Edward took pleasure in their colours every fall.

The Gold Commissioner, a man named Paul Spyles, was holding the position on a temporary basis during the absence of the normal incumbent who was on medical leave. As was common in remote locations, the position of Gold Commissioner came with that of Government Agent, whose duties included Stipendiary Magistrate, Chief Constable, Deputy Sheriff and Registrar of Births, Deaths and Marriages, among other duties. Mr. Spyles was not someone whom Edward looked forward to dealing with. It was widely known that the multiple offices he occupied had led him to assume a status not conferred by the position he occupied. The man had earned a reputation for self-importance and a condescending manner.

As Edward rode into Aldermere, a hamlet of fewer than two hundred souls, he noted that it was becoming a busy place. Numerous men and a few women picked their way along muddy streets, taking care to leave adequate distance between themselves and the hindquarters of horses and mules. Nearly every year someone's lack of attention led to serious injury at the hooves of a tethered animal.

The government office was an unpretentious three-room building with a wrap-around veranda. There being no one in the outer room, which at busier times would have housed a typist, Edward walked right into the recorder's office and knocked on the open door. A middle-aged man with an ample moustache looked up as he heard Edward's salutation: "Good morning, sir."

"Good morning. Pre-emption of land, mineral claims, or legal?" asked Mr. Spyles.

"Minerals. I've come to record some claims."

"I think I recognize you. You've got land a few miles north of here. West of the wagon road. You're a farmer. What's this about mineral claims?"

It was not the question which irritated Edward, but its manner of delivery. His response was polite but measured and firm. "I'm a prospector as well as a farmer. I've just come back from an expedition east of the Babine range. Looks pretty good. I have three claims to record."

"Got your forms? Payment?"

Edward felt himself bristling. "I have all those."

"We get prospectors coming all the time without any idea of what is required. Let's see your stuff."

With no invitation to sit down, Edward took his time pulling his documents from his satchel, and laying them on the desk of the government agent.

"I'll get to them this afternoon."

"I won't be here this afternoon and I understand that part of the process is for me to make a solemn declaration. Also I'd like a receipt, please, with both the date and time. I don't expect competition, but I believe in taking precautions."

Mr Spyles glared at Edward, who met his stare in silence.

"Very well, we'll do it now."

Five minutes later, with receipted copies of his applications in the bag slung over his shoulder, Edward took his leave and left the government office. This was an opportunity to see what was new in Aldermere and the new store in particular. Since Sergeants had set up shop, it had become so much easier to buy new tools or replace those which had worn out. He bought a new grinding stone for sharpening saws and scythes and a haft for his sledgehammer which had broken two days earlier.

As he rode home he went over in his mind the next steps. He was well aware that the next stage would be expensive. He would need financing to drive a tunnel, and most financiers would want a crown-granted mineral claim and the superior title that would accompany that status. He also knew that, even if he decided that the venture was promising enough to justify financing it himself, Florence's disapproval would become more of a problem than he cared to face. With that glimpse of reality in place, he realized that he would have to raise significant funding prior to advancing the claims to the status of crown grants.

Chapter 7 — Securing the Claims

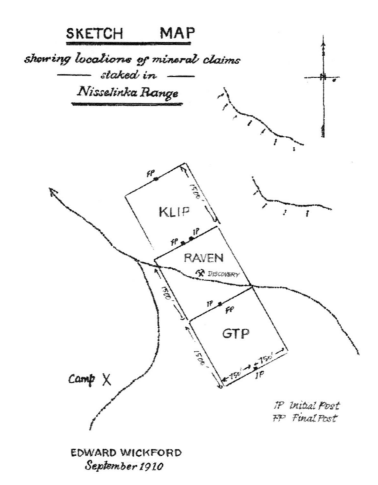

    The Mineral Act of 1896 allowed two years during which a mineral claim could be upgraded to a crown grant. Converting each claim would require a land survey and a minimum expenditure of five hundred dollars. This was a significant sum, but one which would be accompanied by the cost of another expedition to take a Provincial Land Surveyor on a journey to the site. To do this in winter would be especially difficult and expensive. Horses would do well on packed trails but not in deep snow. All the supplies for the time on the trail and at the site would have to be carried by men. To incorporate the survey into the expedition next summer would be much cheaper, and safer. Moreover,

The Nisselinka Claims

it might take time to find financing. On the other hand, it seemed likely that a prospective financier would accept the claims in their present form with the understanding that a survey would be an early priority for the summer program.

Chapter 8

In Search of Finance
March, 1911

On his trips to Aldermere, Telkwa, or Hazelton, Edward was in the habit of dropping into one or other of the saloons to see who was there. Several men in the community were prospectors or followed as best they could the stories, the excitement, the new finds and the disappointments. Late one afternoon in early 1911 he ventured into the Skeena saloon in Hazelton. Waiting for his eyes to adjust to the darkness, he felt a tap on his shoulder. "Ned," said a familiar voice. "Good to see you. What you bin up to?"

"Spud, you look like you're not the only one in need of a drink or a sandwich. Can I join you?"

"Let's take that table," replied Spud pointing to one just being vacated by three men.

Spud Manners was one of the more experienced prospectors and someone whose tales Edward always enjoyed. There was always a lot to talk about. Spud had been prospecting all his life and spent most of each summer away from town. It seemed to be an arrangement which Mrs. Manners tolerated, some said preferred.

"That find of yours," he said as they sat down. "Sounds pretty good. What's next?"

"That's exactly what I've been asking myself. The next step has to be to drive a tunnel, but that's more than I can afford. Where's the best place to get it financed?"

Spud took a while to reply while he pulled a flame into his pipe. "You know, you'll find plenty of financiers in Vancouver and more of them in Montreal and Toronto, but I reckon the best place is Nelson. You get real miners there. They know the difference between an important find and the others."

"That's what I've heard. It's good to hear you confirm it. But that's a long trip. Bulkley Valley back and forth to Vancouver and Victoria, that's one thing but Nelson is in another corner of the province."

Spud nodded. "I know. I've made the journey twice. You've got to decide on your route."

Edward said he remembered a conversation at one of the local agricultural fairs. "It was at Telkwa last year. A feller from the Kootenays told me he came north, the most direct route; by four-horse carriage to Fort George, then by sternwheeler and the Cariboo trail to Ashcroft. That new sternwheeler, the B.X. is supposed to be just luxurious. You go to Soda Creek through Cottonwood. They've made it safe by blasting a channel through the rapids. Then you take a stagecoach to Ashcroft. He said the CPR to Revelstoke is real comfortable."

After drawing on a cigarette, he continued. "That sounded promising until I heard later the same day from another man who'd come north on the Cariboo trail. The stage from Ashcroft to Soda Creek was hell. They were getting stuck every few miles. All the passengers had to get out in the mud and help it along."

The two prospectors laughed. They continued talking for almost an hour without running out of topics. By the time they parted, Edward had concluded that Nelson would have to be one of his destinations. After further research, he decided: the route south from Revelstoke was well established: stagecoach to Arrowsmith then sternwheeler along the Upper and Lower Arrow lakes to Castlegar, which was only three hours by carriage to Nelson. Although it could sometimes be done in less, he was advised to allow ten days each way. And, despite the negative reports about big city financiers, he wanted to talk to the financiers in Vancouver.

At home two days later, anticipating a cool reaction, he told Florence of his plans. As it happened she was in one of her more supportive moods and made it easy for him with a logic he would not challenge: "It's been years since you saw my sisters and your in-laws in New Westminster. From Vancouver it's an easy journey by the CPR, and the boats run to Nelson, don't they? Come back by Soda Creek and Fort George. Avoid the sternwheeler up the Skeena as it's twice the price of the down trip and takes at least a week instead of a day. We'll all go with you as far as Hazelton."

Chapter 8 — In Search of Finance

So that became his plan: from Hazelton to Port Essington, then by steamer to Vancouver. A week in Vancouver would be sufficient time with his in-laws. He would enjoy exchanging stories with his father-in-law, but Flo's mother always failed to conceal her disapproval of the man her daughter had chosen. From Vancouver he would take the CPR to Ashcroft and Revelstoke, then continue by boat and rail to Nelson. The time required for the coastal and inland routes would be much the same, whichever way he went.

And so in mid-April a carriage pulled by two horses left the farm and Edward Wickford started on his journey, accompanied by his family and thirty pounds of samples in his luggage. He would have preferred to go alone, but the opportunity to visit the Hudson Bay store in Hazelton was not something Florence was going to miss. Not only was the store well stocked with the equipment and supplies required by settlers, but recent issues of the Omenica Miner had advertized oranges and bananas, fruits the children had yet to experience. After one night en route and another in Hazelton, Edward said a rather formal goodbye to his family and boarded the *Skeena*, one of the new sternwheelers, for the downstream journey to the coast.

In addition to the mineral specimens, Edward took with him several letters of introduction from the Inspector of Mines, three to mining people in Vancouver and one to the representative of the Wall Brothers in Nelson. Correspondence with a friend during the winter had provided him with a list of financiers in Vancouver. After exchanging letters with five of them, he had made plans to visit three. The first occupied an office on Hastings, near its intersection with Beatty. The building was a three-story timber-frame with a brick façade opposite a major construction project on the other side of the street. A wide staircase with elegant newel posts provided comfortable access to the upper floors, one of which held the offices of Glassop & Krassen, Brokers & Financiers. Inside their office he was greeted by a young lady with an accent revealing her Irish upbringing. "Good morning, sir. How are you this fine day?"

"Good morning. My name's Edward Wickford. I've come to see Mr. Fines."

"Very good, Mr. Wickford. I believe he expected you to get in touch with him this week. I'll tell him you're here."

He was shown into a corner office looking northwest towards the port and the mountains. The view was just visible through a haze of tobacco smoke. A large man with a well-liquored complexion, pipe in hand, rose from his chair and came around his desk, his right hand outstretched: "Sebastian Fines, Mr. Wickford. I'm glad to see you. In fact, we're always glad when prospectors come to see us."

The greetings over, Mr. Fines returned to his desk.

Edward settled into the chair facing him. "That's good. Most prospectors need, sooner or later, to finance their discoveries."

"How was the trip? I've never been up the coast but I hear it's spectacular." With a confident and affable demeanour, the man behind the desk carried on with continuous small talk allowing little opportunity for a conversation to develop. "And you've found something east of Hazelton, I understand. We like that country. That new railway is going to open it up. Copper is it? But before we get into that, how about some lunch? There's a saloon two doors away with a restaurant above. Good place to talk. And we could round up some of my colleagues."

The meal provided by the restaurant was indeed a good one. So was the wine. Both Mr. Fines and his two colleagues were diligent in taking opportunities to emphasize the power and influence of their company. Mr. Fines did most of the talking. "There was one prospector we backed who became very rich indeed. His claims were in the Rossland district not very far from the Le Roi mine. He had thirty-five percent of the company we floated so, when it was taken over by the mine, he did very well."

"When was that?"

"I don't remember exactly. Not long ago."

Edward expected them to ask more questions about what he had found, but most of the obvious questions remained unasked. After the luncheon had gone on for over two hours, he explained that he had appointments that afternoon.

"Of course," said Mr. Fines. "Let's return to the office."

Back in his office, Sebastian Fines' first step was to open a mahogany liquor cabinet behind his desk. "A little brandy? I often have one myself at this time of day." And then, gesturing to the wall: "I have a really good Corvoisier in here."

"Thank you, but I have to pass this time. I've more meetings this afternoon."

Chapter 8 — In Search of Finance

"Oh, don't worry. A little tipple never harmed a meeting. So you're talking to others? That's fair, but this is where you'll get the best deal."

Edward smiled and, looking directly at Mr. Fines, said: "Copper and gold. The copper is showing good grades over eighteen inches. I have a few samples in my case, if you want to see them."

"Sure, I'd like to see them. But I'm not a mining man. The main thing's: can it be promoted? Sounds promising. Copper prices are up. The railway will be there soon. We'd start a new company and give you enough shares to get rich."

"The next step is to drive a tunnel and I have to find out what that will cost."

"That'll cost you a few thousand. And that's where we can help. We would issue the shares, announce the company and the find, sell enough shares to the public to pay for the tunnel and whatever else you need. You go and drive the tunnel and report good results. Price goes up. Then we raise more money for more work. Sound right?"

"So you'd take a right-to-purchase on the property?"

"We prefer to buy it outright for shares. Then you and we are co-owners of the claim."

By now Edward was well into detecting a divergence between his own plans and those of Mr. Fines. "What I'm looking for is a financier who will earn an interest by spending a certain amount and then pay to purchase the rest of the property."

"The way we do it is to pay for it with shares. Then you and we are co-owners. We'd float it on the Montreal Exchange. Then you could hold onto your shares or sell them. Whatever you choose."

The two men talked more about the economy of Northern B.C., how both agriculture and mining in the Bulkley Valley would benefit from the railway, the influx of settlers, Chinese immigration, and the policies of the McBride government in Victoria. Before taking his leave, Edward took the opportunity to say again that he was looking for terms which would include sufficient funds being provided to drive a tunnel in the spring or early summer. "So you have my postal address. If you can see your way to providing the funding I need to get started, send me a letter. I can always get down here again to discuss details."

"That we can do any time, Mr. Wickford. Remember to think about the advantages of getting shares early and being able to trade them on an exchange."

"I'll certainly think about it."

With that they shook hands and Edward turned down the stairs.

His next call was to a very different type of office. Located on Howe Street, not far from the post office, it was an all-wood building with wide steps leading up from street level. The ground floor was occupied by the Canadian Bank of Commerce. A doorman directed Edward to a flight of stairs leading to the offices of Gillham Financing Co. Ltd., where a receptionist led him into a windowless boardroom lined with books. Mr. Charles Gillham, with whom Edward had been corresponding, soon appeared, introduced himself and motioned his guest to a seat at the table. They talked briefly about the journey, copper prices, the possibilities for Edward's discovery, and expectations for the Grand Trunk Pacific Railway. After a few minutes, Mr Gillham, a grey-haired man with a studious manner, appeared to become restless, got up and paced around the room.

"Our business in mining is to finance development, but only after we know there is enough ore to pay back the capital. Yours is at a much earlier stage, but tell me just what you are looking for."

Edward leaned back in his chair to be better able to address the man standing on the other side of the table. "The next step is to drive a tunnel to find out how wide the vein is. I'm told that the grades we already have should justify development if the vein is thick enough—at least three feet wide—and continues like that. I've also been told that for an adequate test the exploration tunnel should be at least a hundred feet."

Mr. Gillham listened carefully while continuing to walk around the room. "Access must take a while?"

"Yes, it takes us a couple of weeks to get in with a pack train. But I reckon that, once a good trail has been built, a producer could get the ore to the railway in three or four days. It helps that much of a trail to the railway would be downhill."

"And equipment and supplies to the mine by the same route?"

"Not entirely, and it would take a day or two longer to reach the higher ground," replied Edward.

"As I mentioned a moment ago, we generally limit our investments to properties where at least some ore has been proven. It would take you at least a year to demonstrate reserves. Is that right?"

"Perhaps, but I would need expert advice on that."

Chapter 8 — In Search of Finance

After another half an hour of questions and answers, the financier turned to Edward.

"It certainly looks interesting, but it is too early for us."

Edward disguised his disappointment with a covering of optimism: "That's all right. I may come back when it's more advanced."

"We would appreciate that."

Mr. Gillham returned to the table and sat down facing Edward. "Perhaps I can suggest where you might look for funding. Where have you been and who else are you going to see?"

"I started this morning on Beatty Street opposite that huge building being constructed."

"Sounds like Gallop & Crash."

Edward frowned for a moment while he tried to understand the name, then laughed. "That's good. Glassop and Krassen, Gallop and Crash. I like that. Is that fair?"

By this time Charles Gillham was also laughing. "Perhaps I shouldn't have said that. We make a point of never talking about the competition in any negative way, but theirs is a very different business. They are not competitors."

"There must be more to the story than just a good name."

"About five years ago they backed a property in the Nelson camp not far from the Le Roi mine. Their usual style: put it in a company with the prospector getting a bunch of shares. Then they floated it in Montreal. That one hit and they all made a lot of money when Le Roi bought them out. Trouble is they have tried to do it again several times since then. Each is launched with a lot of fanfare. That's the 'Gallop' and you can image what comes next!"

Charles Gillham was enjoying telling this story, but then he became serious again. "So, I'm really sorry we can't get involved at this stage, but I think your plans to go to Nelson are good. If you're going to talk to the mining companies you may well get a backer. For the last couple of years some of the mines there have been very profitable and they need to find new orebodies."

"Thank you for that advice. And if I am looking for funding after I have demonstrated some reserves, I may well come back here."

"Very good. In the meantime please keep us informed of your progress."

Edward was more successful in Nelson. Mr. Henderson, the mine manager at the Silver King, a role which gave him considerable status in the town, was evidently a cautious person, parsimonious but encouraging. After asking numerous questions, he expressed disappointment that nearby showings had not been reported. On the other hand, he said, he liked the appearance and grade of the material Edward showed him and the potential of land which was virtually unexplored. "I think we could put up some of the money to drive a tunnel next year, but we may expect you people to contribute some of the cost." Then, after a few seconds, he continued. "In any case, I will recommend that the Wall Brothers earn a majority interest by financing most of next year's tunnel. If we allow ourselves three months on site we would hope you would expose some twenty to thirty feet of the vein."

"I believe that would be possible," said Edward. "We would need about ten men on site with extra supplies delivered once every two weeks. I have no experience with estimating the cost of that sort of work, but people have told me we could do a lot with two thousand dollars."

"That sounds about right. We would want to add some to allow for mishaps and mistakes. My employers would be funding the greater part of the expense, but they might choose to bring in a partner. After they have spent a certain amount, or perhaps worked on the property for three years, they would have earned perhaps sixty percent, with the right to reduce your interest—that is yours and your friends—to, say, ten percent. If we don't find what we want or if we don't go back the following year, we will return the claims, one hundred percent, to you. It would be all yours again. You must understand, I am not empowered to negotiate but, on the other hand, they usually listen to my recommendations."

After discussing other aspects of a tunnelling expedition, prospects for the prices of copper and silver, and Le Roi's recently achieved production rate of one hundred tons per day, Henderson asked Edward if he would like to visit the Silver King.

The next day at seven in the morning he was standing at the portal of the Dandy Tunnel, ready to share a ride with the mine manager and three miners in an empty ore truck on its way into the mine. Edward, a man of the outdoors who had never been inside a mine, found himself both repelled and fascinated, repelled by the oppressive confines of the tunnels—the dark, the grime, dust, and smoke—but fascinated by the methods and ingenuity applied to timbering, drilling, blasting and mucking. Three hours later, he

Chapter 8 — In Search of Finance

was glad to see the growing patch of daylight at the end of the tunnel as he and the manager approached the portal.

Edward left Nelson feeling satisfied that he had become acquainted personally with several men associated with mining and mining finance. He felt there was a reasonable chance of obtaining funding for a tunnel the following year. Although he did not expect it, he would have liked, for Florence's sake and the farm's, to receive an offer which absolved him of the need to spend the summer at the site. But Mr. Henderson had made it plain that Edward's continued involvement on the next expedition would be a requirement for financing.

His return by the inland route, although it took only eight days, seemed longer than the journey out, perhaps because the many hours in a bumping and lurching stagecoach reminded him in a painful way of the earlier comfort of *The Skeena* as he had steamed down to the coast.

Chapter 9

The Plat
Early 1911

Soon after his visit to Vancouver and Nelson, Edward sought the advice of George Carthorpe again. During one meeting the Inspector said: "You will have noticed on the claim map there are a couple of crown grants which appear to be within a few miles of your find."

"I did notice it, but I have my hands too full with my own claims to investigate anyone else's."

Straightening his back and frowning across his desk with evident disapproval, the Inspector replied: "That's no way to treat a find, Wickford. You have to search the neighbourhood and do your best to understand the other sites."

"Very well, Mr. Carthorpe, I will try to find it when I am next there."

"Those claims used to be held by a man named Bellford or Bellforth. I forget exactly what his name is, or was. He had them fifteen years ago and he was not a young man then. They were one of the first crown grants to be issued in this district. I remember him telling me he didn't know what to do with them. He talked about gold and he seemed to know his minerals. If he's still alive, you should talk to him. He might want to sell."

"Do you know where he lives?"

"No, I don't, but if he's been paying taxes on those claims, the Gold Commissioner will have an address for him."

They continued talking for a few minutes until the Inspector signalled the end of the meeting. "Now, if you'll excuse me, I have to make preparations for a journey tomorrow to Roche de Boule, where they are making good progress underground. Please continue to keep me informed of your own progress."

Chapter 9 — The Plat

Edward took the Inspector's advice, visited the Mining Recorder and learned that the two crown grants, "Old Sam" and "Newfy Boy," were still in good standing and that they belonged to a Mr. Wilfred Belfrin who lived in Hazelton. It was two weeks before Edward could find the time to make the four-day trip there and back.

As he rode his horse through a late fall of snow, he wondered whether the journey would be worthwhile or whether he was barking up too many trees. The first person he met on the road in Hazelton that afternoon responded to his question with: "Oh yes. That old man. People call him 'Will.' Dunno if that's his real name. He lives in that cabin at the end of Clifford Street, on the right. You can't miss it. It's run down. Bit of a mess. He's hard of hearing and unsteady on his pegs."

The stranger's instructions were correct. The run-down cabin could not be missed. It was of logs with a shake roof and a single chimney from which smoke indicated life inside. It could not have been more than fifteen by twenty feet. No porch or veranda. Edward tied his horse to a fence post and knocked on the door with a piece of wood tied with a rope beside the door. Nothing happened. After about a minute he knocked again, louder. Then he heard some movement inside and, after another wait, the door opened to reveal an old man with a bent back supported by a stout stick held by both hands. His poorly trimmed beard was matched by a heavy wool sweater and very baggy trousers, and his greeting was as rough as his clothing. "Who are you?"

Edward introduced himself and started to explain why he had come but, before he got far, he was interrupted.

"What do you want?"

He raised his voice to compensate for the man's deafness. "I want to talk to you about your mineral claims."

"My claims? You want to buy my claims?"

"That's why I came to see you."

The old man was speechless as his eyes narrowed and an expression of anger flitted across his face. Then, recovering his composure, he took a deep breath and glared intensely at his visitor. "You want to steal them."

Faced with this onslaught of unconcealed hostility, Edward stepped back: "I'm not a thief! I want to buy them. Buy them!"

"That's what they all say. All smiles and charm, and I end up losing what I worked for."

"I don't like to hear that. But, you know, not everyone in the business is a cheat. Why don't you tell me about your claims? Perhaps they're not what I want."

"Of course you want them. Anyone would want them." With that, the old man turned, pushed the door wide and hobbled into the room. "Shut the door behind you."

Edward had already done so.

The old man collapsed into a sofa in front of a stone fireplace with still-smoking logs, and motioned Edward to sit on a chair opposite.

"I've held 'em a long time. Found the vein in '86. I was strong then. Walked those hills for miles and miles looking for prospects. Started after I was laid off by Collins in '66. The line, the telegraph line. You know about that?" Edward nodded but Belfrin continued as if talking to someone too young to know. "It was on its way to the Yukon and Alaska and then to Europe. We had that trail all the way to Telegraph Creek. The line was following. Then they laid us all off. Just like that. They lost the race, they did. Most of us didn't have money to get home. Lots went prospecting. I lived alone for the summer months. Worked my way south along the telegraph trail. Checked every creek I saw, couple of pans at least. Spent two years finding nothing much." The old man paused for breath. "Then there was this little gully with just a trickle. But the first pan! Must have been twenty grains. Good sizes too."

Observing old Belfrin so stimulated by his memories, Edward recognized the enthusiasm he had seen in many prospectors, himself included. After a pause, the old man continued.

"So I traced it upstream and found this vein. Lots of quartz and lots of gold."

While the old man paused for breath again, Edward took his opportunity to contribute. "I like to hear stories like this."

"This is not a good story!" Another expression of anger drifted across the old man's face. "I followed this vein. It came and went for nearly a mile. So I staked a claim. Just one because that was all that was allowed on one vein. Damn silly rule. Must have been dreamed up by someone in an office somewhere. And there was more of the vein a thousand feet to the north. Just sitting there unstaked. So I came back a month later with a partner. Sam was his name. We worked together on the telegraph line. Some people

Chapter 9 — The Plat

called him Old Sam. He wasn't that old, thirty maybe when Collins laid us off, but that seemed old to us. We had fifty percent each of the new claim."

Edward glanced out of one of the small windows at the fading light, wondering how the good story would end.

"Next spring in Hazelton—that was 1870—we met a man from the south looking for claims. He had plenty of money. At least that's how it seemed. Said he had to send someone to check the vein. Didn't want to do it himself. So we spent most of the summer of '71 going back to the claims. Not far, just two or three weeks out of Hazelton. This man, he sampled lots and liked what he saw. So, back in Hazelton, we did a deal. Two thousand dollars! Can you believe it? One hundred dollars when we signed. Then it was to be four hundred the next year and fifteen hundred after that. So we signed and got the hundred. Then we had to register the change of ownership with the Gold Commissioner."

Edward put his hands over his face in unfeigned sympathy. "I think I know what comes next."

"You probably do. We never got a dime after that. Nineteen hundred dollars lost. Gone forever! A year went by and he owed us four hundred. Sam wanted to shoot him. I would have cheered but wouldn't do it myself. Sam traced him to Vancouver but then he disappeared and we understood he had sold the claims. A few years later someone had a mine on it. So by 1875 I had run out of cash. Went prospecting again, this time to the east."

Telling his story was something of a marathon for the old man. He was running out of breath, but his determination to finish kept him going. "Didn't get to Nisselinka country until '86 I think it was. Found a vein. 'Twas narrow, less than half a hand's breadth wide. But it had gold. I could see it. Then I took two samples, crushed them with a hammer, and roasted them, but found no gold. The next sample had plenty of gold. The gold just came and went. Then the vein pinched out to nothing, but there were other veins next to it, very small ones."

"Did they have gold?"

"Some did. Some must have been about a tenth of an ounce, some a lot more, maybe ten, twenty. I don't know."

"Did you have any assays done?"

"No. Always planned it but did other things. Didn't even stake a claim. Didn't go back for years." The old man took a long pause this time, looking thoughtful, perhaps wistful. "Went east again.

Thought I would get to the gold at Germansen by using the grease trails. Stopped somewhere near Fort Babine. Stayed there. No good prospecting. But 'twas a better time. Kept a squaw. Good wife she was. But she died. Then back to Nisselinka in '91. That was when they changed the claims to square. Fifteen hundred feet each way." The old man stopped, and took several deep breaths. Edward was about to end the silence when Mr. Belfrin started again. "Didn't stake them until '92. Did some work, and they granted the claims to me. I did more work and didn't go back. Never will now. But I kept the claims. Paid the taxes. So now you want to buy them?"

Leaning forward and speaking slowly, Edward explained his situation: "I have some claims which may be quite close to yours. So I could try to find yours this summer. Then I could come and see you again."

"That's no good. I may not be here by then. Pay me one hundred dollars for each claim now. If you come back in the fall they will cost you a lot more. I need the dollars now. They won't do me any good when I'm underground."

Feeling a profound respect for the old man and the challenges he had survived, Edward was conscious of the evident logic of this statement. He was tempted by the price, but then he reminded himself that two hundred dollars would buy a man's help on the farm for five or six weeks. Buying mineral claims sight unseen! No one with any sense would do that. "Do you have the crown grant documents here?"

"Of course I do. But, first, tell me what you do. You're a prospector, you say? That ride of yours ... my sight's not so good, but it ain't no prospector's horse. What d'you do? Where d'you live?"

Edward moved his chair closer to the old man. "I'm a farmer, but I have always liked prospecting. And now I have three claims. Copper and some gold."

"Where?"

"Close to yours, in the Nisselinka Range."

"That's good country. So you're a farmer. At least you're not from the city. I need the money, so I'll sell them to you. All cash. All upfront."

"You said you have the crown grant documents?"

"Want to see them?"

"Please."

Chapter 9 — The Plat

Wilfred Belfrin hauled his worn out body off the sofa and shuffled off to a dark corner of the cabin. Edward could hear the rustle of papers. The old man came back, papers in hand. With a shaking arm he handed Edward the sheaf. As he did so, a grey piece some nine inches square dropped out and fluttered to the floor. Edward was leaning to pick it up when he heard a croaky shout from the old prospector: "Watch what you're doing! That's important." Edward was about to place the piece back with the other papers, when he heard Mr. Belfrin take a deep breath in preparation for speaking again. "No. It's not important. Take a look. Just a useless scrap. But it's my plat. It's mine."

Edward, holding the pages in his lap, examined the piece of paper and looked up. "Plat?"

"Yes, a plat. Every prospector knows what a plat is."

"I don't."

"No. You wouldn't. You're just a farmer. A plat is what the surveyor makes when he does your claim so it can be a crown grant. They had to do three. One to go in a post at the claim, two for the recorder."

Edward placed the piece of paper carefully on the crown grant document and studied it as the old man continued talking.

"You see, the surveyor made a mistake and had to do it again. So he threw his first plat away, not quite finished. Then I said, 'Can I have it,' and he said, 'Keep it. Just don't tell anyone.' So I kept it."

Edward examined the plat with interest. The drawing was on linen drafting paper, grey, translucent and shiny. Most of the writing was in black ink, but some was in red. The most prominent lettering was the name of the claim: "Newfy Boy." The claim itself was shown in orange, applied with a crayon to the back of the translucent paper. The surveyor's name was on the last line of the title. He put the little map carefully down and looked at Mr. Belfrin. "Mind if I look at the crown grants?"

"That's why I got them for you. Go ahead. Read them, if they make any sense to you. I've paid taxes on them for sixteen years. They took my money, so the claims must be good."

Edward picked out a yellowed piece of paper titled "MINERAL ACT 1891", followed by a coat of arms, two signatures, one of the Chief Commissioner of Lands and Works and the other of his deputy. Several lines below the printed words beginning "Victoria, by the Grace of God..." he recognized the name "Wilfred Belfrin" written neatly in cursive long hand, and the name of the claim, "Newfy Boy".

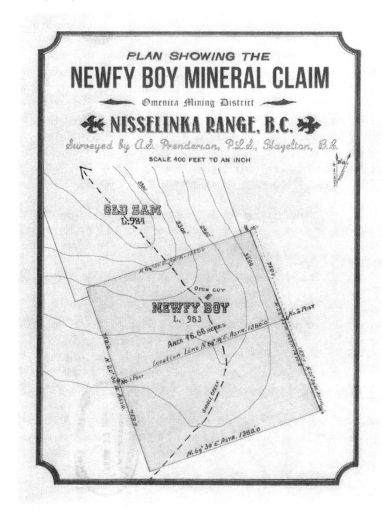

Both this and the second document, for a claim named "Old Sam," were dated 1895. He looked at the time-worn man and pointed to the documents. "Newfy Boy, is that you?"

"Sure is. And I told you about Old Sam. So I called a claim after him."

Chapter 9 — The Plat

The light coming through the windows did not permit reading of the fine print but Edward knew that grants issued in those early years conferred not only the mineral rights but also ownership of the timber and the surface.

"They look in good shape, Mr. Belfrin. If satisfactory to you, I could come back at this time next week with a bill of sale. That will give me time to make a few enquiries at the offices of the Mining Recorder and the Mines Inspector. So the price is one hundred dollars each?"

"That's it until the end of next week. But after that it goes up."

"Very well, Mr. Belfrin, I will return next week. And, if what I find out is all in order, we will complete the Bill of Sale and I will write you a cheque for two hundred dollars.

"Just bring cash."

"If that's what you want. Isn't it rather a lot of cash to keep in your cabin?"

"No one would expect to find that much in my house and you won't tell anyone."

In taking his leave, Edward asked if the old man needed anything brought to him, but the offer was declined with a dismissive wave of a hand.

Back outside, with his hands on his horse's tether and about to untie it, he exchanged "Good evening" with a young lady walking by with a toddler.

"Been to Mr. Belfrin, have you," she said. "That's good. He doesn't get many visitors."

"Yes, just a short visit. Do you know him?"

"Oh yes. Some of us take turns to make sure he is supplied with food and wood. He couldn't manage on his own."

The conversation continued briefly on the community and then the weather, before Edward took his leave saying he had some business to attend to.

Edward stayed the night in the hotel and began the journey home the next day with a few supplies from town. Space for baggage was limited as Finch was a good ride, not a packhorse, and she knew it.

With the children hovering around him, vying for attention, it was hard for him and Florence to catch up on the news from town and the farm. Sensing her husband's irritation, Florence persuaded the children with just a hint of command to go out and play. She and Edward then left the kitchen for the comfort and calm of the veranda.

"Half an hour's peace?" said Edward.

"I doubt it, but how did it go?"

"Well, I think. I met the claim owner. A really old man. He can't do much for himself but it seems he gets looked after by others in the village. Crusty old feller. He wants to sell me the claims, but I have some checking to do."

He didn't mention the price and Florence didn't ask. They both knew the topics to avoid. After telling her more about the trip and others he met in town, he asked if all was well at the farm. Florence told him that nothing unusual had happened except for a strange letter. Then she asked: "Do you have a Great Aunt? Someone called Mabel?"

Edward looked puzzled. "Mabel? She rings a very distant bell. Why?"

"Or Albert Sanders?"

"No. I don't know any Alberts or any Sanders. Do I want to?"

"I don't know. But here's the letter."

Edward took the envelope, noticing the King Edward VII stamps and the London postmark. The letter was written in blue ink in neat longhand.

42 Moore Street,
London, SW
April 7, 1911

My Dear Wickford,

Your great Aunt Mabel, who is connected to my family by marriage and whom I have known for many years, tells me that you have made a discovery of copper in northern British Columbia. Please accept my congratulations and my wishes for commercial success.

I am prompted to write by my interest in such finds and in financing some of them. Having been fortunate enough to have done well with my investments in the Transvaal, I am now looking for other opportunities. My preference is to finance early development work and then to sell most of my interest when production is in sight.

Chapter 9 — The Plat

The Dominion of Canada, and the Province of British Columbia in particular, appear to be destined for a great future. I am well aware that the Grand Trunk Pacific Railway is expected to reach the coast within the next two years and that this will open the part of the province where I understand you are working.

If you should be interested in discussing my involvement, please send me a description of your find and your plans for advancing it towards production. The more you can tell me about the nature of the vein you have discovered and the way you expect it to develop, the better informed I will be.

Yours very sincerely,
Albert Sanders

"How would he know? Who could have told him?" asked Edward of both Florence and himself.

"It's your family. I don't know, but I wonder if it could have been your sister. Meg, I mean. She seems to keep in touch with everyone."

"Well, this could be interesting. Possibly helpful. I think I remember where she fits in. Mabel must be a sister of my grandmother on my mother's side. And yes, Meg does keep in touch with family everywhere." Then he added. "Including me, which can't be easy. And I did tell her about my mining venture. Or, rather, she pried it out of me."

Just then two children appeared, looking very pleased, each carrying a chicken egg.

A week later, Edward replied to Albert Sanders using one of his most treasured possessions, an Underwood typewriter.

```
                              Wickford Ranch
                     Wagon Road, Aldermere,
                              British Columbia

                                11th May 1911
```

```
Dear Mr. Sanders,

I write to thank you for your letter of April 7 and
for your interest in my discovery.
```

59

The Nisselinka Claims

The discovery was made by a native Indian whom I had employed on my farm a year ago. When he showed me what he had found, I recognized that his samples contained chalcopyrite. The samples were impressive, but I was also encouraged by his telling me that he had seen numerous boulders containing considerable amounts of the same mineral. This is exactly what I found when we reached the site last year. We traced the copper-bearing boulders back to their source: a vein of sulphides ranging in width between twelve and twenty inches where it disappears beneath fallen rock and vegetation.

The discovery has been secured with three staked claims which I will raise to crown-granted mineral claims after the necessary surveys are complete. The claims cover over four thousand feet along the projected direction of the copper vein. I plan to add two more claims in the other direction. I am the registered owner of these three claims, now subject to a financing option, but I hold ten percent of my share in trust for the former farm hand who led me to this find. His interest cannot be registered in his name because native people living on reservations are not permitted to own property.

These mineral claims lie some three weeks by packhorse from Hazelton, a Hudson Bay post and an important settlement close to the route of the new railway. Our first expedition with seven men and six horses took twenty-four days to reach the copper find but I expect the next expedition to be faster. As our objective was only an initial examination and collection of samples, we remained on site for only two weeks. The round trip took us just under two months. For the expedition planned this year, we will be better prepared and able to stay longer. We will use mules as well as horses and allow two days to find a less hazardous crossing for a particularly challenging river. I aim to spend a month on the showing. If the vein justifies a commercial operation, we could, I believe, use a large lake for much of the

Chapter 9 — The Plat

transportation and put the copper within a week of the railway. This new railway, which will connect us to both the East and to the Pacific Ocean is going to open up a vast area to settlement and commercial development.

Earlier this year I went to Nelson with the samples and spoke to representatives of the Wall brothers about my venture. I feel that these meetings may lead to sufficient funds for the tunnel we plan to drive. While in Nelson I had the good fortune to be shown around the Le Roi mine. That experience, and learning about the profit it makes, gave me increased enthusiasm to find something similar on my claims.

Yours sincerely,
Edward Wickford

Edward decided to combine posting his letter with a visit to the Union Bank in Aldermere. Recognising one of the bank's valued clients, the teller greeted him warmly. "Good morning Mr. Wickford. What can we do for you?"

"Good morning. Just withdrawing cash, but a little more than usual."

"Very good. That's what we're here for. How much would you like?"

"Two hundred please. I have a purchase to make and it has to be in cash."

"I'm sure that will be no problem, Mr. Wickford, but I'm not authorized to hand out that much myself. I'll see the manager and be back in a moment."

The manager came to the wicket with the teller and greeted his client. "Good morning, Mr. Wickford. It will, of course, have to be in five-dollar bills. They really ought to make tens and even twenties."

"Perhaps they will," answered Edward as he counted out the bills.

Purchasing the old prospector's crown grants required another journey to Hazelton, first to check mineral title at the office of the Government Agent and then to exchange the wad of notes in his pocket for the old man's signature on the records of conveyance.

When Edward knocked on the door of Mr. Belfrin's hut, he was prepared for another hostile reception. After a wait which seemed even longer than on his previous visit, the door opened slowly. Wilfred Belfrin stepped into the spring sunlight and squinted. "Wickford? The farmer? You?"

"That's me."

"What d'you want this time?"

"I've brought the money to buy your claims."

"How much?"

"Two hundred dollars. I have it in my pocket."

"Come in."

It was dark inside but sunlight through two small windows made narrow streaks in the cabin's dusty air. Wilfred Belfrin shuffled over to his chair and dropped himself into it. Edward had anticipated a difficult conversation and had given some thought to how he would handle the transaction. Instead of exchanging pleasantries about health and weather, he had decided on a direct approach. "So, Mr. Belfrin, assuming you still want to sell the two crown grants, I have brought the money and conveyance documents."

Without a moment's hesitation, the old man said, "The money's the important part. Let's see it."

Edward took the bundle of notes from an inside pocket and set it on a small table made from a shingle nailed to a sawn log. "Here it is in five-dollar bills, forty of them. I'd like you to count them."

He watched the notes being counted into piles of ten. While he had little but contempt for the drifters and ne'er-do-wells drawn north by the new railway, his feeling about the man in front of him was one of respect—admiration for his persistence, fortitude and survival. Edward even allowed himself a fleeting moment of pity for a man whose prospecting success had been snatched away by scoundrels.

Wilfred Belfrin looked up, clutching the sheaf of bills. "That's right. Now you have the claims. I'll find the crown grant documents and sign for the sale." The old man struggled to his feet, cash in hand, and limped off to a chest in a corner of the room. He rummaged in a drawer and came back with a handful of papers in one hand, still holding the cash in the other. His return was slowed by the need to steady himself with one hand or the other on various pieces of furniture. Back in his chair, he thrust the papers at Edward. "Here you are. Here are my claims."

Chapter 9 — The Plat

Edward took them. "Thank you, Mr. Belfrin, and I have brought two records of conveyance."

"Read them out to me."

Edward drew breath, held one of the bills up to the light and started.

The old man waved his hand. "Not the whole thing! Not the printed part. Just read out what you've written on it."

It did not take more than a few seconds for Edward to read the inserted words, first for Newfy Boy and then for Old Sam.

"That's right." Mr. Belfrin leaned forward and pointed to a table in the shadows behind Edward. "Now fetch me the pen and the inkwell over there."

Edward did so.

"Now point to where I have to sign."

Wilfred Belfrin signed the first bill of sale, paused to look around, and then signed the other. He handed the pen and ink back to Edward, evidently expecting them to be put back where they belonged. A few seconds of silence followed, and then Belfrin announced: "They're yours now! There's something there, I know."

The old prospector took Edward by surprise by holding out his hand. "Go and find it."

"Thank you, Mr. Belfrin. I'll come back in the fall to tell you what I found."

"Come back, yes, but I'll be gone by then."

After the old man declined Edward's offer to fetch whatever might be needed from the store, Edward took his leave.

Chapter 10

Offers to Finance
June 1911

After returning from Nelson, Edward Wickford had been too busy to spend much more than thinking time on his mining venture. Catching up with work on the farm required long days and, with midsummer approaching, that is what they were. The first crop of hay was ready for cutting. Although steam machines were available in many places, northwestern British Columbia was not one of them. Edward counted himself fortunate to have found three men for a week in early June when the grass in the main meadow was ready and the weather almost perfect. Two of them were locals who made their livings working on the farms and logging camps. The third was a young man working his way around the west before fulfilling his parents' expectations and taking over the family business in Montreal. He had never used a scythe before but, after a clumsy start, he mastered the art: heel almost on the ground, tip slightly higher, advancing just two or three inches with each swing depending on how thick the grass was. The rhythmic swinging of the blades in the hands of the older men made it look easy. The Montrealer's sore back on the first evening attracted remarks ranging from mirth to encouragement from the older hands who made sure that their superior skill and experience were properly recognized. There being little room in the house for more than the Wickford family, the hired hands made themselves comfortable in the barn, but they came to the kitchen for both breakfast and dinner. Florence prepared the workmen's meals knowing they would perform better for being well fed.

A week after the men had left, and while both Edward and Florence were enjoying having the house to themselves again, Edward was returning one evening from the boundary of his property near the wagon road. As he looked towards his house and the

Chapter 10 — Offers to Finance

Bulkley River beyond with satisfaction, he was glad to see that Florence's horse was back in the paddock. She would have bought some groceries and collected the mail, which remained the principal mode of connection with the world beyond the valley.

After a shower in the outdoor washhouse he had rebuilt the previous year, he went to the kitchen where he knew he would find Florence and the children. Among a miscellany of letters was an envelope from Nelson bearing the name of Wall Bros. Ltd. He had not expected to hear from the people in Nelson for another week or two. Telling himself that the early response was most likely to be a turn-down, he ignored the letters.

His wife greeted him with a smile. "Finished the hay?"

"Yes, we got it done. How was the town?"

"Seemed to be busier than usual." replied Florence. "Lots of strangers. People seem to be coming north because they've heard about the railway."

"They say it could arrive within a year. It will certainly help."

"Did you see the mail?"

Edward's response was dismissive. "Had a quick look."

"There's one from Nelson. Must be from the people you went to see."

"That's too quick. Has to be a turn-down. I'll look at it later."

"Go on. Get it over with. Anyway, I want to know."

After exchanging the ghost of a smile with his wife, Edward opened the envelope from Nelson, took out the letter and walked slowly out of the room, deep in thought. A minute later he was back in the kitchen, letter in hand.

"That's extraordinary! They really want to finance us."

"You told me it was good, so why are you so surprised?" asked Florence with a look which conveyed her usual tolerant scepticism of her husband's mining venture.

Edward sat down at the table engrossed in the contents of the envelope and replied without looking up. "Just my way of preparing for disappointment, I suppose. But this is what I was hoping for. They'll take an agreement they call a 'right-to-purchase' one hundred percent of the property by paying for all work at the site. Each February they can decide to continue the right-to-purchase by paying for the summer program, or they can back out. Seems fair."

After a silence while Edward read more and Florence attended to the children, he stood up, waving the letter and said: "This is good. They'll pay me a wage while I am supervising the project. And, if they want to maintain the right-to-purchase beyond three years, they will have to start buying the claim."

Florence responded by summarizing her concerns. "All of which means you will be gone for a month or two later this summer. And back just before the baby arrives!"

The conversation, tense at times, continued until Jeffrey came to his father with a book. The time of day and his imploring look was all he required to explain his purpose.

"All right. I'll read to you in five minutes, if you're in bed."

Jeffrey skipped off, evidently pleased that no negotiation had been necessary.

A month later, after various letters and documents had made the two-week journey from Aldemere to Nelson and back, Edward had in hand both a signed copy of the agreement with the Wall Brothers, and a cheque. In anticipation of its arrival he had made preliminary enquiries about how to find experienced miners. It was not an easy task, as the mining industry in British Columbia was growing fast in response to the demand for copper and coal. He even went to the trouble and expense of advertising for the skilled help he needed in three newspapers: The Omenica Miner in Hazelton, The Colonist in Victoria and The Sun in Vancouver.

The farm provided his family with an adequate living. The region's growing population, much of it attributable to railway construction and expectations of its benefits, added to the value of the land he had purchased eleven years ago. Other young families on neighbouring farms provided a social life for both adults and children, and there were expectations for a school to be built within walking or riding distance. The Wickford farm, like many others, was a good place for children to grow up. There were places to play and the time to do it; a routine, which required helping with household chores, gave them familiarity with the animals and fostered a growing confidence in their own abilities to perform and contribute.

Edward Wickford, now just over twenty-nine years old, was the owner of a farm he had built from little more than a homestead by clearing land and putting back the money it generated. The farm was less able to expand now that it had to compete for cash with both a growing family and a mineral venture. He didn't spend a lot of time with his children. That was, after all, what mothers

Chapter 10 — Offers to Finance

did, and he knew Florence did it very well. He looked forward to the time when Jeffrey would be old enough and strong enough to work on the farm. While his life was centred on family and farm or, rather, farm and family, Edward's other interest, formerly just a hobby, was now also a business. Like many other citizens of this frontier community, his dream was to find minerals to make a mine. Such a find would confer riches on himself and his family. It would also add to respect and status in the community, although these had never been priorities for him.

Although their respective priorities sometimes pulled in divergent directions, Edward and Florence were well matched. She considered her duties to consist of maintaining a home and raising the children, together with some obligations to the community in which they lived. Edward knew he had to provide for his family, but his sense of obligation extended to a wider world. Conflict between duty to his family and duty to others was not a possibility he considered.

Chapter 11

Second Expedition
August to October 1911

By mid-July Edward Wickford's team was taking shape. The Grand Trunk Pacific Railway from the Pacific coast had reached Sealy on Skeena Inlet and was well west of Fort George on its way from the East. The imminent completion of the railway had prompted a flood of labourers, skilled and unskilled, to the north.

Danno the wrangler and his partner, Syd, were pleased to be tasked again with the transportation. Peter Cooper, now living with his new wife in Hazelton and working as a carpenter, was keen to return, but others from the previous expedition were not going to be available. Fred, who had shown himself to be a good worker, had taken a job on the railway, and Rus could not be found. But Harry Wiggin, now seventeen, had been an applicant ever since the "hay thief" incident, as it had come to be known. He and his friend, Theo, were to be the unskilled helpers. Charley Raven had said he would come but had then disappeared. Edward's need was for miners, those with drilling and blasting experience in particular, and a camp cook.

Two weeks after he had placed advertisements in the Omenica Miner and the southern newspapers, Edward was waiting outside the Hudson Bay store in Hazelton. The sky was clear and he was enjoying the sunshine while periodically pulling his watch from his vest pocket as the appointed time approached. He had listed fifteen minutes past noon as a means of conveying his liking for precision. Although he had heard that there were men looking for work in Hazelton and along the route of the railway, he had no means of knowing how many applicants he might get, if any. But at ten minutes past twelve, a man of less than medium height, stocky build under a shabby coat, walked towards Edward. "Mr. Wickford?"

Chapter 11 — Second Expedition

Edward nodded and held out his hand. "You've come for the mining job?"

"Yes. I saw the advertisement."

"You're in good time. I need to wait to see who else may come. Then you and I will take a walk along the riverbank. I need to learn about what you can do and, if I think you can do it, I'll tell you about the job you're applying for."

The applicant pointed to the other side of the street at two men approaching. "I'm not the only one."

By fifteen minutes past noon, seven applicants had turned up, and Edward had started on his interview with the first to arrive. He took no more than a few minutes with some applicants, longer with anyone who appeared suitable. All had experience as labourers. Two, including the first to arrive, seemed to be drifters; only two of the others had brought written references and appeared to have the skills required. By mid-afternoon Edward had made his selection. For the miner it was to be Jim Tunnay, a tall nineteen-year-old with a wiry frame and a seedling moustache. He had been brought up on a farm in Oregon. He told Edward he had worked in various mines on his way north. Edward pointed at the man's left hand where two fingers were missing. "Mine accident?"

The young man nodded and then laughed as if to make light of it. "Yes. Mostly my fault. Rock fall. I shouldn't'a bin so close to the face just then."

"Any trouble with a mattock or shovel?"

"No."

"Hand drilling, blasting?"

"I can do all that."

Both the applicants for camp cook came with references and documented experience.

By the end of the interviews, Edward had three men with credible claims to be hired. As before, he offered them farm work to assess their abilities. At the end of the week he remained very comfortable with Jim Tunnay, the miner. His choice of camp cook, Sebastian Sewell, was based entirely on his easy-going personality.

The team of nine was to consist of two miners, two helpers, two wranglers, a cook, Charley (if he should turn up) and Edward. They would be accompanied by a surveyor and his assistant, who had their own two horses and supplies as they would make their own way back as soon as their work was complete. Tentage, tools, and explosive were to be purchased in Fort George, which had become a thriving supply centre for the new railroad.

At eight in the morning on the last Monday of July, the team assembled again at the Inlander Hotel in Hazelton. Eight packhorses, two of which could also be ridden, would provide the transport for the prospecting team. A gathering of some twenty well-wishers, friends and the curious had assembled to see their departure. Mineral discoveries were commonplace, but one which had attracted financing was worth following. A mine could have a substantial effect on the town and on the lives of its occupants. Real estate prices, already elevated by the expected railway and the hyperbole of the salesmen, could be pushed even higher.

Three members of the previous year's team, Edward, Danno and Charley, who had turned up a week before the planned departure, felt capable of following the trail, most of which was well blazed. They knew where to cross the two rivers, and where to camp. Pete said he preferred to leave trail-finding to others. The miners had been told that their main task would be to expose more of the vein by driving a tunnel into the cliff. The Inspector of Mines had provided Edward with a wealth of information and advice. His estimate had been that each day the two miners and their helpers should advance the tunnel two or three feet. The plan was to spend at least four weeks at the site, longer if a supply run turned out to be possible. Two men, preferably three, would need to be sufficiently familiar with horses to be able to help the wranglers when necessary. Edward knew that Harry Wiggin and his friend Theo had looked after and used horses all their young lives. Most of the prospecting and the search for the Belfrin claims would be carried out by Charley and himself, sometimes on foot, sometimes on horseback.

Edward realized that much would depend on the skill and attitude of the miners. Once on the property, there would be no opportunity to replace them. Engaging Jim Tunnay and the two applicants for camp cook to work on the farm for a few days had again been a good decision, though he remained aware that, whoever he hired, there was always a chance that some suppressed and damaging character trait would be released by circumstances beyond his control. He knew accidents were common in any type of mining and the consequences of a serious injury could include having to abort the expedition and report failure to advance the tunnel. But after seeing Jim Tunnay at work around

Chapter 11 — Second Expedition

the farm, Edward was confident that he had made a good choice; having been injured once he seemed unlikely to take unnecessary risks again. Peter, a steady man and seasoned underground miner had proved himself the previous year.

Over supper in the saloon on the evening before departure, Edward had been talking about his plans and asking questions. "What's the trail going to be like, Syd?"

"It'll be pretty good most of the way up the Suskwa. We've been there twice since we took you last year. That trail gets plenty of use on the way to the Omenica gold fields. It's well cleared. Only problem we had in May was in the swampy patches, but they should be dried out by now. After we branch out on our own trail I can't say. There may be a lot of deadfall. We managed it last year."

"We did, but I like to think that river crossing won't be so difficult."

"The trouble with that one is the size of the boulders. It's a matter of luck where the horse puts its hoof. Unless the water's clear, he can't see exactly where they are. Danno's going to ask for a better place this time, if one can be found."

And so it was. As expected, they made good time up the Suskwa, but once they branched off on their own trail to the Nisselinka Range delays, mostly for deadfall, were frequent. But despite the problems the men and horses completed their journey in three days less than the previous year.

They set up camp where it had been a year ago. The rings of stones for the fires were still there surrounding charred wood, ash and the remains of tin cans. Neatly piled a few yards away, and well preserved by the long winter snow, were the tent poles. These would save time since ridge-poles of twelve to fifteen feet were hard to find among the local trees. Some of those from last year had been made by thinning and trimming the conical shapes abundant at that altitude. Most of the fences used to corral the horses were still standing and any damage was repaired within a few hours.

Two days after arriving at the site, Edward had the satisfaction of watching Pete and Harry clean out the first drill hole in the trench which had yet to become a tunnel. After working for four hours, they were twenty-five inches into the granite. Then Pete inserted one stick of dynamite followed by a four-foot fuse into the top of the hole. He stood up and stretched, before noticing Edward looking on. "We're ready for the blast, sir."

"That's good, Pete. Where do you want us?"

"We'll all go behind that big boulder. That's where Harry and the other young'un will be."

Behind the boulder, Edward found Harry and Theo. After a minute or so, they were joined by Pete who was counting out loud: "Thirty, thirty-one, thirty-two—it'll go at about sixty—thirty-five, thirty-six…"

He had got to fifty-six when they heard the explosion, followed by the rattle of rock fragments falling to the ground. Pete was the first to speak: "We'll wait for another minute. Just to be safe. Then I'll go. You all wait here until I call you."

After several days of trenching, the miners reached the cliff. Now the tunnel had been started, there was room for only one miner and his helper. Each pair would be assigned to tunnelling for no more than three days. Then they would be on prospecting and other tasks before being rotated back to hand steeling, blasting and mucking.

On the second day of tunnelling, while a miner and helper continued the cycle of hand steeling, blasting, and mucking out, Edward and Charley headed east on foot. The plan was to find Edward's recently purchased crown grants and the vein which they covered. Once the vein had been found, a trail could be cleared for both people and horses. The first challenge was to find the approximate location of the vein which old Wilfred had staked. Edward had traced the sketch maps attached to each of the crown grant documents, but such maps were often of limited use unless they included easily recognizable landmarks in the vicinity. The larger rivers and mountains were often named but lesser geographic features were usually nameless. Names, where they existed, could be misleading, as many places had been honoured with more than one name by other prospectors and surveyors.

Every day Edward and two or three of his team would head east in search of the crown grants. Their route took them over the same ridge into which the miners were driving a tunnel and then onto a plateau where trees were sparse and walking easy. They then dropped down into a gully with close-spaced pine, including deadfall with patches of salal. Progress was slowed by the need to clamber over branches or fallen trees. Such places would be impassable for horses until a trail could be cut. After crossing a

Chapter 11 — Second Expedition

slough they turned north in the expectation that the source of the water within it would be the creek shown on the sketch map. A small creek was found but its turns and bends did not seem to match any in the map. Another creek farther east yielded the same lack of encouragement. At the end of every day for the first week the prospecting crew had to turn back without having found any feature which could be related to the geographic features traced from the government records.

The day it was their turn to go prospecting, Peter and Theo spent an hour reaching the place to be searched and another four working back and forth across the only creek which appeared to fit the sketch map. When it came time for a break, Pete settled on some pine boughs lopped off a nearby tree. With his back against the tree, he put a cigarette in his mouth and held out the package. "Smoke?"

Theo pulled a small canvas bag from his leather pack and shook his head. "I'm gonna eat first."

The two men formed a good team. Pete's curiosity made him a good prospector. Theo took pride in his strength and ability to provide a strong back whenever required. Staring at his own copy of the copy which Edward had made of the original sketch in the recorder's office, Pete was talking more to himself than his companion. "It's got to be somewhere around here. It just has to be."

Theo's grunt was his only reply as he tucked into a handful of bread and beef jerky.

Undeterred, Pete continued talking to his map. "The creek takes a bend to the east and then another back to the south. That little cliff fits perfectly."

Looking up from his sandwich, Theo pointed towards a place where the stream squeezed itself around a large outcrop. "See that rock? Could it be on the far side of the stream just about level with the rock?"

"We've been there. Saw nothing. Just scrub and grass."

"We've looked everywhere."

"Then the scrub and grass have to go!" said Peter emphatically.

Theo signalled his acceptance, even welcome, of the physical challenge with another grunt and a short declaration: "They *will* be gone." And then, after another mouthful, "Give me just a few more minutes."

They continued eating in silence, enjoying the short rest and a welcome sun after several cloudy days. Recognizing that it would be all too easy to succumb to a nap, Pete pulled himself up, walked slowly to the stream, splashed his face and took a drink from his cupped hands. He returned to find Theo holding a cigarette in one hand and offering the package with the other.

"Time for another?"

"Sure. And then we're going to find the old man's gold."

"D'you think Ned got conned?"

"No idea. This is the first time I've worked as a prospector. I hear it happens."

They finished their smokes and Theo was about to pick up his pack when Pete said: "We'll leave our stuff here. You work down there and I'll go upstream to see what else fits the map. There's no need to strip off every bit of green. Just a few lines to expose the rock. I don't think it'll be very far. Don't go deeper than a foot or so."

Theo dropped his bag, grabbed his mattock and shovel and strode down the slope to the low bench of the river they had already walked across several times. He pointed to the other side of the gully and gestured to Pete.

"This way?"

"That'll do. If it's too deep, move on." Pete headed upstream with only his map. When he returned half an hour later, Theo, stripped to his waist, had cut a shallow trench twenty feet long from the creek to the bank of the gully.

Leaning on his mattock, he pointed to the other end of the trench. "Just boulders there. Big ones. No outcrop."

Pete looked up from his map with a startled expression of disbelief. Then his gaze locked onto where Theo was pointing. His next words were yelled. "That's it! The bloody stream! It's moved!"

Theo's puzzled look prompted Pete to explain: "You see? It used to be where you found the boulders. Now it's here. So we've been looking on the wrong side. Dig on the other side and we've got it!"

Still puzzled, Theo shouldered his tools and was across the stream in a couple of steps and a leap. He had already moved some sod and shrubs when Pete joined him with his own mattock. Within ten minutes the two men, working away from each other for safety, had each exposed some ten feet of rock.

"What's this, Pete? You said you wanted broken rock."

Pete dropped his tool and examined what Theo had exposed and started to mark out a rectangular area with broken twigs.

Chapter 11 — Second Expedition

"That could be it. We need to see more. Let's clear between here and here."

In contrast to the smooth surface of most of the rock they had exposed, they were now looking at whitish rock with angular fragments and sharp corners.

"I think this must be it. You see this groove following this little quartz vein? I think that was done by someone."

Two hours before sunset Theo and Pete had cleared enough to show that someone had hollowed out the entire width of a ten-inch quartz vein leaving the bordering rock untouched. In one small crack there was even some rock dust one would expect to be left by anyone working an outcrop with moil and hammer.

The discovery of the Wilf Vein, as it became known, led to a happy evening at the camp. Edward produced a bottle of rye whiskey from his personal baggage. The celebrations for finding an old prospect of unknown merit echoed those of winning teams throughout the ages: the buffalo killed, enemy defeated or the pirates' treasure discovered.

Later that week, the trail between Pete's discovery and the camp had been brushed and cleared sufficiently for easy walking by both man and horse. The journey now took less than half an hour on horseback. Equipment assembled on the vein came to include shovels, sledgehammers, drill steels, moils and crowbars. Edward, who had seldom missed an opportunity to learn from prospectors and mining professionals he met, wanted not only the vein but also the enclosing rocks exposed. This requirement led to a trench across the vein, instead of along it, revealing some twenty feet of whitish, rather friable rock, bearing numerous small quartz veins, none of which appeared to have been sampled. It was obvious that such small veins could never be economic, but Edward knew that veins could change character along their lengths. He also knew that a vein which was uneconomic in one place could improve within a few feet or that the missed promising vein could be hiding outside the claim boundary. Although he was uncertain about the best ground to acquire, he staked two claims next to the Belfrin crown grants.

With four additional mineral claims to add to his holdings, Edward had to start planning the next stage of exploration on the new claims. Wilf Belfrin's vein would require a lot more excavation and sampling, with tunnelling probably to follow. The work would need additional funds for which he would approach the

The Nisselinka Claims

Wall Brothers who had financed the Raven claims and who had first rights to any new discoveries in the vicinity. The first question they would ask would be about assays. He could divert his two miners for a short period, but any extension to the program would require resupplying the camp with food and explosives. For these essentials he would have to send a party back to Hazelton or possibly Fort George. But Edward felt they had achieved enough for the year and additional work would have to wait for the following season.

Conditions for writing in the camp being far from ideal, his initial report describing the discovery was short enough to fit on a single page. He would mail this to his financiers from Hazelton. They would get a full report later.

It was not until November, when Edward was back in the comforts of his home, that he sent the complete report. He also wrote to Albert Sanders.

```
                                         Wickford Ranch
                                   Aldermere, B.C., Canada
                                         15 November, 1911

Dear Mr. Sanders,

I write to report progress on the Raven vein and to
tell you of another discovery.

Prior to this year's expedition, I took a chance on
purchasing two crown grants belonging to a prospector
of advanced years who is no longer capable of reach-
ing his claims. While we were driving the tunnel on
the Raven vein this summer, we succeeded in finding
the claims I had purchased. Instead of a single vein,
there are several small veins distributed over a
width of about fifteen feet. Although there are some
signs of copper, the importance of these veins lies
in the gold they contain. I don't believe that what
we have uncovered could be economic, but the vein
certainly warrants further exploration. I sent ten
samples to the assay laboratory in Nelson and was
gratified to learn that the gold (some of which is
visible to the naked eye) ranged up to 0.4 opt.
```

Chapter 11 — Second Expedition

We spent nearly four weeks on driving the tunnel on the Raven vein. It has now reached forty-five feet into the mountain. Where exposed by nature, the vein is some thirty inches wide. Over the length of the tunnel it pinches down to four inches in one place but then swells to three feet at what is now the end of the tunnel. I took twelve samples for assay in Nelson but am yet to be notified of the results. By our estimates they ranged in grade from two to four percent of copper. I believe the most significant sample is one taken near the end of the tunnel over a width of two-and-a-half feet. We estimate the grade to be among the highest we have seen. You will, I trust, understand my enthusiasm.

The Annual Report of the Minister of Mines for 1911 is expected to be available early next year. I expect my property, which was visited by the local Inspector of Mines, may be mentioned in his report. If it is, I will send you the entire Annual Report as you may find it interesting. It would be useful to you to see a description of my vein by a knowledgeable and independent person.

I have added to the purchased crown granted mineral claims (named Old Sam and Newfy Boy by the prospector) with another two claims (not yet surveyed). You can see my five Raven and the four Eastern claims on the enclosed map, which I copied by tracing the government map and adding the new claims. In accordance with my agreement, I have offered the Wall brothers an opportunity to finance this new showing. With our experience on the first tunnel, I will be able to make reasonable estimates of the costs per foot. I have told the representative in Nelson with whom I have been dealing that with contingencies I would need about $3,000 for the first year, during which we would aim to drive forty feet. I have asked them to take a right-to-purchase whereby I would be carried to production, at which point my interest would be an undilutable ten percent.

The Nisselinka Claims

I will, of course, keep you informed on the progress of these negotiations.

With great respect and consideration,
Edward Wickford

Chapter 12

Tunnels Continue
1912 and 1913

In the absence of any communication from the Wall Brothers to say that they would renew the option, the first two months of the year 1912 were difficult and uncertain times for Edward. He did not know whether the late summer would see him on the farm or in the hills. Hiring and planning for the next expedition was on hold. His energy, normally so well directed, was wasted on a pile of unpleasant possibilities. His discontent was not lost on the family. The two older children were more than usually cautious in his presence, Florence even more tactful than usual.

In mid-March, fifteen days before the renewal date, confirmation came that funding would be provided. This welcome news was followed by more. The Annual Report of the Minister of Mines contained, as Edward had hoped it would, a description of his Raven claims. Then, when the expected cheque for fifty percent of the budgeted amount arrived in the mail, Edward's burden was lifted. The family could now enjoy a more relaxed version of husband and father.

In addition to recovering his energy and drive, Edward made minor adjustments to his daily routine. He spent more time with his children, especially Jeffrey, and he would indulge in such luxuries as coming back to the kitchen for a mid-morning snack. To his wife's surprise, he made a habit of helping in the kitchen.

"Where does this go?" he asked, holding up a saucepan.

"On the second nail up there," replied Florence pointing towards the top of a pillar.

"See anyone in Aldermere today?"

"Yes. I talked to Jill," Florence replied, chopping carrots.

"Any news?"

"She's just back from Hazelton, a bit disappointed."

"Why?"

"The Bay was meant have a shipment the day before she was there. She went to get some new clothes."

"That shipment is bound to arrive soon. Want to go?"

"To Hazelton?"

"That's right. Let's all go."

Florence put down the knife, walked round the table and embraced her husband and stepped back smiling. "That would be wonderful, just wonderful. Annabel needs a new dress."

"And what about you? When did you last get yourself a dress?"

At that moment Jeffrey and Annabel came into the room, covered in snow and mud.

Edward laughed. Florence exclaimed: "What on earth have you two been up to?"

Jeffrey, his cheeks red from the cold, answered, "We're digging a tunnel." Then he turned to Edward. "We're going to find copper, just like you, Father."

Edward looked very pleased: "Are you, by Jove! Will you show me?"

Annabel said "Come!" and turned towards the door.

Florence, smiling happily, watched the three of them leave the room. Then, deciding she didn't want to miss the event, she checked that Penny was still asleep in the crib, grabbed her coat and boots, and followed the others.

Now that he was less pressured, her husband had became more open to reading stories to the children, more interested in what was happening in the community, more available for time with her. One day, he built a toboggan for the children and banked up a pile of snow to improve the run. On another, towards the end of the evening meal, he took them all by surprise. "Jeffrey, tomorrow's Sunday. Let's go fishing after church. It's a little early in the year, but the ice is off the river and we might catch something."

Jeffrey beamed. Annabel frowned. "Me too!"

Edward's response was not what she wanted: "Do girls like fishing?"

Even as she was speaking, Florence had misgivings about the way she had chosen to intervene: "Yes, some girls like fishing, and I'm sure your father will take you, and then you can see if you like it."

Chapter 12 — Tunnels Continue

To her relief Edward's response was to say to Annabel. "That's right, you come too. See if you like it."

In early April, two letters arrived from Albert Sanders. They had been written six days apart but must have been on the same boat.

41 More Street
London
11th March 1912

My Dear Wickford,

The Annual Report of the British Columbia Minister of Mines for 1911 arrived yesterday by the Royal Mail, only five weeks and two days after you posted it in Hazelton. For this I am indeed grateful. In my opinion, the report is first class and an excellent description of mining in British Columbia. I read the entire document and am now well informed about the considerable amount of mining and exploration being carried out in the province.

It will be no surprise to you to be told that I read the section on your discovery with considerable interest. I believe the reported grades will allow you to continue with financing, provided you can demonstrate sufficient quantity. As is the case with any mining venture, transportation is the key. For that you are well positioned by the new railway to the coast and the opening of the Panama Canal. In my opinion there will be continuing demand for copper ores. Most of the nations in Europe are spending vast sums on armaments, for which metals, especially copper, are required in quantity.

If you seek financing on any other ventures you may have, please remember me. Although copper is my primary focus at present, I remain particularly interested in gold, with which I have more experience.

With best wishes for your success, I remain your attentive and grateful friend.

Albert Sanders

And in the second envelope:

The Nisselinka Claims

41 More Street
London
18th March, 1912

My Dear Wickford,

Thank you for sending me your encouraging news.

By the time you receive this you will probably have received mine of a week ago. I am writing again to tell you that I remain very interested in taking a financial interest in your recent purchase. If your current financiers decide against extending their purchase right to your new eastern claims, please inform me (by telegraph if possible). I remain in correspondence with several of my partners with whom I benefited from our investment in the Witwatersrand, and I anticipate no problem in raising the funds you require for development of this new vein.

I write this in haste as the mail goes in half an hour and I have a meeting in the City this afternoon.

With best wishes for your endeavours, I am your attentive and grateful friend,

Albert Sanders

These letters, which provided Edward with the comfort of being less dependent on a single source of financing, prompted a regular correspondence between the two men. Generally, with the letters taking between three and four weeks, each would write every other month. As Edward came to understand the depth of experience of the older man, Albert Sanders took on a role of adviser on mining matters. There had been no opportunity for Mr. Sanders to finance Edward's venture as the Wall Brothers had not only continued to renew their option on the Raven claims but had also chosen to incorporate the eastern group into the right-to-purchase and increased their funding accordingly.

Journeys to Hazelton continued to be necessary both for supplies and for filing work on the mineral claims. Sometimes they would leave the children with the Milfords, take the stagecoach and return with a load of staples, tools and a few luxuries that could be found in the Hudson Bay store. On other occasions

Chapter 12 — Tunnels Continue

Edward would ride alone. By stagecoach or alone the journey would take two days each way.

For Edward, riding alone was a good time for thinking. Although the journey could be arduous, and in bad weather far from comfortable, he looked forward to the days on horseback and recognized that he would miss them when the railway made them unnecessary. As he approached the emerging railway town of New Hazelton on his journey north one day in late April of 1912, the work crews and piles of lumber and steel brought to mind the reality and imminence of the engineering achievement that would change life for his family, his farm and his mineral venture.

Weary when he reached Hazelton, he was relieved to find a room at the hotel far enough from the saloon for a good night's sleep. As usual he went across the street in search of a drink and conversation with whomever he met, but preferably with miners or prospectors. As his eyes adjusted to the dark and the smoke, he saw that all the tables were occupied. Then he noticed a man sitting at a nearby table looking at him. The man got up.

"Ned. You alone? Come and join us."

Without remembering the man's name, he recognized him as one of the surveyors who lived in town and kept busy with land acquisitions and mineral claims.

"There's just two of us and room for one more."

As the pair squeezed their way across the room, Edward kept hearing snatches of conversation and the word "Titanic." This was old news as it had been the headline in the paper for two consecutive Saturdays. He didn't particularly want to talk about it again. He was appalled by the loss of life and the ship, but it had happened a continent and half an ocean away, and to people who led very different lives from his.

The two men sat down.

"Ned, this is my friend, Sooty. The rest of his name can wait. And this is Edward Wickford who has the Raven claims."

Sooty picked up the thread on the mineral claims and then changed the topic to international news: "I don't know much about your claims but they sound good. I hear you've been travelling, so you may not have heard the news of the shipwreck."

"I know about the Titanic. Just awful."

"Yes. But today they published the list of who died. It included Mr. Hayes. It came to the telegraph office just a few hours ago."

"Hayes? The GTP boss?"

"Yes, him."

Edward's look of distant regret changed to one of direct concern.

"I met him once. Just briefly. In Port Essington, I think. He seemed keen to develop the spur line from the Telkwa coal fields."

The three men paused, each with his own take on the disaster and its impact.

Edward continued: "That's a real shame. A project like that needs a driving force. And he was it."

After only one night away, and some time spent with the Gold Commissioner, Edward was able to head for home the next day, all too aware that the outside world had demonstrated its reach to his remote corner of Canada.

An ocean and a continent away, Edward's correspondent, Albert Sanders, was in a comfortable leather chair next to a ceiling-high bookcase in the smoking room of his club. When he arrived that day he had been irritated to find his favourite chair by the fire already occupied. But, comfortable enough in the chair he had found, he was scanning the Illustrated London News for world events. An unopened copy of The Times was on the table next to him, his to read before anyone else could claim it. But just as he was turning a page, he heard a familiar voice.

"Morning, Albert."

In most such salutations his acknowledgement, although polite, would have failed to conceal that he would rather have been left alone with his pipe and his papers. But in this case his response was genuinely enthusiastic. "Morning, Charles. Where the hell have you been? Have a seat."

The visitor took his time moving a chair to within hearing distance of his friend and eased himself into it with a sigh of satisfaction. Then he waited for the newspaper to be folded and put on the table before opening the conversation. "Still chasing copper in the colonies?"

After using his folded newspaper to move a cigarette tray on the table, Albert Sanders turned to face the visitor with a look of mock exasperation. "Charles, I have to think you are making light of my ventures. You must first tell me where you have been for the last month, or is it two?"

"Almost three. Had to go to my place in Ireland. This Home Rule business is getting absurd. If they get their way, my place

Chapter 12 — Tunnels Continue

there will be in a foreign country. Just like that. And it's been in my family for generations! "

"Not much you can do about it. At least if that's what they all want."

"I dunno what they want. It was hard to get anyone around where I live to talk about it. I didn't go to Dublin, but I hear it's different there."

Albert Sanders, who could be seen as often reading a book as a newspaper, enjoyed his reputation as someone who took an interest in history and who could be counted on for opinions on almost anything that ever happened. "Well, you see," he began, "they're all Catholic and most of us are not. It all started with Cromwell, who thought he could make them into Protestants. They didn't like it. Can't really blame them, can you? But old Olly behaved like a bully and a tyrant and now we have to pay for it."

Charles Mansthorp was not about to debate the origins of the crisis. "Well, that's enough about history and enough about Ireland. Let's talk about something encouraging. What about your copper venture? Are you going to let me in on it?"

"As you know, Charles, it's a mining venture and that means risk. You'd be welcome to join me, if I get a chance to invest, but I think you should wait until it is on firmer footing."

"Somewhere in Canada, isn't it? I think you said West Coast."

"It is. Do you know anything about that part of the world?"

"Canada, yes. Big country, all the way from the Atlantic to the Pacific. You see, I'm not that ignorant."

"All right, you passed the first level. How about the next question. Do you know how big it is compared to Britain or other countries in Europe?"

"I'd just be guessing. Tell me."

"British Columbia, that's just one province. You could fit most of France and Germany into it. Or three Great Britains."

Watching to see his friend's reaction, Albert continued, "Assuming, of course that Ireland is still with us."

"We're not talking about that. Back to Canada. Next you'll tell me there are not many people there in British Columbia."

"Only four hundred thousand. And much of the province is unmapped. Who knows what could be there." Albert the Enthusiast was emerging from Albert the Reader. "You see, most of the population is in the south near the American border, where there are roads, railways and towns. But four hundred miles farther north there is going to be a new railway crossing the centre of the province. That will be another link between central Canada and the Pacific Ocean, opening up prime agricultural land, hundreds of square miles of untouched timber. The settlers have just started to arrive and the mineral discoveries have only just begun. The development of that part of the country must be half a century behind the south."

Charles was attentive and looked impressed. "Sounds encouraging. I suppose you want to be part of the first discoveries just like you were in South Africa."

"Of course I would. Can you imagine finding another Witwatersrand?" Albert's enthusiasm faded as he changed topic. "But, like you, I'm getting older."

Charles adjusted his position in his chair. "I know all about that. It get's worse every month. You know, I'm still hunting. As a young man I used to fall off almost every year. Just got back on. I hate to think what will happen next time I fall. But I don't take those wild jumps any more."

"You're ahead of me. I don't mount a horse any more unless I have to."

"But you still acquire minerals somehow. And you haven't told me what you've got."

"Nothing yet. I've been corresponding with someone called Wickford who seems a reasonable fellow. He has some claims over a copper vein and some others with gold. They're both being financed locally so I haven't had a chance. But that may come and, if it does, I'll jump in. The gold interests me more than the copper. They're both in mountains called the Nisselinka Range, and not too far from the new railway I told you about. And, as you may know, the west coast of Canada and America will all be connected to Europe by the Panama Canal in a couple of years."

The two elderly gentlemen continued their amicable conversation without either of them changing the other's different understanding of world history and current events.

In an unimportant part of the New World, the small community of Aldermere, which had always provided the Wickford family with supplies and connections to other settlers, was yielding to Telkwa, the railway town on the west side of the river. Along with other farmers on the east side of the river, the Wickfords started going to the Telkwa stores instead of those in Aldermere. Florence

Chapter 12 — Tunnels Continue

always enjoyed the weekly half-hour trip to town, especially with the pony and trap which Edward had given her the previous year. The pony, Nigs, and the "one horse shay" as she called it, gave her more than transportation. They gave her an independence which no horse alone could have provided. Capable of taking two adults comfortably, the shay had room for one adult and the three children, as well as items purchased during her weekly trip to the village.

One afternoon, Florence was watching through the window as Edward returned from New Hazelton. Despite the growth of Aldermere and Telkwa, he continued to find it necessary to make occasional trips to both Hazelton and its emerging rival, New Hazelton.

After kicking off his boots and leaving them outside, he came as usual straight to the kitchen. Florence looked up from using a heavy wooden spatula to pull a new loaf of bread from the oven. "You'll have to tell us all about your journey." Then, pointing to the fresh bread: "And I'm sure you'd like to sample this. You can, but the children have to finish their vegetables first. Easy trip? No adventures I hope."

Hearing the "adventure" word, all three children looked up.

"Sort of. Not what I expected."

Jeffrey got in ahead of his sisters. "Anything exciting?"

"Yes, young feller. You'll be interested to hear what happened."

Edward continued, with the attention of the entire family: "I was walking to the bank in New Hazelton."

Then addressing Jeffrey, "It's another bank like the one you go to with your mother."

"What happened?"

"I heard all this shooting."

"Shooting?"

"Yes, shooting. Lots of it."

"Why?"

Still addressing Jeffrey: "Some robbers stole some money from the bank. They shot one of the bank people. Then some other people shot at the robbers. And they got some of the money back but not all of it."

"Did you shoot the robbers?"

"I didn't have my gun. So I couldn't do anything."

It was now Florence's time to ask questions. "Any fatalities?"

"Six. One bank employee and five bandits."

"How horrible! Good thing you were not armed."

Edward looked towards her and responded with emphasis: "Yes, dear. I think you're absolutely right."

Jeffrey hadn't finished. "It's good to shoot robbers."

"I agree. But you have to make sure they really are robbers."

"When can I learn to shoot?"

"When you're a little older. Don't worry. I'll teach you."

Florence took the stage to terminate the conversation: "Now, children, here's a slice of the new bread and you have time to play before bed." And then, turning to Edward: "That will be the headlines on Saturday."

"And telegraphed all over the world."

After the excitement from his tale had died down and the children became restless, Edward addressed Jeffrey again. "How was your trip to Telkwa, young feller?"

"We went to a bank but there were no robbers."

"Did you get any money?"

"Mumma did."

And then turning to his wife: "That must be the new Union Bank in Telkwa?"

"That was it."

"I suppose that's where all the stores will be soon. Then Aldermere will just die. Shame, but the railway will make life so much easier for most people."

Florence nodded. "You can tell that from the construction. It's everywhere. The rail bed's in place and they've started on the new bridge. Streets and lots are all laid out for development."

"Aldermere has served us well. Mind you, Aldermere may have the last laugh. Telkwa's on the river plain. Damn silly place to put a town. Unless you like floods."

"Another thing I learned is that the Agricultural Fair is also going to be across the river this year."

"I suppose that was bound to happen. So all of us, at least all of us this side, will have to get our horses across the old bridge. How does Nigs take it?"

"Didn't seem to mind. Just walked on. But we watched a pair after they had been unharnessed from the stagecoach. They just refused to cross."

Chapter 13

Disappointment
April 1914

With the work on the claims funded by the Wall Brothers, the annual exploration of Edward's claims would henceforth take advantage of the experienced miners, woodsmen, wranglers now available in the northwest. Edward planned to spend at least one of the three snow-free months at the site before the camp had to be shut down in September. All he had to do at this stage was to select the right people, establish objectives, meet the payroll, and make sure that all the reporting requirements were met. There were now two tunnels being driven, one on the original Raven claims in the west, the other on the crown grants he had purchased. Of the five Raven claims, the original three had been surveyed and application for crown grant status would soon be submitted. By the end of 1913 the lengths of the tunnels had reached sixty and twelve feet respectively. The copper vein on the west pinched and swelled and pinched again from as little as a few inches to just over three feet. The gold vein on the east continued to produce impressive grades, but over frustratingly narrow widths.

During the winter, especially when the snow was thick, the Wickfords' visits to Aldermere and even Telkwa became less frequent than in other seasons. When a journey was required they usually used horse and sleigh. Horses could slip on the ice and the consequences were less dramatic for people in a sleigh than a saddle. A horse-drawn sleigh was an efficient way of travelling, and once outside the boundaries of the farm the trail had usually been flattened by other travellers.

Life on the farm, though hard, was rewarding and the family was mostly self-sufficient in vegetables, milk and meat. Agricultural products of the farm were in demand. Travel to the south by steamer from Prince Rupert was becoming faster. The population

The Nisselinka Claims

of the Bulkley Valley was growing. Copper prices were down but that was not expected to continue. Thanks to the railway, due for completion within a few months, towns like Smithers, New Hazelton and Prince George were growing fast. Others, which the railway had bypassed, such as the original Hazelton and Fort George, had not been so fortunate, but their occupants adjusted by moving to the centres of growth. The previous year having ended well, both Edward and Florence felt that 1914 would be a year of achievement, with prosperity not far behind. But their optimism became constrained by a series of events, first from within the province and then from the world beyond.

Although Edward Wickford was a full-time farmer, much of his creative energy was directed at his mining venture. Since returning last summer, he had been thinking about the next expedition to his two groups of claims, some of them already elevated to crown grant status. With the snow in the mountains expected to last through most of May, the earliest time to begin work on the tunnels would be June. Most of the planning had to be completed long before then. He had got as far as sending letters to the two miners, who had gone south for the winter, and arranging to meet Syd the wrangler in Smithers. Other members of his team, being easier to replace, could be reached later.

Then, one day, when collecting his mail from the post office in Telkwa, he noticed an envelope from the Wall Brothers in Nelson. It was not what he expected nor was it what he wanted to hear:

```
                              Wall Bros. Ltd.
                              Baker Street,
                              Nelson, B.C.
                           3rd February, 1914

Dear Mr. Wickford,

We regret to have to tell you that we have decided
not to renew our right-to-purchase on your Nisselinka
claims this year.

Our decision is no reflection on the potential of
your mineral properties. Instead, it is a conse-
quence of uncertain copper prices and our need to
make substantial capital expenditures in our mines in
southeast British Columbia.
```

Chapter 13 — Disappointment

```
The veins on which you are driving the tunnels have,
in our opinion, an excellent chance of achieving
commercial grades and width and for this reason we
expect you will be able to find alternative sources
of finance for continued exploration.

We wish you continued success with your endeavours.

Yours ............
```

Edward read the letter again, muttered to himself, and folded it into his pocket. The half-hour journey back to the farm gave him plenty of time to think about the Wall Brothers and how their decision would affect the coming summer. Being able to devote the entire summer to the farm had advantages. And he looked forward to being with his family. But putting his dream on hold was not what he had planned and was going to be difficult to accept.

As soon as he walked into the kitchen, Florence, recognizing that something was troubling him, sent the children out of the kitchen. "Difficult day in town?"

Smiling at his wife's thought-reading, Edward responded, "You're too perceptive!" and after a pause while he walked around the table, "Yes. The Wall Brothers have withdrawn."

"So that means no funding for this year."

"That's it exactly. No funding. Keeping the claims is not a problem. We've done enough work to keep all the claims and to take some of them to crown grants. It's just that we don't make any progress."

"That means we'll have you here for July and August," said Florence with a laugh.

"Yes. You'll have to put up with me."

"The children will too. They'll be delighted."

Edward acknowledged his wife's attempt at humour by raising a single eyebrow. But it was not a moment for levity. He left the room still wounded by the loss of funding. He then remembered that the letters from Albert Sanders had included a request to inform him by telegraph if his current financiers withdrew. But there was no urgency and another journey into town within the week was not required. The telegram could wait until next week.

The message he sent the following week was short. There was no point in spending money on unnecessary words.

The Nisselinka Claims

TO: ALBERT SANDERS
4 More Street
LONDON SW1
WALL BROS WITHDRAW FROM BOTH
LETTER TO FOLLOW Wickford

The letter which followed explained in some detail the status of the claims, now five crown-granted, and four unsurveyed, most of which had had sufficient work applied to them to be "in good standing" for three years, some for five. Edward also explained how one of the quartz veins in the Belfrin claims had expanded to a width of seven inches at a grade of 0.7 ounces per ton at a distance of twenty-two feet from the portal. But when the next round had been mucked out, the miners found that the vein was no longer there. There was some evidence from surface that it had been displaced by a fault and would be found again with a short cross-cut.

Despite the setback to funding, April started well. The trains were running and villages like Telkwa and Smithers were on the map and connected to the Pacific Ocean in one direction and to the rest of Canada in the other. Having to visit Hazelton to complete documentation on his claims, he took the opportunity to ride the train. He had heard of the tracks being flooded and cars being derailed but he was curious and wanted to travel the new railway himself. Luck was with him. Instead of two days by horse, the journey from Telkwa took him little more than three hours, all of them spent in considerable comfort. From the station at New Hazelton he took a cab the four miles to Hazelton.

Like most of his kind, this cabbie liked to talk. "Come again next year, sir, and you'll be able to take one of those motor cars."

"And you'll have to learn to drive it."

"No sir. No way. They cost a lot more than horses. And they tell me that you keep on paying to fix them. There're two here already, but the drivers seem to spend more time underneath their wheels than I spend above mine."

Despite his interest in the new machines, Edward decided to be supportive. "I hear that they bring them on the railway because they can't make it on their own. Roads are too rough."

"And you heard about the one that won the prize a couple of years ago? First automobile to Hazelton. They got it here but they had to bring it in pieces on horses!"

Chapter 13 — Disappointment

"Yeah. I heard about it."

Conversation ceased while they crossed the Hagwilget Bridge, a hazardous contraption over a threatening drop to the gorge below.

As soon as they reached the north side, Edward's posture relaxed. "You know, I've been over that bridge I dunno how many times, but I'm always glad to get across."

"It used to be like that for me." And then after tapping his whip on the rail of the cab to prompt a faster pace up the hill, the cabbie continued, "You know, sir, I think I recognize you. D'you mind if I ask if you're in the mineral business?"

"That's right. But I'm a farmer most of the time."

"I saw you in town last year. You were with your pack team heading for your property."

"That sounds right."

"Copper, is it?"

"Yes. Mainly copper in one of our tunnels. Gold in the other."

"Gold, too. That's good. Another mine would be good for Hazelton. Roche de Boule brings a lot of business. I did a bit of prospecting myself as a young man. Exciting and interesting, but tough! We almost got trapped for a winter up on the Finlay. Came back thin and hungry. Could hardly walk. Then I decided I'd had enough. Found myself a wife and settled down. Been driving a cab ever since."

Neither Edward nor the cab driver said anything for a while until Edward pointed to the Wrinch hospital: "It's good to know it's there."

"You're right, sir. Was in it myself once, and very grateful I was to the good reverend doctor."

"And Doctor Wrinch still runs it, I believe."

"That's right, sir, he still does."

"First he built it, now he runs it."

When they reached Triangle Street, Edward stepped down onto the wooden sidewalk and tipped the driver.

"Thank you, sir. And good luck with your mine. I hope you make it big!"

"I'm sure you'll hear about it, if I do."

Chapter 14

A Distant War
September 1914

True to his stated intention, Albert Sanders had stepped in to fill the funding gap left by the Wall Brothers, and work on the two groups of claims had continued for a fourth season. By late September the horses were back in Hazelton, the crew had returned to their various homes, and Florence, by now accustomed to Edward's absence every summer, was enjoying having her husband back on the farm.

One cool September day when Edward had gone to Telkwa on an errand, Florence was inside the deer fence picking runner beans when she heard what she had been expecting, the sound of horses hooves on a rocky patch of the cart track. She was in the prime of life as a wife and mother, but her contentment was soured with apprehension. The news from Europe had been getting worse. The Germans had invaded the Low Countries. Newspapers were reporting facts and patriotic rhetoric. For reasons they had both begun to understand, she and Edward hadn't talked much about how it would affect them. In some respects, talk was unnecessary. They both knew that if the war continued for more than a few months, it would only be a matter of time before ordinary citizens, including those in remote places like northern British Columbia, would hear the call to arms. Florence knew that, sooner or later, Edward's sense of duty would call him in the same direction.

Basket in hand, she headed towards the driveway. Edward slowed his horse to a walk, swung his leg over the animal's rump and jumped down without waiting for it to stop. He tied the reins to the saddle, loosened the bridle so as to remove the bit from the horse's mouth, and left it, knowing it would prefer the grass at the side of the road to wandering very far. Edward's expression told her that he had news from town which she didn't want to hear.

Chapter 14 — A Distant War

Putting an arm round her, he didn't try to soften the news: "It looks pretty bad, Flo. The British Expeditionary Force has engaged the Germans in Belgium and the French are fighting in the Ardennes. The newspapers say that casualties on both sides are heavy. As you know, Canada declared in early August. Some of the unmarried men in Telkwa have already left for Vancouver."

She gave him an anguished look. Looking away, he said: "I'll unsaddle Finch and then be in."

As he walked towards his horse, he heard her say: "There's hot stew and fresh bread," but he did not turn round.

Three days later a neighbouring farmer, Roland Price, a man in his forties who owned a neighbouring farm, came by on his horse to drop off some mail and newspapers he had picked up for the Wickfords. As Florence expected and also hoped, he accepted her offer of a cup of tea. Edward was not expected back until later.

"Tell me how bad it is," opened Florence without needing to mention the subject.

"It's about as serious as it could be. All the major powers are involved, Britain, France, Germany. All of Europe has mobilized, now the Dominions."

"Are you going to go?"

"Well, I have to do my part. Being unmarried is difficult. I don't know what will happen to the farm. I just hope that I can get back before too long and carry on."

Florence just listened, saying nothing. Roland continued: "I hear that a lot of the young men have volunteered already."

"That's what I've heard too," said Florence slowly.

"And did you hear that Hans Menzel sold his business and has left the country?"

"Hans with the tackle shop? Of course we know him. Sold? Why?"

"So he could sign up, I suppose."

"But why would he do that? He's not…" Florence paused, then said, "Oh, my!"

Roland sensed her discomfort. "That's the way it works. The pull is strong. Same for him as for us."

"They say it could be over by Christmas."

"I've heard that too. But can you imagine either England or Germany throwing in the towel after only four months?"

"You're probably right." She took in a breath as if to say something, then paused.

"I know what you want to ask," said Roland. "Will Edward have to go?"

She nodded slowly, looking at the table and saying nothing. Roland continued talking but without conviction. "I can't imagine Canada calling up men with families to support. They will start with the young. Edward must be early thirties by now? That's getting on for military service. As for whether he will volunteer, that's up to him. Perhaps you will have a say?"

"I don't think I will have much influence. If he sees it as his duty there is nothing I or anyone else could do to stop him."

Florence walked out with Roland to his horse and watched him leave. Then she walked slowly back to the house, sat down at the kitchen table, glanced at the headlines of the Omenica Herald, put her elbows on the table, her head in her hands, and imagined the agony of family and farm with Edward away for years, perhaps for ever. Then she remembered what her mother said at times of difficulty. "Pull yourself together." She did just that and went back to preparing the evening meal.

The following months were a time of uncertainty for the Wickfords and their neighbours, indeed, for most citizens of British Columbia. Young men were signing up. The headlines in the newspapers trumpeted battlefront successes and mentioned setbacks in smaller typeface or on a later page. Itinerant recruiting sergeants could be seen in towns and hamlets across the land. On rare occasions Edward would say to his wife that he might have to join, and he would then talk about the farm and his relatively advanced age. Florence would bring their children into the conversation and talk about their upbringing. Once she made reference to sons needing fathers as they grew up. But that touched too raw a nerve and served only to terminate the conversation and add to Edward's lonely agony.

By midsummer he seemed less troubled, but it was another month before Florence heard from him that he had made up his mind. Duty called and he had to go. It came as no surprise to her. She had already concluded that he was bound to go and that it was just a matter of time before she would be told.

Chapter 15

On the Boat
December 1915

It was now well into December and Florence had been expecting a letter from England for what seemed like a long time, but in fact it arrived less than four weeks after Edward had left the farm.

Flo', my Dear,

Nov 21

We are now on board the Saxonia. She began life as a Cunard liner in 1907 and must have been quite luxurious then. Now she is a troop ship and has been going back and forth across the Atlantic for several months. I will write a few words every day and then catch the mail as soon as we're ashore. Most of us expect we'll dock in Plymouth; others expect Liverpool. There seems to be some secrecy about just where we will land.

By the time this reaches you, my letter from Halifax should have already arrived. Just in case it has gone astray, I will mention that it was mainly about the train journey. Although there were a few civilians, it was very much a troop train. Half the regiment was on board. An advance group had left Vancouver about a week earlier, and another group followed us two days later. So almost the whole regiment is together now on board this ship.

The C/O, Lt Colonel Crandon, is an impressive man, one of only three career soldiers. Most of the other officers are from militia units around the province and most of the men seem to come from the Kootenays, having signed up with the Kootenay Rifles. Quite a few are from Vancouver Island, many from the coal mines in Nanaimo and Cumberland. I am one of only three officers with no militia training. We think we were selected for a commission because we were older than most recruits and had demonstrated our ability to think for ourselves by having run our own businesses or farms.

I have met several in the mess whom I look forward to getting to know. One of them (his name is John McCormick) has a ranch just south of Fort George (Prince G. now, I suppose), where he runs about 50 head of cattle. He has left it in the hands of his wife, who sounds very capable, but with three children is going to be very busy. As you can imagine, he and I have a lot to talk about. Although most of the officers in the regiment no longer think that the war will be over very soon, they expect us to be home next year. In the evenings, especially at meal times, the officers seem to split into two groups, the married men at one table and the bachelors at another. The married men talk about what they will do when they get home, while the bachelors are looking forward to something best described as an adventure. My company commander is an interesting fellow. He has spent most of his adult life in Burnaby, where he established an accounting practice, specializing in both fishing and forestry.

When not occupied with regimental drills, I read a lot. And, as you might expect, I spend much of my time thinking about you and the children. After making allowances for the time differences, I think about what you are all doing. As I write (an hour before midnight by the boat's time) I believe it's about 8:00 in the evening with you, so you must be reading stories before bedtime.

Nov 24

Much of yesterday was spent getting used to the shipboard routine. We start the day with lifeboat drill followed by gymnastics on deck. Then there is breakfast, and by that time we all have a good appetite. The food is fine and I have no complaints. Between 9:00 and 10:00 we have rifle drill one company at a time. Some of this involves shooting at floating targets with live ammunition. As a second lieutenant, I command a platoon of 28 men, all of whom I am getting to know. I have to say that,

Chapter 15 — On the Boat

with a couple of possible exceptions, these are fine men and I regard myself as privileged to lead them.

Nov 26

More of the same today: gymnastics, which I enjoy, also target shooting. I find it interesting that just about everyone is familiar with guns. So many were raised in the country, many of them on farms. Our routine keeps us busy for most of the day but there is plenty of time for reading in the evenings. I also spend time thinking and planning the next stage of the mining claims. Tell Jeffrey I look forward to the time when he is old enough to come with me on an expedition. But I like to think I will get back long before he is comfortable on a horse and safe with an axe.

Nov 27

We must be just about in the middle of the Atlantic. For much of today there was a stiff breeze from the north with a strong swell. Quite a few men were seasick, but it doesn't seem to bother me. Gymnastics on deck when the boat is pitching and rolling was a challenge and not without its humorous moments. I often think about how fortunate I am having you and the children especially. Life on the farm is hard, but I wouldn't want anything else. Then we have our mining claim and all the excitement which it brings. Now I find myself being part of an important and noble mission, but I would give anything to be with you again.

Nov 29

It seems to be Plymouth. We are only a mile or so from the shore and can see the town and some of the countryside. In a few moments we will be called to parade on deck with kitbags and nothing left on board. I expect the next few days to be hectic with few opportunities to write. So my first task when I get a moment's free time will be to buy stamps and send this.

With all my love,

E.

Chapter 16

London Meeting
December, 1915

Although the early December day was grey and damp, Lieutenant Edward Wickford was enjoying the sights of London from the motorized taxicab he had hired at the railway station. He could have taken one of the horse-drawn Hackney cabs which were becoming outnumbered by the new machines, but motorcars were something of a novelty for the farmer from northern British Columbia, and he had chosen to be modern. He was riding in a Unic, a box-like machine, which was the most common variety on the streets of London at the time.

Edward was in uniform because civilian clothes had limited uses for a Canadian soldier stationed at Bramshott, and because men in uniform in the England of 1915 were treated with ready respect. Moreover, the opening moves of any conversation with a stranger were made easy by his Canadian shoulder badge.

He was looking into Green Park and its wintered trees, when he heard the driver change gear and slow down. Shortly thereafter the vehicle made a sharp turn. Then he noticed a large "IN" inscribed on the gatepost at the entrance to the semi-circular driveway of what he knew to be the Naval and Military Club, usually referred to as the "In and Out Club".

As he walked up the front steps of the club, an officer, his seniority evidenced by the red rim on his hat, came out of the club. By now well-trained, it did not require a moment's thought for Lieutenant Wickford to put up a smart salute and a "Good morning, sir". This was politely acknowledged as Edward entered the club.

"Good morning, sir," said an elderly concierge.

"Good morning. I've come to meet Albert Sanders."

"Oh yes, sir. He's in the coffee room. You must be Mr. Wickford. Shall I take your coat?"

Chapter 16 — London Meeting

"Thank you," said Edward, handing over his coat, hat and scarf.

The concierge led the way into a large room with a high ceiling, tall windows and numerous leather chairs, most of them occupied by gentlemen reading papers. As he passed a table with various newspapers and magazines, his attention was captured by a copy of the Illustrated London news folded to show a picture of an anti-gas respirator. It was similar to one recently demonstrated to the regiment during training at Bramshott. When Edward looked up he saw that the concierge was heading towards two chairs and a table next to one of the windows. The man in one of the chairs, who appeared to be in late middle age, seemed likely to be his host.

"Mr. Sanders, Mr. Wickford is here."

"Thank you, Symes," said Mr. Sanders as he rose from his seat with some difficulty.

"Good morning, sir," said Edward as he stepped in front of the concierge and held out his hand.

Albert Sanders, who was older and more stooped than Edward expected, greeted his guest with a firm voice. "I'm very glad you have been able to make it here. It is good of you to come. How was the journey?"

"It has been very easy, thank you. One train and one cab."

Mr. Sanders waved a hand to the other chair. "Do sit down. Did Symes know what to do? Bring you straight here?"

"Yes, indeed. He was very efficient. Knew exactly where to find you."

"That's good. He's a fumbling old codger. Don't know where they found him. We used to have younger men, but they had to go. Coffee? Or we can go into lunch in about an hour."

"A coffee would be really welcome. Thank you."

Mr. Sanders glanced at the concierge who, after a shallow bow to indicate that he had heard the request, turned towards the other side of the room.

"Well, it's really good to meet after exchanging letters with you for quite a few years now. I'm sorry it has to be war which has caused you to come. I suppose you have a family you've had to leave behind?"

"That's right, a wife and three children. We've been living on a farm since we got married."

"That will be difficult for your wife. How is she managing?"

"She seems to be coping. One of the problems, of course, is shortage of labour. It's hard to get men for the farms. Same with the forests and mines."

"Yes, I understand. How's the army treating you?"

"We're camped with the rest of the Canadian Division at Bramshott. It's a lot more comfortable than at Comox on Vancouver Island. The camp there was put up in a hurry after just about every able-bodied male in the province signed up."

"Yes. I've read about the percentage of Canadians who are volunteering. How's the training going?"

"Much as I expected. We do lot of route marches with full packs, digging trenches, rifle practice, bayonet practice and all that. Both officers and men get shuffled from one regiment to another, which is not very satisfactory. And drafts get pulled out and sent to France to replace the casualties."

"When do you expect to go?"

"We have not been told. I suppose it could be any day, which is why the training is intense."

"I don't suppose you have much time to think about your mineral claims?"

"Well, I do. Not a lot of time goes by without thinking of the family, the farm or the claims. Of course soldiers always think and talk about what they are going to do when they get home. In my case that is just it: family, farm and mineral claims. My wife knows that but she might expect me to put mineral claims first."

Mr. Sanders laughed. "I know what that's like. I've been in the mineral business myself."

"I remember, you wrote about that. South Africa must be a fascinating place."

"Yes. Like a lot of young men in the seventies, I went there. Others went to Australia or Canada or America to look around, but I chose Africa. Took a boat to Capetown and never went north of the territory which is now known as South Africa. Wonderful country. Ever been there?"

"Not yet."

"Miles and miles of open country. Good for ranching or riding. And then there are the minerals. A friend of mine knew George Harrison who found the reef."

"Reef?" asked Edward, looking puzzled.

"That's where the gold is. At least that's the word everyone uses. It's not a vein. Just a bed of white pebbles."

Chapter 16 — London Meeting

"I'd better watch out for white pebbles."

"Yes, and yes again. You've got all that unexplored country. If you find any pebble rock with gold, you'll have no trouble getting backers. Starting with me."

Sanders paused to get his breath. "So, as I was saying, I had this friend who told me he was putting up a small amount of money to tie on to the Harrison find. Did I want to join him? Of course I wanted to. The money wasn't much, but I had very little at the time. So I found, I should say raised, the cash, only a couple of hundred pounds, and went into partnership with my friend. It wasn't long before I sold it for thousands and I put that money back into getting more ground."

"This sounds like what I am trying to do."

"I thought you'd find it interesting," responded Sanders with a knowing smile.

"Tell me more."

"Well then it got more difficult. I was living in Jo'berg at the time. The Boers didn't like all us foreigners in their republic, so they squeezed us with taxes and gave us no vote in running the growing city. That's what triggered the Jameson Raid. Silly thing to do, but I understand why it happened. And the second Boer war followed. Like a lot of others who had benefited from the gold rush, I signed up and was in uniform for a couple of years. Miserable little war. But not so little, really. Lots of excitement, hurry, wait, hurry again, water shortages. I don't ever want to be thirsty again. Rather be shot at. Friends get killed. Bloody awful business. Now this one you're going to sounds even worse."

Edward was about to say something when Sanders continued. "When it ended I still had my money, so I headed back to London and put most of it in gilts, but continued to invest some on the gold fields. So, like you, I went from prospecting to military service."

"Now you specialize in financing mining ventures?"

"Not really. I have enough to live on, so I don't need to work, but ventures like yours can drag me back. It's hard to give it up." Sanders looked at his pocket watch. "It's almost one. If we go to the lunch room now we should be able to get a table by the window."

The table to which they were shown was evidently one favoured by Albert Sanders, who renewed the conversation as soon as he sat down. "I find this a very good club. Suits me well. I would be glad to propose you for membership, if that's what you would like. Finding a seconder will be no problem."

"That's very good of you, but I don't think I will have much chance to use it. That may change of course."

"Well just let me know when you're ready. Tell me more about your prospects. This gives me a chance to dig a bit deeper than the occasional letter allows. As you know I have taken a great interest in copper since I first learned about your discovery. And look at the price now. Did you see it yesterday? It seems my instincts were right. But, despite my interest in copper, I remain fascinated by gold. And, as you now know, it was the source of my good fortune."

Edward was about to tell his host about the old prospector's search for gold when Albert raised his hand. "Before I forget, I want to thank you for continuing to send me those annual reports. The last one for the year 1914 was particularly interesting for me because of the map of Hazelton and surroundings and the new railway line. I know your claims are a long way to the east of the map, but it was good to see the Suskwa river where your trail goes, also the wagon road up the Bulkley Valley. That's where you live isn't it?"

"That's right. Off the map on the east side of the Bulkley River."

"Sounds wonderful country." Albert sat back. "So, please tell me about the claims you bought."

"As you will remember," replied Edward settling in to his favourite topic, "we are working on two discoveries less than a mile apart. First came the copper on the west. Then, a year later, the gold in the east, where I acquired the claims by purchase."

"Yes, I remember one of your letters, but that one again, please. From whom?"

"A prospector who must have been over sixty when I met him. I had known that there were crown-granted mineral claims somewhere near mine, but I had done nothing about them. Then, in the early summer of 1911 the Inspector of Mines chided me for not being more diligent in finding out about neighbouring claims. And he gave me a lead by telling me that they used to be owned by a prospector whose work he respected. He also suggested that the claims might be for sale. So I found an address for the owner and went to see him in Hazelton. He was certainly old, lived alone and was very unsteady on his feet. He talked about gold on his claims. He told me in a rather crusty, combative manner that he would

Chapter 16 — London Meeting

sell the claims immediately for a hundred dollars each, but that if I waited until I had seen them, later that summer, the price would be much higher. He said he needed the cash. So with some misgivings I visited the bank and made the payment. When I returned to town later that summer, I was told that the old man had died. He had held those claims for nearly twenty years."

"Twenty years!" exclaimed Sanders. "And dreamed that they would make him rich!"

"Just like I am doing now." Edward paused and then continued: "Encouraged by you!"

"That's how it works. So let's make yours come true. Would you describe the gold veins?"

This was a topic Edward always enjoyed talking about. "We made quite a bit of progress last year. We've now got twenty-two feet on the vein, or I should say veins. The main one pinches and swells. At its widest, which is eight inches, it runs just under an ounce."

Sanders held up his hand. "Hold it a moment. I'm more comfortable with pennyweights. So that must be nearly twenty on my scale? That should be minable. On the reef they are mining about thirteen pennyweight over two feet and that's horizontal mining which is more expensive. Go on."

"When it's narrow the grade drops to about a quarter of an ounce. The interesting thing is the cross cuts. We did just two of those, each for six feet. They show more veins, all of them very small. Their grades are good, but they're too small to mine. We've had lots of discussion on what they mean."

The back and forth continued throughout lunch and then into the smoking room. Edward had always enjoyed the occasional cigarette, usually one he had rolled himself. Albert said he preferred pipes and cigars.

"So we've both signed the letter agreement. You've got the money. The next step is a proper agreement."

Edward nodded. "That would be good."

"There are a couple of changes I would like to make. All to your benefit, I believe."

"That sounds generous. I have to say the terms as they are very acceptable to me."

"The main change I suggest is that, if we are successful and it can go to production, I think you should continue to have an equity interest, minority of course, but something."

Edward felt obliged to say that he would not be able to contribute to any financing. "I don't think I would be able to fund that."

"You could do that out of revenue. You don't have to agree to anything just now. If acceptable to you, I will have my solicitor draw up a draft. And I need to do some more thinking about it. Then you and I can discuss it when you are next in London."

"I've no idea when that will be, but I look forward to it. As you know, my time is not my own. The regiment could be sent to France at any day."

"I understand that and it brings me to my next point." He hesitated, tamping down his pipe. "The agreement would have to cover the possibility of, heaven forbid, your demise. We have to recognize that the life of an infantry officer at the front is always at risk."

"That I understand. We guess at the casualties from the numbers they pull out of the regiments in training."

"In the event of your death and the claims becoming valuable, your family would, of course, inherit the value." Edward nodded in agreement without saying anything. He was about to mention that this would be covered by his will when his host continued. "As I told you in one of my letters, I speak for three of us on this venture. The focus of this particular syndicate is gold, so your eastern claim fits very well with our objectives."

Edward's response came with evident feeling. "And having you as financier fits well with mine."

"Very good. Then I'll arrange for the initial draft of the agreement for your review when we next meet."

Edward stared out of the windows, his mind on the farm for a moment. Then he said: "I suppose that an agreement drawn up here could be registered in British Columbia."

"I certainly think so, but that is a point I will investigate with my solicitor."

Edward Wickford took his leave shortly before four o' clock in the afternoon so that he would have time to catch the train back to Bramshott. While they waited for a cab on the steps outside the main doors, Albert Sanders said, "I have your address at the camp and I will send you the draft agreement as soon as it is ready. I look forward to meeting again. In the meantime look after yourself."

Chapter 17

Back from the Front
April 1916

For one of its periods of rest and recovery the regiment found itself on the outskirts of a small, rural town some twenty miles behind the front. The big guns could be heard only when the wind was from the east. Accommodation for both officers and men consisted of a series of tents and wooden huts in a once-grassy field now crisscrossed by boardwalks over the most-travelled pathways. Two other regiments, both from eastern Canada, were benefiting from this all-too-short respite from the guns, wire and slaughter of the trenches. Though far short of peacetime standards, the officers' mess, a commandeered barn, was appreciated for its basic comforts: hot meals and the ready supply of liquor. Some of Edward Wickford's fellow officers, especially the younger ones, spent most of their time in search of women and entertainment in the local town. They knew that lives were likely to be short and that no opportunity should be spared to experience the pleasures of existence while it lasted. Although he had participated in forays into town when they first arrived, Edward preferred the barn, his books and conversations with the older men he knew or met in the mess.

Despite the rules on what he could say, he cherished the opportunities to write letters home. At first, both Edward and Florence had been diligent with their correspondence. Within the limits permitted by the censors, he described not only the places and living conditions wherever the battalion found itself, but also the amusing or insightful antics of his fellow soldiers, their likes, dislikes, strengths and foibles. Florence, in addition to telling stories about the children and the types of person they were becoming, kept Edward informed on the local news and the characters involved, at first in and around Aldemere and Telkwa, then increasingly in Smithers as it grew from a swamp into a railway town.

But now Edward was finding letters home difficult to write. The battalion had experienced its first major loses on the front line and, recently relieved by an Imperial unit, along with the rest of the division, all ranks were trying to enjoy their first days of rest. Conditions for letter writing should have been good. The soldiers had time to themselves. Where they slept was warm and dry, and food was provided at regular intervals. Edward's problem lay in describing what he had been doing and seeing. A few sentences could have given an adequate description of what it had been like, but he was glad that he would not have been permitted to tell Florence that two fellow officers, whom he had described in previous letters in some detail, were now dead, and that one died on the wire in no man's land. Or that Sergeant Swindon, whose quick wit he had mentioned in previous letters, had been declared missing in action two weeks ago and that the day before yesterday his arm, identified by a wrist watch, had been disinterred during a bombardment. Or that the chances of a junior officer in an infantry regiment surviving unhurt for more than a month were slim indeed. So he decided to tell Florence about the rats and the mud and the nights without sleep.

At times of rest behind the lines, the CO required platoon commanders to write letters to the bereaved. Some carried out these duties with ease and efficiency, but for others it became a major task. Edward, who was ten years older than most of the subalterns, found himself playing the role of mentor to those having difficulties. He pointed them to various stock phrases they could use to describe the merits of the deceased, in most cases well deserved. It reminded him of what teachers had told him about writing report cards, except that in these cases, everyone described had excellent marks.

One afternoon, after watching a team from his regiment compete in a brigade football competition, Edward was sitting alone with a glass of beer and a week-old newspaper, when he became aware of two men approaching his table.

"Ned, I believe you've met Bill Dyson," said his CO as he introduced a young man with ginger hair and the shoulder badges of a second lieutenant.

Edward stood up, motioned the two visitors to the vacant chairs around the table, and shook the hand of the younger

Chapter 17 — Back from the Front

man. "Yes, indeed. I saw your name on the last draft. Posted to A company, if I remember correctly."

The CO then made it clear that he was not going to stay. "I have a mound of paperwork to get through. But I've just learned that Bill is a qualified mining engineer, so I told him that he had to meet another miner. I'll leave you two to talk."

"Beer?" said Edward as the CO left.

"Thank you. Just what I need."

In response to Edward's raised hand an orderly in the uniform of a Canadian private soldier arrived at the table.

"What can I get you, sir?"

Edward pointed to the cast around the soldier's left foot. "How serious is that?"

"Not at all. I was lucky. Just a piece of shrapnel into a toe. They had to remove the toe, but I'll be fine. Probably saved my life."

"How so?"

"I missed one of those advances. The regiment gained a hundred and fifty yards but most of my buddies didn't make it."

The delayed response, while both officers considered what to say, gave the orderly the opportunity he wanted. "Was that two beers you wanted?"

Edward glanced at his half-empty glass. "Thank you. That would be good."

After looking towards the orderly as he walked away with an uneven gait, Edward turned to his companion. "So you're a mining engineer."

"Yes, but without much experience. I had only three months on a mine, before I felt I had to sign up. The CO said you're a miner, too."

"Not exactly. I can't claim any professional knowledge. I'm an amateur. Most of the time I'm a farmer, but I get in some prospecting when I can."

"Someone, I forget who it was, said you have made an important find."

"That's good to hear and what I like to think. I've been lucky enough to raise money to drive a tunnel, so someone else must think so too. What about you?"

Bill Dyson sat back in his chair before replying. "I was raised on a farm in western Ontario. Rocks and minerals always fascinated me so I worked underground in Timmins and then joined the opening class at the Haileybury School of Mines. When I graduated there were lots of jobs in the east, particularly in Northern Ontario, but I liked what I heard about B.C. Nelson sounded like a good place to live and work. Plenty of mines, mountains, lakes. So I went there. That was a good move. I had so many opportunities. Silver or copper, big mines and small. I took a job sinking a four hundred foot shaft. I knew the theory, but actually doing it was all new to me. I had half of it done before I left and without a single fatality. The old timers seemed impressed. Things were going well for me. But it was hard to get miners. They were all signing up. Eventually I felt I had to go too."

"I know the feeling."

"I left a girl in Nelson. I am sure she'll wait for me, but I can't promise her I'll get back. How long d'you think this will last?"

"I wish I knew. But it can't go on forever. I've got a wife and three to go back to. And a farm. And my mining project."

The beer arrived in two pint-sized tankards. After a nod and thanks to the orderly, Edward raised his glass: "To B.C. and our return."

"Amen to that."

"The C.O. told me it's a vein you've discovered. I think he said copper."

Edward needed no more encouragement. To be able to describe his find to a knowledgeable listener was particularly gratifying. "We've got this vein, mostly copper with some gold, in the Nisselinka Range."

"You'll have to tell me where that is."

"We get to it from Hazelton, which you can reach by steamer up the coast and then a sternwheeler up the river. From Hazelton we go with horses. It takes about two weeks, sometimes a bit more. We start along an established trail to some well-known gold fields, then along trails we've had to make ourselves. It's north of the Grand Trunk Railway and, I think, if we can make it into a mine, we could pack-train the ore to the railway in less than a week."

"What sort of grade?"

"The copper ranges between two and four percent. The gold comes and goes but is usually about a tenth."

"Of an ounce?"

Edward laughed. "Yes. But, you know, I was talking to someone in London who is financing us. He is from South Africa and all his thinking is in pennyweight! So, yes, ounces."

"What about widths?"

Chapter 17 — Back from the Front

"Pinches and swells. It's thirty-four inches at the end of our tunnel. Appears to be getting wider."

"Steeply dipping?" asked the mining engineer.

"About seventy degrees."

"That's good. Those shallow-dipping veins are nothing but trouble. What's the hanging wall like?"

"Granite. Or something like it."

"That's good in a hanging wall. You shouldn't have problems with granite. At least, unless it's badly fractured. Not too much dilution. You wouldn't want to drive a tunnel through it."

Second Lieutenant Dyson paused for breath and continued, evidently enjoying a chance to talk about his chosen occupation to someone who was interested. "If you can get three percent, or even two at present prices, and keep it over thirty inches, you should have a mine."

Their conversation continued, touching on pack-trains, tramways, raw-hiding, smelters and smelter charges, the Grand Trunk Pacific Railway, life in British Columbia and much else, until they were interrupted by a rowdy bunch of young men returning from a spell of leave in town.

A week later the regiment was back at the front. April was about to yield to May and even the shell holes and trenches showed signs of spring.

Captain Wickford was using the hour he had before a nine o'clock muster parade to review the list of reinforcements which had arrived last night. The four officers and eighty-five men would replace those lost in the last two engagements and bring the regiment close to full strength. Most of the men came from towns in the Kootenays, with a few from Vancouver, but Edward's eye rested on one from Telkwa, a Corporal Sam Finning. This was not a name he recognized, but it was one he was sure to remember along with the company to which the man had been assigned.

The regiment was deployed in a series of trenches behind the front line, ready to take over from the Imperial battalion which had relieved them two weeks earlier, when Edward took the opportunity to visit C company, commanded by a captain he knew well.

"Where can I find Captain Reynolds?" he asked a saluting private soldier.

"He was here just ten minutes ago. He's probably in Sparrow trench. That's the next right and then left."

It took Edward no more than ten minutes to work his way along some three hundred yards of trench. The damage caused by shelling the previous day had been repaired, and the casualties removed. Duck-boarding and planks covered the worst of the mud. As it was a warm day with still air, the smells were particularly invasive. At times the stink would take him back to the farm, but only for a fleeting moment. They were not the same. Then he was reminded of butchering an animal, but that, too, was different.

The soldier's directions were good and led directly to the captain, who greeted Edward warmly. "Good to see you, Ned. What can I show you?"

"I noticed you have a Samuel Finning from the recent draft. He's listed as coming from my neck of the woods in the Bulkley Valley so I'd like to talk to him, if that would be allowed."

"Sure. Go ahead. I'm sure he would be glad to talk to someone from his home. Down this trench, second right and first left. You'll find him at the machine-gun position. Let's talk on your way back."

Corporal Finning was sitting on a piece of wood placed on a bucket. He stood up and saluted. Edward returned the salute. "I noticed that you are listed as a Telkwa man. That's close to my farm, so I thought I would come to see you. Is that where you're from?"

"Yes, sir. I was there with the railway crew in 1913. I liked what I saw so I managed to get back in 1914. Didn't last long with all this going on."

"I know all about that. What did you do there?"

"Various jobs. Some farm work. Some logging. Helped out selling saddles and bridles as I know quite a bit about horses."

"Would that have been Hans Meizel's tackle shop?"

"That's it. Good place to work. Then he sold it."

"You know why?"

"Not really."

"To sign up. Same as you and me. But the other team."

Just then their conversation was interrupted by the whine of shells going overhead followed by the sound of the guns behind the lines.

"The right direction," commented Edward.

Both men held further comments until they heard the explosion of the shells.

"How far was that, d'you think, sir?"

Chapter 17 — Back from the Front

"About five hundred yards. Somewhere near their front line. Perhaps that's where Hans is. Keeping his head down in some muddy trench."

"Crazy, isn't it, sir. Just think of all the good work we could be doing back home."

Conscious of his commission from the King, Edward thought that the drift of this conversation could become prejudicial to good discipline. So he brought it to a close, wished the corporal well, and started working his way back along the trenches, some of them merely damp, others filled with muddy water. Between returning salutes and the occasional greeting, he was thinking about the Corporal's brief comment. Yes, Samuel Finning, Hans from the other side, and Edward himself were all needed in the Bulkley Valley, where there was so much to do, so many opportunities. Without the war, men in both armies could have been engaged in productive activities, instead of this waste and destruction. But wars were a fact of life. Loyalty to king and country and one's own people had to come first. If another nation wanted to march all over you, it had to be stopped. Suitably fortified by the certainties of life, Captain Wickford continued his journey along the trenches to regimental HQ.

Chapter 18

At the Front
June 1916

They were waiting for the wind. It had been blowing in various directions for the last hours and now at last it seemed to be coming from behind them. The enemy trenches lay about a hundred-and-fifty yards away on the other side of two lines of barbed wire. The Canadian infantry battalion from British Columbia was to storm the trenches after the enemy had been attacked with gas. The equipment and the procedure for the release of gas were experimental. Sergeant Rackham, who had been entrusted with managing this new weapon, approached Colonel Crandon, a tall man who, despite his moustache, looked too young for the rank he held. The sergeant saluted.

"All cylinders in place, Sir, and ready to operate!"

"Thank you, Sergeant. We'll stand by until the wind settles down. Do we have any sailors in the regiment? They might be better at guessing how the wind will behave."

"That's a good idea, sir. I'll find out."

The night sky had given way to a grey dawn. The sentries were stamping their feet to beat the cold. A full company was on standby in the trenches. If they were attacked without warning the enemy could be on the wire in less than a minute. And if he were not repulsed at the wire, he could be through it in another minute. The rest of the regiment was in dugouts connected to the trench. One company was in a parallel trench fifty yards to the rear, connected by a communications ditch. Captain Wickford, the duty officer, looked along the trench and was generally satisfied with what he saw. Apart from the occasional shell, the front had been quiet for two weeks. During this time the regiment had had plenty of time to work on the trenches. The timbering had been re-enforced and additional corrugated iron placed where it was needed most. There was nothing much they could do about the rats. They were

Chapter 18 — At the Front

just there. A well-aimed blow with a piece of wood or a bayonet sometimes yielded a dead one, but there seemed little point. There were just too many. The smell was bad but Captain Wickford had experienced worse. The latrines were under control thanks to the quartermaster keeping up a good supply of Chlorox. Bodies were always hard to handle. They were frequently unearthed by a shell or just by digging. And then they had to be disposed of, back into the ground with a prayer, perhaps to be exposed again by another shell a few days later.

After two days of waiting for the wind to turn, the colonel and his advisors decided at five o'clock in the morning that the wind, after blowing mildly to the east for an hour, was going to stay in the same direction. The first release had been planned for five-thirty, but that had been postponed. Now, half an hour later, the CO gave the order for his company commanders to assemble again. The revised plan was to release the gas at six-thirty and, in compliance with orders from brigade HQ, to follow it with an assault. Dawn was breaking when the canisters were opened. By this time the entire regiment was standing by in the trenches ready to advance. Edward, acting as Assistant Adjutant and not attached to any of the three companies, had requested permission to go over the top with A Company. He would be acting as second in command to Major James Fraser, who was short of officers. As the gas was released Edward looked through the periscope, swinging the instrument from one end of the regiment's lines to the other. A low fog of green drifted slowly away, hugging the ground. He wondered why it had to move so slowly. Was the wind slowing? Then he watched in horror as the green cloud started drifting sideways. Would it come back? He considered a warning to don masks but decided to wait. As he watched, the cloud started to inch eastward again and finally hit the enemy lines three hundred yards from its intended target, opposite 3rd Division lines.

Two hundred yards away, on the other side of the wire, Karl Hermann was looking through a small telescope at the enemy trenches. Nothing new. In fact nothing much had happened for several days except the occasional batch of artillery shells. Apart from one which had killed three and seriously wounded four others, the shells had not inflicted much damage. The trenches and tunnels were well constructed, supported with timber and, in some cases, with concrete. The lull had given him a chance to write letters and to read some of the books which reached the trenches from time to time. At twenty-one, Karl frequently found himself wondering what he would be doing had he not become a soldier. Along with numerous other young men in the engineering class at the Technische Universität Berlin, he had heard the speeches and exhortations which accompanied or replaced the lectures on the engineering subjects he had come to hear. There was no doubt that the Fatherland was being challenged. He and his classmates had been told again and again that their country needed them. They were required as soldiers. Engineering could wait until the war was over. Then they could get back to their chosen careers. Karl had been reluctant, a feeling he had confided in only one friend. He did not want to be accused of disloyalty to his country. That would be unthinkable. The defining day had come when one of the teachers announced at the end of the lecture that he himself was leaving to sign up and that the following week classes would be taken by a former teacher who had been called out of retirement. During the next day a rumour circulated the classroom that two other lecturers had announced they would be leaving to join the army. Within a week, the network of commitments, obligations and expectations which made the university had started to fray. The call to arms had overcome resistance and all but a few, most of them physically impaired in one way or another, had taken leave of the institution from which they had expected qualification for a productive and rewarding life. Karl had been no exception. He and three good friends had joined this infantry regiment, one in which a great uncle of his had served in the Franco-Prussian war.

After basic training, which was much as he had expected and probably no more boring or brutal than in other armies, the four friends found themselves in a Bavarian Division in the first battle of Ypres. Because the affairs of state had not been one of his interests, Karl had been no more than partially aware that the standing armies of the European nations were supported by militias involving large proportions of the male population of military age. Nor had he known that in 1914 his country had two million men under arms and the French over a million. But by now, although still unaware of the numbers, he knew that the opposing armies had already succeeded in slaughtering large numbers of their enemy. Unlike previous European wars, which had been fought by professional soldiers, the majority of his companions in the trenches had been civilians before the war.

Chapter 18 — At the Front

Karl had been recognized for his bravery and leadership in the battles of November 1914 and was now a battle-hardened soldier with the rank of Leutnant. Not a day passed without him remembering the friends with whom he had volunteered. They were no longer with him. Hans and Gustav had been killed attempting to take an enemy trench in one of the first encounters; Gregor had been repatriated with wounds which would leave him a cripple for life. Karl was thinking of them as he put down the periscope. Then something, he knew not what, prompted him to peer through the lens again.

He followed his usual procedure, to direct his gaze first at the far left field of view, then move his line of sight along the enemy lines from left to right. His line of sight had just passed the centre when his gaze became focused on two places. He had stared for no more than three seconds when he realized what he was seeing. This was not one of those observations which required calling for an senior officer or a sniper. He knew exactly what he had to do. With his voice at full parade-ground volume, he called for action and gas masks. Immediately the trenches within hearing distance sprang to life. He heard with satisfaction the orders being barked. A few seconds later he could hear shouted orders from more distant trenches, then the sound of men emerging from the bunkers, gas masks on and bayonets fixed. By now the officer to whom he reported was looking through the same periscope, while he and others were peering over the parapet for a few seconds at a time. It was unmistakable now: the ground-covering fog of green was drifting slowly towards them. They watched it for several minutes, then watched it drift south along the barbed wire. They could hear the regiment on their left flank called to action. After half an hour the wind picked up and, as far as they could see, the green cloud was dispersing before it could do any damage or justify an assault by the enemy.

Edward was disappointed by the failure of the experiment, but he was relieved that they would not have to attack that day. He saw from a distance that the company commanders were assembling for a conference with the CO. A few minutes later, the commander of C Company, Patrick Trahern, whom Edward had met briefly in Nelson in 1911, squeezed past him in the narrow trench. "We are going to attack in half an hour. No gas, no guns. Bloody stupid, of course, but the colonel says he has to follow orders."

Edward felt a tightening of his stomach. But he prided himself on being a good soldier and doing what he had to do. He forced himself to address the problem at hand. How were they to minimize casualties between the two sets of trenches? The wind had now turned into a steady breeze towards the east but there was no more gas to use. A patch of blue heralded clearer skies. Visibility was excellent. He heard the order rippling down the line: "Stand by to advance in fifteen minutes."

As the order to advance was shouted down the trenches, six hundred men climbed in three waves out onto the open ground. Almost immediately they came under rifle fire from the opposing lines. At first it was not threatening, just an almost regular crack and thump as the bullet went by. But not all went by. A few men fell. Not until they reached midway between the trenches did they hear the machine guns. Edward was near the middle of A Company's three lines. The men were running forward, but as some fell the lines became ragged. Men could be seen forming clusters where the wire was being cut. Some used armalite bombs to break through, others threw wooden ramps on the wire. Some were lying down and attempting to return the fire. Then the regiment's bugler sounded the retreat, and B company on his left started back. At the same time he noticed James Fraser lying on the wire, his head thrown back, his face covered with blood. Edward realized he was in command. There was no time to think of James as a person. He had become just another lifeless feature of a fast-changing scene of devastation. Edward called for smoke from the bombardiers.

With the smoke forming thick blankets obscuring the field of fire, soldiers of A Company retreated in order, some doing their best to provide cover by firing into the smoke from positions on the ground, others running back past their comrades and in turn adopting firing positions. The machine guns were still firing but with less effect. It took five minutes to reach the home trenches. Of the six hundred who participated in the assault, ninety had been left on the battlefield. Eleven of these were picked up during a truce later in the day, though only six would survive their wounds. Later that morning the Colonel, his arm in a bandage, came to A Company's HQ to congratulate Edward for his handling of the situation.

Chapter 19

Another Front
April, 1917

Major Edward Wickford looked at his watch. It was five o'clock. In exactly thirty minutes the battle they had all been training for would begin. The enemy was well dug in and well prepared to defend a ridge which provided a commanding view in all directions. The four divisions of the Canadian Corps had practised the assault at a place well behind the lines, where the layout of trenches to be attached, the wire and the landmarks had been replicated. Thanks to elaborate training, every man knew the plan: wave after wave of infantry were to advance behind a creeping barrage laid down by the heaviest concentration of artillery ever assembled. At five-thirty the 102nd (North Vancouver Island) and 87th (Montreal) were to advance behind the barrage and take the first four lines of trenches. Then Edward's battalion and the 87th were to advance through the four lines already captured and take the next four.

Rain, changing to snow and sleet, was falling continuously. Major Wickford and his men were cold. Half of them he knew well from his days as a captain in A Company. The other half had arrived during the last weeks to replace those killed or wounded in the previous month. Edward couldn't stop thinking of his family. Florence had been good with the letters and packages, the last of which had arrived only three days ago. The family had let the land to a neighbouring farmer and were now living in Vancouver. It was nearly eighteen months since he had seen any of them. Jeffrey was now nine, Annabel almost eight and little Penny at six might scarcely remember him. Enough of day-dreaming. He pulled out the green handkerchief Florence had given to him and tied it to the button of his left breast pocket as he mocked himself for his superstition. He looked down the trench. Some men were standing, some leaning against the sides. Fifteen minutes to go. He walked slowly down the narrow passage, greeting each man as he passed.

"Good morning, sir," said Captain Stewart, saluting. Fred Stewart had arrived recently. He seemed to be competent and the men evidently respected him. Everyone knew that his job was to take over when Major Wickford was killed or wounded. After that it would be Lieutenant Granger, then..... Five minutes to go. Then it would start. For the first thirty or perhaps sixty minutes the regiment would be waiting, then its turn would come.

A minute before zero hour, flares from the enemy enabled Edward and others, peering over the sandbags, to recognize the features they had come to expect. Then as he watched the minute hand pass the start time, Edward was aware of the sky behind the lines light up as the heavy guns fired. Seconds later he heard the rumble of a distant noise which grew louder until it was impossible to hear anything else. At almost the same moment the enemy lines ahead of him were illuminated by exploding shells. After several minutes he saw the first men of the 102nd emerge from trenches in front of him and move forward in a line, rifles at the ready, bayonets fixed. The sounds of rifles and machine guns were almost lost among the explosions. Edward, watching the advancing line, saw men fall forward; some were knocked backwards; others swerved to avoid patches of enemy wire which had survived the shelling. In the flickering light of the eighteen-pounder shells now landing a hundred yards beyond them, he saw the round-arm action of the bomb throwers. Then the line of soldiers, now about half their former number, disappeared into what he believed to be the first enemy trenches.

After about an hour, Edward recognized the three-flare signal that indicated the first objective had been achieved. About a minute later he received from the CO the signal to advance. By now scattered shells from enemy guns were exploding on the ground just crossed by the 102nd. As planned, men of B Company now climbed out of their trenches and advanced in open order across the former no man's land, now a patchwork of interlocking craters filled with mud, water and, in most of them, dead or wounded men. Coming in towards them were walking wounded and parties of prisoners with their guards. Little was left of the enemy trenches. Like the surrounding ground, the trenches had been converted to shell holes with broken timber, bent fragments

Chapter 19 — Another Front

of corrugated iron, as well as shredded clothing, the wounded of both sides, the dead and parts of the dead.

When the men of B Company reached the positions now held by the 102nd, they could see the open country beyond. Continuing over captured trenches, they found themselves within one hundred yards of their objective, the next line of trenches, where the shells were now bursting. Then the signal came to wait until the barrage moved forward. After seeing his men take cover, Edward found himself in a shell hole already occupied by a private soldier, his arm covered in blood. Noticing Edward looking at him, the soldier said, "Nothing serious, sir".

The barrage lifted and in response to the CO's signal the regiment continued its advance. Edward and the remainder of B Company, now some forty men, moved towards the enemy trenches as fast as the mud and water would allow. A machine gun opened up on their left. Several men were hit. A moment later, Edward was aware that the gun post had been overrun by men of A company on their left. As they advanced, Edward and those near him were slowed by a series of interlocking shell holes. With only thirty yards to go to the trench ahead of him, Edward glanced to his right, where he could see some of his men jumping down into a trench, bayonets fixed. He looked again at the trench ahead of him, and then….

Some time later he became aware of rain falling on his face. He opened his eyes to see a grey sky. He could feel straps across his legs and chest. He could also see the back of a helmeted man near his feet. The man's loping stride threw him against the straps, first to one side and then the other. He was not aware of anything else until, still on his back, he could see the roof of a large khaki tent. Doctors and orderlies were going in every direction, ignoring him. He could hear heavy guns. A nurse, looking like an angel, passed by him. He called out. Then a man came by, lent over his bed and said: "Major Wickford. Can you hear me?"

"Where am I?"

"Field dressing station Number 84. You're going to live. We'll get you out of here as soon as we can."

He tried to sit up, but the strap around his chest and a shooting pain stopped him.

Chapter 20

Revision
July 1917

Edward never remembered much about his time in the first hospital, just a blur of nurses, white-coated doctors, and being wheeled around. But he did remember being shown a bullet which had been extracted from his leg, and three pieces of shrapnel from his chest and abdomen. The surgeon said the bullet must have hit something hard, probably metal, before reaching Edward, so it had entered sideways thereby doing damage to his muscles but not to the bone. He learned, too, that the break to his leg had been caused by blast, not by impact.

The first two weeks after his transfer to the Canadian Convalescent hospital in Bromley was a welcome respite from the trenches, but he soon became restless. He wanted to get out, to see his comrades in the regiment, or at least to hear how they were doing, and to rejoin them as soon as he could. He wrote to them and received replies, but their letters were constrained by army censorship. He wrote frequently to Florence and she to him, but their letters took at least two weeks each way and some never arrived.

Eventually he was told that at the end of a further two months convalescing in Britain he was to report for administrative duty at division headquarters. He had applied to rejoin his regiment, but had been told that that was unlikely. In the meantime he was free to travel. He took the opportunity to find relatives he knew only by name and to catch up with people he had come to know, Albert Sanders among them.

On one of his visits to London, when he was talking to Albert in the smoking room of the Naval and Military Club, the topics included the usual: mining, votes for women, and Irish independence, but inevitably came back to the war and recent casualty

Chapter 20 — Revision

figures. Their conversation then lapsed while both men retreated into the cloud of tobacco smoke surrounding them. Then, Edward noticed Albert's expression through the haze. He looked as though he was grasping for solutions before he spoke.

"We have to face reality." Although Edward believed he knew what topic was going to be introduced, he waited for the older man to explain himself. "We both know that the life of an infantry officer is dangerous and can be short."

Edward helped him out. "Of course, I have to recognize that. If they let me back with the regiment, my life could end any bloody day."

"And it all but did, just a couple of months ago. So let's plan accordingly. The right to purchase your mineral claims will, of course, survive your death and, if we find anything important, your family must benefit, even if you're not around."

"Yes, that's covered in my will."

"But I don't suppose your wife knows much about mineral claims."

Edward smiled. "You are quite correct. And I think she would prefer to keep it that way." After a pause he added: "And so would I."

Albert chuckled and then became serious again. "And there's another factor we have to take into account."

Edward waited again, this time not knowing what to expect.

"As I'm more than twenty years older than you, I could go first. It wouldn't need a bullet. Old Father Time will come when it suits him."

Albert drew on his cigar before continuing. "You see, like many in the business, I would like to find a really big orebody before I die. It would give me and, I am sure, you, enormous satisfaction as well as make us rich."

"There may be nothing there."

"That's my next point. If there's nothing there, so be it. What we both want to avoid is missing a big one and leaving the wealth for some other sod to find."

Edward signalled agreement by nodding slowly and waiting for the older man to continue.

"All this means is that I should put enough money into the venture to see it through. The gold claims, I mean, the ones in the east. Or at least give them a fighting chance. I think copper will drop after the war so gold's my main focus."

Edward nodded.

"So that means," Albert went on, "that even if neither you nor I are still around, your wife would have the money to continue. All she would have to do is hire the right people to continue the work."

Edward had enough experience in business to know the boundaries which typically separate two parties engaged in negotiating terms of an agreement. He now saw his counter party and part-time mentor further blur the differences. "That would be most generous of you. But are you intending to look after my interests as well as yours?"

"Your family's interests, as well as mine. You are fighting for King and country. If you die, I will owe you something. Which means helping those you leave behind."

"What about your own family?"

"If we are successful, we both benefit. We would both get rich. As for my family, I don't have one. I was married for a few years. We had no children. But I have a nephew who is showing a lot of promise. There are also some cousins I don't get on with too well. A couple of them think they can sponge on me whenever they need a few pounds. Just because I have more than they do, they expect to be able to share whatever I have. I started with very little and took some risks which they don't begin to understand." Albert's anger was coming to the surface but, after a pause to draw on his cigar, he continued. "So what I'm thinking is this. I put enough money into a fund for work on the claims to continue for, say, six, perhaps eight years. The money I put in would earn me a majority, vested ownership. Your interest would be carried. Then, if my side can't continue to move ahead with the venture—I mean if I've gone and my nephew's gone too—there will have to be a way of your family getting back the claims. If you survive the war, you will be able to apply that money to the claims; if not, your wife should be able to engage the right people. And she wouldn't have to go and raise funds or negotiate new deals."

"That's a generous offer, very generous. You know, many times I have stood in some miserable trench wondering what happens if the next wizbang gets me. My wife would have to sell the farm, and the mineral claims would certainly have to go too. Do you really want to do this?"

"I do indeed. This is not a thought of the moment. It is the product of many hours. And I'm not finished yet. The nephew I mentioned, he's only eighteen but has the makings of a fine young man. I'll leave him everything, including my interest in your mineral claims."

Albert paused, staring at the smoke he had exhaled. "If he survives, of course."

"He's in the trenches?"

"Still training. He could go any day. But if he dies before me, then I'll have no one to take what I leave behind."

Edward, listening intently, did not respond. Albert continued. "So, if he survives he can continue with the option, and if it makes money, leave it to his sons, if any. Even daughters, I suppose. But, if that family ceases to exist, you get the whole thing back. I don't know quite how to do it, but I'll get the agreement to you as soon as I can."

They continued talking until Albert's cigar was just a stump. Minerals and mining remained the principal topic, but the war intruded from time to time.

Albert closed off the discussion on the claims agreement. "So I will get my solicitor to draft the new agreement or amend the old, whichever way he wants to do it. We can sign it here and you can get it registered in British Columbia."

"I will do just that … and I remain very grateful," was Edward's reply as stubbed out the remainder of his cigarette.

Chapter 21

Return to Canada
January, 1919

The five-day crossing of the Atlantic on R.M.S. Mauritania was uneventful. Many of the officers and men who had been encamped in Belgium after the armistice, and then in England at Bramshott waiting for a troopship, were on board. Three of the officers, two majors and a captain, had served with Edward long enough to become good friends. Only one of them, John McCormick, now Major, had been with Edward on the Saxonia from Halifax nearly three and a half years before, when they had both been junior officers. He had lost touch with the others who had been on that crossing. Those who had survived had been transferred to other regiments or invalided home.

There was much about the return voyage to remind Edward of the previous crossing—the bunk beds, the safety drills, and the food. But gone were the physical fitness sessions and the rifle drill and the bayonet practice. Also absent was the sense of adventure. The excitement had been replaced by relief, accompanied by something akin to guilt for being a survivor. Conversation was now about what homecoming would be like. Several, including Edward, were apprehensive about re-establishing relationships and adjusting to an utterly different life. Music helped. In the evenings after dinner someone played a piano and the singing began and usually lasted until midnight. Then the lights went out as evidence that the army still set the rules. They were still soldiers and would remain so until the final dispersal.

On most evenings when the weather was fine, Edward would go to the upper deck and look out across the open ocean and reflect on his last three years, his mortality, and how he would use the future. His thoughts dwelt on the luck that had kept him alive, unlike many of those with whom, in the misremembered phrase of

Chapter 21 — Return to Canada

a half-forgotten poem, he had "toiled and wrought and fought". He thought of Florence, their children, the farm he had left at the age of thirty-two in the prime of life and health. He thought of his and Charley's discovery and the possibility of wealth. Then, imagining himself in the woods on his way to his "mine," he thought of his leg. In the context of what he had seen, his was a minor wound which troubled him only occasionally. More troublesome was his lack of breath from those few seconds when he had breathed air tinged with gas. He thought of what he would have to do on the farm. The house would, he was sure, need work and the family would demand attention.

After disembarking at Halifax, men from British Columbia, the majority on the boat, said goodbye to a few from the Maritimes before boarding the train for the West Coast. The Canadian scenery rolled past, mile after mile of coniferous forest and deciduous trees of Quebec and Ontario still devoid of foliage. Some twenty men and one officer left the train in Toronto and several more in Winnipeg. Then they were in the big-sky prairies. As they rolled farther west, Edward felt gradually unburdened of both the obligations and discipline of regimental life and he started thinking again about the Bulkley Valley and his claims in the Nisselinka Range. He knew the farm was in good hands but, when Florence had first proposed leasing it and moving to Vancouver, he had been strongly opposed. Then he had yielded to her arguments: education for the children, especially Jeffrey who was now almost twelve. Florence had finally convinced him with her news about the shortage of labour all over the province. So many had signed up for the war that the mines, forests, and farms were all short of workers. His neighbour, Henry Milford, who had been too old for military service, had agreed to look after the farm. In return he had the right to the hay and any crops he could grow. He would keep an eye on the house and make sure it wasn't taken over by animals.

Florence's letters describing their new home in Vancouver had convinced Edward that the $1,600 they had spent on the house in Kitsilano had been a good investment and the move a sensible decision. It had seemed like a lot of money at the time, but trying to remain on the farm would have been made very difficult by the shortage of labour. All the children were now at school. The family had neighbours, other families with children of much the same age. If Florence needed help, there was a community she could call on. She had described how she had been able to lend support, on more than one occasion, when a neighbour had received one of those dreaded telegrams. What if she were to get one? No longer on a remote farmstead, in Kitsilano she was close to her siblings, and there were wives, mothers and widows nearby to whom she could have turned.

At last the distant horizons yielded to the confines of snow-covered mountains. The slow grind up the mountain passes changed to the downhill of the western Rockies and then the pine and sagebrush of the dry belt before reaching the Coastal Mountains and the Fraser Canyon. Scrubby pine gave way to larger trees and then the magnificent Douglas firs of the Fraser Valley and the coast.

He hadn't seen his family for over three years. He expected from her letters that Florence would be there at the station with the children. She would recognize him, but would the children? As the train emerged onto the Fraser delta and then slowed through New Westminster the demobilized soldiers started exchanging goodbyes. They all knew that once on the platform in Vancouver, there would be no more opportunities.

Scanning the crowd as the train drew into the Canadian Pacific station, Edward caught a glimpse of Florence flanked by three children looking at the carriages. She looked just as he had been remembering her, but she was staring at another part of the train and had evidently not seen him. Seeing her before the train stopped was not what he expected, and somehow brought his emotions closer to the surface than he was ready for. He had imagined the meeting time and time again and it had always been after he had worked his way through the crowd. In a minute or so this was exactly what he would be doing.

Once on the platform he knew where to find them. But she was looking in the opposite direction. He called out. She turned and started towards him, arms outstretched. The younger two children stayed close to their mother. Jeffrey just stared.

The house was much as he had expected. A timber-frame building with a small porch, shingle-clad and shingle-roofed, thirty feet from the road, and with a backyard against a lane. It took a day or two before the children became used to this strange man in their house and rather longer to settle into a comfortable and happy routine. As part of a community, Florence's and Edward felt their happiness clouded by knowing other families who would never

Chapter 21 — Return to Canada

be able to welcome a returning husband and father. Florence was good friends with two widows. One had three children, the other, having been married for only a few months before her husband signed up, was all alone.

He found it easier than he had expected to become used to his new routine—fixing the house, walks with the family, socializing with other couples and other families. But, despite having returned from sufficient challenges for a dozen lifetimes, he continued to feel the need to strive and to achieve. The farm was part of him and so were his mineral prospects. Shortly before joining the army he had completed as much work as possible to put the unsurveyed claims in good standing for four years. The crown grants required only payment of annual taxes, which were not onerous. And now, with Albert Sanders having committed to funding for several seasons, he was well positioned to continue work on his claims. Although copper prices had collapsed with the end of the war, gold was still worth mining and base metals would no doubt recover in due course.

At one of the family's evening meals, Jeffrey asked the question, "Father, are you going back to the mine again?".

"I'm glad you asked, young fella." Edward looked around the table, then back to his eldest. "And the next thing you'll tell me is that you want to come with me!"

"Yes, I want to come. I want to see the farm and the mine."

"I would like that, as soon as you are ready. I will talk to your mother about it. We have to make some plans. Our first objective is to get the farm going again and that is going to take a lot of work."

"Will we move back to the farm?"

Florence joined the conversation: "Don't forget, Jeffrey, you and your sisters have to go to school. We have to make sure that you will get a good education. We don't know much about the schools up there. How much of the farm do you remember?"

"I remember the horses. Also the grass, which was as high as me before it was cut. And of course I remember the house."

She turned towards her husband. "I sent a letter to Jill last week asking what state the place is in. We should get a reply soon, perhaps next week. I asked her about schools."

"We could go there for the summer," said Jeffrey emphatically.

His father nodded. "That would be a good plan."

Chapter 22

Return to the Farm
1919 June

The Wickford family would return to the farm for the summer of 1919. Edward would have liked a permanent move, but he recognized the force of arguments against it: the children were in school, the farm had probably become run down during their nearly four years of absence, and his capacity for physical labour was no longer what it was.

Preparing for the summer triggered a range of emotions: excitement in the three children, Edward's relief that he was actually going to see his farm, and Florence's gratitude for the second homecoming for the husband she had expected to lose. Edward's anticipation was mixed with realism about what would be required to get it working again. Florence looked forward to the expedition as a family holiday, and to the long-anticipated reunion with the Milfords, particularly Jill, with whom she had been corresponding since moving away. Not only had Henry and Jill been looking after the house and farm, but before the war the two couples had been very close.

The journey was easier than it had been when they'd first moved north. No longer did it require stagecoaches and sternwheelers up the Fraser River to Fort George, followed by stagecoach again to the west, or a hazardous journey by sternwheeler up Skeena Inlet. This time they took a steamer up the coast to Prince Rupert and then a train on the Grand Trunk Pacific Railway to Smithers, which still showed the scars of the construction site it used to be. From there it was less than an hour to the farm.

They had a choice of vehicles at the station. Edward, having set aside his usual take-charge approach to such decisions, let the family decide. Their unanimous choice was an automobile. The

Chapter 22 — Return to the Farm

driver of the first car in line welcomed them, helped with their baggage, and then asked Edward the destination.

"To a farm on the wagon road, just west of Stone Creek. If the owners are in, that's where we'll get off. If not we'll need to go to another farm a mile down the road."

The cabbie looked concerned. "I don't normally go that far out of town, guv. It's a really rough road even at this time of year. I'll have to charge you extra."

"That's fine. Let's go."

As the automobile bumped and lurched along the wagon trail, they looked out on a field of tall grass ready for haymaking on one side and at grazing cattle on the other. Edward pointed first to one side and then the other. "Nice to see Henry's doing well." Then, after a few seconds of silence, while all members of the family were taking in the scenery, he turned to Florence. "Are you sure they're expecting us?"

"Oh, yes. At least sometime this week. I doubt they'll be at the farm, having enough to do at their own place, but I've mentioned it in my last two letters. No need to send a cable."

"That's good." Edward waved both arms as if to capture the landscape on both sides of the car.

"You know, all this is just like I've been remembering it. Let's go to our place first."

Florence's only response was to put a hand on his knee and to conceal her emotions.

As they came to the end of the drive they could see that their house, the barn and stables were still there, though evidently unused. Weeds were abundant in the driveways and walkways. The children, having heard about the farm continuously since they'd left, were agog with expectation and fascination. After they had clambered out of the carriage, they could be seen cautiously peeking around, in and out of the outbuildings, while Edward and Florence approached the house.

Edward looked around with an impassive stare. His comments, when they came, were brief: "Needs attention." "That will work." "Stood up well." "Windows still there." He put his hand on the latch of the front door and pushed gently, expecting to find it locked. But it opened and swung easily. The air had the musty smell of an unoccupied house. He took off his hat and threw it with a spinning motion to the end of the hall where it hit a rack of moose antlers holding two hats. The spinning hat dropped to the ground. He muttered as he picked up the hat: "Out of practice. Used to get it every time."

Florence smiled and then pointed to one of two pictures on the wall. "Remember that seascape?"

He nodded. "You gave it to me. Long time ago."

"Yes, just after we were married."

"Why didn't you take it south?"

"Not much room. Thought we'd be back."

As they moved slowly towards the kitchen, the two adults could hear the children scurrying about in the other rooms and making a lot of noise.

Florence ran her fingers along a shelf. "Seems very clean."

"Yes, Henry must have done a lot," said Edward, pleased at what he saw.

"More likely Jill."

They both laughed. As they entered the kitchen, they saw a bottle labelled "Blackberry, 1918" on the kitchen table holding down a note saying: "Welcome home! We are expecting you all. Beds ready. Jill".

"Well that takes the pressure off," said Florence.

"Do you suppose they know we're bringing the whole family?"

"Oh yes. I told you I wrote twice to tell Jill."

Florence was walking around the room with an owner's eye. "They've even got us a supply of candles."

"And the lamps are fuelled up," added Edward as he picked up the oil lamp to assess its contents.

Edward's arrangement with the driver had been to wait for an hour and then take them on to the Milford farm. Once there, the cabbie accepted a drink to augment the food he had brought, thanked Edward for the business and took his leave. Henry told the children where they could and couldn't go. There was little temptation to ignore instructions given by a man even older than their father. The field with a bull was out of bounds and so were all the farm implements. Otherwise the children felt free. Penny and Annabel, hand in hand, followed Jeffrey who was doing his best to elude them.

The adults, having much to talk about, split into two pairs. Henry and Edward left their wives in the kitchen and walked out towards a wooden fence from which they could see across a field of grass with a few sheep. Leaning on his fence, which might have

Chapter 22 — Return to the Farm

been designed for the purpose, Henry filled his pipe and said what was evidently most on his mind: "I'm sure glad to see you back!"

Edward, pulling on a cigarette, smiled. "And there's been little else I've been thinking about."

"You well?"

"Mostly. My breathing's sometimes difficult. So's the leg at times."

"I noticed you have a bit of a limp."

The conversation stopped for what seemed like a long time, each man with his own thoughts.

"We were sorry when Florence and the children left, but knew she had to do it. She might have continued at the farm, if help had been available. But they all disappeared. All the young men and then the older ones. Like you. There was a time when I wondered if we would be able to hang on ourselves."

Edward's response was slow in coming. "We all felt we had a duty to go. There wasn't any choice."

"That I know. I watched it happen. Three men I used to employ went, one in 1915, the others a year later. I've heard nothing from two of them. The other wrote to me from Vancouver to say he had found a job as a clerk. It was what he wanted as he has only one leg."

Edward grimaced saying: "Too many of those." Then he changed the subject: "Looks like you kept your place in good shape."

Henry stepped back from the fence post he had been leaning on and turned to face his friend.

"Yes, I'm proud of what we've been able to do. But, you know, the land isn't worth as much as it used to be."

"Mine too, I suppose."

"I fear so. That railway bankruptcy has been a blow, although a lot of us saw it coming. All that enthusiasm and capital—you will remember it—is no longer around. It just disappeared during the war and hasn't come back. Of course hay doesn't sell so well, but I have to admit I like my motor-car. They're so much easier to handle than horses."

Henry then added, "When they work, that is!"

Edward smiled. "Lots of changes, but it's so good to be back."

Looking out over his fields, Henry responded, "And we've both been praying for this day." Then placing his back against the fence post again, "You know, we've been so lucky. I was too old to go to the war and we had no sons to send. But, hey, change of subject.

Come and see my tractor. Seemed a huge expense at the time and it takes a while to get its steam up, but it sure saves a lot of labour. Will you take on the farm again?"

"Of course that is what I'd like but it's a decision we still have to make. This summer will tell us a lot."

"And I suppose you've still got your mining claims?"

"Damn right, I have. I've got to get back there as soon as I can. The price of copper has dropped so it could have been hard to find the money for the first vein, but I got funding for it and the gold claims in London."

The two men continued talking until called for supper.

Chapter 23

Back to the Claims
1920 July

In the early fall of 1919, before going back to Vancouver, Edward visited the Mining Recorder, now located in Smithers instead of Hazelton, to check on documentation for his claims. The clerk brought out a folder containing the affidavits for claims in the Nisselinka Range, including those Edward had staked and the two he had purchased. Attached to the back of each affidavit was a sketch map showing the location of the claim in relation to nearby geographic features and other claims.

"You probably know about these. As far as I can tell they are tied on to your Raven claim."

Edward looked at the sketches with a mixture of disappointment and anger. He turned each form over to display the second page with the signature and date.

"So these were staked in the summer of 1916?"

"That's right. All of them at the same time."

"So while I was away in France on the King's business in some stinking trench, someone goes and stakes right next to my claims. And right on the trend. Who is he, this son of a bitch?"

The clerk pointed to a name on the first page of one form and then the next. "I think you'll see that they were all staked by the same person. He's no one known to us. Not a local. Gives his address as Prince George."

"I see. Samuel Rhynes. That's a name I'm not going to forget. Wait till I meet him."

"You know, sir. We have no reason to disallow his claims, unless of course he failed to mark them properly on site."

"Yeah, I know that. On the other hand he must have been there because of my discovery. Not quite claim jumping, but not the way to behave. I'll check his work when I'm there next summer. How long are they good for?"

"Just over a year. Unless, of course, he applies more work."

Edward and the clerk then reviewed the documentation on the Raven and the two claims he had staked next to the old prospector's crown grants. The work so far applied was sufficient to keep them in good standing for another three years. The crown grants needed only the payment of annual renewal fees.

Since returning to Canada, Edward had continued to exchange letters with his financier, Albert Sanders, the holder of the right to purchase the claims. With Sanders' enthusiasm for gold, there was no question that the tunnel should continue. The quartz vein on which it was being driven contained impressive grades of gold, although too thin to justify mining. Widening (albeit only from four inches to seven) over the last fifteen feet had provided additional optimism for continuing.

Although Albert Sanders had been very understanding of the difficulty of finding experienced people and also of Edward's need to get his farm operating again, the correspondence with his financier had made Edward uncomfortable with his inability to report progress. But Edward had at least been able to confirm soon after his return that the agreement on his claims had been registered with the Mining Recorder. It was a generous arrangement under which Albert Sanders would provide funds for continued tunnelling for the next few years. All Edward had to do was report progress and call for funds, when needed.

It had taken a lot of organizing, but Edward had finally been able to put together a team capable of continuing work on the claims. The two miners who had worked so well for him before the war had both joined the 102nd regiment and neither had survived the second battle of Ypres. In the search for suitable men, Edward had been to visit George Carthorpe in retirement in Victoria. Now frail, but of sound mind, the former Inspector of Mines had provided useful suggestions as to who might be available to work on the claims. These leads had led to three men: Andy, an experienced miner from the Kootenays, whose medical condition had prevented him joining the forces; Alfonse, an itinerant miner from Quebec; and a young man who had worked in the Cumberland coalmines for two years. By mid-February Edward had finally been able to assemble a team capable of continuing the

Chapter 23 — Back to the Claims

work on the claims, with Danno and Syd handling the transportation again. Prompted partly by a wish to expose his son to some of the less comfortable aspects of a man's world, and over his misgivings as to whether a twelve-year-old would contribute more than he consumed, Edward had included Jeffrey.

Much as he wanted to join the men on their adventure, Jeffrey, too, had his misgivings. He had doubts about whether he would be able to match his father's expectations as there had been several recent incidents when Edward had become angry at him, pointing out his errors or shortcomings.

The expeditions to the claims just before the war had remained on site for over two months, with a mule train every three weeks to keep the crew in supplies. But for this first expedition since the war, Edward decided on a single month on site with a single supply run. He expected problems with the trail because it was bound to be overgrown, and problems on-site because his crew was untested. The expedition was assembled for departure on July 7 from Old Hazelton. As in previous years, a few citizens turned out to wish them well. Everyone in the vicinity was well aware of how much an operating mine could do for them and their community.

The trail, last used in 1913, was still recognizable, but until they reached the subalpine levels, the going was difficult. Seven years of regrowth imposed serious impediment on both men and horses. Particularly troublesome were large trees which had fallen across the trail. In some places there was an easy way around. In others it could take two men with a small cross-cut saw as much as two hours to cut and roll away the segment blocking the trail. Edward's leg troubled him, especially in the afternoons. Syd, having noticed the limp, persuaded him to accept the relative comfort of a horse for three or four hours towards the end of each day.

Four days after arriving on site and setting up the camp, the miners had hand-steeled six holes into the face of the Wilfred tunnel. Each was horizontal and about two feet in length. With limited room to swing a hammer, drilling holes in a tunnel was never easy, but the miners had sufficient experience to make good progress. The explosive was dynamite, used extensively for building the railway and now readily available.

With two sticks in each hole and the detonating cord attached, all was ready. Edward, who had joined the four men waiting outside the tunnel, took satisfaction in hearing the explosion at exactly the intended sixty seconds. The blast had shattered the rock for three feet at the end of the tunnel. It would now be mucked out in preparation for the next round of drilling. As far as they could tell the vein continued with much the same width.

That evening, when Edward had not appeared for the evening meal, Syd went looking and found him sitting on an outcrop about a hundred yards from the tunnel looking very pale.

"You all right?"

Edward looked up at the man leaning over him and shook his head.

"You look pale."

Shaking his head slowly, Edward answered. "It brings it all back. The blasting, I mean."

Syd was puzzled. "Hurt your ears?"

"No. No, not that. It's like being shelled again."

And then, while Syd was wondering how to respond, Edward explained: "Must be some sort of shell shock. Seen it in others. Never thought it would happen to me. I just need to lie down."

Syd led Edward back to the camp and to his tent. "Get some sleep," Syd told him quietly. There's no more blasting today."

Edward saying nothing, lay down on his bed, and pulled up a blanket.

The next day Edward felt fine but remained unnerved by his experience of the previous day. He spent most of his time prospecting the nearby hills until the camp was closed ten days later. By this time the Raven tunnel had been driven another six feet and the Belfrin had a ten-foot cross cut which showed plenty of quartz veins spread over a width of eight feet. They were all very narrow, but the presence of gold in most of them had been demonstrated yet again by crushing and roasting some of the quartz.

Edward's reaction to blasting continued to distress him even after his return to farm and family. In his world men should not give way to weakness and now he had been overwhelmed by a weakness which, until now, had generated in him no sympathy for anyone who had yielded to it. He found himself forced to recall his participation in the disciplining of soldiers who had succumbed. His consequent loss of self-confidence and self-esteem made it easier for Florence to persuade him to spend another winter in Vancouver.

Among the tasks he set himself for completion before heading south was a visit to Prince George to confront the man who had

Chapter 23 — Back to the Claims

staked claims adjacent to his Raven group during the war. He told Florence that by using the now-bankrupt but functioning railway, the journey from Smithers to Prince George would take only two days each way. Florence regarded this mission as unnecessary and vindictive, but she was in a mood to humour him as long as he continued to agree to wintering in Vancouver.

The taxi driver at the Prince George station had no difficulty finding the street.

"The number, sir?"

"1446."

"That'll be in the next block. I'll have you there in a moment."

Indeed he did. The automobile pulled up next to a small bungalow with a white picket fence surrounding a patch of lawn.

"Thank you. I don't think I will be more than ten minutes, if you want to wait."

Edward walked up to the door knowing exactly what he would say, once he had identified the occupant as Samuel Rhynes.

At his knock, the door was opened promptly by a young woman who acknowledged her visitor with a polite, "Good afternoon".

"Good afternoon. I'm looking for Samuel Rhynes. I believe I have the right address."

The woman paused before answering. "He's dead."

Edward's response was automatic. "Oh. I'm very sorry to hear that."

"He was killed in France one day before the armistice."

Edward was taken aback. "I'm sorry. I'm very sorry. Then I have no reason to trouble you."

The woman stepped back into her house and closed the door. Edward turned towards the taxi. But the taxi had gone.

Chapter 24

Soldier's End
1921—22

After the winter in Vancouver the family repeated what was to become an annual migration. Edward went north at about the same time as the geese, in late April or early May. The rest of the family followed as soon as school was over in June.

Even Edward's diminished health and the depressed local economy could not destroy the joy of the first summer back on the farm. It fulfilled the family's dreams. The children remained happily unaware of the clouds forming beyond the horizon; but for their parents the looming problems were very real. Any price they might get for the farm was no longer what it had been in the boom days before the war. The earning power of the farm was reduced by horses yielding to cars on the wagon road past the farm. Edward made light of his ailments, but he could not conceal them from Florence.

One late afternoon in July she watched him return from the Meadow. His slight but regular limp was evident even at five hundred yards. She remembered him a decade earlier, returning to the house at the same time of day. That was when his stride was strong, and with energy to spare. Today she watched as he paused for a moment, removed his hat and wiped his brow.

One morning, some three weeks after the return of the annual expedition to advance the tunnels, Edward spent a few hours sorting through the hand specimens collected that year. The bulky samples for assay had been shipped to Nelson soon after the expedition reached Old Hazelton, its starting point. The specimens taken back to the Wickford farm had been selected to show certain features of the two veins, in some cases evidence of impressive grades, in others the spectacular nature of the minerals, some of which would be used to support applications for further financing.

Chapter 24 — Soldier's End

This was work he enjoyed, sitting on a high stool labelling rocks laid out on a bench. As he didn't have a lot of energy that morning the work suited him well. There were numerous other tasks calling for his attention, but there was one he had to do before he went in for lunch: transferring some bales of hay onto a four-wheel hay wagon, originally built for horses, now adapted for a tractor.

An hour later, with lunch ready on the table, Jeffrey and his sisters were waiting and anxious to get started. So was their mother.

"Where's your father?"

Jeffrey was accustomed to taking the lead. "I'll go and look."

He was back in less than a minute. "He's in the barn. Sitting on a bale of hay. Doesn't look well. I think you had better come, Mother."

"What did he say?"

"He didn't say anything."

Florence frowned. "That's odd. Not like him. I'm coming."

Followed by the children, and throwing off her apron as she left the kitchen, Florence walked fast and then ran to the barn, her frustration at having to wait for her husband now replaced by concern. As she entered the large, open doors of the barn she paused for her eyes to adjust to the darkness. Jeffrey ran past her to his father who was slumped on a bale of hay. His mother caught up with him. "Are you all right?"

Edward's response was slow. "I'm fine. Just not feeling well."

"Can you get up?"

"Probably. I'll try."

Very slowly Edward hauled himself up, stood for a while and put out a hand on Jeffrey's shoulder to steady himself. Then he started walking slowly through the barn doors. A pitchfork lying on the ground in front him was an obvious hazard but Annabel quickly picked it up. Penny started to cry. Florence hovered, offering an arm, but Edward evidently wanted to show that he could manage without help. He got himself to the kitchen and collapsed into his favourite chair, but without taking his boots off.

By the next morning he had recovered and Florence was already thinking that his collapse in the barn would confirm her case for another winter in Vancouver. There was no longer any livestock on the farm and the expense of having someone keep an eye on the buildings would be manageable.

By early September after a snowfall which was not expected to stay, the family had packed up the house, closed and locked the outbuildings and handed the keys to the Milfords. Despite the railway's bankruptcy the trains continued to run on time. The Skeena Valley was as spectacular as ever though not as exciting as it had been in the days of the sternwheelers.

The Wickford family's return to the house they knew, and to neighbours who knew them, was a happy affair, but for a man so accustomed to a very active life, whatever he was doing, Edward found it difficult to adjust. Making improvements to the house, including building a new wing, provided him with welcome distractions, but at the end of these projects Edward took to long walks. He would go as far as English Bay, turn left and, if the tide was out, take the shoreline or the Point Grey road past Langara to the wireless station at the Point. Sometimes he would leave in the morning and not return home until dusk. Florence recognized she had a caged bear on her hands. She knew he would be happier in the north year round, but the thought of temperatures twenty-five degrees below freezing shut the idea from her mind.

But the idea stayed with Edward. The call was not just for the farm, the open fields, the fall colours of aspen and birch, the sense of building something he owned. It was also for his mineral claims. On his long walks he thought of the copper vein as it headed into the ground beyond the reach of the tunnel. It had been pinching and swelling as they had exposed it during four seasons of work. What if just beyond the tunnel it expanded to over four feet? It was rich enough. Thanks to Albert Sanders there was enough money to continue work. Edward knew that Albert's commitment to the Raven claim was limited by the depressed price of copper. But he also knew of Albert's faith in gold and his enthusiasm for the eastern claims. Remembering his financier, mentor, and friend, Edward recalled yet again the last meeting in Albert's club while he was convalescing in England. Albert had thought that the pencil-thin veins might coalesce into one larger vein. While anxious to see work on the tunnels continue, Albert was well aware that Edward would need time to get his strength back. They still corresponded, though less than previously. Albert's mentioning of his age in his last two letters had prompted Edward to wonder how much longer his financier would have. Memories of the conversations with Albert seemed so often to lead to memories of the war. And when the war scenes and incidents barged into his

Chapter 24 — Soldier's End

mind, he would start walking faster. The scenes appearing from his past ranged from the brutal to the humorous; they included machine guns and destroyed bodies, but also football games and camaraderie. At times he remembered the men with shell shock and his intolerance of their weakness. This led to him remembering his own experience of delayed shell shock, and he suffered the agony of being unable to apologize to those he had rebuked or disciplined. Then, when he realized he was walking at an uncomfortable speed, he would slow down and force himself to think of something other than the war.

After one of his long walks, Florence had made a suggestion. "You know, I was thinking and had an idea."

"Not about me, I hope."

"Yes, dear. About you. You're the only husband I have."

Edward waited, his curiosity aroused.

"With all your experience building houses, you could start that again."

"That was flat out, hard, hard work. I don't have the physical energy any more."

"You could put together a team and do the supervision and administration."

Edward took time to reply. "Let me think about it."

He did indeed think about it. It was a good and practical idea. The trouble was that it would be a commitment which would make it doubly difficult to get back to his claims. But his thinking about building houses, the farm, the war and his mineral claims came to an abrupt end on the cliffs southeast of Point Grey. He set out after lunch one day but failed to return.

The search party found his body beside the trail. The coroner said it must have been a heart attack.

It was a civilian funeral and to no one's surprise the church was full at the appointed time, three o'clock on a Saturday afternoon. Florence's family had been parishioners for nearly two decades, so the family was well supported in their loss. With her siblings and cousins, Florence's extended family accounted for five rows of pews. Friends accounted for another five rows. Both men and women were in black or sombre grey, many of the women wearing veils. Then there were the soldiers. Three who had served with Edward in France attended in the uniform of his regiment. Two of them served as pallbearers and the third delivered a homily citing the deceased as an exemplary citizen soldier. Others from the 102nd, the 29th, and the 54th, some in uniform, some in mufti, filled another pew. A full church, a talented organist, and well-known hymns touched the emotions of many, but only a few allowed themselves to show what they felt until, as the coffin was carried out of the church, the mournful and penetrating notes of the Last Post overcame their resistance.

The headstone in the churchyard captured in words how he had more than once told Florence he wanted his life to be summarized. *Edward Wickford, farmer, miner & soldier, 1882—1922.* When she visited his grave a week later, she looked at the new gravestone and wondered whether she had remembered his instructions correctly. But she also recalled that they had been not so much instructions as thoughts spoken long before he began to see his life ending. On one occasion, when she and Edward had been with friends, he had said, "Prospector, soldier, farmer." Sometimes, when Edward had been in a good mood, truth and jest had been hard to separate.

Chapter 25

Between the Wars
1924—1939

Within two year's of Edward's death, Florence had sold the farm in the Bulkley Valley. Jeffrey, then sixteen, protested at the loss, but selling it gave the family the financial stability needed to keep their house in Vancouver. Florence was able to find part-time work with the Department of Lands. This allowed her to be home each afternoon when the children came back from school.

Although the death of his father had hit him hard, Jeffrey recovered quickly, not least because several boys in his class at school had the same misfortune to cope with. He was an average student but, as a talented athlete, he came in contact with a capable group of young men with whom he remained friends. His sisters found it harder as they had both begun to establish a rapport with their father. On the other hand they had each other for support and it was not long before they settled into the new realities of family life.

Having grown up in a family which had struggled as pioneers in the north, and having seen the damage wrought throughout the country by an economy in retreat, Jeffrey's instinct for survival suppressed most of the ambition that might have pointed him in other directions. At nineteen he spent almost a year travelling alone across Canada and back through the United States before taking a position with a large insurance agency in Victoria. In this capacity he came to know most of Vancouver Island and much of the Sunshine Coast. Like many young men of his generation, he joined the militia, selecting the Seaforth Highlanders of Canada, one of the units based in Victoria. He enjoyed the camaraderie of the army and participating in activities with his friends. A steady income and harmony with the people he knew were among his priorities, as was keeping up with his sisters and his nephews and nieces.

1934

At the age of twenty-six Jeffrey married Celia, a friend of Penny's who came from a farming family with land on the coast south of Nanaimo. He had now been five years with the insurance company and this experience gave him the intent and some of the confidence to open his own agency offering specialized service to the agricultural business. Although sceptical at first, Celia eventually came cautiously on side, but they both recognized the very real practical problems, chief among them maintaining a reasonable family income. This being the "dirty thirties," jobs were being lost in nearly every industry. To walk away from steady employment seemed foolish. In the end, the decision was made for them when Jeffrey was informed that his employer was closing its office in Victoria and would manage the Vancouver Island business from its office in Vancouver.

Jeffrey was now on his own in the middle of the worst depression of the economy in living memory. But behind the lines of unemployed he continued to see what he perceived as the outlines of an opportunity. He had long believed that the small farmers could be better served and that the premiums they had been paying were not justified by the risks they faced. For almost six months he corresponded with underwriters in Montreal and Toronto and talked to as many farmers as possible by attending every agricultural fair gathering on the island. Two years after losing his job, he and Celia had a small business which did little more than pay the rent. But it was growing.

1936

For some time Florence, now living on her own in Kitsilano, had wanted to unburden herself of the responsibility for the mining claims. With the funds made available by Albert Sanders and the skills of a retired railway engineer, she had arranged for the work to continue. Now, a few years later, she decided it was time to hand over the responsibility for directing further work. She knew

Chapter 25 — Between the Wars

that, without continuing work, all that would eventually remain of the two claim groups would be the five crown grants.

At Thanksgiving dinner, Florence laid out the paperwork on the kitchen table.

"You've heard me talk about your father's English friend Albert. Since your father died, I've corresponded with Mr. Sanders about the exploration programs he's been paying for. He has now earned a majority interest but has always wanted us to continue managing the work. He seems to like the way I've been handling it. But, as you all know, I've been looking after this business for over ten years now."

This was no news for the children, who had been aware for some time that the claims had become a burden for their mother and that Jeffrey had been reluctant to take them on.

Annabel, who had always been close to her mother, looked at Jeffrey. "Couldn't you manage it now? I'll do what I can to help."

It took no more than a few minutes discussion before Jeffrey, although hesitant to take on another task, agreed to look after them. The claims were assigned to him in 1936 on the basis of an agreement, documented with the help of the family lawyer, that if he disposed of them within the next ten years, each of his siblings would share in the net value of the sale. Thereafter both the burden and rewards would be all his.

With the economy so depressed, financing for such early-stage mining ventures was rare indeed. The price of gold was static. The gold producers were doing very well, but risk capital for exploration projects, even for gold, was not available. The crown-granted claims were inexpensive to maintain, but unsurveyed claims, if he were to stake any, would require either cash payments or annual work programs, which Jeffrey knew he did not have either the money, time or knowledge required.

His business earned enough to keep his family, now three, in reasonable comfort until, despite the counsel of his more rational self, he decided to venture some money on gold by adding six claims to the eastern group. But he soon discovered that raising funds to explore them was beyond his reach. The enlarged claim group caused enough of a drain on his cash to prompt Celia to question the expenditure. Sometimes she referred to the claims as "your other family".

1938

The ongoing issue of whether to keep the claims would be discussed from time to time, but a decision on what to do remained elusive. One evening in the winter, when Jeffrey and Celia were sitting reading, the topic came up yet again. Jeffrey had put down his book and was staring into the fire.

Celia broke the silence, "A penny for your thoughts." She knew that such offers were usually declined, but in this case she was wrong.

"Just thinking about our mineral claims."

"Do you see any chance of getting our money back?"

Jeffrey's reply was, as usual, non-committal. "Maybe ... I like to think we can, but it will have to wait until there is a real market for mineral claims."

Normally, with both of them realizing the conversation would lead nowhere, they would steer it back to other topics or go back to reading. But on this occasion, the conversation went further, perhaps because Celia felt she needed to know more. She closed her book and placed it on the table next to her. "But letting them drop would be difficult for you. Wouldn't it?"

"Yes, yes. I often think about that but..."

"Because they belonged to your father?"

By this time Jeffrey had also closed his book but it stayed on his lap. "Yes, but it's more than that."

Celia said nothing as she waited for him to continue.

"He put all that work into them. Money too. He had a vision or dream, whatever you call it. And he couldn't finish the job. So I feel I just have to do it for him."

"Is that what he would want, if he could see you now?"

Jeffrey looked up at his wife: "Not just want. He would expect it. I don't know whether he would say it, but he would think that it was my duty."

"Duty?"

"That was part of growing up. I was made aware that, when I grew up, I would have to be tough and do my duty, whatever it was. Nothing specific. And, of course, I had to be honest, but that was taken for granted because everyone else was. Except for the scoundrels—and we all knew that they were quite different."

"Your father's beliefs, I suppose. And your mother's?"

"Yes, both. Except for being tough. Sometimes my mother would say my dad was being too hard on me."
"Which he was?"
"Perhaps, but I don't suppose it did me any harm."
"So, taking all that into account, what are you going to do with the claims?"
"Keep the crown grants, drop the others. There's no alternative."
As she picked up her book Celia closed off the conversation. "Thought so."

By the time war broke out in 1939, Jeffrey had been in the insurance business for twelve years and running his own agency for nearly half that time. He had built a loyal group of clients, most of them on Vancouver Island and the Sunshine coast. He and Celia with their two daughters, now eight and six, were living in the house they had bought three years earlier in the Fairfields part of Victoria. His mother, still in the Kitsilano home, kept in close touch with his sisters and their families.

Canada having declared war in September, the militia units were mobilized and Jeffrey was called for active service in 1940 as a junior officer with the Seaforth Highlanders. Training exercises in central Canada were followed by the regiment being posted to England, where it participated in coastal defence and further training. After Operation Husky, the landings in Sicily, Jeffrey found himself in late 1943 with the Canadian First Division pushing north along the east coast of Italy. Early in 1944 senior officers in the regiment recognized in 2nd lieutenant Jeffrey Wickford an uncommon ability for planning and organization. Some two months into the campaign he was no longer leading a platoon into battle. He was now a full lieutenant and Assistant Adjutant, soon to be promoted again to a staff position at Brigade HQ. Although the brigade was involved in several gruelling battles, first in Italy then in Holland, and although he lost a number of friends, Jeffrey, to his own surprise and gratitude, remained unscathed.

Chapter 26

After Another War
1945—59

Jeffrey returned to Canada in 1945, settled back into married life in Victoria, and took up his former occupation as an insurance agent. During his absence, his business had been managed by a friend and former colleague who had been willing to put his retirement on hold. Although he hadn't been able to keep all Jeffrey's former clients, he had kept the business alive and now handed back a functioning organization.

In 1946, Celia gave birth to their third child and first son, Kenneth. Caring for him was made easier by his two sisters who were old enough, at nine and seven, to take a hand looking after their baby brother. Civilian life was easier for Jeffrey than it was for many returning soldiers. He picked up the threads of his insurance business one by one. Like him, many of his former clients had seen their farms or other businesses disrupted for four or five years. Each was adjusting in his own way. Getting back in touch with his clients and hearing their stories of the war years was an aspect of his business which the returning soldier enjoyed.

A group of some eight veterans, Jeffrey among them, liked to meet at a bar in downtown Victoria in the evening on the first Thursday of every month. Originally all from the Seaforths, the group now included two from the Loyal Edmontons, both of whom had moved to Victoria after the war. In their post-war, civilian lives, all differences in military rank had been bridged by bonds of mutual respect. Gus and Ernie, whom Jeffrey knew well, had formed the basis of a friendship despite their very different ranks while serving in Italy. Ernie was always a corporal because he had refused numerous offers of promotion to greater responsibility. A retiring, studious type, he now ran a second-hand bookshop. Gus, promoted to Major after the crossing of the Moro River, had

Chapter 26 — After Another War

commanded the same company until the end of war in Holland. He had first noticed Ernie while watching in awe and admiration as the corporal led his section in the rescue of a wounded soldier from an almost impossible situation on the first day of the battle for Ortona. Ernie came to respect Gus as an efficient officer, known to take all reasonable precaution to safeguard each soldier under his command.

Other regulars in the group included Len who, having served as a sergeant for all of the Italian campaign, ended the war as a warrant officer. Within a year of returning, he was working for an automobile dealer in Saanich. Four years later he owned his own Ford dealership. George, also a sergeant, had been mentioned in dispatches in both the Italian and the Holland campaigns. After returning, he took a degree in civil engineering and joined the provincial Ministry of Transport. Walter joined the Seaforths as a twenty-two-year-old subaltern in time for the campaign in the Netherlands. He was now a teacher of history at a private school in Victoria.

These old soldiers formed a corps of six regulars who managed to attend nearly all the meetings. Another three, all comrades in arms with Jeffrey in the Seaforths, attended frequently. Others came when they could. At the first meetings, after returning from Europe, conversation consisted mostly of shared memories of war-time incidents and comrades they had lost, but later it became tacitly agreed among them that talk should be more about their current lives and plans for the future than the war they had all experienced.

The original participants stayed in touch year after year. By the mid 1950s some, George among them, had dropped out, but came back a couple of years later. Others joined. While the only qualification required was overseas service in the Canadian military, most members of the group continued to be those who had served in the Italian campaign.

At one of the meetings towards the end of the decade, when most of the participants were learning to cope with the challenges of middle age, the conversation began, as usual, about work, families, news from elsewhere in B.C. and their plans for the future. Then Ernie started on the old topic. "I was dreaming last night about one of those villages in Italy."

Len leaned forward and stubbed out his cigarette with a rather forceful gesture. "You don't expect us to talk about the war again. It's over and we're back."

Ernie, who was one of the more retiring members of the group, said nothing but looked at Gus, who could be relied on to oppose any strongly held opinion.

Gus obliged. "You know, Len, there are times when some people, and that includes me, need to talk about it. Some of those scenes go round and round in my head. I can't talk to just anyone. We need to talk to one another—people who were there and who can listen and understand. And that means you."

Suitably reinforced, Ernie came back in. "Gus's right. I need to talk about my buddies, especially the ones that couldn't come home."

It was time for George to take the lead. "Then let's do it. There were good times as well as bad. I will always remember when the quartermaster somehow came up with two sheep and the cooks roasted them in the open. I don't remember ever enjoying food so much."

His memory of those distant events triggered, Len, despite what he had said earlier, had to say something. "Then we were joined by the people from the village, and all those girls."

"Yeah, that was...." Ernie just smiled without finishing his sentence. "But after that it got tough," Len said. "At times I thought we'd all meet our ends in that town."

Gus removed the pipe from his mouth. "I was lucky. I replaced a platoon commander who'd been wounded or killed. I even forget his name, but he must have been a good officer ... or maybe it was the sergeant. That platoon, the one I took over, was one smooth machine. They had that mouse-holing down to a fine art. We'd have one section in the upper room of the house. Occupants gone, thank God. Family stuff all around. One charge laid against the wall, retreat one floor. Charge goes off and we'd be through that hole in just a few seconds. Sometimes we'd throw in a grenade first. Then we'd secure the house and do it again. Remember that, Len?"

Len, nodding slowly, said: "Never forgot it."

Jeffrey had been following the conversation but heard no more than the first few words of Len's reply. His mind was back in Italy. Len's response was no more than a string of words in an inaudible conversation. He was remembering events he had tried to forget.

Chapter 26 — After Another War

After a while he came back to himself, half aware of who was speaking but barely registering who was talking, or the meaning of his words.

"They, the Huns, knew what they were doing. That parachute brigade we were up against were good fighters."

"Yeah, and Hitler had ordered them to hold that line at any cost, 'to the last tree and house' or something like that."

"I certainly know now they had been ordered not to retreat, but I can't remember whether we knew it at the time."

"They had had time to prepare. All those tank traps and defensive positions."

"We lost a lot."

"So did they."

"And the civilians. I think that's got to be the worst part of war."

"Does any of it ever keep you awake?"

The word "awake" aroused Jeffrey from his reverie.

"Sometimes, but that's rare," Walter was saying. "But I do daydream, when I'm on a bus or driving over a bridge, about those canals in Holland. I don't know how many canals and rivers we crossed. Just about every one was contested. And I get them all mixed up, except for the Ijssel River."

"One thing I remember about those crossings was how good our gunners were. They kept improving their system so that even after a rapid advance, they always had at least two batteries ready to support us. Whenever we called for it."

Len said, "And I'll never forget, when it was all over, marching through Apeldoorn. We could talk about that, but let's move on."

Gus picked up his glass. "I think it's good to talk about the war sometimes, but that's enough for now. I want to hear about Jeff's mining claims."

Jeffrey smiled and lifted his own glass. He welcomed the opportunity. His claims had become a nagging item of unfinished business. The mineral claims had come to occupy increasing amounts of his thinking time. The talk about the war had brought to mind a torn and muddy paperback with missing pages. He had read it in an abandoned farmhouse in Italy, while trying to take his mind off an advance his company was due to make in a few hours. The book had been about a family which had fallen on hard times. They possessed only one significant asset: a stone house, not quite a mansion, but elegant, and in need of repair. The sensible step to take, to sell the asset and move on, was out of the question. It would have been an act of disrespect to the ancestors who had bequeathed it, and a deprivation to the generations to come. His ownership of the mineral claims came with similar obligations.

Once again, he explained to his friends that only five claims, all crown granted, were left of the ones his father had once owned. Aware that a property had to be of a reasonable size in order to attract significant venture money, he had added a few staked claims to each of the claim groups shortly after the war, but had been forced to abandon them a couple of years later when renewal was due.

"I have to say I have done little except for paying the taxes every year. I feel I have to keep what I inherited, but I'm damned if I know what to do with them."

"Why bother?" said George. "Why not just let them go?"

Jeffrey looked back at George while the others waited for his response. "Easy question, and I have asked it myself many times. But the answer is not so easy. It comes down to what my dad put into it and why he couldn't finish. There were three things in his life: family, farm and minerals. He left them all when he signed up in 1915. He was in his early thirties at the time. When he came back he tried to start up the farm and the mineral claims, but too much had changed. He was dead three years later. The farm was sold. My mother kept the claims as they didn't cost much to keep. So his sense of duty to King and Country led him to leave everything that was important to him—his life's work. I might be able to buy back the farm, but that's not my line. In any case it wouldn't be profitable now. So my sense of duty tells me to focus on the claims."

Someone said, "Before it's too late?"

Someone else said, "Go on."

"When I was a kid, these claims seemed almost more important to my dad than his family or his farm. We never dared question their importance. Then he went off to war and couldn't finish the job. Now it's up to me."

"But, Jeff," said Gus, "you can't do it alone. Ernie and I met someone recently. His name is Justin, I think. Is that right, Ernie?"

Ernie nodded. "Justin Chisholm. All he really said was that mining's picking up and he was looking for some promising properties. We thought of you. Want to meet him?"

"Maybe," said Jeffrey. "Put him in touch. But tell him I'm unlikely to do much."

Chapter 26 — After Another War

"As I see it, if you've got something you're doing nothing with and someone wants it—there's an opportunity for a deal."

"It might make you rich!"

Jeffrey leaned back as he responded, looking at his friends: "Or poorer!"

"I know nothing about minerals and all that," said Gus, "but they tell me that the smart people use other people's money."

Len took the floor and summed up the considered wisdom of the friends. "There you go, Jeff. If this guy wants to use his money, go for it."

Justin Chesham did indeed get in touch with Jeffrey. They met at a café not far from Jeffrey's office. The coffee was stale but the place was convenient. After the usual introductions and do-you-know-whos, Justin, a man of average height and beefy build and of similar age to Jeffrey, steered the conversation to the purpose of the meeting.

"I've been following the mining business for several years now. There seem to be opportunities for owners of good claims to make a bit of money. I've seen this type of situation before and I've got friends who've done well from them."

"So your main business is not mining?"

"That's right. I've always been in real estate. But there are similarities."

"Except that real estate always has value. Mining claims sometimes do and sometimes don't."

"Yes, I suppose that's true. How long have you had yours?"

"To be honest I should tell you that I don't know much about mining. I'm in insurance. I inherited these claims."

"Well. I hope you don't mind, but I've taken the liberty of doing a bit of research on the Nisselinka Range and I've read about your property, or properties, I should say."

"You have? Find anything interesting?"

"Yes. You've got quite a copper showing. It's got a tunnel into it. And there's a couple of claims, also crown grants, with some gold, and a tunnel about a mile away from the copper."

"I've got only three now. I sold the other two before the war. So, what now? What do I do?"

In answering the question Justin began to sound like an authority on the topic. "You need to stake a few claims to extend what you have now. And then you'll have a package more likely to be of interest to companies which want to do some exploring."

Jeffrey felt a twinge of suspicion. "Sounds expensive. I've already tried adding claims. But they cost me too much to keep so I had to let them drop."

"That's where I could help. If you and I could agree on a joint venture, I could fund the staking and perhaps an exploration program. We would then look for a company which would spend some serious cash."

"Interesting. I believe that is the sort of arrangement my dad used to make to pay for the tunnels."

"Your father must have done something like that. Unless he was very rich."

"He wasn't. He was a farmer. He may have made a bit of money on his claims, but it couldn't have been much."

"So our objective, our joint objective, yours and mine, is to make the claims into an attractive package for one of the mining companies. They would pay us something every year and if they find an orebody they would buy us out."

"Very well, but that first money sounds risky."

Justin replied, "It is, but that's for me to worry about."

"So you would finance that?"

"That's what I do—with partners. We would have to stake claims and do some sort of magnetic survey, also perhaps dig some prospecting pits. Paying for that work is how I would buy into your claims."

"And what would you get for that?"

"Twenty-five percent for the initial expenditure and then, if I can get another party in for major exploration, I get another twenty-six percent."

"That would give you control."

"That's correct. Generally speaking fifty-fifty is not a good idea. Do you have strong feelings about the percentage I would earn?"

"I'll have to think about that."

"All right. Think about it, and if you want to talk again, send me a note or try a phone call."

Celia always liked to hear about Jeffrey's "old-soldier" social meetings. They formed a sort of counterbalancing topic for them to share: he had his soldier friends; she had her book club; except that Jeffrey had given up asking about the books reviewed and

Chapter 26 — After Another War

what was discussed in those sessions. She knew he'd had a lunch meeting that day with the man Gus and Ernie had put him onto. Someone who might take an interest in the claims.

"How did it go?"

"His name is Justin Chisholm."

"Honest? Is he?"

"Don't know. Seems okay."

"Be careful."

"I will. He suggests earning an interest by paying for some work. That much makes sense. He says we have to stake more claims and then do preliminary work on them. Magnetic surveys and something called geochemistry. He would pay for all that. Then we would try to interest a mining company in drilling it."

"What would that leave us with?"

"Well, Chesham wants twenty-five percent for funding the preliminary work. Then he'd get more if he finds a company which would make a serious commitment, but we haven't agreed yet on just how much. He doesn't sound too greedy. That gives me some comfort. Then, of course, our share would be reduced further when the big money gets spent."

"And, if it didn't work out, you'd have a bigger block of claims."

"Yes. I meant to mention that. It could be a huge advantage if the work is filed for assessment. The claims might be good for three years, perhaps more, without any more work."

"I've always known you'd have to do something with those claims, but the last attempt didn't work out. Is this an opportunity or a trap?"

"There's another aspect. My fly-fishing friends tell me there's a wonderful stretch of river a few miles away."

"I'm all for you going fly-fishing, but don't let that influence your judgement on this Chesham person and his proposal."

Jeffrey laughed. "Wouldn't dream of it."

Chapter 27

First Try
1960—61

During the month of March 1960 Jeffrey and Justin met over several lunches to discuss the terms of an agreement. As he became accustomed to the possibility, and then the expectation, of some serious work on the claims, Jeffrey began to feel optimistic as he listened to Justin's growing enthusiasm. The realtor told Jeffrey he had been a cautious man for most of his life, but this might be the moment to take a chance for his day in the sun. Here was a chance for them both to make their mark and perhaps get rich.

Initially reluctant to assign even a minority interest to any party other than a recognized mining company, Jeffrey gradually became more comfortable with Justin and more interested in doing something with the claims.

Justin Chesham had a confident style made more effective by evident familiarity with the basics of the business: "Our main objective is to get the claims to a stage which will attract a major ready to spend big bucks."

But Jeffrey needed to know more and continued asking questions. "That makes sense, but what happens if we do the staking and the other stuff and then we can't get any serious money into the project? Then I'm left with less than a hundred percent and it would be hard to do anything with the claims."

Justin thought before answering. "That's a reasonable concern."

Then, after pausing for further thought: "Tell you what. If, by the second anniversary of your agreement with me, we have not got an agreement with a commitment to spend, name a sum, my percentage will revert to you. You will be back to one hundred percent."

"I think that would work."

Chapter 27 — First Try

They continued with lunch and covered other aspects of their agreement. Justin then outlined the steps ahead. "I will draw up a draft for you to look at. I'll get it to you within the week. There's one other idea to run by you. I have been planning to hire the stakers and the crews for the line cutting and other work. I should be able to find them in Prince George or somewhere like that. But it occurred to me that you might like to get involved. You could hire the stakers and make a small markup on the side. I would have no objection to five percent because it would save me some management time. You would have to make some site visits for quality control, but you might find that interesting."

In Jeffrey's mind the mention of "site visits" triggered an image of water sliding over gravel beds in unspoilt streams, with snowy mountains in the background. "That might suit me very well. I could count on you to advance the money?"

"Yes, of course. I would advance enough for half the job, with the rest payable at various stages which we would agree on. If it helps, I could give you copies of staking contracts I've used in the past."

"I'll take you up on that. I think I might like getting involved. At least to that extent."

The two men parted with a firm handshake and a commitment to meet at the same place in two weeks time.

At dinner that night, Jeffrey told his wife about his discussions and the opportunity to participate by taking a role in the field work. To his relief, Celia was supportive. "Combining it with a fishing expedition sounds good. Your travel costs, or some of them, would be covered, I suppose."

"Exactly."

"You'd have to have the money advanced, or you might be left holding the baby."

Jeffrey smiled with satisfaction at his wife's cautious approach to business. "You've got it just right. We discussed that. Fifty percent up front, the balance at various milestones towards completion. Same sort of thing for the line cutting."

"It sounds good. How much have you learned about this Justin fellow?"

"I checked two of his references, both real estate people, and they both said he was fine and they would deal with him again. He was in the army during the war, somewhere in France, but I don't know what unit."

"Well, if you've checked him out, I think you should follow your instincts. With a good agreement, of course. And the other thing I was thinking about—I know from you and others how much these claims meant to your father. Giving them a real test might ease your burden, if that's the right way to put it."

"Yes, that much I know. My dad's mineral claims were in some ways more important to him than his farm. He was convinced he had found something important. So, as you know, I have always felt I couldn't just abandon them."

The agreement was just a three-page letter signed on behalf of Chesham Minerals to be countersigned by Jeffrey. Justin's company could earn twenty-five percent of the claims after spending $20,000 and a further fifty percent if he was successful in finding a company to take on the claims and spend at least $250,000. After Jeffrey counter-signed the agreement, they went to a lunch which lasted a lot longer than usual. His initial hesitation had been replaced by enthusiasm. "I look forward to getting up to the Nisselinka country. I went once as a kid. I know fishing on the Bulkley is good and I like the idea of fitting it in with a business trip."

The upshot of that lunch meeting was that two weeks later, Jeffrey took on the preparations for the staking and line-cutting work. Justin Chesham was to pay an advance, and then more at each stage as the work progressed.

Jeffrey liked to keep his family up to date on the mineral claims they had heard so much about so arranged to do it at a Sunday dinner soon after he had reached agreement with Justin Chesham. Unfortunately, both daughters, now living away from home, were unable to come, but Jeffrey was pleased that Kenneth would be present as he particularly wanted to see a spark of interest from his son, now a fast growing fifteen-year-old.

After they started on the roast of beef, Jeffrey opened the subject. "Ken, you'll be glad to hear that I have got someone to spend money on the claims."

There was no response until Celia came to the rescue. "And your dad is going to help with the work and combine it with some fishing."

Kenneth looked up. "Fly-fishing? That could be fun."

Chapter 27 — First Try

"Yes. It looks like we'll be up there in mid-August. Want to come?"

Ken fidgeted before answering. "Not really, Dad."

"Oh, that's a shame. Busy summer?"

"Yes. That's it. My friends will be in town and we've got band practice three days a week. I can't miss any of that."

By mid-summer Jeffrey Wickford had two agreements in place, one with Chesham Minerals and the other with a group of cheerful, scruffy young men calling themselves Northern Linemen. He had checked and found their corporation to be genuine, and that the men themselves were well known in the mining fraternity of Prince George for both staking and parties. Their references were all positive, as was his impression of their leader, a lanky young man who introduced himself as "Des," and whose informality disguised a sharp attention to the details of his business.

The number and location of the claims to be staked had been agreed with Justin, and a map of the claims-to-be formed part of both agreements. After completion of staking, the pattern of claims would connect the eastern and western crown grants, and form a roughly rectangular block some two miles long.

Justin made an initial payment one week after the agreement was signed. Another payment would be made as soon as Jeffrey reported that half the staking was complete. A final payment would be made after Jeffrey had inspected the completed claims and written to confirm that all was in order. Jeffrey's agreement with Northern Linemen had similar terms, a payment up front followed by cash calls on completion of each stage.

Jeffrey's careful scheduling would give him six days on the Bulkley River between the middle of the staking and its completion. After a two-day drive from Vancouver, he checked into a motel close to the Bulkley River and a day's drive from the staking. He spent the night there and left next morning. Driving for several hours, mostly on logging roads, took him to the stakers' camp that evening. During two days at the camp he reviewed the new claim boundaries on the map and in the field. Concluding that the staking, by then half complete, was satisfactory he returned to the motel. A phone call to Justin called for the second payment to be made to his account. Arrival of the funds was confirmed by telex to a local branch of the bank the following day. The next days spent fishing were among the best Jeffrey had ever experienced.

The trouble began two weeks after completion of the staking and half way through the line cutting. The claims had already been filed with the Mining Recorder in Smithers and the final staking invoice paid along with the first phase of line cutting. But Jeffrey had not received the cash for the second phase of line cutting a week after it was due.

He had written the cheque for the line cutters' second invoice but held on to it until he knew the cash was in his account. But each time he checked, the money from Chesham had not arrived, and phone calls to Justin were not answered. Having scheduled another day on the river before his flight back to Victoria, he went fishing as planned, but his mind was on the money owed to him and the man who owed it, not on the fish. That evening Des Bucklin, looking like the woodsman he was, but with his hair brushed, came to his room at the motel to present another invoice and to collect a cheque as he had done before.

Jeffrey, a man accustomed to paying bills on time, was most uncomfortable. "I'll send the cheque from Victoria as soon as I have the money in my account. By this time next week at the latest."

"You were very prompt paying all invoices to date, so I hope you won't have any trouble with this one."

"Don't worry. You will have the money within the week, even if I have to find it myself."

Des looked at him with a surprised expression. "I have complete trust in you, but I didn't like what you just said. I've been through it before. Someone who owes you is depending on someone else."

"That's exactly where I am. I expected the money to be in my account by now. But, as I said, if it doesn't arrive soon, I will take it from my own resources."

Jeffrey extended his hand. Des's handshake and his expression were firm and confident. "Very good. I look forward to hearing from you. You know my address." He turned and left the room.

Jeffrey's first task, once he had returned to Victoria, was visit to Justin's office. It was closed. As it was a one-man office with occasional help, this was not unusual, but in the circumstances the closed office only added to Jeffrey's concern. And his concern was not one which could be kept from Celia.

"Everything okay?" she asked.

Chapter 27 — First Try

"No. I can't say it is. The staking went very well, also the first part of line cutting. So did the first three of Justin's payments. They came in as planned, on schedule."

"Oh no. Don't tell me he hasn't paid the next one."

"That's it, exactly."

"And you can't find him?"

"Doesn't answer phone calls and his office is closed."

"And you—we—owe money?"

"Yes."

"I don't think I want to know how much."

"No. You don't."

The situation did not improve. All methods of locating Justin—letters, telegrams, visits to his apartment, conversations with his landlord—led to nothing. At the end of the week, Jeffrey sold some bonds, wrote a cheque, put it in the mail, and sent a telegram to Bucklin at the Linemen's office to say the cheque should arrive mid-week. In one sense this was money he could afford. It was in his possession. On the other hand, he had earmarked it for a holiday on the Oregon coast for a belated celebration of their twenty-fifth wedding anniversary and Celia's birthday.

A month later, Jeffrey was at the intersection of Blanshard and Fort Street, waiting for the traffic to stop at the light, when he saw a man who looked like Justin cross the street in the same direction on the other side of the road without waiting for the light to change. As soon as the light turned, Jeffrey crossed and turned left dodging two cars to catch the retreating figure. Without being certain of the man's identity, he called out, "Justin!" but the man, appearing not to hear, continued head down at an increased pace. Jeffrey broke into a run, overtook the retreating figure and looked him in the face. "Justin!"

The man did not respond and continued walking. Jeffrey seized the man's coat and forced him to look him in the eye. It was indeed Justin, but with a haggard and haunted look he had never seen in this man, who used to be confidence personified. Jeffrey pointed to a café. The place looked cheap and run down, but he steered his prey towards it and guided him forcefully through the door. The guided man did not resist. They went to a table near the wall on the right. Four men, an elderly couple, and a group of three young women occupied the other tables. Before either man could draw breath a waitress arrived.

"Coffee?"

Jeffrey, knowing Justin drank it, replied, "Two, please."

The two men sat in silence, Justin staring at the sugar dispenser, Jeffrey at Justin, until the silence was broken by the man who had said nothing. "I'm sorry."

"So you can't pay what you owe?"

"That's right."

"Why? You signed the agreement."

The waitress brought their coffee and paused for a moment. "Would you like anything else?"

Jeffrey shook his head. "Not now, thanks."

After what seemed like minutes of silence Justin faced Jeffrey for the first time and spoke again. "I'm tapped out, cleaned out. I have nothing left. No money, no assets. Nothing."

"Your real estate?"

"Going fast. Can't make the payments. Bank will take it."

"Tell me what happened."

Picking up his coffee cup with an unsteady hand, Justin replied, "I had a backer who was going to support your project and two others. All agreed to. Agreements signed." He paused. "But he left me holding the bills. When I challenged him, he just said 'Sue me.' He knows I can't do that. I don't have the money. Any money."

"What a god-awful mess!"

Jeffrey looked again at the wreck of a man across the table. His own loss was serious, but nothing to compare with the situation Justin was in. The feelings of frustration and anger which had been driving him for nearly three weeks were now replaced with something like pity. "Can I buy you a meal?"

A flicker of gratitude passed over the haunted face. "Thank you. I'd like that."

During the next month, Jeffrey managed several meetings with Justin. Having long since given up any expectation of recovering his money, his principal objective at the meetings was to see the option to purchase his property cancelled. In most circumstances Justin's failure to perform would have been considered sufficient evidence for termination, but Jeffrey wanted to remove any grounds for a later challenge. Apparently guided by both remorse and shame, Justin cooperated fully in unwinding the option, but he was less than forthcoming when asked about the financier who had let him down so badly and who, in Justin's mind, continued to pose a threat. Despite legal fees being yet another cost in a losing

Chapter 27 — First Try

venture, Jeffrey did not begrudge what was required to protect his title.

A year later he had found enough money to pay for the anniversary trip, but the loss of a useful amount on his foray into mineral exploration continued to hurt. The topic came alive whenever claims had to be renewed or taxes paid on the crown grants. Because the exploration had never been completed, the claims which had been so expensively staked lasted only one year. On several occasions Celia made the case for not spending additional money. With exploration activity in the province at a cyclical low, the force of her argument was not lost on him, and the claims staked for Justin were allowed to lapse.

"Those eastern crown grants, they have only gold, don't they?" asked Celia while she and Jeffrey were walking along a wild stretch of Oregon beach.

"Yes. That's all."

"Is anyone looking for that?"

"Not really. The price is fixed and you'd need a good grade to make a mine."

"Ever thought of selling them?"

"Not really."

"Did I read somewhere about Canadian gold mines being subsidized by the government?"

"They are. Mostly in the east, just to keep them going."

The claims and their cost were raised by Celia again a few days later when they were home again, preparing an evening meal. "I was thinking about those gold claims and wondering what your dad would have done."

"I was wondering that too. I can't imagine him giving up the Raven claims. They still make sense as copper is wanted."

"Would it make sense to sell the gold claims to support the copper?"

"I suppose so, especially if we could get enough to recover our losses on the copper. Let me think about it."

Satisfied that the idea was well planted, Celia changed the subject.

Chapter 28

The Early 1960s

In 1961, although he was too young to retire, the idea of the next natural stage of life occupied a fair amount of Jeffrey's thoughts. His conservative inclinations and his upbringing in a family which had to pinch its pennies forced him to think about future finances. The mortgage on the house was paid off. He had a very modest pension from his time in the army, and equally modest savings. But the Canadian economy was buoyant, and standards of living were on the rise, as were expectations for continued improvement. His two daughters were married and no longer a responsibility. Ken was at university, but seemed to have no trouble finding sufficient summer employment to cover his costs. Jeffrey and Celia worried about Ken's lack of focus— as he seemed to be interested in everything and in nothing—but that was a matter no longer under their control.

To the soldier friends Jeffrey still met for workday breakfasts, lunches, or for a drink at the end of the day, had been added several in the mining business. Among them was a prospector named Solly Flynn, who managed to make a living from finding and selling mineral claims. One Friday in late summer Jeffrey, Gus, Len, Solly and two friends met for an end-of-week drink at the Old Trapper Inn. Each was enjoying the company of the others, the buzz of numerous voices, the smoky haze, and the opportunity to be heard by an uncritical audience.

"Copper's up," announced Solly, raising his glass.

"Saw that," said one of his friends. "Makes things everyone needs—pipes, electric wires, telephones. Even cars, I suppose."

"Bullets, too," said Gus.

To which Jeffrey felt compelled to add, "We've seen enough of them for a lifetime".

"But we can't let our guard down. The Russians would march all over us."

Chapter 28 — The Early 1960s

But Solly, who never liked talking politics, had a more immediate interest. "You know what I've been watching?"

The smoke disappeared from two cigarettes and a moment later reappeared through noses as the men waited for their companion to answer his own question.

"There's a company called Bethlehem Copper that thinks they can mine less than half a percent from a big hole in the ground."

One of Solly's friends wasn't going to let that go unchallenged. "That's ten pounds, about three dollars a ton. No way."

"It's been done in the States," said Solly. "You need big shovels, big trucks and a big mill. Seems a long shot to me but, if they can do it, just watch what happens in this province."

Jeffrey, aware that Solly was known to keep himself up to date with the industry, was always alert to news which might help him with his claims: "I heard something similar and just put it out of my mind. If that's for real, then I'd better put a few more claims onto my property in the Nisselinka."

"So you still have the claims that son-of-a-bitch didn't pay for?"

"They've expired. And I had to sell some crown grants to pay for that fiasco. But, you know, he wasn't a scoundrel."

"Oh?"

"He was just imprudent. He rushed in where others would have been more careful. And I blame myself for getting involved. I liked the idea of participating, but..."

"Oh yes, wasn't it something about the fishing?"

Jeffrey smiled to acknowledge the hit. "Yes. That was it."

"And the fishing was good?"

He nodded as he stared at nothing in particular. "You know that miserable business was almost enough to make me abandon those claims for ever."

Looking horrified, Gus exclaimed, "Don't do that!" Then he continued in a calmer tone. "You just need one win. But watch out for the real scoundrels. They don't screw you by mistake. They just execute their plan to take what you have."

"I'll stay away from people like that," responded Jeffrey, "but the trouble is they don't wear uniforms."

Although Solly was someone who would never have called himself a "professional," the others always paid careful attention to his statements out of respect for the way he continued to persuade others to spend useful sums on his claims. "It's not easy. After a couple of painful lessons I never take on a cash

The Nisselinka Claims

commitment myself. Even when you know someone is a hundred percent honest," he went on, "you don't know who else can pull the rug from under him."

"Back to your claims, Jeff," said one of Solly's friends. "I think you should make sure you cover quite a bit of ground. I know some of the big mining companies have crews all over B.C. I even heard of an oil company, I don't know which one, setting up a minerals subsidiary in Vancouver."

This and other such conversations with his friends during the winter led Jeffrey to decide he should build up his claims to the size of a land package which a major company might like to acquire.

But his previous forays into mineral exploration had left their scars. Finding the money, keeping the family on side, and deciding how to proceed in an industry not his own, made postponement the easiest route to take.

A few months later, Bethlehem Copper's announcement that they were in production at their new open pit mine in the Highland Valley prompted headlines in the daily papers as well as the mining press. It was not long before good times for mines convinced oil companies to spawn mining subsidiaries, all with generous budgets. This seemed an auspicious time to try again to get his mineral properly worked. Because he enjoyed being in the bush and liked to be careful with his money, he decided to do the staking himself. With the assistance of a local man he had engaged for three days, he staked enough claims to surround his crown grants.

Although the staking cost him less than he had expected, Jeffrey did not look forward to sharing the information with his wife, but it was a step he had to take. One evening as they were having a drink before the evening meal, he took the opportunity. "The mining business is really picking up. Copper seems to be what everyone wants now."

Celia looked up from her knitting and peered over the top of her glasses. "When I hear that sort of comment I get worried. The next thing is you will propose spending some money on new claims."

This was not the way Jeffrey wanted the conversation to begin but he decided to bull ahead. "The main thing with the mineral business is to grab opportunities, and that means being prepared with sufficient claims."

Chapter 28 — The Early 1960s

"So how much do you plan to spend?"

"Two thousand, or just over. And I've already done it."

The next moments of silence were enjoyed by neither party.

"So that's cash we won't have for our retirement."

"If I'm right, I'll get it back in spades."

"And your record to date?"

More silence before Celia gave voice to more of what she was thinking. "If you had one of those big company pensions, I wouldn't worry. But we're on our own and all we will have is what we've saved."

Jeffrey had to choose. A mea culpa was out of the question. A stone-wall defence was a possibility, but he decided he had to get Celia to acknowledge his case.

"Look. I beaver away at the office day after day. I have good clients, and we have reasonable savings. I don't spend much on myself, no late nights drinking with my buddies, no expensive golf memberships, no boat, no mistresses. Give me a bit of slack."

Celia looked up with no hint of what she would say.

"No mistresses? Keep the claims. They're less expensive."

She smiled and they both laughed.

One evening, when Celia was out with her bridge-playing friends, Jeffrey and his son were to have dinner on their own. In many ways Ken at nineteen was typical of his age, enjoying sports and parties and discovering girls. He lacked the focus and lifetime plans of some of his friends, but was becoming more interested and curious about the world he was about to launch into. Jeffrey's relationship with him was mostly good, although they both knew it could be knocked off the rails for reasons neither of them ever might understand.

Celia had cooked a roast for them. Jeffrey's job was to carve it. Ken's only job was to lay the table and mash the potatoes, if that is how he wanted them. Although it would have been easier to have their meal in the kitchen, his mother's instructions had been to lay the table for two in the dining room. Ken had always been aware of his father's mineral claims, but he had never needed to know more. On this occasion his awakening curiosity and the opportunity, sitting across the table from his father, prompted him to ask a few questions. "Dad, those claims of yours, do you think they will come to anything?"

Jeffrey smiled at the question and took a few seconds to frame a response. "That's something I have asked myself many times, so I should be able to tell you."

"I know you've spent quite a bit of money so you must think there's something there."

"It's not as simple as that. I have no idea whether it's worth spending another dime. Nobody knows what's there and certainly not me."

"So you could just let them go?"

"I could. Then someone might put money into them and walk away with a fortune. I would prefer to bring home that fortune myself. And that would be good for you and your sisters, as well as your mother and me."

"Yeah, we'd all like that. But it's a gamble, right?"

After they had been eating and talking for a while. Jeffrey pulled the dish of mashed potatoes towards him, added a scoop to his plate and offered some to his son. "You did good work with these."

Ken nodded to signify he would like more, and to acknowledge the compliment. "Mother said to add butter and milk and pepper so that's what I did."

"You see, always do what your mother says and you won't go far wrong."

Ken laughed. "Does Mum want you to let them go? The claims, I mean."

"That's a good question and not so easy to answer. Even if I knew there was almost no chance of making money, I would find it hard to drop them."

"Because of Grandfather?"

"Yes. And because I don't like to give up."

"I think I understand. Grandfather must have believed there was something there. Did he know or just hope?"

"That I can't answer. We know he put his heart and soul into those claims and he persuaded others to put their money at risk."

Ken, whose plate was now empty, shifted in his chair. "What was Grandfather really like? I often wonder."

"That's another question I can't answer easily. I never knew him as well as you know me. He went to war when I was seven. I was eleven when he came back, and he died before I was fourteen. Your grandmother would have been able to tell you a lot more."

Chapter 28 — The Early 1960s

Ken looked thoughtful. Jeffrey continued. "And he wasn't quite the same when he came back."

"Different? How?"

"He didn't have the same drive or energy. He liked to be alone a lot. Could be short tempered. I never knew when."

"The war?"

"Yes. I'm sure of that. But I believe he was always a hard man who drove himself and others hard, including his family. I always knew he expected a lot of me."

"What did he expect?"

"I had to be tough."

"Does that mean strong?"

"More than that. Able to put up with hardship, even pain. It was all about manhood. And duty."

"Duty?"

"Oh, yes. Like a lot of his generation. That came first. That's why they all signed up."

"And that's why you signed up?"

"No. I was in the militia. We were all called up. There was no decision to make."

"If you hadn't been in the militia?"

"Yes, I suppose, if I'd been a civilian I would have felt an obligation to join. A lot of men did exactly that. Yes, it's a kind of duty."

"Duty to what? For what?"

"To one's country, or to a principle. Look at all those people who signed up for the Spanish civil war."

"I always wonder about 'duty.' How it works for each generation."

"Back to your Grandfather, I'm sure he was a fine man, committed to his family, hard working, but he had some objectives which he was intent on achieving."

Ken said nothing for a while, before responding. "Thought he might be like that."

Jeffrey waited to hear more but Ken soon signalled that he had learned enough by looking at his watch and saying. "I've got to go in half an hour. Meeting my friends. Is there any dessert?"

"I'm sure there is. Look in the oven. I believe there's a pie."

Within a couple of years of first hearing about mining copper from big open pits, Jeffrey had added more claims to make a package of seventeen, including the crown grants. They looked impressive on the map and he was proud of what he had done but now, in his mid-fifties, he acknowledged to himself that the next attempt to find a buyer for his claims would be his last. He scheduled a day at his office to devote to sales and then phoned the seven oil companies he could find with mining offices in Vancouver. Four of them took his name and some details of the claim location and said they would get back to him. Two of the companies asked him to send a claim map and a description of their mineral occurrences. One, Namco Minerals, a subsidiary of Namco Oil, expressed immediate interest.

"Did you say the Nisselinka Range?"

"That's right."

"You had better talk to Patrick, our chief geologist. He was mentioning that area recently. Hold a moment, please. I'll try to put you through. If it doesn't work, just phone back."

Jeffrey waited with the phone to his ear.

"Patrick speaking."

"Good morning. My name is Jeffrey Wickford. I'm phoning to see if Namco might be interested in some claims I hold in the Nisselinka Range."

"We could be. In fact I was reading about that area just recently. Tell me what you have. I assume you have it all staked. We don't care to hear about anything on open ground."

"Yes, it's staked. My claims are four wide running for about a mile along the west flank of the range. They include some crown grants which have been in the family for a long time."

"Copper?"

"Yes, copper. There's a tunnel which shows it quite well. Gold too, but in a different place."

"Sounds interesting. Can you send me any maps or reports you've got? We prefer to have copies, not originals. Mail will be okay. Or you could send it by KZ Courier. We have an account with them. Just tell them it's going to the Namco office in Vancouver, for attention Patrick Krandle."

"I'll do that."

"Thank you, Jeffrey, or d'you prefer Jeff? That's with a J is it, or G?"

"It's a J and Jeff's okay."

"That's good. I look forward to reading what you send."

Jeffrey drove home that evening feeling satisfied with the phone calls he had made that day.

Chapter 28 — The Early 1960s

Celia looked up at her husband as he came into the living room. "You look like the proverbial cat. Good day at the office?"

"Yes, didn't do much insurance today, but I made phone calls to all the oil companies I could find with minerals offices in town. Seven in all."

"A bit of a long shot?"

"Actually, they seem to be very keen on copper. Some of them are going to get back to me. But one wants all the data. Seemed to know something about the Nisselinka Range."

Celia was pleased. "That's encouraging."

With her information up to date, she changed the topic of conversation to their youngest daughter and her family.

Chapter 29

Oil in Minerals
Late 1960s

Two weeks after Jeffrey had sent the package of maps and reports to Namco Minerals, he received a phone call at his office.

"Good morning, Jeff. This is Patrick Krandle."

"Good morning. I trust you got the package."

"We did indeed. And that is the purpose of my call. I would like to visit your property in the Nisselinkas."

"Any time. I can give you directions. It's easy to find."

"Well, I would prefer to go with you. Property examinations are so much more effective with the owner. Would that work for you? We will pay your travel expenses, of course."

In dealing with anyone expressing even preliminary interest in his mineral property, Jeffrey was automatically on his guard. But he was also aware that most major companies, in their own best interests, were meticulously open in their dealings with claim owners. After his experience of ten years ago, it was the part-timers and would-be financiers he was determined to avoid.

"That would be fine. So you would cover my return flight to Smithers and my other expenses?"

"Absolutely. I'm going there in any case. I have several properties to visit in that neck of the woods."

"I'd be glad to show you around. Most dates would work for me."

"Weekends better?"

"No, as long as I'm not away from the office for more than a week."

The conversation continued until they had agreed on a date to meet at Smithers.

Three days later Jeffrey walked away from the PWA flight which had brought him from Vancouver scanning the group of people

Chapter 29 — Oil in Minerals

waiting to meet the passengers near the shed labelled "Baggage." He noticed two, either of whom might be the man he had come to meet.

"Patrick Krandle?"

"Not me."

For his second attempt, he approached a man who looked like a better bet for middle management: late thirties, holding a leather briefcase, and looking around the room as if to find someone.

"Easy flight?" said Patrick, as they shook hands.

"Oh yes. No problems. Comfortable. On time."

"Good. I've checked you into the Taku Motel where I've been based for the last few days. We can go over your reports and maps tonight, find ourselves a good meal, and then be back over there tomorrow morning."

Jeffrey followed Patrick's outstretched hand pointing to a building labelled 'Telkwa Helicopters' on the other side of the runway.

"So we're flying in? That's good."

"It's also the only way. With one of these machines I can get to the eight properties I have to see in five days. Otherwise it would take me two weeks."

Conversation at breakfast the next day was relaxed but businesslike, each man using the opportunity to find out about the other.

Jeffrey started on an easy topic. "I know nothing about the oil business but my son would be interested to learn his dad is meeting an oil man at the same time as he's working on a drill rig in Alberta."

"Good for him! No matter what career he takes up, that's a good thing to do. How old is he?"

"Twenty-five and showing no sign of what he plans to do with his life."

"That's okay. Young men go on to all sorts of occupations after trying life as a roughneck."

"I'm glad to hear that," replied Jeffrey. "How long have you worked for an oil company?"

"I've been in mining since graduating, but this is my first time with an oil company."

"Notice any difference?"

"You bet! Main thing is the way they spend. Unlike most mining companies they don't count their pennies. Once they've decided to do something, they just do it; they need something, they get it."

175

"That must make your job easier."

"Up to a point. I can get what I need. But then they expect results quickly, and that's not so easy in mining. But this is a good job and I enjoy it. What about you?"

"You have to call me an amateur. I inherited a few crown grants from my dad."

"You mentioned that he had driven some tunnels. I found some government reports on them. It will be good to see what they were following."

"He was an amateur like myself. A farmer, but he rounded up some serious money to drive those tunnels. Trouble was that when he got back from the war he wasn't as fit as he had been. And the copper price was right down."

"That must have been a bad time for miners. He can't have been the only one struggling to hang on to mineral claims."

"I am sure it was just like that. He got back to the tunnel for one short season, but his health got worse and he was dead within a couple of years."

"What a shame. Let's hope you're the owner when the mine is found!"

Jeffrey was enjoying the conversation. The young man's enthusiasm and their shared interest prompted recollections, stories and laughs. "Yeah, let's hope. And I hope you like what you see today."

"That's my job, trying to spot the winners using only a limited amount of information."

Patrick signed the bill for breakfast, finished his coffee by upending his mug and appeared ready to go. "Shall we meet at the truck in half an hour? You can pick up your pack lunch at the desk. It will take about twenty minutes to the airport. You have an extra coat? These machines can let us down and leave us out for the night."

"I can think of worse than that. Yes, I'll be ready."

They arrived at the Telkwa Helicopter shed fifteen minutes ahead of the time scheduled for departure. As they walked towards the office door, they could see a helicopter being wheeled out of the shed towards the pad.

"Not my favourite type of chopper," said Patrick, "but that's all I could get this week. They're very noisy."

"Safety record?" asked Jeffrey, more to provide a reply than out of concern.

Chapter 29 — Oil in Minerals

"I don't know, but I always figure that the pilot's more important than the machine."

Jeffrey, sitting on the right behind the pilot, enjoyed watching the ground retreat beneath him. After half an hour the helicopter descended and began to circle around. As it did so, he was able to recognize the Raven tunnel clearly revealed by its pile of yellow-and-red spoil. There seemed to be plenty of places to land, but the pilot took his time, circling around several times. Once the preferred site was selected, the landing was faultlessly soft.

The two men walked hunched over until they were some hundred yards from the aircraft, and waited for the engine to be switched off. As soon as the noise had subsided, Patrick commented: "Cautious pilot. That's what I like, even when it does take extra time."

"Suits me. I have had enough excitement for a lifetime."

"The war?"

"That's it. Like many my age."

As the geologist and the owner walked across the patch of level ground selected by the pilot towards a pile of course scree with large boulders, the rolling country to the left and the mountains in the distance reminded Jeffrey of his first visit as boy. But he was drawn back to the present when he noticed that Patrick was waiting for directions. He took the lead, stepping carefully over the scree as they headed towards the tunnel.

Patrick was soon looking at the changes to the topography wrought by the tunnellers. "They must have been at this for several years. At least that's what the size of that dump tells me."

"I believe the tunnel was started in 1910. I have childhood recollections of my father talking about it at home and then disappearing for the summer. The government records are more reliable than my memory, and they say this tunnel was worked for three years before the first war. After that he had another go at it and there was a bit of work done after he died, but I don't think they made much progress."

There was little to see at the tunnel as the entrance was blocked by fallen rocks. After spending some two hours looking at surrounding outcrops and examining rocks in the dump, Patrick announced that he had seen enough. "Jeff, is there anything else you want to see while you're here?"

"No. That's just fine, thanks. You know there's another tunnel about a mile away? Used to be mine."

"Yes, I read about that, but it's just gold isn't it?"

"That's right."

"That's what I thought. We'll take the gold if it comes with copper, but it's no good on its own."

They picked up their backpacks and headed slowly back towards the waiting helicopter. Patrick looked at his watch and then turned to Jeffrey. "There's one more place we could see this afternoon. It's beyond your claims just five minutes north of here."

"That's fine by me."

Once in the aircraft and strapped in, Jeffrey watched the dials as the rotors picked up speed. After a few minutes the pilot pulled on the collective and the machine lifted, tilted forward, and gained velocity and height over scrub timber before swinging to the north. Jeffrey looked down in search of features on his claims. He recognized an island of four pine trees at their northern boundary. A minute later they were well beyond any familiar features and the pilot was circling again in search of another landing spot.

After forty-five minutes on the ground Patrick announced that he had seen enough and turned back towards the aircraft. "I've seen what I came for, so it's time to head home. Jeff, would you like to take the front? I'll sit in the back and make some notes."

"Sure. I'd like that."

They flew over sub-alpine terrain with its wizened pine trees, grass and scree slopes, and then over thicker trees as the landscape sloped to the south ahead of them. Jeffrey's thoughts strayed to his career in the insurance business, and he found himself wondering whether a life in mining would have been more interesting than insurance. It would certainly have been more exciting at times. His day-dreaming ended abruptly when Patrick's arm came from behind him on his right to tap the pilot's left shoulder. The pilot turned his helmeted head to look at Patrick's pointing finger and then up to the plexiglass bubble. There was a small patch of oil on the plexiglass. Although never a natural mechanic, Jeffrey knew enough of the basics to realize that oil appearing anywhere was not a good sign. The pilot looked above his head, then at the instrument panel, then again above his head.

During the next few minutes, Jeffrey's gaze flitted between the oil above, the ground ahead, and the instrument panel in front of him. Among the several clock-like dials, there was one which looked likely to be the oil-pressure gauge. As far as he could tell, the other dials were for air speed, tilt, fuel, and something he could only guess at. On closer examination, a rather hard-to-read "psi" on the first dial confirmed his guess. The needle was at one o'clock, at the left-hand end of a strip of circle marked in green. There was no obvious movement in the needle but, as if playing to the three pairs of watching eyes, it inched past the edge of the green toward the sector of the dial marked in red. Whenever Jeffrey glanced away and then back at the needle, it had moved.

Although still too slow for any movement to be seen, the progress of the needle was inexorably towards the red.

To his surprise the machine seemed to be climbing as they headed south. Then he noticed the pilot tilting his head, looking first to one side of the plane, then to the other and then back to the front. For reasons that puzzled him later, Jeffrey felt more curious than concerned. Looking for a place to land, he thought. That's what he must be doing. More height meant more options, more places within range. By now they were over thick forest above low ground North of the Prince George highway. The needle was touching the red. Then Jeffrey looked up at the plexiglass roof to see, not just a few specks of oil, but a sheet trying to flow down the sides before being pushed back by the upward current of air at the axis of the rotors.

The needle was well into the red when the highway came into view some two thousand feet below. He had just glanced again at oil on the roof when he heard the engine go silent as he felt the sudden drop. The next minutes lasted a long time. The pilot's objective was becoming evident: a branch road running south of the main highway. As they descended, the only noise came from the blades as they picked up speed. Jeffrey was watching the road as it came to occupy more and more of his field of vision. It was unpaved, wide enough for two vehicles, and empty, except for a cloud of dust in the distance which had to be caused by a vehicle of some type. This time there was to be no circling around to double-check the landing site. They were descending directly and rapidly towards the road, when he felt himself being thrust into his seat and then forward against the shoulder straps before the machine thudded into the gravel with a hard bump.

The pilot turned to him with a grin and gave first Jeffrey and then Patrick a thumbs-up. Then he signalled to Jeffrey to get out, pointing him in the direction to leave. Then he did the same for Patrick. The passengers walked heads-down until they were a good hundred yards from the aircraft, where they stopped, straightened up and looked back at the silent chopper. The blades were still turning, but slowly, their energy all spent on arresting the drop.

Patrick's first words were to the point. "Good pilot."

Jeffrey said nothing. After a few minutes of watching, they saw the pilot remove his headset, climb down and then walk towards them.

Patrick, looking at the pilot, was the first to say anything. "First time you've had to do that?"

"Yes. Except in practice."

"It worked well."

"It did. But it was no sure thing. I kept the engine going as long as I dared. It could have blown at any time."

Jeffrey had to ask. "So the engine didn't cut out? You switched it off?"

"Switched off. You saw the oil. Right in the red and still dropping. I didn't know what would happen if the engine seized. By that time I could see this road and we had the height. So it was an easy auto-rotate. Done it many times for practice. But never for real."

Patrick expressed appreciation for both passengers. "Well, we're sure glad you did all that practising. I'd be happy to fly with you again."

Then after a few seconds, the pilot, staring at his machine, said emphatically, "But not in one of those birds. They've killed too many. I'll be glad to see them all go. We're getting turbines in a couple of months. They're much more reliable, and quieter."

The conversation was brought to an end when all three men noticed a logging truck and its cloud of dust coming towards them from half a mile away. The pilot looked mildly concerned before dismissing the threat.

"He won't get past us. He'll stop. It'll make him mad when we tell him we can't move it."

"Yeah," said Patrick. "We'll probably get a bill from the logging company. But that's okay."

As the truck came to a halt the noise of its diesel engine was drowned by a louder sound. A helicopter had landed behind them.

"That's to take us back to base," explained the pilot. "I sent them a message as soon as we were in trouble. It's good to have a response like that. We'll offer the trucker a lift. His truck will have

Chapter 29 — Oil in Minerals

to stay here until tomorrow. Our chopper will have to wait till they get a flatbed out. No way it can be fixed on the spot."

One week after their shared experience in the plunging helicopter, Jeffrey received a phone call from Patrick to say that he was recommending that Namco Minerals offer an option on Jeffrey's Raven property. Only three days later Patrick phoned again to say that his recommendation had been accepted and that a letter would follow. When the letter arrived, Jeffrey reviewed the terms, which were close to what he had been led to expect. His cash payment would start at $5,000 and then increase annually on renewal of the option. In the event, which he knew to be unlikely, of the option to purchase being exercised, he would become wealthy. After discussing the terms, first with Solly Flynn and then with his wife, he had no hesitation in accepting. In fact he felt very comfortable with the situation. After years of headaches, false starts, sunk cash, and family arguments, his claims had finally been put in the hands of a company with the resources to explore them properly. If they found something, well and good. If not, he would be able to abandon them with a clear conscience.

On more than one occasion, by phone or letter, Patrick had urged Jeffrey to visit the office of Namco Minerals when he was next in Vancouver. Accordingly, before one of his periodic trips to the big city, he wrote a note to suggest such a visit. It took place later that summer. The two men, the experienced geologist in mid-career, and the insurance agent nearing retirement, had a good relationship, founded on their shared objective, finding an orebody, and somehow strengthened by their shared experience in the helicopter.

"Did you ever learn what they did with the machine?"

"Yes. We use that outfit quite frequently so I keep in touch. The engine was replaced. They have the machine flying again, but they are getting rid of their entire fleet and replacing them with the new 206s. Suits me."

"I keep wondering what would have happened if the pilot had not turned off the engine."

"So do I. So does my wife. I discuss that sort of thing with my colleagues here, but no one seems to know. My wife was asking me. I could honestly say I didn't know. Best not to discuss such things at home."

Jeffrey smiled. "Makes a lot of sense."

"Let me show you round the office. Drafting room first. We can't look at the maps, but we can just peer in."

He was shown a large room, windowed on two sides, with large tables, sloping drafting boards and some half dozen men and women on stools working at maps.

"With the nine geologists we have here, we keep these people very busy. What I can show you is how your claims fit into our Nisselinka project. Let's go to my office."

In his office, with its window looking onto Burrard Inlet, Patrick waved his hand at a map on the wall. "Here are your claims. You will recognize the boundaries." Then pointing first to the bottom of the map and then to the top, he demonstrated the extent of the Namco holdings. "We have acquired just about everything in this belt. Three blocks are under option, like yours. The rest we staked. So we have nearly twenty miles of the belt under our control one way or another."

Jeffrey was impressed, but disappointed that his claims would have to share the oil company's attention. "That's a lot of ground!"

"It is, but that's how oil companies think. The land you hold is everything. Head office was very pleased with this one."

"And now what will you do with it?"

"All the usual stuff. Systematic exploration, airborne geophysics, geochemistry, mapping. We will work at it steadily and it will probably take a few years."

"You have an objective? I mean what do you expect to find?"

"We do indeed. It has to be large. I mean a large, open-pit copper deposit. If there are some small ones in the belt, we don't mind missing them. In fact, when we get to drilling, we will space our holes so that they will catch a big one if it is there. Of course we acknowledge that a little one might be missed in the gaps."

Jeffrey responded with a look, only half feigned, of resignation and disappointment. "Then, if it's only a small orebody on my ground, I have to find another backer and start all over again?"

Patrick smiled while his hands gestured an inability to change reality. "That's the way it works. Let's go have a bite."

Chapter 30

Passing the Baton
Late 1970s & Early 80s

During the years of Namco's option on his Raven claims, Jeffrey Wickford followed progress with a comfortable detachment. His claims ceased to be a worry, or even a concern. They had generated some income but, he had to admit, only a fraction of his annual expenditure. The reports received from Namco describing work on his property alluded to regional work on Namco's extensive holdings in the Nisselinka mountains. From these reports, and even more so from the mining press, Jeffrey came to realize that the greater part of Namco's enthusiasm was directed at a mineralized zone a few miles north of the Raven claims.

In fact, during his now annual migration to the north to cast flies at steelhead trout, he often met people in the business of servicing the Namco camps. They told him of the large camp and two drills now operating on this other discovery. It soon became apparent that his Raven claims were not the main focus of Namco's attention. That was fine. Perhaps they would get to his claims in due course. In the meantime Patrick had been offered a more senior position in Chile, where Namco was opening a new minerals office. Before leaving for his new post, Patrick had told him that the Raven claims merited more attention than they had been getting, but that his company, like any in the exploration business, had to "play its aces first."

Jeffrey's business ventures were taking second place to family matters. His daughters, one in Victoria, the other in Vancouver, had started to occupy much of his and Celia's time by producing grandchildren. Another part of their attention was directed at keeping track of Kenneth, whose occasional phone calls and rarer letters kept his parents only vaguely informed of what he was doing. So they were taken by surprise when, soon after leaving the Alberta oilfields, they were told of his engagement. The girl was one they had not heard about. Along with their daughters, they attended and enjoyed the wedding in Saskatchewan.

In 1978, by which time Namco had held its option on Jeffrey's claims for six years, Solly referred Jeffrey to an article in one of the mining magazines about the oil companies in the mineral business. The author's principal theme was that the oil companies had yet to be successful in their adopted business and, moreover, their culture, founded on successful drilling leading quickly to cash flow, was poorly adapted to the multi-year process from discovery to production typical in mining. Jeffrey's consequent concern turned into reality when Namco sent him a letter announcing that they would not renew the option on its anniversary the following year. Namco would return the claims with three years of assessment credits in hand. This meant there would be no immediate need to apply more work to keep the claims in good standing, and for the next three years he would not have to invent ways of gently telling Celia about how much they had been spending on the claims.

Shortly afterwards, Namco and two other oil companies, both US-based, pulled out of minerals altogether. By now most of the oil companies remaining in mining were pursuing uranium, since that particular mineral was a better fit with their primary business of selling energy.

A couple of years after having the claims returned to him, Jeffrey was in the process of selling his accounting practice and was enjoying the slower pace of life, and freedom from most responsibilities. The time bought by the assessment credits from Namco had been useful but had eventually run its course. Except for renewing the crown grants, he was not about to spend more money on the claims. Kenneth occasionally expressed interest in taking them on but, whenever asked and for reasons he rarely explained, had never been ready to do so.

Though never frequent or detailed, Kenneth's letters home kept his parents aware of where he was and what he was doing. Three months after the wedding he announced that he and Jill would continue travelling for a while.

Jeffrey and Celia followed, through his postcards, the extended honeymoon as the young couple spent over a year exploring

Chapter 30 — Passing the Baton

Europe. It was good news when he announced that they were back in Canada and he was working for a junior mining company, while Jill set up house in Regina.

A year later, they were delighted when he told them that he and the family, now three, were returning to B.C., but their pleasure became tinged with concern when he reported that he was going to earn his living as a prospector. Jeffrey knew that unless he could find another company to take on the claims, all except the crown grants would become too expensive to hold. No easy decisions came his way. That the claims had been worked by Namco seemed to deter prospective optionees, many of whom tended to infer that such a large company would have made a well-informed decision in letting them go. Just as Jeffrey and Celia began to think that the three crown grants would remain theirs for life (and only a few months after Ken had last told them that he was too busy to take them on), they were relieved to hear that their son would be glad to add them to the inventory of B.C. properties which he had assembled from his new home in Smithers.

By this time, all except the three crown grants had lapsed. On the claim map they looked lonely, the more so for having lost their former companions, which Jeffrey had sold to cover his costs on the Chesham fiasco.

One day in early 1983, Jeffrey went into town, to the office of the Mining Recorder to sign bills of sale transferring ownership in the three crown grants to his son. He came home early and was sitting by the fire reading a newspaper, when Celia came into the room.

"Transfer go okay?"

"Yes. A very simple process. They are now legally his. Our son, believe it or not, owns the claims!"

"And the responsibility!"

"I'm not sure how he'll treat that part"

"He took them on because he felt he ought to? Or did he see some opportunity?"

"A bit of both, I suppose. At least, that's what I like to think."

Jeffrey leaned further back in his chair. "I hate to think what I spent on them."

"Don't add it up. You did what you could. Your father would have approved."

"But not of letting go those two crown grants on the east...."

"From what I know, which is not much, I expect his main interest was in the copper claims."

"I hope so. At least they're in the hands of a prospector, someone who ought to know what to with them."

"But, our prospector still has to raise money to work them."

"Prospecting's not a real career."

"But it might be right for someone like him."

"That's true. For a rolling stone, driven by curiosity."

Celia, now sitting down, voted for optimism with her next comment. "Maybe Jill will keep him on track."

Jeffrey raised a hand with fingers crossed.

Book 2
Public Company

Chapter 31

Kenneth

At the end of grade twelve, like most of his friends, Kenneth Wickford had anticipated a professional or academic career and had been accepted by the University of Victoria into its geography program. His first year was, from his perspective, a great success, not least because of an active social life. But for reasons he never fully understood, he became restless in his second year. He experimented with a variety of other courses, including English literature, mathematics, even philosophy, but found only patches of satisfaction. Before what would have been the start of a fourth year, he and his backpack were well on their way around the world—Thailand, Nepal, and India. Then to Australia where most of the young man's time was taken up by a wild affair with a Canadian girl. Although they continued to correspond for a couple of years after he left Australia, they eventually lost touch with each other. His journey took him to Africa and Europe. Returning to Canada at the age of twenty-four with an empty bank account, he replenished it by working as a roughneck in the oilfields of Alberta for three years. Marriage to Jill led to further travel—an extended honeymoon exploring the cultures of Europe—before a chance meeting with a high school friend found him a job with a staking contractor. He was soon working in Saskatchewan during the uranium rush while Jill set up house for the family of three, then four, in Regina.

His new understanding of how mineral title could change hands at impressive prices prompted him to ask his father about the mineral claims of which he had heard so much. He had known of them since early childhood as they, and the significant sums his father had spent on them, had been a frequent topic of family conversations. In fact, his mother's objection to those expenditures had made them something of a family issue. As far as he knew, there had been no return on the sums expended. He was not ready

Chapter 31 — Kenneth

to take over responsibility for the claims but had become sufficiently interested in the mineral business in general to move his family to Smithers. He knew of his grandfather's association with the town but his main reason for selecting Smithers was its role as a hub for mineral exploration of central and northern B.C. It was a community town and he had taken to it on his first visit. As a hockey player and a member of the Smithers Exploration group, he fitted quickly into the life of the town, as did his family. Now lured to a constant search for treasure, he became a full-time prospector, a life which suited his restless curiosity and his love of the outdoors.

After a slow first year, hard work and a lucky break brought him the cash to buy a small ranch south of the town and the confidence to take on the family claims. Having been surveyed and elevated to crown grant status, they appeared as parcels of private land on the government's topographic maps. Locating them on the maps was easy. Access was another matter. By now an accomplished bushman, he applied those skills to many weeks of prospecting within and around the crown grants and then to staking additional claims next to them.

Within a few years, Ken Wickford became established in the community and concluded that he was unlikely to leave. Summers, when he spent long spells away from home, were especially hard on his family. The stresses on Jill eventually led to their separation. Fortunately both of them had their children's interests in mind when they drew up the agreement.

Chapter 32

Two Assists
May, 1986

During the winter and spring, when the hills and forests were covered in snow, Ken Wickford took great pleasure in playing hockey. Nothing serious. Just the "beer league" for players who had advanced beyond youth, but who refused to abandon a sport they had loved as kids. Many of the players remained in partial denial that their joints and muscles could no longer perform as they had in earlier days. While growing up in Victoria, Ken had taken skating lessons and in his late teens had played with a school team, but it was not until he moved to Smithers that he had become committed to the game. Although he enjoyed watching the professionals, the spectator side of the sport could never deliver the thrill of being on the ice himself. He liked the exercise, the excitement, the camaraderie and the friendships which came with the game. His club, the Smithers "Old Timers," one of a network across the country, fielded at least one, sometimes two, teams. They played against nearby towns and places as far away as Prince George in the east and Prince Rupert on the coast.

The sole rink in Smithers had to accommodate skating lessons, school hockey, junior hockey, serious amateur teams, even skating for seniors. Competition for the rink meant that time for amateur teams was limited to the late evening twice a week. Housed in an old aircraft hangar moved to the town in 1947, the rink and the building itself were prominent features in the life of the town.

At a recent game against a team from Terrace, Ken had taken great satisfaction from scoring the tie-breaking goal. In the second period, after a typical stretch of scrappy play by both teams—missed passes, falls, and collisions, deliberate or otherwise—it all seemed to go right for a few magic seconds. Playing on the left wing, Ken had positioned himself for a pass which he knew had

Chapter 32 — Two Assists

little chance of actually happening. Then he saw his friend Will Herman break away from a knot of players and take the puck forward across the centre line. Seeing a shot at goal blocked by two players, Will sent him a fast pass. Despite the risk, he took a slap shot and, to everyone's surprise including his own, it passed over the goalie's shoulder and dropped at the back of the net.

An hour later, several members of the team were in the Taku Inn savouring their win with a drink or two. Later that evening, when most of the team had left, only Ken and Will remained, sipping their drinks next to the bar. Their conversation, having covered all aspects of the recent game, moved onto other topics, including Will's career as a helicopter pilot, and then to the mining business. On that topic Ken had a request to make. "With the flying business a bit slow, you must have some time on your hands?"

"Not a lot. There's always maintenance, procedures and that sort of stuff. And someone has to be there for the phone call that might get us a few more hours."

"Can you spare a day? Want a good hike?"

"What's up?"

"I've got a bit of staking to do."

"Sounds interesting," said Will, "Go on."

"There's some ground I've had for a long time, but I slipped up and didn't renew."

Will waited without saying anything for the explanation which appeared to be on its way.

Ken, never comfortable sharing his personal life even with a close friend, continued: "You may remember, a couple of years ago, Jill and me, all that separation business. It really hurt. Some things I should have done just didn't get done."

"Yeah. I remember. You were in another world. Hard to talk to."

Ken explained: "You know, looking back now, I have to recognize I made it difficult for her. Coping with the kids when I was away for months at a time. So, we just agreed to live separately and see how it works. It was all very civilized, the separation, I mean. We continue to share time with Phillip and Sarah. I like to think we could put it back together one day."

Will said nothing.

Then, with his next sentence, Ken came quickly back to the present and what he had to do. "The claims I let go and which someone staked will almost certainly come open again on Friday next week, so I want to be there at first light on Saturday. They are right next to my crown grants so I have to re-stake. I can easily get a helper, so don't come along unless you really want to."

Will, unlike many helicopter pilots, was quite willing to walk. In fact he hiked for pleasure. "Sure. I'll come. I can get a standby to look after the base for Saturday. Tell me where to meet you and what to bring."

"That's good. It will be hard work but I think you will enjoy the experience. We start off in the trees for an hour or two then break out into the alpine. Just magnificent country. You can see for miles."

"What do I bring?"

"Just your lunch, rain gear and the usual emergency stuff. We might have to spend the night out, but I don't expect to."

Saturday morning was overcast and cold as Will, Ken, and his mutt Spike emerged from the truck at the edge of a long-disused logging road running through a stand of pine some twenty years old. Will put down the tailgate and was standing holding his backpack with one hand and a gun case with the other. He was looking at Ken for an answer. "Need this?"

"Hell!" said Ken. "I'd rather travel light. It's been with me many times, and I've used it only once. But I did see a dead moose last time I was up here a couple of weeks ago."

"I'll carry it," said Will, taking the old Lee Enfield jungle carbine out of its case.

"Okay, if you wish," replied Ken. "Clip's in the pouch."

From the end of the logging road their route lay along a zigzag of skidder trails through an old clear-cut. The alder had made progress recolonizing the ground once occupied by mature trees and was now over head-height. Spruce and pine three or four feet high provided a link with the forest that had once been there and a promise of another, eighty years in the future. A light frost held to leaves and branches still in the shade. When the trail came to an end Ken, Spike and Will were at the edge of uncut pine and spruce. Patches of snow remained on the north side of some trees.

Ken checked his compass and set it for fifteen degrees, a bearing which would bring them in half an hour to a ridge he knew well. Without a trail their pace slowed. Salal concealed much of the ground, and deadfall, especially in the gullies, prevented any rhythm in their strides. The only wildlife to make the hike more

Chapter 32 — Two Assists

interesting was a whiskey jack flitting from tree to tree and a chipmunk running over a log.

Forty minutes later and eight hundred feet higher, the trees were noticeably smaller and farther apart. Walking was easier. After half an hour, they broke out of the forest and out of the shade. Just ahead was a ridge. Beyond that a scree slope led to the valley and forest below. A glimpse of mountains, a gentle breeze and broken sunlight made this a location for a break. They faced east toward the view. Beyond a small gully a few feet ahead the trees stopped and the down slope began.

By mid-morning they were at 4500 feet above sea level in subalpine country where few of the trees reached to more than twenty feet. Another half an hour of easy hiking took them to a grassy knoll surrounded by scrub pine.

Ken pointed to a small pine tree some twenty feet away. "Ah! See that blaze. We can start here." He walked over and examined the line he remembered cutting. "This first line should be easy. It was part of a smaller claim I staked a couple of years ago." The prospector, pack slung over one shoulder, looked around as if assessing the situation. "Normally I would suggest each taking separate lines, but I'm thinking of that dead animal I saw last time. It would be safer to stay together."

After three hours of walking, blazing trees, and tying orange flagging tape to trees and scrub, they were back where they started. They had travelled two kilometres to the west, one and a half to the north, and then the same distances east and south. Ken completed the tag on the post and, to Will's relief, suggested lunch.

"Lunch? Yes, that's just what I need after a work-out like that."

The two men, each with a small tree to lean against and with their backpacks beside them, sat on the ground enjoying both the rest and the view.

Ken pointed towards the east. "This side of that low ridge in the middle distance are two crown grants my grandfather bought and drove a tunnel on, but my dad had to sell them."

"Buy them back!"

"Tried that, but the price was absurd. That was his second tunnel. The first is north of us here, but it's been covered by a scree slide, so I've never seen it."

The sandwiches, prepared by Dolly at the Evergreen Cafe and always something to look forward to, paused the conversation. Then Spike, who had been the first to flop onto the ground, rose and looked expectantly at his master. Ken responded by pouring some water into a plastic sample bag pushed into a depression in the earth. After lapping it up, Spike trotted off to check the smells. Ten minutes later they heard a distant bark.

Ken's relaxed demeanour gave way to irritation: "What the hell's he doing? Must be half a mile away."

"Wish I had that energy," said Will. "Got to bring that pup of mine along on one of these trips. Maybe he'll be ready in a couple of months."

A few minutes later the barking became more frequent and closer. Then they heard the cracking of broken sticks and saw Spike, in evident haste, running towards them. He went straight to his master and barked back at the woods from which he had emerged. Shortly afterwards there surged into the horrified gaze of two men and one dog, the unmistakable shape of a large grizzly. It, or she, as they both began to realize, came to a sudden stop as the gentle breeze they had been enjoying carried their scent towards the puzzled animal. By this time Ken and Will were standing up and rapidly surveying the nearby trees for branches they could reach. But the trees were small and the branches thin and high. The bear was now rearing on its hind legs and sniffing the wind. As she did this, two cubs came out of the woods and stopped just ahead of their mother. With them to protect and with a threat identified, the she-bear charged.

Time expands in the face of danger. A minute lasts an hour and each second gets counted in hundredths. Ken seized the rifle with his right hand, banged the base of the magazine with his left to make sure it was locked in place, pulled back the bolt, pushed it forward and felt it come to a slow halt before it could be closed. Without looking, he knew exactly what had happened. The rim of the top round had caught behind the rim of the one beneath. He needed only two seconds to fix it. But the bear was only ten feet away and the gap was closing fast. He stepped back behind the tree he had been leaning against and moved to his left as the bear came round the right of the tree. He heard Will shout "Here" from twenty feet away on the other side of the small gully. Using the momentum from his swing round the tree Ken flung himself at another tree as the bear changed direction behind him. Grabbing the tree with his left hand, he used his right to pitch the gun to Will.

Pointed skywards for its entire trajectory, the rifle traced a graceful arch across the gully.

Chapter 32 — Two Assists

Will snatched it out of the air by seizing the stock with his left hand, removed the offending shell and closed the bolt. Aiming at the bear with Ken so close was out of the question. He fired two shots in rapid succession at the ground.

The bear stopped. Ken stopped. Then one cub, followed by the other, started climbing one of the few larger trees in the vicinity. Reminded of her cubs, the mother bear bounded to the base of the tree they had climbed.

Ken crossed the gully to Will with a jump he didn't know he could make. Spike had not stopped barking.

Will pointed to a prominent outcrop with steep sides which looked as though it could be defended. To this they retreated with frequent glances backwards.

"Thanks for the assist", said Will with a grin.

"One of my better passes. But I'm glad you didn't score."

"Why?"

After a thought-filled silence, Ken responded. "Her territory." And then, looking back to where the bear had surprised them, Ken continued. "You know, even though we haven't finished, I think it's time to quit. I planned to start on more ground to the east, but we've put in a good seven hours and to continue would be asking for trouble now that we know someone has taken ownership of that dead moose."

Will looked relieved. "Makes sense to me. What's left to do when we come back?"

"A couple of days will do it. The south was covered. We've done most of the next one. My claims there are okay. I'll be a bit worried about northeast of what we did today until I have it re-staked. But there doesn't seem to be much exploration around here just now. I'm still kicking myself for letting it lapse."

"Is that where you were looking for a tunnel?"

"No, the northeast is where the other claims are, the ones my dad sold. The tunnel has to be on the crown grant, and that's safe. What I have to secure is right next it. So it could be important."

"I suppose cost didn't come into it?"

"Not really. The first plan was to renew by applying work. Then I was thinking about enlarging the claim. It was just procrastination. And distractions."

"Happens to everyone," said Will.

"I suppose so, but I wouldn't want anyone else to grab that ground."

"It's not a hot area is it? Not much activity?"

"Right. I should be able to get away with my lapse."

They shouldered their packs, climbed down from the craggy bluff to which they had retreated and set off in single file along an animal trail towards lower ground, each man with his own thoughts, but each more than usually attuned to sounds or movements in the scrubby woodland that lay on either side of the trail.

Chapter 33

Tennis
June 1986

Some four hundred and fifty miles to the south, while Ken Wickford and Will Herman were retreating from their encounter with the bear, four people were assembling on a tennis court in West Vancouver. The residence next to the court was an imposing building. A sensitive observer might have glimpsed the tall shadow of an ego lurking behind the pillars. The same observer would have wondered whether to credit the architect or the owner, Sydney L. Poulter, a man with some achievements and several enemies to his name. He worked hard towards more of both. Slightly less than average stature, of muscular build, he looked like the pugilist he was. Known as "Slip" to his associates and to the mining press, he enjoyed the good life, his friends, camaraderie and, whenever possible, being the centre of attention. For most of the late 1980s he was between wives, a status that made his philandering less complicated than being married.

"You and I will play together," said Sydney to Victor a wiry twenty-eight-year-old with an intense expression and a neatly trimmed goatee beard. "You have to make up for my shortcomings. Those two are good."

Victor looked across the net at the other pair on the court, Sydney's neighbour, Jim, and Julie, his girlfriend. "I'll do what I can. D'you like left or right?"

"Right," replied Sydney as he walked towards that side of the court. Then he spun his racquet as he looked across the net at the other pair. "Your call."

Julie responded. "Up."

"Okay, we get to serve. You start, young man."

Victor's serves were very hard but not precise. In the first game there were three lets, and two double faults. But he knew he was a useful player, fast on his feet, and able to back up his older partner by taking shots Sydney had missed. Julie's youthful figure and graceful movements, well displayed by her tennis whites, were not lost on him. He found himself placing his male opponent in the category of rival. His hardest shots were directed at Jim. When the time came to change server, he sent the balls he was holding down to Jim at the other end, the second slightly faster. He then picked up two more. To Jim's irritation, the first two balls landed at his feet together. He caught one and had to let the other go to the net behind him. Victor sent two more, again hitting the second harder than the first. They arrived at the same time. Jim picked up one. The other rolled to the back of the court.

In the third game Jim, who was at the net, had to protect himself from a very hard shot by Victor. To Jim, who parried it successfully, the direction appeared to be deliberate. The ball bounced off his racquet and went out of court. The young couple won the set 7 - 5.

As he handed Victor a glass of water from a cooler at the side of the court, Jim opened the conversation. "You play hard."

"I try to win."

Julie evidently regarded Victor's answer as inadequate. With a smile and a quizzical look, she lobbed a question. "At any game?"

"Yeah. Losing hurts."

After another set, Julie and Jim left, and Victor and Sydney sat on the patio on the other side of the house overlooking Burrard Inlet, where half a dozen empty freighters waited at anchor. Victor looked around at the dwelling and liked what he saw: the pool, the ample space, the emphasized opulence. It was a lifestyle he wanted and was determined to get.

"I've heard some stories of how you got started," Victor said, as Sydney poured him a drink. "But I'm never quite sure what to believe."

"Started as a floor trader in the late fifties. Got my first real break with Afton. Ten years ago that must be now. Maybe more. Time flies. Got in between twelve and eighteen cents. Somehow had a feeling this was the real thing. Committed more than I should have. I was trading all the way up and was in and out several times, but still had plenty of it at ten dollars. So I ploughed that block back into some start-up companies, two of which did very well."

Chapter 33 — Tennis

"You've a knack of picking winners. How d'you do it?"

"I do my homework. Talk to the geologists. Find out why they disagree. Try to guess the odds. Structure of the company is always vital, shares out, who owns them, the float. And then, of course, there's the promotion. You can have the best property and the best technical team in the world, but without good promotion it won't fly. That is where I get involved. A good promoter doesn't need a hand from Mother Nature. I start the buying and bring in more. And then there are the news releases." Poulter paused to light a cigarette. He took a deep breath and continued. "News releases written by geos who never stick their necks out. I have to supervise those. Often rewrite them from scratch. And they go out over my name. Now I seem to have quite a few followers, so it is easy to get the price up. Then, when my investors are up fifty percent I tell them to sell. They usually ignore my advice. Some go on to make a fortune. Others lose it all but are in no position to blame me. The big picture, of course, is that lots of people put lots of money into finding new mines. So everyone benefits—even the goddamn government."

"You've certainly made a name for yourself. Why are you interested in me? What can I do for you?"

"I need an assistant. I've got lawyers, geologists, promoters, brokers all working for me, even a regulator for a while, but I need someone to backstop most of what I do. Must be energetic, smart, able to see through the bullshit, able to get along with people. They tell me you can do all that. You'd have to work long hours, answer the phone at any time, day or night, know almost everything and everybody I know and...." Sydney looked out to sea and then at Victor, with a smile. "Some people would say you'd have to be able to put up with my rages, but they're not that common."

"Yeah, I've heard about them."

"You're single, I believe?"

"Very much so."

"Anything permanent?"

"No. I like to play the field."

"You can't have them all, you know. Same with stocks."

"But I enjoy the game and I like to keep score."

"And the girls, what do they feel?"

"That's up to them. I give them a good time."

"Why would you want to work for me?" asked Sydney, looking directly at Victor.

199

"I'd like to learn from you and make a buck."
"Owe any money?"
"Some. Nothing significant."
"Penny stocks?"
"Quite a few. I'm ahead on most of them."

After both men had paused for what appeared to be thought, Victor continued: "Your investors, who are they mostly?"

"All over the map," replied the older man. "Many know the game. Some don't."

"Do you worry about those that don't?"

"Not at all. Mining exploration is high risk. Those who play the game should know that. One way to look at it—investing in mineral exploration I mean—is to think of it as a kind of voluntary tax for development of northern Canada. How else would all that new wealth be found? Government couldn't do it."

"Loyal investors must be a key to your success."

"That's probably true. The pros do well enough, some make a lot of money."

"And the others who don't understand it and lose money?"

"Then it becomes a tax on stupidity, and that's a good thing to tax."

Victor chuckled. "And your priorities for me?"

"Take some of my load. Align your interests with mine. Loyalty is key." After waiting for a response, Poulter added: "And, of course, look after the shareholders."

"Yes, that's what they taught us in business school."

"Believe it?" asked Sydney.

In a moment of mutual understanding, they both laughed. The conversation then continued for another half hour before Slip Poulter signalled they were nearing the end. "So if you want to make money and can work hard and be smart, this will be good for you. It can get a bit rough, but you look as though you could handle that. Do you want the job?"

"Absolutely. I would be honoured."

"Good. I tell you what. Come and work with me for a couple of months. Trial basis. See if you can put up with me. Title will be personal assistant. I'll get you to do all sorts of things. You'll have to learn on your feet. Won't be easy, but I promise you it won't be dull."

They discussed pay. Poulter offered rather less than Victor was expecting but the upside on the options more than made up for it.

Chapter 33 — Tennis

"So we have a deal?"

Victor responded with enthusiasm. "Yes, Sir! I have to give two weeks notice. Start next month?"

"Yes. Make it the first Monday in July. I'm always in my office by six, but for your first day you'd better wait till seven. Now with that settled, help yourself to another drink. I'll be back in a minute."

Victor got up, poured himself a gin, and stood staring at the lights of the city and the ships, and felt the thrill of starting a journey towards a destination he longed for, but also feared.

In Victor's apartment an hour later, Peri Shifron, a petite young woman, fashionably dressed, and Victor's lady-of-the-month, sat on the sofa flipping a magazine.

"Five minutes," said Victor as he walked across the room tucking in his shirt. "I have one call to make, just a short one."

Listening was interesting for Peri, a lawyer in the securities division of Lindrop Samuel. She was one of those confident young women, well-launched on a promising career. Having spent a decade successfully attracting (with one still-rankling exception) all the men she wanted, Peri was now feeling the need to settle down. Victor might be the one, but she had only known him for a short time.

Victor was speaking into the phone. "Yes, it went very well. No, we didn't talk about that."

Peri was trying to form an image of the speaker at the other end, friend? colleague? relation? as she listened for more clues.

"At the beginning of next month. So I'll give in my notice next Monday." The slightly deferential tone, which didn't seem to fit Victor's normal demeanour, surprised her. "Yes, personal assistant. Yes, I understand." After a pause, while she continued to listen: "Yes. I'll be in touch next week."

Peri was ready with the questions as soon as Victor put down the phone.

"Who's that?"

"Just a business associate interested in my new job."

"Tell me more."

"There's not much to tell. We ought to leave or the restaurant may not hold our table."

Chapter 34

Property Examination
July

Ken Wickford was showing one of the several mining properties he owned to a visiting geologist. He and Bob Tranich, a geologist in mid-career, had been driving along miles and miles of unpaved roads, nearly all of them built for logging. Those nearest the paved road were wide and well maintained but now, each time they turned off one road, they found themselves on another that was narrower and rougher. After one and a half hours, they were proceeding slowly to avoid overhanging branches, mostly of alder. From time to time they had to stop to clear a fallen conifer, either by hauling it to the side or, if unmovable, by starting up the chain saw.

Ken's passenger had recently taken a job with Sydney J. Poulter, the well-known mining promoter. On this assignment, Tranich had looked at two properties north of Prince George. These had been submitted to Poulter's private company, which provided office and personnel for several junior public companies. Now, after one day on the road and a night in Smithers, he was being taken out to see the Bobcat claims belonging to Ken Wickford. Like any market, the demand for mineral properties waxed and waned. At this time, the market was reasonably robust. Junior mining companies on the Vancouver Stock Exchange needed properties on which they could raise money. A good property provided drill results which excited the market, raised the share price, and allowed promoters to raise money without giving away too much of the company. Some promoters genuinely intended to find an orebody. Others were more comfortable taking money from the public, raising enthusiasm for the shares, and then selling their holdings at an elevated price.

Chapter 34 — *Property Examination*

Bob had taken the Poulter job with some misgiving. The major mining companies for whom he had worked since graduation were not hiring. This job would involve looking at many properties for a stable of different junior companies, all run by a man with a reputation for injecting excitement into his "plays." Poulter was the object of both adulation for his achievements, and something akin to hatred by those who decried his methods and scorned his successes. While no one assumed he was an innocent, no accusations of shady practice had ever lasted, and more than one journalist had lost a libel case against the man known as "Slip." Bob had welcomed the technical challenge that seemed likely to come with the job. In his moments of doubt, he told himself that he knew the game, and by being alert he would keep his reputation clean.

Ken Wickford slowed his pickup to a halt. There being no room to park it off the road, he left the truck where it was. "Safe enough. This trail has little chance of ever seeing another vehicle." He pointed to the right: "There are two ways to get to the places I want to show you. The shortest is to cross a stream just to the right of us. The other way is to continue on this road for another mile or so and then hike around the far side of the hill."

Bob, who had experienced treacherous terrain in many parts of the world and had a young family in Vancouver, was not about to commit. "What's the crossing like?"

"Best if you have a look at it. It's the route I usually take, but I have to admit, I sometimes wonder whether I'm doing the right thing, especially when I'm alone."

"How far to the river?"

"Five minutes. We may as well take our stuff. But don't let that influence your decision." They each pulled a pack from the back of the truck. Ken lifted a football-sized boulder, placed the key beneath it and looked up to speak. "Spare key's under this rock."

Many years ago he had slipped on a patch of clay while climbing down into a gully no more than ten feet deep. The fall had not been serious and, apart from a bruised knee, he had sustained no damage. But, when he was back at his truck two hours later, the key to his car was no longer in his pocket. A twenty-mile hike at the end of a long day in the field had not been forgotten. He was also well aware of the possible consequences of having a useless vehicle when someone was hurt.

The prospector led the way through a stand of cedar, ferns, salal and deadfall. As they mounted a slight rise, the quiet of the forest was broken by the sound of water which became louder as they descended. The geologist listened carefully. He was young enough to enjoy the more adventurous aspects of his work, crossing mountain streams among them, but he was old enough to avoid risks he would have shrugged off as a younger man. This was a time to say what he was thinking. "Not sure I like the sound of that."

"It's not as bad as it sounds. You'll have a chance to see in a moment."

By now they were zigzagging down a steep slope as the roar of the river became loud enough to drown out conversation. Looking up, Bob could see from the small patches of sky visible through the trees that they were coming to an opening in the forest. Then the water came into view, a torrent of white cresting from boulder to boulder in a channel ten feet wide. Noticing a large cedar that had fallen across the creek, he wondered whether this was where he was expected to cross. As the tree was sloping up towards the far bank at about twenty degrees, they would have to walk uphill. Not ideal, but manageable. The bark was still in place so a good foothold was not going to be a problem. Nor was balance likely to be difficult as the log was over two feet across. But, if either of them were to fall off the log near the centre of the stream, the chances of being able to hang onto a boulder were minimal, and the chances of being swept downstream, bouncing from rock to rock, were high and unpleasant to contemplate. He imagined for a fraction of a second what his demise would mean for his daughters and decided on the long hike. He faced his guide who, with a knowing grin, pointed to the stream and signalled that this was not where they were headed.

Five minutes later, after following an animal trail running parallel to the river, they came to a place where the torrent had become a quiet pond. At the far end, just upstream of another stretch of wild water, was a rocky island connected to each shore by well-placed logs. Both were narrow and smooth, but the consequences of a fall would not be too serious. Bob chuckled to himself, and then smiled to Ken, in acknowledgement that this crossing was acceptable.

Their route on the other side of the stream lay up a south-facing slope on which the trees were fewer and more widely spaced than in the valley. For half an hour they walked in single file with hardly a word spoken, the geologist keeping an eye on the changing rock

Chapter 34 — *Property Examination*

types. After knocking off a fragment from an outcrop at the side of their trail, he confirmed to himself that they were crossing volcanic rocks of no great significance.

As the trail opened into sunlight and a view of faraway mountains, they no longer had to walk in single file and conversation became easier. Bob could start asking questions: "What brought you here?" he asked.

"I was prospecting on horseback. It was four or five years ago. Eighty-two or three, I think. We stopped for an overnight camp at that creek down there." Ken pointed to the southwest. "You can see where the river is from that line of darker trees. I noticed some copper stain on a small rock at the edge of the stream. The next day we followed it upstream for a mile or so, and had no trouble finding several pieces at most of the places I checked, then I lost it. Came back to camp and rode up the hill. We checked the creek, or what we thought was a tributary of the creek about five miles from where I had camped. Not a sign of any copper. We spent several days that summer trying to find the source. No luck. That winter I ran some of the pieces I had found in the stream. They had silver as well as copper. Some of them had quartz that looked vein-like. Wasn't sure what I was chasing. By the middle of the next summer I had covered, with different helpers at different times, an area almost thirty square miles. Then we found it!"

"Must have been quite a day! What did you see?"

"We spent the morning checking every outcrop on a ridge about two miles long on the southwest side of a small valley. Just after lunch—I remember it exactly, even what we ate—we started on the other side, the east side of the creek. We had just pushed our way through a clump of scrub willow when we came to an outcrop about fifteen feet high. All I had to do was look at the rubble at the base: copper stain all over. Every piece I broke was different. Then Bud, he was my assistant then, managed to break a big piece, eighteen inches or so across, and I realized it was a breccia. Chalco all over the place. Prospector's dream!"

The geologist echoed Ken's enthusiasm. "Aren't breccias fascinating! Fragments in fragments, multiple histories in one rock."

He enjoyed hearing such stories. He had great respect for prospectors, especially for professionals like Ken. Their dedication, knowledge and self-interest had supplied the Canadian mining industry with many (some would say most) of its mines. Some prospectors had become wealthy and famous. Others had toiled for a lifetime and faded into oblivion. All were driven by a dream, the big find.

"So you spent the rest of the afternoon rooting around to see how big it was?"

"You might think so, but we didn't. It was obviously important so we decided we would need to be on that spot for a few days. We went back to our camp, about two miles away, and spent the rest of the afternoon moving it up to the find. Felt good that evening. We even broke open our bottle of rum, something we normally left until the final night."

"Will we see that outcrop today?"

"Oh, yeah."

A few minutes later they were both sitting on an outcrop looking downhill towards some trenches easily seen among the grass and scrub of a south-facing slope.

Ken pointed. "Bud and I dug the one on the left. That was the discovery. The others came later after I had found a company to take it on."

Bon Tranich pulled a notebook out of his pocket. "I need to get the history. So you had it optioned out soon after you found it?"

"Yes, it was picked up by a junior called Mindy Mines. Terms were okay. I got a bunch of shares. But they were a rinky-dink outfit. They just pissed around for the entire summer, a couple of trenches, just three holes, all of them with that little Winkie machine. I never thought they really knew what they were doing."

"Who was running the program?"

"Geologist called Toby... I forget his other name. Must have been about thirty. I think he knew what was required but he had to deal with a bunch of turkeys in the office. He was hired just for the project, but they never gave him his head. I don't think they ever had enough money."

"Shame, but it happens. Did you get a report out of them?"

"Yes. I brought it with me. Show it to you when we stop."

By this time they had rounded a spur of rocky ground and were looking across a small valley about three thousand feet across. Ken pointed to a low cliff on the other side of the valley. "There it is! That's where we found it. I'll get out the maps and give you the overview."

They found a patch of grass from which they had a good view of the other side of the valley.

Chapter 34 — Property Examination

"This is my map so you can take it with a grain of salt," said Ken laughing as he opened out a sheet some eighteen inches square. "This is at one to five thousand. The limits of the breccia are shown in red. As you see, we get it in four outcrops. Volcanics on all sides. I think there is a fault up that gully, but that's just my opinion."

"Three drill holes, I see. Looks as though they tested only one side."

"Exactly. Left the east side untested. Idiots. I don't think it was the geo's fault. He had six holes spotted, but they never gave him the money to finish the program."

For most of their way to the other side of the valley the trails were good enough for snatches of conversation.

"Looks like a good map you made. Any formal training?"

"Just a couple of prospecting courses. But I've always been fascinated by maps, ever since I was a kid."

"Why didn't you become a geologist?"

"I often wonder that myself. I took English literature, which is what I thought I wanted to do, but it wasn't right for me, so I veered off onto other subjects. All that took three years. Then I took off round the world. After that I had to earn a living. Did some contract staking. Wouldn't want to do that for the rest of my life. But it gave me an introduction to the minerals business. By that time I had realized I wasn't going to like working in any kind of institution. Got into prospecting. Had a bit of luck so I decided to buy a ranch, just a small one, outside Smithers. Got to know the local people, including the miners. Then, when my dad was getting old he handed me some crown grants. They had been in my family for two generations before me. That led me to learn more about prospecting, mining, geology and things like that."

"So this is not your only mineral property? Or are the crown grants here?"

"No, they are part of another property. And, yes, I have more than this property, three main ones and a couple of others that I have yet to do any serious work on."

They approached the east side of the valley through a thicket of scrub willow and then emerged onto a corridor of grass separating the scrub from a cliff some fifteen feet high.

"Here we are," announced Ken. "This is just about what we saw when we found it ten years ago. You might want to leave your pack here. I'll show you around for an overview, then we can come back here and spend some time on this outcrop."

There was a gentle breeze blowing. The sky was mostly clear, but some dark, brooding clouds over the mountains in the west removed any confidence they might have had about getting back to the truck in the dry. A climb up a forty-degree slope for some fifty yards led them to a place where the ground had been cleared over an area about twenty feet square.

"This is the third and last drill hole," said Ken, pointing to the north: "The others are beyond that small shrub. They drilled all three holes to the southwest at an angle of forty-five degrees. Each was only about fifty metres."

"And they got?"

"Quite a lot of point-threes and point-fours. Copper, I mean. A two-metre sample ran zero-point-nine with a trace of gold."

"That's not a bad start. I suppose it's all in the report, but do you remember what the best hole averaged?"

"Point-two-six over fifty metres," answered the prospector.

"It'll need more than that in this location. Do you think that the other side is going to be any better?"

"Can't say, but there is, or was, a small outcrop about fifty yards above us with some promising grades. I managed to get one-point-five from a bunch of random chips. Let's head on up there."

After a short climb they reached the site. There was no longer any natural outcrop remaining. What was left was a hand-excavated pit about three feet across cut into the slope. Much of the rock, a brecciated volcanic, was copper stained.

"Looks encouraging," said Bob as he arrived on the site, slightly out of breath.

"I think so too. Which is why I want to see the east side of the breccia pipe, if that is what it is, properly tested. I tried digging through the overburden north of here to expose it again, but the cover is too deep."

"Tried magnetics?"

"I brought out one last year and did a couple of traverses expecting to get a clear indication of the boundaries of this pipe. Hardly showed up, so I haven't suggested it since. Might work."

"It seems from your map that you have the breccia pinned down quite well with these outcrops of volcanics. Mostly unaltered, you say?"

Chapter 34 — Property Examination

They worked their way to the north looking at the outcrops. The geologist, following their route on the prospector's map, made his own sketch in his notebook. "The breccia is nice-looking stuff. Problem is to get some size into it."

They spent the rest of the afternoon examining all the outcrops in the vicinity. While it displayed some encouraging quantities of copper and was a promising indication for the region, the property was not what Bob Tranich had been hoping to find. There was little indication of a big enough deposit at the grades the prospector had found. In situations such as this his style was to let the prospector down gently, even though, in this case, he was dealing with someone who was aware of the shortcomings of the property.

Ken Wickford had been keeping an eye on the time. "Seen all you want? Ready to head back? We could probably fit in another half hour, if you wish. But I would prefer not to walk those logs in the dark."

"Me too. Let's go."

They shouldered their packs and headed back across the valley, walking in single file in some places, abreast where the terrain permitted.

"How long you been working for Poulter?" asked Ken

"I joined about seven months ago. It's just one of several companies in the office, all under him. I'm sure you've heard of him."

"Certainly have."

"So you probably know how he operates. Poulter must have at least a dozen companies. Sometimes I go to make an examination without knowing which of the juniors is going to bear the cost. In this case, I believe they want a property for one called Chilko. It has a bit of cash and the two properties it had last year have not proved up. Needs something new. But you never know. If I recommend something, they might put it into a different company."

"Did I hear you say you had worked mostly for the majors before?"

"Yes. Six years with Anaconda in Australia and the surrounding islands, and then a further five with Noranda based in Toronto."

"Why did you join Poulter?"

"Good question. Sometimes I ask myself. I was getting a bit fed up with the majors. You know, politics, jockeying for power. Things like that. I wanted to see how the juniors worked and this seemed likely to give me a chance to see a lot of different geology."

"And it's working out as you want?" asked Ken.

"Pretty much. I've no complaints. I do my thing. Tell 'em what I see. Slip's okay. He has a few wild ones hovering around him, but I think I can keep myself out of trouble. And the good thing, of course, is that he can raise lots of money. His companies are well funded and, to his credit, most of the money seems to go into the ground. I don't believe he sticks too close to the rules, but I don't think he would do anything outrageous. Interesting fellow. But I wouldn't want to get on the wrong side of him."

Ken liked to express opinions on promoters and developers. "We need people like that. Without a few slightly crazy promoters, we wouldn't have a market for our properties and I'd have to find something else to do."

They talked when the trail permitted until the light began to fade and then they fell silent. It was dark on the way down to the river, but they crossed the logs without incident and twenty minutes later were in the truck and heading home.

"Drop you off at the motel?"

"That would be fine."

"If you have time tomorrow morning, I'd like to show you a few rocks from another property. I've got some more work to do on it later this year. It would be good to have your opinion."

"That's okay. I should leave for Prince George by eleven. Meet for breakfast at the restaurant just opposite the hotel? I forget its name."

"Taseko Inn."

"That's it. Seven?"

"See you there."

Over pancakes and bacon the next morning Bob Tranich got right to the point. "I've seen several breccias like the one you showed me. Those in Arizona are closely associated with the porphyry being mined all round them. Those in the Highland Valley are a mile or so away from the main orebody. I think you've got a very interesting occurrence, but I don't think we can make a mine of something as narrow as that."

"But I'm hoping you will fund the next stage which will be to look for the big one next door."

"That would be fine and it would be a good program, but my job on this particular trip is to find something we can move a drill onto quickly. With the Bobcat you're a year or so away from a serious drill program, assuming the next program outlines a target."

Chapter 34 — Property Examination

"So I should keep plugging away at the area until I find something bigger that you guys can drill?"

"That's about it. I'd like to be able to tell you we will take an option to explore the vicinity. Might be possible in some markets, but not this one. Some promoters would like to drill down the centre of your breccia, but Slip is at the stage in his life when he wants more than just a spectacular drill hole."

After breakfast they went as planned to Ken's farm. Behind the barn was a large shed, once a workshop, now used by Ken to house his rock collection. A table near the centre was flanked on both sides by racks of shelves holding boxes, all of them labelled. Ken pulled down three. "I would like to get your opinion on these."

Bon Tranich picked up pieces of core, examined each with a hand lens, then held a sample under a light at the centre of the table. "Hey! I like this."

"That's what I like to hear," said Ken as he came down the ladder. He dusted off his hands and picked up one of the samples from the box Bob was examining. "Oops! I gave you the wrong box. Let's start again." With a touch of urgency, he picked up the samples and put them back in the box.

"But those are really interesting. Will you show me that one in the field?"

"Eventually, yes, but I'm not ready. Why do you like it?"

"Potassium alteration, chalco in micro fractures and disseminated, a mineral that could be scapolite. Looks like an alkaline porphyry. But it also has quartz. Any size to it?"

"Yes, I think so, but I've got a lot more to do there, including quite a bit of staking."

"Well, when you're ready, give me a call and I'll be there. Don't tell me where it is. But I have to ask: access okay?"

"Should be no problem once we get going. I hike in, but the first round of serious exploration would probably use a helicopter."

"Had it a long time?"

"Ages. In fact as long as I can remember, but that's another story." Ken headed up the ladder.

"Well, I look forward to seeing it whenever you're ready. Meantime, I'd better get moving."

"I've got it!" said Ken from the top of the ladder. "Here's the one I want you to see." He passed down a single box.

Bob held the samples one after the other under the light. "Chalcocite?"

"Yes, and quite a bit of it and some good grades. It all seems to be in this volcanic stuff. I read about a property at Sustut that seemed to be the same sort of thing. Quite a bit of work was done but it didn't seem to come to anything."

"As you probably learned from your research, these tend to be concentrated near the tops of volcanic flows. The difficulty, same as the Bobcat, is to get enough size. You might get someone to take it on, but it is not the sort of thing we would, unless the price of copper were to jump. But each case is different. Most of the class may be too small, and then someone finds the exception. Any mapping?"

Ken was putting the box away. "Not yet. That's another one I have to get back to. Coffee before you go?"

"No thanks. I'll stop at Burns Lake or one of the places on the way. But thanks for the offer, and thanks for the trip yesterday. Enjoyable and interesting, and I look forward to the next one."

Chapter 35

Back at the Office
July

Bob Tranich ran up the steps to 750 West Hastings Street and punched the elevator for the 15th floor. With several passengers, each with a different destination, the elevator took longer than usual and Bob used the time to review the day ahead of him: the usual correspondence, some property submissions, more research on that copper-cobalt occurrence in Mexico, and a letter to Ken Wickford. He wondered whether to mention the unknown property. Probably not, he decided. Then he remembered he had to plan his trip to Flin Flon next week to review a former producer that was probably a non-starter but had to be checked out.

A few minutes later he was sitting at his desk, reviewing his correspondence and dictating letters. Through the window to his left he could see across Burrard Inlet to the sulphur piles waiting for shipment and, beyond them, North Vancouver and Grouse Mountain.

One coffee called for another. He walked down the corridor to where Tanya, who rarely emerged from the drafting room, was talking to someone he didn't recognize. They were waiting for the coffee machine to finish its process. After pouring his own, he headed back down the corridor. Coming in the other direction were his employer, Sydney Poulter, and the new man, Victor Dubell, whose job, he understood, was executive assistant.

The promoter opened the exchange. "How did it go? Find a winner?"

"Not this time. But the property was interesting and..."

"Goddamn geogolists!" responded Sydney Poulter in a tone of good-humoured scoffing. "What's 'interesting' got to do with it?"

Bob Tranich was unfazed by his boss's bombastic style, which a person with less self-confidence might have found threatening.

"Nothing wrong with a property being interesting. I went to see a prospector I hadn't met before—Ken Wickford. He knows his stuff and is someone we ought to keep in touch with."

Sydney was not going to let go. "Anything useful to us? If not, don't waste time on him."

"He's the sort of person who is capable of bringing us just what we need. In fact he already has a property I want to see as soon as he has it ready."

"Go to it! I've got to go. Got to meet some people about financing the Sabre Mines play. Find us a porphyry!" was the promoter's last comment as he left without the coffee he had come to collect. His departure left Bob Tranich and Victor Dubell to continue the conversation. With no need or desire to talk to his new colleague, Bob was about to head towards his office when Victor Dubell addressed him with a look of puzzled annoyance. "What do you mean, 'as soon as he has it ready'?"

"It makes sense. Prospectors like to work their claims to the point at which they are ready for market. In this case, I don't think he has it all staked."

"How come you like it so much when you haven't even seen it?" asked Victor.

"Some of the samples I saw looked typical of a copper-gold porphyry. You know, like Afton, Similkameen. They're like the other porphyries, except they have gold instead of moly."

Victor's irritated curiosity now changed to real interest. "Could be useful for Chilko. In fact, it could be just the sort of property we need. Money's available, mostly flow-through, that we are committed to spend. Do you have any idea where it is?"

"No, and I deliberately told him not to tell me."

Victor rolled his eyes, let his shoulders sag and held both hands down in a gesture of incredulity. "You mean there's some patch of forest out there with indications of tens or hundreds of millions of dollars worth of copper and gold sitting under the ground, and you don't want to know where it is?"

His tone was rising in a mixture of disappointment tinged with contempt.

"That's absolutely right!" replied Bob emphatically, as he felt his anger rising. "I know this business is new to you, but you have to understand some of the rules."

The geologist looked directly at the younger man, who was staring impassively back. "Prospectors are a vital part of the

Chapter 35 — Back at the Office

business. We—at least that goes for most of us—don't try to cheat them. Ken Wickford knows I am very interested in this property. When he has it staked or mapped, or whatever he plans to do, he will get in touch."

Victor showed his exasperation: "That's hard to take. We're in the business of making money for ourselves and our shareholders. And we're not going to do that by being Mr. Nice Guy."

Bob started toward his office before turning around to face Victor. "In that case, you and I are playing by different rules, different standards."

A moment later, without another word, Victor responded by turning in the opposite direction.

Once in his office, he shut the door and stood staring out at the city.

Later that morning Victor Dubell went to Leonard Marsden's office.

"Morning, Len. I need to know how this claims business works. D'you have time to explain it?"

Leonard Marsden, a middle-aged and balding man who had put on weight since he had starting doing less field work, had held several conversations with Victor since their boss had introduced them a couple of weeks ago. Insofar as this short time was any guide, theirs was not a naturally comfortable relationship, but each man had a job to do and neither was going to let minor issues interfere.

Len, remaining seated, looked up from his desk at his visitor. "Yes, I can do that. I have no plans for lunch. Do you want to discuss it over soup and a sandwich across the way?"

"Sure. Let's do that." Victor glanced out of the window. "I see the rain's stopped. See you at the elevator."

At the restaurant they spent little time on trivial matters before Victor got the conversation onto his topic. "This claim staking business. I need to understand it."

"That makes sense. Penalties for getting it wrong can be serious, even loss of an orebody. Where do you want to begin?"

"Start from scratch. How would I stake a claim in this province?"

"First, get yourself a Free Miner's Certificate. It'll cost you twenty-five bucks. Then get yourself some claim tags. Look at the claim map to see if the ground you want is open."

"Open? What's that mean?"

"It means not already staked."

"Okay, go on. Assume I know what I want and no one else has it."

"Now you have to do a bit of planning. Under the MGS system—."

Victor interrupted. "MGS?"

"Metric grid system."

"So I've now got to do some planning. Go on."

Len pushed his plate aside and turned over the paper tablemat to expose the blank sheet of paper. Pulling a mechanical pencil from his pocket he drew a small square. "You acquire ground in units, each five hundred metres square." After drawing a north arrow on the tablemat, he added: "They have to be aligned north-south and east-west, like that. A claim can be up to twenty units."

"That would be four units by five?"

"Right."

"Or two and a half by eight."

"Negative. No half units." Len drew a claim four units north-south by five units east-west, then looked directly at Victor. "Next, the hard work begins. You go to the place you want to claim and you cut down a tree and square it with your axe."

"Or I could pay someone to do this?"

"That's correct. Then you, or the person or contractor you've hired, walk around the perimeter of your claim marking your line with blazes or tape. Every five hundred metres you put in another post."

"So I walk through the woods cutting trees and marking them with my axe. Sounds primitive."

"I suppose it is," replied Len, "but it works. It's been going on a long time."

"And this procedure, which we agree is primitive, can give me the ownership of something worth hundreds of millions of dollars?"

"In principle and sometimes in fact," answered Len, "It also takes luck."

"That means we have to seize opportunities. That goes for all of us, right?"

"But you need to know about all those other claims you will see on the map, staked under a different system. And you have to know about crown grants."

Chapter 35 — Back at the Office

Victor stood up and picked up his coat from the back of his chair. "That's all I have time for now. Thanks for Lesson One. The other types of staking will have to wait until I have more time."

Len got up too. "Very well. See you back at the office. I have some banking to do."

The next morning Victor walked through the drafting office in search of Fred Colborne, a geology student working in the office for the summer. Spotting the young man, he went directly to the drafting table. "Ah! just the man I was looking for. Do you know much about how to research claims in B.C.?"

Fred was working, head down, pen in hand. He looked up, evidently surprised by the visitor. Then he stood. "More or less. I know the basics, but I'm sure there's a lot I don't know."

"Great! If you would drop by my office in five minutes, there's a claim I'm trying to find and I'm not sure how to go about it. You can spare the time, I hope."

Fred worked for Leonard Marsden, who guided the geological work for most companies in the Poulter stable. As Fred was junior to everyone in the office, and as Leonard had not been keeping him particularly busy, Fred did not dispute Victor's right to ask for some of his time.

"Sure! Nothing I'm doing now is all that urgent. In five minutes did you say?"

"That's right. See you then."

Victor returned to his room, made a few notes, and then answered a phone call. He was still on his phone when Fred arrived. He motioned him to a chair, completed the call with a "Yes, that's right. No, no. Okay, Do it," before addressing Fred. "Can you get me a list of claim owners in the province?"

"Yes. I believe that could be done. It would be quite a big job. Do you mean in all the mining districts?"

"No, that's a good point. Just one district, I suppose. How many are there? I'm looking for a claim in northern B.C. Smithers is the closest town of any consequence."

"That makes it almost certain that it would be in the Omenica Mining District. Much easier than searching the whole province. So you don't know the name of the claim?"

Victor shook his head. "No. Just the owner's name."

The Nisselinka Claims

"I think I can do that. I need to go to the Mining Recorder—up at Robson Square. So what you need is a list of claims belonging to—."

"Yes, a list of claims—" Victor dropped his voice just enough to prompt Fred to lean forward. "—belonging to a fellow called Wickford, Ken Wickford."

"That shouldn't be too difficult. If he has hundreds of claims, it will take a while, but that can't be too likely."

"How long will it take you?" asked Victor.

"A couple of hours, maybe four if I run into difficulties. What company shall I charge my time to?"

"Oh yes. That's a good point. To tell you the truth, I'm not quite sure. Put it down to Sabre Mines, but I may have to ask you to change that later."

"Tomorrow morning okay?"

"Yes. That's what I need. Come and see me after lunch and let me know how you got on."

Fred had no trouble finding Ken Wickford's name among the list of those holding a Free Miner's Certificate. Among the FMC holders in the Smithers Mining District, Ken Wickford was listed as being the registered owner of seven claim groups including BOB 1 to BOB 6, CASO 4, 7 and 9, and NIS 1 to NIS 3. Most of the claims had sufficient work credited to them to be in good standing for two years or more. Two of the NIS claims had passed their due dates but had probably been renewed. Although he was not by nature a particularly organized sort of person, Fred was keen to impress, and he was sure of what was required. He made a neat list of all the claims in alphabetic order, with their claim number, date of staking and due date.

Bob Tranich was returning from a meeting with a joint venture partner on Centaur's project in Nevada. As he walked into the elevator at the ground level below the Poulter offices, he noticed Fred holding the elevator door open for him. With his other hand Fred was holding a roll of maps.

"Thanks. Fred. Let me guess. Mag maps from the GSC? Claim maps from the Mining Recorder? Or…" But Bob's guessing was interrupted by Fred saying:

"Right on number two! Claim maps. Just giving Victor a helping hand."

Chapter 35 — Back at the Office

Bob Tranich paused for a moment while a look of concern flashed across his face. "That's what we like to hear: teamwork!"

The elevator arrived at the fifteenth floor and both men walked out into the office. By this time the conversation was onto the Canucks and their chances for the next season. "I bought season tickets last year."

"Will you do that again?" asked Fred.

"Yes, and they'd better perform," said Bob as he wheeled off into his office.

Fred went on down the corridor to Victor's office and knocked on the open door. Victor, sitting at his desk, motioned him to a round table in the corner. "How did you get on?"

"I think I've got what you need. Here's a list of all the claims he owns in the Smithers district. At least, these are all the claims registered in the name of K. Wickford. He may own a part of other claims that are registered in someone else's name. Also I've got four maps and they cover the three of Wickford's properties that we identified." Fred opened up the roll of maps and pointed to a patch on the top right hand corner of the map covered by a chequerboard of overlapping squares. "The Bobcat claims are here." He explained, tracing the outline with his index finger. "The boundaries of other Wickford claims are here and here."

"Just a moment," said Victor. "Let's mark them with a colour pencil. I've got one in my desk."

Fred was enjoying the opportunity to display his knowledge. "So in this group he has three claims, all called BOB. There is one of twenty units, one of sixteen and one of twelve, for a total of forty-eight. The claims are called BOB 1, BOB 2 and BOB 3. People who do quite a bit of staking prefer short claim names because they have to be written out again and again on metal tags and forms."

"These figures here '6,' '12,' what are they?" asked Victor.

"That just shows the month when they were first recorded. These four digit numbers give us the claim number. This tell you what you need?"

"You've done everything I asked for. So far so good. I'm looking for claims he has held for a long time. Can we tell that?"

"Not from the map. But the list I prepared this morning gives the date the claims were first recorded. You see," said Fred leafing through his notes, "the mineral claims held longest were staked in '82. There appears to be nothing older than that."

Still searching for the information he needed, Victor asked another question. "So if he had held claims for a long time, they would to show up on this list?"

Before Fred could answer, Victor continued: "Let me look through them tonight. Leave the list with me. I need to go through them slowly. What, by the way, are these smaller claims at various different angles?"

"Those are older claims staked under a different system. Most are crown granted mineral claims, a completely different system, more like real estate. Some of them date back into the last century."

"What a bloody crazy system! So this means some claims are handled by the Ministry of Mines and some by another ministry. Is that right? None of the other type, grants or whatever you called them, appeared on your list, did they?"

Fred shook his head. "No. As I mentioned they wouldn't show up at the Mining Recorder's office. They are handled by Land Titles."

"Okay. That's enough for now. Are you in tomorrow, in case I need some more help?"

"I'll be here."

As Fred got up to leave, Victor added: "Just one other thing. Please keep this work confidential, even within the office."

"I understand," replied Fred with restrained honesty.

Victor put the roll of maps and Fred's notes on his desk, sat down in his chair, swivelled round to look at the cityscape before him, and thought. Why wouldn't that idiot, Tranich, have bothered to find out about the property that looked so encouraging? Didn't he know how they would all benefit from a really good mineral property? As an employee, Bob would have options on shares in most of Slip's companies. What was he waiting for? This boy-scout attitude to prospectors—it could ruin a chance for all of them to make a bit of money. He got up, walked down the corridor to the receptionist, and asked her for the day-by-day copy of the outgoing correspondence for the current week. She handed him a board with two inches of paper attached to it and asked him to sign for it. Back in his office, he flipped through the pages, starting with those on top, the most recent. After only fifteen or so pages he

Chapter 35 — Back at the Office

found what he was looking for. In an internal memo to Sabre Mines by Bob Tranich, one paragraph caught his eye.

"Other properties: Ken Wickford is a capable and knowledgeable prospector with whom we should keep in touch. He has at least one property that could be of considerable interest to us, when it is available. From samples he showed me by accident, I believe it to be a copper-gold- alkaline porphyry associated with a vein which he has held for some years. There may be some workings on the property and they may be quite old. I believe he has some sampling and perhaps some staking to complete before he will be ready to bring it to us. He knows of our interest."

Victor folded back the pages he had turned and handed the file back to the receptionist with a "Thank you," but without a glance in her direction.

Chapter 36

Conflicting Interests
July

"It's for you," said Denny, the engineer at Burns Lake Helicopter's base, as he passed the phone to Will Herman.

"Will Herman speaking."

"Are you the base manager?"

"That's my job, when I'm not flying."

"My name is Victor Dubell. I'm with Poulter Investments in Vancouver. We need to put out a crew of eight either tomorrow or the next day. We may need the machine all day. Is that possible?"

"Tomorrow we have both machines fully booked, but on the following day I've only got a drop off at 7:30 and a pick-up in the afternoon. We could fly several hours for you on Wednesday. Where do you want to go?"

"I'd rather not say, right now."

They talked about crew size, type of terrain for landing, travel arrangements, and price.

"It would be best if you could tell us a bit about your plans," said Will. "I'm sure you understand we are used to keeping things confidential. If you could tell us the direction and roughly the distance, I might be able to save you some money by arranging for a fuel cache."

"Yes, I understand you have to know. But can you assure me that it doesn't go any further than you?"

"Until we fly, of course. Then the staff here has to know where we are going."

"We have a job to do east of Smithers. The contractor's already engaged. They'll put four men in your chopper and drive another four to a place nearer the site. They will be picked up as soon as the first is out."

Chapter 36 — Conflicting Interests

Writing down distances and map features Will continued with routine questions. "Will you want moves during the day?"

"Oh yes. We'll need you all day. You'll probably be moving a two-person crew every hour or so."

"In that case I'd better get a couple of drums dropped off. Would a few miles north of Spindlers Creek on the Nisgon Lake road be close enough?"

"You'd be closer on the other side of the ridge and ten k farther north. Cache the fuel somewhere near there if you can."

As Will heard this and glanced up at the aeronautical chart covering the entire wall opposite his desk, he felt almost sick. Will liked flying, liked chalking up the hours, and liked his base to do well. But he had fielded many orders for staking crews and he recognized the signs: short notice and secrecy. "So you'll be working at the headwaters of Nisgon river, on the south flank of Siwell Peak?"

"Yes, that's it. But please remember you've got to keep that to yourself until the day we fly."

"I understand," said Will.

He felt tired. There was little room for doubt that the area to be staked was the location of Ken's claims, those his friend had been working on for years, was worried about, and intended to enlarge with further staking. But Will had a professional duty to guard the confidentiality of his client and he had his own and Burns Lake's reputation to look after. Snapping his thoughts back to his job, he continued.

"Are you staying in town Tuesday night?"

"Yes. We will arrive on one of the evening flights."

"Want me to meet the flight? You could leave gear at the hangar instead of taking it all to the hotel. Helps to keep a low profile."

"Great. I'll phone you when we have everything arranged."

Will got up slowly and, with all the enthusiasm of a man faced with choosing between two disasters, he wrote on the wall calendar for Wednesday: "Poulter Investments."

"Big job?" said Denny, looking up from his desk.

"Could be several hours," said Will as he left the office.

On Tuesday evening, Will was at the base when he heard the PWA flight from Vancouver touch down. He waited five minutes and then drove his pickup the couple of miles and parked close to the arrivals door in the small terminal. Northern's crew were easy to spot among the dozen or so arriving passengers, unkempt young men with bush shirts and beards and two older and rather better dressed men in plaid shirts and heavy boots.

"Stu Wrangle?" said Will addressing the first of the four.

"That's the guy you want," was the response directing Will's attention to the bearded man behind him.

After introductions, Will walked with them over to the baggage rack. "You're welcome to leave your equipment at the hangar, if you wish. It's just a couple of minutes drive from here."

"Good. That's what we'd like to do," replied Stuart. "I don't want too many people in town trying to guess what we are up to. We'll leave the field stuff and the trunks with you."

Within a few minutes the doors behind the baggage rack opened and suitcases, boxes and packages of all types started to arrive. Among them were four backpacks, two with axe handles protruding, and an aluminium trunk. When these and some hold-alls had been thrown in the back of his pickup, Will climbed into the cab. "These will be waiting for you in the hangar. Seven-thirty okay?"

"We'll be there," said Stuart, as he headed towards a taxi to take his crew into town.

Will had a late hockey practice that night. Usually he phoned Ken and drove by his house at 8:30 to pick him up. With ten minutes for the drive, that left enough time for them to change and put on their skates. At 8:00 he phoned Ken at home.

"Look, I can't make the practice tonight. Too much on. Got to go back to the shop."

"Wow," said Ken. "Never known you to miss one. Must be important. I'll catch up later and tell you how it went."

After a hurried meal at home, Will walked the mile to the hangar. Driving would have taken him five minutes instead of thirty but he needed time to think. There was no work too urgent to wait for the morrow. At the office he put on a pot of coffee, let himself into the hangar, took a polishing rag and wiped the already-clean windshield of the Jet Ranger. He then went to his desk, put his feet up, and stared at the chart on the wall. A friendship or a career? An expensive staking expedition wasted because of a pilot who could not be trusted with a confidence? Perhaps even an orebody lost. A close friend abandoned in a time of need? Perhaps a fortune lost. The tentacles of circumstance had him bound.

His thoughts were shattered by a loud knock on the outside door to the office. Who on earth? At this time of night? He went

Chapter 36 — Conflicting Interests

to the door, opened it to face Ken, in the red lumberman's jacket he often wore going to and from the rink. "You didn't sound right, so I phoned from the rink after the game. No reply so I decided to come here. What's up?"

Will shrugged. "Just got a lot to do."

Ken put his head to one side, in a manner which could only be interpreted as disbelief. "Lot's of flying?"

"Yes, all day tomorrow," was Will's response.

"It's cold out here. How about letting me in? Any chance of a coffee?"

Will stepped back, opened the door wide and indicated that his friend should enter. Not much was said as he started the coffee machine. A minute later both men were sitting, Will in a chair at his desk, Ken in a sofa against the opposite wall. As Ken leaned back, he glanced past his friend's shoulder through the door into the hangar. He stood up and walked slowly through the door into the hangar, towards the helicopter. Will followed.

"Bird in good shape? Knowing you and Denny, it has to be. Good that the work is rolling in. Timber cruising, I suppose."

As he said this, Ken was staring towards the side of the hangar, at the row of four backpacks, and at the protruding axe handles. Next to them lay a pile of rough-cut lumber some four inches square and five or six feet long. He turned to face Will, looked him in the eye, and said nothing. Will stared back, blankly. Each man knew what the other knew. Without letting up on his stare, Ken broke the silence. "Looks like competition for someone."

Will responded slowly. "Could be." Then, after moment's pause. "I'm sorry."

"Not your fault," said Ken. "I'd better be going. Much to do before the morning, and even more to do tomorrow. See you."

"Good night," said Will as he turned back to his office.

Ken let himself out.

Chapter 37

Team Staking

July

Stuart Wrangle, leader of a team of eight stakers, climbed into the seat on the left of the helicopter pilot, Brent Sanford. Brent had been asked by Will Herman in a late phone call the previous evening to take on this job. Will had said he had too much paper work to do. The three others in the staking crew, after putting their packs in the hold, climbed into the rear seat, adjusted their seat belts and headsets and soon heard the pilot on the intercom. "I expect we'll have a bit of a tail wind so this shouldn't take much more than an hour or so. Everyone comfortable?"

"Just fine," and a couple of grunts was sufficient answer.

The machine detached itself from the concrete outside Burns Lake Helicopter's hangar. Then, as the pilot moved the stick forward, it gradually picked up speed, crossing a runway for small aircraft, then hay fields, then mixed conifers and deciduous trees, until they were flying at about one thousand feet over what seemed to be endless forest.

After assembling at the hangar at 8:00 am, Stuart and his crew had spent three hours waiting for low cloud to burn off, an uncommon situation at this time of year. The wait was particularly frustrating for Stuart as he saw his opportunity to complete on time disappearing and with it the bonus the client himself had suggested. His men were happy enough. They were being paid, albeit at a standby rate, to wait, drink coffee, look at magazines and talk. But it was a relief to all when Brent finally announced they could fly. By this time, unbeknown to Stuart, who thought any competition unlikely, Ken Wickford and his single helper had completed their two-hour hike up the hill and had started their desperate effort to stake as much as they could before being overwhelmed by the competition they feared.

Chapter 37 — Team Staking

Stuart Wrangle was an experienced staker, as was his entire crew, except for one rookie, a wiry twenty-year-old from Burns Lake who came recommended as a good worker and someone who could handle himself in the bush. The assignment was typical—to acquire all the open ground between certain coordinates. The area the client required was large, over ten kilometres across, some nine thousand acres. Taking into account some pre-existing claims and crown grants and the constraints imposed by terrain, Stuart had divided the area into five claims of maximum size, 2 x 2.5 kilometres, and some smaller ones, if time permitted. With the other half of the crew due to be waiting for him at the end of a logging road close to the ground to be staked, and with the helicopter available all day for moves, he had calculated he should be able to complete the job in one day. With the morning's delay it would still be possible, but he would require just about every minute of the summer daylight. On his lap he held a map on which he had marked the claims to be staked. The client, to whom time seemed more important than money, had wanted it done in a hurry. Accordingly, this was a cost-plus job with a bonus for early completion. Stuart took on fixed-cost staking only when he knew the terrain or had time to check it out. The men would be working both in pairs and singly. When working together, the lead man would set direction with a compass and measure distance with a thread dispenser attached to his waist. The second man would check the direction his partner was taking, and then mark the line by blazing trees and tying tape.

Stuart had spent most of the previous two days preparing for this one. Each staker had been assigned a route involving directions (one of the cardinal points of the compass), distances (in multiples of five hundred metres), and pre-inscribed metal tags, each of which had to be nailed to a post at a given location. In some cases the route encompassed an entire claim, in others it involved a side or sides of a claim, the other sides being left to others in the team. The sites for dropping off and picking up each pair of stakers had been selected from air photographs. Each pair carried a radio for communicating with the pilot and with each other.

He knew his plan was good. He also knew he could trust his crew. The leaders of each pair of men had worked for him on previous contracts. Although some of them had to be kept out of the bar on the night before work, the helpers were all good field men.

But even with good planning and a first class crew there were always uncertainties. A site which appeared on the air photos to be suitable for landing might turn out to have a leaning tree that could be dislodged by turbulent air. A pattern of low shrubs might pose a threat to the tail rotor. If the pilot said he did not like the site, he would get no argument or attempt at persuasion from this seasoned bushman, who knew enough about the dangers of taking helicopters into difficult situations.

The first stop was a rendezvous with the other half of his crew, which should by now have arrived by truck at the closest point of road access to the claims.

Stuart spoke into the microphone held by the headset next to his chin. "Should be on the other side of that clearing."

"Roger!" replied Brent as he eased his machine slightly to the right.

"Our truck is a black Suburban. Should be there by now."

After a couple of minutes, during which the altimeter had dropped from 2600 to 900 feet, they could see the clearing and the truck they were expecting. On the other side of the clearing was a red vehicle, which as they came closer could be seen to be a pickup.

"Stu, that yours too?" asked Brent.

"Nope!" said Stuart, annoyed at the unexpected presence of anyone. "No hunting yet. Any fishing around here?"

"Don't know of any. Could be forestry of some sort," said Brent. The pilot was hoping that the electronic processing of his voice would conceal his lack of conviction. He had seen that truck before and was well aware it had nothing to do with forestry work.

As they circled around the clearing, they saw four men get out of the Suburban and congregate on the side away from the only place for the helicopter to land. Moments later it touched down, blowing dust everywhere. As soon as the engine noise had faded the pilot's voice came over the intercom. "Shut down?"

"Yes, but we'll be only a few minutes. Just a quick confab on the plan." Stuart climbed out of the machine, collected his pack from the hold and walked in front of it at a crouch until well clear of the blades. The other passengers followed. They walked towards the black Suburban where the four men had been sheltering from the wind on the lee side of the vehicle. The stakers appeared from behind their truck.

Chapter 37 — Team Staking

"Good navigating!" called Stuart. "Sorry about the delay. We were socked in by low cloud. Who's our companion?"

"No idea. It was here when we arrived. Judging by the tracks, it must have come in this morning. Nothing to see in the back or in the cab."

"No matter. Nothing to do with us. Let's just review the plan. Geoff, Mark, Ben and Francois to Site A in the first set out. You all ready?"

A few grunts and one "Let's do it!" signalled assent as the first four picked up their packs and axes and moved slowly towards the chopper.

Some ten minutes later the machine was circling a natural opening in the forest occupied by salal bushes and scrub willow and a patch of grass growing at the edge of a small pond. As he banked the machine the pilot spoke into the microphone: "I can get you down by that pond."

This prompted responses from two of his passengers: "Looks like wet feet to start the day, but that's okay," and "Oh, shit!"

But then, as his machine whipped the water amongst the grass into dancing wavelets, Brent moved it slowly sideways onto drier ground and settled his craft onto the grass. "Dry start, everyone. Good luck."

A couple of hundred metres to the south, Ken Wickford was running his staking line due north with all the energy and stamina a fit body of thirty-nine could produce. He had heard the helicopter circle twice and then land ahead and to his right and now, after a minute of relative quiet, he heard it take off and then fly directly over him. He stopped for a few seconds to look, but all he saw was a glimpse of the underside of the machine as it picked up speed some hundred feet above him.

As far as he could judge from the sound, which he knew could be deceiving, his route was taking him closer to the point where the helicopter had landed but not directly towards it. He suspected that it had ferried in a staking crew of two or four men and would pick them up at a different location. He knew his staking lines and those of the competition would almost certainly cross and that he and they might meet. The advantages were mostly theirs. He could think of only one for himself, the ability to change his staking plan on a whim. He would try to redirect his helper, but communication with the walkie-talkies they each carried was a chancy business.

Some six minutes after hearing the helicopter take off he had blazed and flagged his line to what he thought would be its closest point to the landing spot. This, he believed, was now about a hundred yards directly to his right. Thereafter his line would take him away. Thinking he could hear voices, he paused and listened. He heard the sound of an axe against a tree. Two or three minutes later he heard a tree crash, followed by more chopping. He continued on his northerly course, stopping frequently to listen. Then he heard the axe or axes coming closer. All staking lines being along cardinal points of the compass, he knew that the line approaching his would be heading west and it would intersect his some fifty yards behind him. He stopped and waited. Sure enough, as expected, he caught a glimpse of a man travelling west across his line. He waited for a second staker, saw none, and attributed this to the thick undergrowth restricting visibility.

After the ringing sounds of axe against tree and the occasional shout suggested they were well beyond the intersection, Ken moved back to the new line and followed it east towards the landing site. His time was precious but so was knowledge of the directions in which his opponents were staking and the size of their claims. Their east-west line was well marked with frequent blazes and flagging tape. By this time, he could confirm what he had already surmised, that the sound of chopping after the helicopter had landed had been to cut a tree and square it off into a post. As he neared the place where he expected to find the post, he could see from the break in the trees that a clearing was close. He moved up to the edge of forest from which he could see the open ground. Covered with orange flagging, the post was easily visible. Not wanting to be seen by a second crew, if there was one, he waited before walking over to the post. Inscribed on the red metal tag were all the details of a Legal Corner Post, the definitive marker for a claim. From this he learned that four claims covering an area five kilometres long by four wide were to be staked from this post, and that the people for whom the claims were being staked were Victor Dubell, a name he did not recognize, and Sydney Poulter. He also noticed that the stakers expected to return to this post to complete the finishing time. Ken knew what he had to do: stake smaller claims within what his opponents intended and finish them sooner. He turned back to pick up his line where he had left it. He was about to re-enter the forest when he heard a shout. Looking behind him he saw a man with an axe

Chapter 37 — Team Staking

by the corner post. Assuming that the opposing team worked for a professional staking crew with whom he had no reason to quarrel, he turned back. The two men converged, then greeted each other cautiously.

"Hi. My name is Mark. We're just doing a bit of staking. You must be the guy with the red truck?"

This was information Ken had no reason to conceal. "That's right. Who are you working for?"

"Can't say," replied Mark. He nodded at Ken's axe, tape and compass. "Sorry mate, but I don't think you've got a chance. We've got eight men and we'll have it done in no time."

"I guess we've both got work to do," responded Ken. "Perhaps we'll meet again—in the bar."

The two men parted, Ken returning along the line to the west and the other man towards the south.

As he returned to his own line, Ken thought through the changes he had to make. Instead of cutting his line for two kilometres, placing a post and turning west for two kilometres, he would stake a smaller claim and would try to reach his helper and tell him to do the same. Estimating he had three hours to complete his claims before his opponents could finish their larger ones, he would use the remaining time, if any, to stake spoilers to the east to put himself in as good a negotiating position as possible. But even for this, time was short.

The next morning Stuart Wrangle groaned when his alarm woke him at the usual 6:00 am. The day before had been a long one. The helicopter had picked up the last pair of stakers as the light was beginning to fade and it was well after dark before he was able to confirm that the four men in the truck were back in town. Compiling their notes on completion times had taken him until well after midnight, and rather less than five hours sleep was far short of what he needed. But he had work to do. His client had made it clear that he wanted to be phoned with a report at the start of business after the first day of staking.

Stuart's notes included some on competing claims where his men had come across other lines or corner posts, but the information was incomplete. Despite another two hours and several cups of coffee in his basement office, he could not form a clear picture of how much ground he had acquired. At 8:30 he put the call through to Victor Dubell at the office of Poulter Management.

"Competition?" yelled Victor Dubell into the telephone. "What do you mean, competition?"

Stuart paused a moment before answering. "We had no reason to expect it, but when we arrived there was an unidentified pick-up truck at the clearing where we met the rest of my crew. Then, soon after we had been dropped off by the helicopter, my guys came across a staker, apparently working alone. We don't know how many there were or what they succeeded in getting, but they were certainly after the same ground."

"That's outrageous. Fifteen hundred dollars to pay you and that much again for the chopper and you're telling me that we have a botched job? Damn it! Who did you tell? It sounds like a leak!"

"Perhaps, but not from my crew. I went through the staking plan with them the night before, but we were dealing with lines on plain sheets of paper, like I always do. The first they knew of the location was when the ground crew got a map from me yesterday morning."

"Jeez! What a mess! You say you don't know what we got and what they got?"

"That's right. But we will know as soon as they file at the recorder's office."

"Know who they were?"

"No. One of my crew said that he met one of them on the line but he didn't get his name. Whoever he was and who he was working for will come from the mining recorder. Do you want me to record our claims now or wait? Some people like to wait but my recommendation is that we get in first."

"Go ahead. And phone me soon as you know. You understand? I want to be kept informed."

"Will do." The contract staker put the phone down slowly, as if it were fragile or dangerous.

Chapter 38

At the Mining Recorder
July

While Victor Dubell and Stuart Wrangle were having their short conversation, Ken Wickford was at home in the room he used as an office. He had already spent an hour drawing sketch maps to show the boundaries of the claims he had staked. Then he took half an hour to complete the Ministry of Mines forms by which his new claims were to be recorded: Name of Claim, Staker, Free Miner's Certificate number, along with the size and location of the claims and other details. Had he been able to stake the claims without competition he would have found satisfaction in completing documentation of the many hours and many miles of axing his way through the bush. But filling out the forms now gave him only an empty feeling of time wasted and opportunities lost. His principal sentiment was of betrayal. He had been betrayed by a geologist in whom he had trusted and, even more painful, he had betrayed his own family, who had discovered the mineral and maintained the ground for most of a century. Some of the events that had delayed his re-staking were beyond his control. But not all. Months after the separation he had continued to procrastinate. That hockey match in Prince George had taken precedence. Sure, he enjoyed the games, and he hadn't wanted to let his team down, but he had let down his grandfather and father. And if there happened to be a fortune beneath the claims, he might even have let down his children, too. He could have staked after the hockey, but the weather had been foul and that would have made the work dangerous. His fault, but not his fault. Damn it. This was going nowhere. Enough of looking back. It was time to file the claims, find out the damage, and see what he could salvage.

233

He drove slowly to the government offices in the centre of town; a brown paper envelope containing his application forms and sketch maps lay on the passenger seat beside him. Normally this would have been the final and satisfying act of a long and arduous process, something like scoring a goal. This was different, a bit like going on the ice in the last sixty seconds with your team down 3—2 and an empty net behind you.

Until the prospector entered, the first-floor room housing the office of the Mining Recorder had been empty of visitors. A bell at the counter allowed him to announce his presence. After a few moments he heard sounds of someone moving at the back of the office.

"Hullo, Ken," said a middle-aged woman appearing from behind a row of high, stand-alone office shelving. "We haven't seen you for a while. Used to be we could count on you coming in once a month."

"Hi, Mary. I know. I seem to have had a lot to do, at least enough to keep me away from prospecting."

"You're probably not missing much. We notice it's been a bit slow. What can we do for you today?"

Ken had known Mary Branson and her husband for several years. He was relieved that she didn't ask him about his kids. Most of his friends knew how hard the separation had been and stayed off the topic.

"Just a few claims to file."

"That's a good sign. At least with you I won't have to worry about the forms and maps being up to scratch."

"I should hope not. Dunno how many I've filed over the years, most of them here."

"Okay, let's see what you have got. Let me have the NTS and I'll pull out the latest."

Ken told her and then spread out the forms and maps on the counter. "South end of the Nisselinka Range. I staked them yesterday and ran into a bit of competition. So you may get more than one application for the same area, if you haven't already."

They looked at the claim map, a two-by-three feet sheet of white paper covered in parts by a mosaic of small squares with some triangles. Ken put his finger on the map to point to his claims. "There are my crown grants and the claims I put next to them a few years ago. This new batch is also around the crown grants and replaces one I let expire." He looked up at Mary and pushed the

Chapter 38 — At the Mining Recorder

completed forms towards her. "I'll leave these with you, but I'm sure some of the ground is going to be contested. I had planned to cover a lot more, but as soon as I realized what was happening we limited ours in order to get earlier completion times. I also ran a line of two-post claims through the middle of the competition's ground. They won't be pleased."

Mary laughed. "Two-posters! I know all about them. I spend a lot of time sorting out the problems they cause."

"Sorry about that. I just had to get that ground."

"I know. Don't worry. I'll plot it all and see what happens."

Mary sounded slightly distant as she recognized she might be the first to pass judgement on the relative merits of rival claims. She had been in her job long enough to realize that innocent-looking forms and sketch maps such as these could become objects of scrutiny in a court of law. While contenders for ownership of mineral claims could often settle their differences cheaply before anything of worth had been found, it was a different matter once mineral assets worth hundreds of millions of dollars had begun to emerge.

"Thanks, Mary. You'll phone me if—I should say 'when'—the others apply for the same ground."

"As you know, Ken, I have to go by the book. If there is overlap, I will write the usual form letter to both of you. But, yes, I'll phone both of you."

Ken smiled ruefully and left.

Ken had been back at his farm for no more than half an hour when the phone rang.

"Ken?"

"Yes?"

"It's Mary Branson. You were right about the competition. They have applied for much the same ground. I told them there were overlapping claims. What we like to do in these cases is to get both parties together to see if it can be sorted out without involving the claims inspector. I would like you and the other party to meet here so each of you can see what the other is claiming. They could be here at 10:00 am tomorrow. Can you?"

"I'll be there. Thanks, Mary."

Stuart Wrangle phoned Victor Dubell that evening. "Sorry to phone you at home, but I need some instruction."

"Go on," was the abrupt reply.

"The Mining Recorder has confirmed that other people were staking the same ground. She wants me to meet the other side at her office in the morning to try and agree on a boundary. Do I have authority to negotiate?" Stu waited for several seconds before he heard Victor respond.

"They had, did you say, two stakers?"

"I don't know. We only saw one."

"And no helicopter?"

"I believe not."

"And you had eight stakers and a helicopter?"

"Right," replied Stuart, feeling he knew what was coming.

"And you started about the same time?"

"Yes, more or less."

"Then don't negotiate. Claim all you can and make it quite clear to the other side that we won't put up with any nonsense from them. Who are they anyway? Small-time prospectors?"

"I don't know for sure, but I believe his name is Ken Wickford. If so, he is a well-respected prospector. He does a lot of staking and selling of claims. I would prefer not to make an enemy of him."

"Listen, Mr. Wrangle. You have a contract with us and we require you to get that ground. I don't mind what you do or how many enemies you make, just get the ground you contracted to stake."

By now Stuart, who had been running his own business for ten years, was feeling resentful as well as uncomfortable. "Mr. Dubell. I understand your instructions. I will do what I can and get in touch with you after the meeting."

Ken was at the office of the Mining Recorder the next morning. He was apprehensive about how much ground the competition had claimed and more than curious about the competition. On that depended whether negotiations would be possible, or whether challenge and counter challenge would be the only way forward. Mary came to meet him at the counter.

"Good morning, Ken. We're going to be in the meeting room. The other staker has not arrived. I think it might be better if you waited here until he does."

"Can you tell me who is coming?"

"Stu Wrangle," replied Mary, "I understand he comes from Vanderhoof."

Chapter 38 — At the Mining Recorder

"Stu Wrangle. He does quite a lot of contract staking. I think I've met him. Certainly don't know him well."

Ken felt a sense of relief that he was dealing with a professional, someone more likely to be reasonable than some part-timer. He glanced at his watch. It was two minutes to ten. Just then a bearded man of average height arrived in the room. Ken introduced himself. Stu Wrangle responded and they shook hands.

"This doesn't happen often, and it's a pain when it does," said Ken. "I'm sure it's just the same for you."

"You're damn right it is," replied the contractor.

Mary spoke from behind the counter. "Good morning, Mr. Wrangle. Would you gentlemen both like to come through that door on your left. Then we can go to the meeting room."

She met them as they came through the door and led them to a room labelled "Room 108." Its bare walls were relieved by only one window which overlooked a back street. An oak table, probably made in the fifties for a more prestigious government office, was surrounded by six chairs of a later age. A roll of maps had been placed at one end, along with four bean-bag paper weights. Ken Wickford and Stuart Wrangle took chairs on opposite sides of the table and waited for Mary Branson, sitting at the end, to begin.

"As you gentlemen know, you have both staked the same ground. The purpose of this meeting is to see if we can resolve this amicably. The alternative is for all the finishing dates and times to be scrutinized and for me to come up with an opinion on who owns what. The result, even if not contested, is likely to be messy. There will be single or small groups of claims isolated with those belonging to the other party, and vice versa. Then it can be hard to get a clean enough patch of ground to justify any work."

Ken Wickford was the first to respond. "So you want us to agree on a boundary?"

"That would be ideal," replied Mary. "Much the best solution from my point of view and, I believe, from yours. Let's have a look at the maps."

The Mining Recorder rolled out two maps, upside down to her, for her guests to see from either side of the table. Each showed the same area. Map frames, topography and several patches of claims were the same. The two maps covered exactly the same area but were different in one respect: one showed the ground claimed by Wrangle, the other by Wickford. It was obvious at a glance that the two maps told very different stories.

The Nisselinka Claims

"If I may make an observation," Mary said as she adjusted the weights on the corners of the maps. "Your claims, Mr. Wrangle, predominate on the east. Yours, Mr Wickford, are concentrated on the west. And neither of you own those two crown grants to the east."

Ken, seeing them surrounded by Wrangle claims and aware of how useful they would have been if his father had not sold them, said nothing. Waving her hand down the middle of the map, Mary continued: "A boundary to separate them would make each more workable."

Ken was staring at the magnitude of the Wrangle staking. Although it came as no surprise, it was nevertheless a shock to see much of the ground he had planned to stake, some of which had been held by his family for years, now claimed by others. He knew the country well, every creek, every vantage point and every outcrop. Protected by different legislation, the crown grants were secure, and he had effectively protected the ground to the west. But the promising ground in the valley farther to the east and the ridge where he had looked again and again for evidence of another copper showing had been taken. His tactic of making his first claims smaller than he had intended had probably worked by cutting into the opposing claims. Even more effective had been his line of two-post claims marching into what he could not help regarding as enemy territory. The claims staked by his helper, who had been working to the north, might or might not have been completed in time. It seemed that the opposition had succeeded with about two-thirds of what they had planned to stake. He had less than half of the ground he intended to cover and a lot of it was contested.

While each man took in the information displayed about his opponent's claim, no one spoke until Ken broke the silence. "Stu. I was staking for myself with one helper. I haven't seen your affidavits but I assume you were staking under contract for someone else?"

"That's right, for a private company in Vancouver."

"Are you able to negotiate, or would you have to refer all decisions back?"

"You and I could probably agree on some boundary line on the map, but I don't think my client will want to back off very far. My instructions are to hold on to what we have. But I will, of course, pass on any proposal you'd like to make."

Chapter 38 — At the Mining Recorder

"It seems then," said Ken, looking at Stu, "that we have to leave it to Mary to go the next step and plot up the claims according to finishing dates." They both looked at the Mining Recorder, as if to give her the floor.

"I'm sorry that it can't be worked out. There are procedures that we now follow. I will write you both a letter informing you of the conflict. I will then make my own judgement on the status of each claim and plot the maps accordingly. Each of you has the right to challenge either my judgement or the validity of your opponent's claims."

After a round of polite thanks the two men left. Before heading off in different directions outside the government building, Stu Wrangle said, "I'm sorry it has to work out like this. As you know, I have to follow my client's instructions."

"I know," said Ken before turning and walking towards his truck.

Chapter 39

Opening Moves
August

Leaning on a fence behind his house, Ken Wickford was in too much of a reflective mood to pay attention to the horses now looking at him. His mind was elsewhere. He was, as they say, "in a bind." A key asset, one with enormous upside potential, as well as very real sentimental standing, was being wrenched away from him. The land grab, for that was how he regarded it, was being perpetrated by people, whoever they were, with unsavoury business practices. But, well aware that he himself had allowed it to happen by delaying what he knew had to be done, he was conscious of a feeling of guilt, a sentiment which always reminded him of the separation. Fortunately, Ken Wickford regarded himself as a survivor. His life had already had its ups and downs, and he knew he would come through this downer, but that didn't lessen the pain of wounded pride, lost opportunity, and the bow wave of work ahead of him.

In situations like these, he took comfort from the books he had read, most of them long ago when he was a floundering undergraduate trying to find a direction in life: some classics, history, science fiction, and numerous biographies. Struggles, he had noted, were essential components of all but a few of the interesting lives he had read. His own life just now was entering a phase of struggle. Would that make it interesting enough for someone to write about? No, but he was in no doubt that his was an interesting life. His particular mix of occupations was one he would not trade for any other. Land disputes were part of the prospecting and exploration business. He was just becoming embroiled in one such dispute. No big deal. He had no alternative to seeing it through. That's what he would do. So, having talked himself into readiness for the struggle ahead, he felt better prepared to take it

Chapter 39 — Opening Moves

on. Although he would have had difficulty admitting it, part of him almost welcomed the scrap looming ahead of him.

First he had to take stock of the situation. In the three years preceding the First World War his grandfather had staked three claims and advanced them to crown grant status. Two others had been purchased, but they had been sold by his father some twenty years ago to cover losses on the initial group. He had tried to buy them back but the price had been too high. His claims were now partially surrounded by the claims staked by his opponents because he had let lapse a key claim and had failed to follow up on his staking plans at a time of personal stress and disorganization two years ago. During his recent rushed staking he had given a high priority to the ground close to the crown grants, both his own claims and those his family used to own. He'd hoped, by reducing the area he had initially planned to stake, to cover most of the key ground before the competition had completed their larger claims.

Of the five crown grants held by his family seventy years ago, three were still in his hands. So was his grandfather's tunnel on the Raven claim, even though he had been unable to find it. Just how much of the rest of the ground he had tried to stake was now his, he did not know. The ground to the north and east of the crown grants, which he regarded as particularly prospective, would have been covered, if he had had his way, by at least twenty claim units. Instead he had attempted to stake less than half as much. The "enemy," the term which best described how he thought of them now, had tried to surround him on the north and east. Farther to the east, on ground he had also planned to acquire, the enemy had a further forty units over low ground with no outcrop. But cutting across these units was his dagger-like line of two-post claims. According to Mary Branson's calculations the first was his, but the other two were not. That left the competition with all the south-east.

If he owned all the ground he had intended to acquire, he would have a saleable package of land. But now the only party likely to pay for his ground was his neighbour and enemy. His package was small, possibly fragmented by claims he did not own, and its title clouded by uncertainty. There didn't seem much point in challenging Stu Wrangle's staking. It was probably good enough to withstand scrutiny. Nevertheless, someone might have made a mistake, particularly under the pressure of competitive staking. So that was one option: take the conflict right to the enemy and challenge his staking. That task would require several laborious days examining and recording the details on every one of their claim posts. He could rely on the nuisance value of his two-post claims. Other options? They were not lining up for consideration.

By now his horses, having come to realize that their master was not bearing carrots or apples for them, had wandered over to a distant fence. He opened the gate and crossed the field. With renewed prospects of reward, both horses trotted up to him. He gestured that he had nothing and slapped the pockets of his jacket to convince himself and the horses. To his surprise, he found an old carrot in his right pocket and was able to justify the animals' expectations.

He returned to the house by a circuitous route and went back to his study to make plans for examining all the opposition's claim tags in the field. The light on his answering machine indicated a message. He pressed the button and listened.

"Mr. Wickford. This is Victor Dubell in Vancouver. I understand you have some claims overlapping some of ours. If you are interested in selling yours, please give me a call. My number is.... "

Ken thought for a moment, told himself that there was no harm in listening, and dialled the number. A female answered for Poulter Management Services, and put him through to Mr. Dubell.

The introductions were short and gave Ken the impression that Dubell was businesslike and polite, but with a hard edge.

"Yes," said Ken. "My claims are, in principle, for sale." Then he heard himself express a sentiment in which he did not always believe. "As a businessman you will understand there is always a price."

"Then we are mostly on the same channel," said Victor. "Price is, of course, everything. Personally, I don't know what else there might be. Can you name what you want?"

Ken was not ready for this. "Not immediately. I would want some cash, some shares, in staged payments would be okay, then a royalty if it ever makes a mine. And a perimeter clause."

"Except for the last item, you seem to be on the right track. The difficult part will be to come up with real numbers. A perimeter would not be possible. That only applies when we are introduced to the area."

Ken's reply introduced what both of them had avoided. "I've first got to figure out what is yours and what is ours. Tell me, am I

Chapter 39 — Opening Moves

right in thinking that one of your geologists examined my Bobcat claims earlier this year?"

"Could be. What has that got to do with the price of the ones we are talking about?"

"No direct connection. I'm wondering what attracted you to that area."

"We have geologists researching all the time. I don't know the details of this one. Someone must have picked it out as a good place. As for the terms, I think it would be best if we wrote you a letter with an offer. Would that be acceptable?"

"Yes, go ahead."

The letter arrived the following Monday. It was written on superior paper, a faint cream colour, with the engraved letterhead of Poulter Management Services.

750 Hastings Street,
Vancouver, B.C.
3 September, 1986

Dear Mr. Wickford,

Further to our conversation last week, we are pleased to offer you the following for an option to purchase a 100% interest in your claims. These, listed on the attached, include all of your claims whether or not they were completed after one of ours.

- a cash payment of $5,000 payable on signing,

- a work program of $50,000 during the first 12 months of the option.

The option may be renewed annually by making the following payments...

The letter continued for three pages. Not only were the terms skinny, but there was no recognition that any of the disputed ground might be Ken's, or of the role he had played in introducing Poulter Management to the ground. In the event of an orebody being discovered on his property, Ken would make a useful amount of money. But a mine, unlikely at best, would be years away and the interim payments were minimal. And if a mine were to be found on ground his family used to own, his take would be small.

He decided he would make his final decision tomorrow. But then he picked up a sheet of letterhead notepaper and, in a neat hand, wrote a polite rejection of the offer. That done he made a phone call to the house of a good friend, someone who had provided grubstake backing in his early days of prospecting. It was answered by a voice he knew well.

"Hullo, Betty, Ken here. I've got some difficult decisions to make about my Nisselinka property. Do you think you could spare Lester for a hour or so after supper?"

"I sure can. All he will be doing is building something in the basement. It can't be important. At least it usually isn't. Do you want to come here? Anyhow you're welcome, if that's what you would like. I'll get him."

"Thanks."

"Lester here. What's up?"

"I need a good discussion on these claims. Then I need to sleep on it before making a decision. Do you have time after dinner?"

"Sure? Where? Here if you like."

"If it's all the same to you, how about the Whiskey Jack? Good place to talk. Music's not too loud."

"Seven o'clock okay?"

"Great. See you there."

Ken always enjoyed his conversations with Lester, a local businessman who seemed to go from one sure-footed decision to another, and who was always generous with his time to people and causes he approved of.

"The trouble with making a counter offer," said Lester holding his glass of rye and soda, "is that, unless they are forced, they are not going to offer terms you really want."

"Getting an interest in their ground?"

"Exactly."

"Then you agree that I should write and say no deal?"

"Yes, but you don't have to slam the door. I think you have to bring into the open the business of how they learned about the mineralization. Otherwise it sounds a bit unreasonable for you to ask for an interest in their ground."

"Thanks for that. I think you're right. At least, that's what I wanted to hear. It's good to get your opinion before starting a

Chapter 39 — Opening Moves

fight. But it's going to be a tough one to prove. The reputable companies would bend over backwards not to be seen to be screwing a prospector like this, but these guys seem different."

Lester nodded. "Takes all sorts. And with what may be megabucks at stake, some people are going to play rough. What was the name of that geologist who didn't keep a confidence?"

"Bob Tranich. Not a name I'm going to forget in a hurry."

Chapter 40

Pressure and Precautions
September

Ken Wickford was just about to leave his house when the phone rang. Although anxious to complete some errands, he picked it up.

"Mr. Wickford?"

"Yes," said Ken cautiously. He thought he recognized the caller's voice.

"It's Victor Dubell. Do you have five minutes?"

"Yes. Go ahead."

"We think we know why you were staking at exactly the same time as we were."

"Is this important?"

"Indeed it is. We have eliminated all other possibilities and are left with the conclusion that you were informed of our plans by William Herman, manager of the helicopter base."

Ken inhaled slowly and found himself tightening his grip on the handset as he said, "William Herman is a professional who wouldn't dream of risking his job by leaking a client's secrets, even to a friend. And I'm the first to admit that he and I are friends."

"Exactly. Because he is a friend of yours, you would not want to see him damaged. I don't suppose his employer would be happy to hear of what happened."

Ken then asked a question to which he knew the answer only too well. "Why are you telling me this?"

"We know you can help him. We don't want to see anyone hurt, but we have to look after the interests of our shareholders. Just now they don't have clear title to the claims they have a right to believe are theirs. So we have to do something. If you can see your way to a reasonable deal, we would have no need to investigate this leak any further."

Chapter 40 — Pressure and Precautions

As he listened, Ken Wickford felt his freedom of movement constrict around him. Whichever way he turned he faced the reality of having to choose between his friend's job and his own dreams.

After seconds of silence, the caller spoke again. "Are you still there?"

"You have no proof."

"We don't need any." After another period of silence, Victor Dubell ended the conversation. "Call me any time, office or home. But don't leave it too long." Then he hung up.

Ken sat down and thought of his friend. Will had been appointed acting manager of the base a year ago. It was a job he had worked towards for years and one he loved. His two children were happy in school. Will and his wife had many friends in the town. Ken had often heard them say they would not want to leave. Would Will be able to get another job in B.C. if this got out? The deal Ken had been offered for his claims was not that bad: enough cash to make a real difference and shares enough for the upside. He could accept the offer and Will could keep his job. Or he could tell Dubell to get lost. If he did so, Will would almost certainly lose his job, and each might lose a friend. And he would still have a fight on his hands.

Ken leaned back in his chair and stared at the wall. After five minutes he picked up the phone again and dialled Burns Lake Helicopters. "Hi Denny, it's Ken Wickford. Is Will there?"

He left a message for Will to call him and then walked slowly out to his truck.

Victor Dubell smiled with satisfaction as he put down his phone.

"How did he sound?" said Sydney Poulter from a chair on the other side of the desk.

"Pretty uncomfortable. I think that two-bit bush rat will come to heel. I'll give him a couple of days and then tighten the screw."

Sydney Poulter stood up. "Victor, I think I would like to talk to him next time."

"If you wish. I can be tougher with him, if you like."

"That's not the point. I want his ground. But I want him on side. Much of the success I've made comes from having a good relationship with prospectors. I'm not about to blow it." Sydney Poulter then got up and walked towards the door. As he did so Victor's narrowing eyes followed the older man out of the room.

By the time he had told Will about Dubell's phone call, Ken had already decided to turn down Poulter's offer. The threat to his friend gave him further resolve. His letter to Victor Dubell was short, polite, and business-like. As is often the case, taking action was a relief, but it also made him realize that he was signing on for a rougher game than he was used to. He was not prepared for the incident a couple of days later at the Taku Restaurant. He was sitting at a table for four waiting to meet a friend for lunch, looking at a tattered copy of the local paper, when two men, both strangers, took possession of two of the other chairs. One was in late middle age, the other much younger.

Mr. Wickford?" asked the older man.

"That's me," replied Ken, very aware that he had not concealed a look of surprise and concern.

"Just a bit of advice," said the older man. "Your claims in the Nisselinka area. It would be much better to option them. The other team would be good partners. You don't want them as enemies."

Ken's response was no more than a reaction: "Who are you?"

"Never mind. That's all we have to say. We have to go. Thank you, Mr. Wickford."

At home, later that day, Ken felt threatened and indecisive. The situation was eroding his usual composure. He took some comfort from the usual routines at home, some satisfying, some a chore, some a pleasure, but his mind would too frequently revert to a gnawing uncertainty. Dubell's phone call would come to mind and so would the strangers at the restaurant. He found himself taking a flashlight with him when he walked Spike on a night lit with a full moon. He threw both bolts instead of just one when he closed the front door. He laughed at himself, but that started the thinking again. They might stoop to cheating and threatening, he thought, but this had to be his imagination going too far. They wouldn't enter his home. Or would they? He picked up a book, but then watched a movie instead before going to bed at midnight.

But Ken did not sleep. He had become a player in a game for which he did not know the rules, except that the opposing side might be unconstrained by any. He tried to focus on the prospect of his son Phillip's visit the next day. This was always an event to look forward to. He found himself remembering a year ago when they were on the Bulkley River, Phillip had hooked and then landed a three-pound trout. The picture of the seven-year-old at

Chapter 40 — Pressure and Precautions

a moment of such achievement was one he would never forget. Then his half-awake mind reverted to the present and he saw Phillip helping in the barn or listening to stories. Then came the possibility that his child could be in danger. But that was absurd. Or was it? Only after he had reluctantly made the decision to phone Phillip and his mother to ask that the visit be postponed for two weeks did he sleep.

He awoke to a feeling of emptiness and disappointment which was not relieved by the phone call he had decided to make. He did not tell Jill all his reasons for the change in plan, nor did she ask. Although the separation had been painful, their shared custody of the children had become an amicable and workable arrangement. With his son's visit postponed, Ken spent the rest of the morning venting his anger by bucking logs and splitting the rounds into firewood for the winter.

Chapter 41

Challenge
October

Letters or notices from the B.C. Ministry of Mines, Energy & Petroleum Resources were not unusual in his mail, but this envelope from the Gold Commissioner's office in Smithers immediately gave Ken an uncomfortable feeling. After staring at the envelope for a couple of seconds he ripped it open.

> Ministry of Energy, Mines, and Petroleum Resources,
> Office of Government Agent
> Alford Avenue,
> Smithers, B.C.
>
> 6 October, 1986
>
> Dear Mr. Wickford,
>
> We have to report that the validity of two of the claims you filed at this office on June 10, 1986 have been challenged. As you will see from the enclosed, the complaint, filed under Section 50 of the Mineral Act, is based on measurement of the dimensions of two of the legal corner posts (Tag nos. 3560 and 3561) being less than the required 4.0 inches.
>
> We are making arrangements for our claims inspector to visit the sites in question.
>
> Your rights as the challenged staker are set out in Section 50, a copy of which I enclose.

Chapter 41 — Challenge

The letter, which continued onto a second page, was signed by an acting Inspector of Mines for the Omenica Mining District, not a person known to Ken. The attached complaint was on the letterhead of Poulter Management and signed by Victor Dubell. Ken put the letters down on the table, thinking to himself, No surprise. Thought they might try something like that. Unlikely to work; my LCPs are pretty good. But it puts a cloud over my title.

Two days later Ken Wickford was following his trail of blazes at a less pressured pace than when he had been staking three months ago. With the leaves now off the deciduous trees, his route was easier to follow. The bugs had been put to rest by the first frosts a month ago and, in spite of the burden of his contest with Victor Dubell and cronies, there was much about the morning to enjoy.

Just before noon he arrived at the first of the two corner posts cited in the challenge. His tape measure set against the top of the post where it had been squared showed just under three-and-three-quarter inches on all sides. But why the error? Why had he made it so small when the lower part of the post, the lower part of the tree with all its bark, showed that the trunk had been large enough with at least an inch to spare? He looked at the post from all sides, scratched his head metaphorically, and then literally.

Then he noticed a difference. Each side had been squared off the same way: with an axe, but the colour of the wood on the side with the aluminium tag was darker than on the other three sides. He stepped back and looked down at the slivers of wood scattered around the base of the post. Then he spotted what by now he was expecting to see. Some of the slivers were not the same shade of white as others. Most were light on one side and darker on the other, but on some the darker side matched the wood on the side of the claim tag, while others were light coloured on both sides. Evidently the darker wood, that had been exposed to the air longer, had been cut during the staking contest three months ago. The lighter wood had been exposed more recently when someone had reduced the size of the post.

A few hours later, after he had photographed the top and base of both of the challenged posts from all sides, he was making his way back to his truck. Instead of following his staking blazes, he took a shorter route on a compass bearing direct to the place on the logging road where had left his truck. His thoughts were on how to play the card now in his hand. He had no doubt about who was responsible for altering his claim posts.

Chapter 42

Hard Decision
November 1986

Ken knew it would be coming because Victor Dubell had left a message two days earlier to say they were sending a final offer by courier, that it would be their last offer and, if he refused, he would have reasons to regret his decision.

The package, just a letter-size envelope bearing the logo and address of Poulter Management Services, contained only two sheets. The covering letter was formal and businesslike:

> Poulter Management Services,
> 750 West Hastings Street,
> Vancouver, B.C.
>
> 7 November 1986

Dear Mr. Wickford,

Please find enclosed our final offer for an option on your Nisselinka claims, listed on the attached.

This offer is not open to negotiation but, if you have questions, we will be glad to answer them by phone or in person. The shares will be in a public company with less than 20 million issued.

On receipt of your written acceptance, we will arrange for preparation of a formal agreement.

Yours truly, V. Dubell.

The offer itself was simple:

The Nisselinka Claims

	Cash	Shares
On signing	$10,000	100,000
1st anniversary	$15,000	100,000
2nd anniversary	$20,000	100,000
3rd anniversary	$50,000	200,000
4th & subsequent anniversaries	$50,000	
On production	1% Net Smelter Return buyable for $1 million.	

The cash, thought Ken, would make a useful contribution to his income for the next three years. Thereafter it would make him comfortable in his inexpensive lifestyle. If the property delivered an orebody, the shares might make him comfortable for life. Also, he would avoid what would no doubt become a bruising relationship for himself, and could also damage the career and family life of his friend. Nor would he have to fight the challenge to his claims. Acceptance would be the least onerous choice.

But just as he was reaching a decision he was reminded, as if by a gentle tap on his shoulder, that most of the ground belonging to Poulter should have been his, and he had been cheated out of it. He was all too aware that his position would have been stronger if the two crown grants, Old Sam and Newfy Boy, had not been sold. He wondered whether his several attempts to buy them back would have been successful if his offers had been slightly higher. If he had not procrastinated on his staking...

The three generations of family involvement with the claims made the obvious choice, the sensible business deal, hard to take. But perhaps he should accept the offer anyhow. Whichever way he jumped, it was going to be difficult. There was no need for a decision today and he needed time to think about it. So he would sleep on it, and that is what he did.

The next day, a cold November morning, he was feeling reasonably comfortable with a decision to accept, and to get on with his life. This decision provided a degree of relief. He had decided, or almost decided, to accept Poulter's offer. Not having to fight

Chapter 42 — Hard Decision

for his claims would lift his sense of being besieged. Not putting his friend's job in jeopardy would be another load off his mind. The cash payments would be very useful. A third of the shares would come on signing, the rest over the next two years if Chilko continued to hold the ground. He was cautiously looking forward to not having to struggle against a persistent opponent with substantial resources and a willingness to stoop to practices that he himself would not contemplate. Whatever he thought of Poulter and Dubell, he believed in the asset they were about to acquire. But, for a man who had decided to accept this quantity of cash, as well as shares with a lot of upside potential, Ken Wickford was a surprisingly discontented man.

He had several errands to run but, as most of them involved shops or offices in town, he would have to wait. They would be closed for Remembrance Day. Ken liked to attend the November 11 ceremonies not in Smithers itself, but at the war memorial in a small community to the south. He had managed to attend all since he had come north. Today he had nearly four hours until the ceremony, and he wanted time to think, so he decided to check the cattle fence between his property and the crown land to the north. He liked to ride along each fence every month or two but it had been much longer since he had last done so.

His old horse, a bay named Mr. Brown, came trotting over from the far side of the paddock, consumed the offered carrot, sniffed for more, and then agreed to be led to the stable. As they knew each other and the procedure well, saddling up was quick. In less than five minutes horse and rider were crossing the big field to the west of the house at a trot which soon became an exuberant canter.

Riding for Ken was a time to think. It consumed less of his attention than driving and he welcomed the opportunity to review progress through his current crop of problems. Looking back on the last few months, it seemed to him that his reluctance to make a deal must have been responsible for a substantially better offer than he might otherwise have obtained. Now he would be able to enjoy the product of the difficult times he had been through. He wondered for a moment whether his unease came from thinking he could have got a better deal, but he soon dismissed this as unlikely. This was one of the best mineral deals he had made. Selling something that had been in the family for so long made him feel uncomfortable, but his children would benefit and that, surely, was the purpose of it all.

Such were his thoughts as he rode along the fence marking the northern limit of his property. Most of his fences, the standard round-milled four-inch posts with three strands of barbed wire, had been installed a couple of years ago after an unusually profitable season. Although he knew that maintenance was required, he did not expect to find anything broken. Perhaps a place where the wire was holding up a fallen branch. After a quick mile mostly in open grassland, the trail was less regular. In places it ran next to the fence, in others it diverged around trees, or rocks. Coming to a place where the fence crossed a small gully, he noticed the underbrush appeared disturbed. This was probably where a steer had gone in search of cool ground on a hot day. He nudged his mount closer to the fence and peered at the barbed wire. All but one of the strands in the panel he was looking at were hanging loose. There being no room to turn around and being apprehensive about what he might find, he backed up his mount to the main trail, threw the reins over Mr. Brown's head and tied them to a low hanging branch. He then went back down the trail on foot. At the lower end of the panel with the limp wires, he found the cause. All strands except the top had been cut.

Ken was angry as he rode back to the barn. He was also mildly worried. Cattle rustling, although a periodic problem in the neighbourhood, was not common. And cutting this particular fence in this particular location seemed an odd and unproductive way to go about it.

He would mend the fence but there was no hurry.

Two hours later, he was driving his truck along what passed for a main street in a small town that had seen better days. Glancing to his right from the stop sign, Ken could see the backs of some two dozen people facing away from the road, and above their heads the top of the war memorial he knew so well. First established around a sawmill at the end of the last century, the town had been a thriving community until the nineteen-fifties when larger and more efficient mills had taken its principal business away. The community's problems had been compounded when a new highway bypassed the village and took most of the traffic with it. Since then the population had steadily diminished. Young people left, returning only for visits. A few large wood-frame houses,

Chapter 42 — Hard Decision

though short of paint and poorly renovated, managed to display some evidence of their former status.

Ken turned down a partially paved side-street, parked his truck and walked towards the crowd. Several people, most of whom he recognized, turned to see who else had arrived. He greeted them all and took his place standing on the grass of a bank raised about three feet above the level around the memorial. A damp breeze moved briskly under the heavy November sky. Several in the crowd had pulled their collars tight. To his right and forming two lines stretching away from the crowd, were fourteen men in uniform. Four of them carried musical instruments, two drums, one set of pipes and one bugle. Two other veterans carried flags, the Canadian Maple Leaf, and a red ensign, faded and frayed enough to have been through as many battles as the old and bemedalled man holding it.

Except for the bugler, a young man in Air Cadets uniform, all the men on parade were elderly or middle-aged. Three of them, all in the front row, looked frail, as if their rows of medals were almost too much to carry. Ken recognized one of them. Rod Bensham, or Mr. Bensham, as he had been known to Ken the teenager when delivering the newspaper in Victoria, had always had a kindly smile for the young man and had once said: "Your grandfather was a fine man. I knew him well." Once, during the afternoon of a hot August day, Ken had been about to put the paper on Mr. Bensham's porch, when the old man called from his seat under a shade tree. He had been in a talkative mood. They talked about school, sports, and what Ken planned to do after leaving high school. "Well, I'll always follow with great interest what any Wickford does. Your grandfather and I were in the Kootenay Battalion together. Though he was quite a bit older, we knew each other well. We went through good times and hell together, and I was with him soon after he got that bullet in his leg. He often talked about his mineral claims in the Nisselinka. Does your dad still have those?" Ken had been somewhat overawed by the old man with the friendly but gruff manner, and had asked few of the questions that came to his mind now. There was Mr. Bensham again, with a straight back and a full row of medals. Ken looked at his watch: 10:50. Should be starting soon, he thought. They shouldn't keep these old fellers standing here too long.

A middle-aged man in the uniform of a warrant officer and carrying a baton under his left arm, called out: "Colour party, form ranks." And then after a pause of a few seconds, "Colour party, At-ten-tion!"

Torsos stiffened and came to a ragged attention.

This was not the parade you would find in the larger towns and cities, with brass bands, disciplined ranks of the RCMP and cadets, or the cheer of boy scouts and girl guides. Ken had been to those and, moving though they could be, found them too similar to a victory parade. Here, in this homely and lonely tribute by an ever-dwindling band of participants and their families and friends, he found a more satisfying way of paying his respects. On this occasion, in a way he could not quite fathom, the event was made more poignant by the impending sale of the mineral claims that his grandfather had owned and worked so hard to develop.

A community elder, whom Ken knew by name but little else, stepped forward, turned and faced the crowd.: "We will now sing 'Abide with me'." Then, facing the band, he raised and lowered his right hand. On the third beat the band played the opening bars, paused and began again, this time supported by voices from the small crowd. At the end of the hymn, the elder read from the book he was carrying: "We are gathered today to remember...." Ken's thoughts drifted to battlefields of not so long ago, to trenches, mud and blood, to men broken in body or broken in spirit, to barbed wire and machine guns, to his grandfather returning home and trying to pick up again where he left off, to the claims he had found and to the threat they were now under. He was awakened from his reverie by the clear notes of the bugle playing the Last Post. When it ended there was no need for this small and practised group to announce the start of the minute of silence. The minute seemed an eternity. To Ken, who had been born twenty-four years after his grandfather died, it was always hard to grasp that a contemporary of his grandfather, albeit much younger, could be participating in the parade in front of him. Then the bugler played "Retreat" followed by the drummer beating the slow march. Then, after what seemed like several minutes of the sad-paced beat, the piper playing "Flower of the Forest" joined in with the same slow time. The sergeant then signalled for the music to stop before calling out, "Colour party, quick march". To the quicker tune, thirteen former soldiers and one air cadet, marched in double file, mostly in step, past the memorial, along the pathway towards the community hall.

Chapter 42 — Hard Decision

Having much on his mind and much to do, Ken would have preferred not to stay for the sandwiches and coffee he knew would have been arranged. But he felt obliged to do so. He stayed long enough to talk briefly to those he knew. Two people asked him to dinner but, within the hour, he was back in his truck heading home.

The trouble with the deal, the term that troubled him most, he decided as he neared his home, was the inclusion of all the crown grants. Still uncomfortable about this term of the deal, he turned into his yard. As he came to a halt, he saw in his mirror a green van pull in behind him. Recognizing Will's vehicle, he climbed down from his truck and went to greet his friend.

Will wound down the window of his truck. "Just back from the parade this morning?"

"Yes," replied Ken, "I try to get there every year. I think of all those guys and that hell. My grandfather was one of them. He was never the same after he came back."

Will got out of his truck before saying more. "I know, mine too."

"In the trenches, I suppose?"

"Yes. Somme, Passchendale, and others."

"Survived?" asked Ken.

"Physically, yes, but…"

Will did not finish.

Ken replied slowly, as if appraising every word. "I didn't know. Yours too. Same war, same battles, same misery. Just different sides. And your dad. He must have been the right age for the second?"

"Yes. He was with a parachute regiment in Italy. I don't know too much because he would never talk about it, except the name, Ortona."

"Ortona? So he would have been fighting Canadians?"

"I think so. And my grandfather, too. As a child I heard about Canadians. Something about a gas attack. But I was too young to ask questions."

"Ortona was where my dad was. Those same battles."

"Wow! For two generations!"

"And we're the third. And not trying to kill each other. What would they think?"

Will Herman took time to respond but he did so with conviction. "They'd approve."

Ken nodded. "You're right, and you know what? Both sides should be at those memorial parades."

"Yes. Of course. But it's going to take another generation for that to happen."

"Time for a coffee?"

"I do, or something stronger."

"What's up?" said Ken.

"I got a call from Mr. Dubell—"

Ken interrupted: "And?"

"He said that unless I could persuade you to accept their terms, he would have to make a written complaint to our head office in Calgary."

"Bastards! That settles it. Poulter gets the claims, you keep your job, I get a deal I ought to accept."

"Thanks, but you don't need to go that far," said Will as he followed Ken into the house.

They talked late into the night. Several hours on, with a glass of rye in hand, leaning back in an easy chair, Will continued to insist that the threat to his job was not credible. "I have a good relationship with my boss. He would have nothing to do with a threat like that."

"So what you're telling me," said Ken, "is that I should reject their proposal and continue to fight for something like justice."

"That's what I'm saying."

His mind over-active, Ken found it hard to get to sleep that night. By any normal standards, the offer was generous. They were putting a value on his property far greater than the current information suggested. Did they know something he did not? Perhaps, but they hadn't even started to explore. Why not take their offer? It would provide him with the best part of a year's normal income, with enough upside to make him rich, and they would cease to threaten his friend.

The rational decision based on the facts and his knowledge that few of these situations actually led to orebodies was absolutely clear: accept the offer. He could talk it over with others. His old friend, Lester, would provide a balanced perspective and sage advice—but Ken knew what it would be and he knew he would be wasting his and Lester's time.

Chapter 42 — Hard Decision

But the rational decision would require putting his pride on the shelf, accepting defeat, rewarding some cheats, submitting to a bully, and abandoning a dream.

Head and heart: the old protagonists. But he was old enough and sensible enough to shun the blandishments of sentiment and make the sensible choice. Somehow, he knew that, on this occasion, the heart would call the shot and, where the heart takes charge, reason tends to follow. He was looking for reasons to tell Dubell and co. to get lost. He knew that business decisions were often driven by egos, and he did not regard his own as overgrown. He knew that decisions based on emotion could lead in dangerous directions. He remembered a girlfriend of his youth, a goddess to behold and to hold, but with a character flawed enough to goad his more sensible self every day. But that was when he was young and letting his emotions lead the way. Now in his age of wisdom was he leaning towards indulging his emotions and, in so doing, making the wrong business decision for nothing other than sentiment?

But it wasn't that simple; if he followed his feelings, he would be in step with his friend, his self-respect would remain undamaged, and his pride would remain in place. Head and heart were not in step.

Two stressful days later, Ken Wickford ended a conversation and put down the phone. He had told Victor Dubell that he would not accept Poulter's new offer.

Chapter 43

In the City
March 1987

Ken Wickford did not like big cities. Prince George was bad enough. Vancouver was to be avoided. Too many of the city folks were slick or rich, and ignorant of those rural parts of the province that provided the source of their wealth. But, having agreed to meet Mr. Poulter, he now found himself in the heart of downtown Vancouver. He had arrived the previous day and arranged to stay at the Georgia, one of the less ostentatious of the downtown hotels. Except for the incessant traffic noise, it was comfortable. Located only three blocks from Poulter's office, the hotel was convenient for the job at hand.

Over breakfast he tried to read the paper but his mind kept wandering back to the reason for his trip and the case he was going to make. He was aware of Sydney Poulter's reputation as a successful, outspoken, hard-driving promoter. He had heard rumours of sharp practice but knew of nothing tangible. Several of his friends, one of whom was a lawyer in Smithers, had offered to accompany him to the meeting in Vancouver, but he had decided to come alone, partly to avoid additional expense, partly because he felt that this particular dragon should be faced alone.

Opposite the elevator from which he emerged were two large oak doors. Beneath "Poulter Management Services" in gold-coloured letters was a list of some fifteen public companies. Feeling he would rather be pushing the old and squeaking door of his hay barn, he pressed the brass handle and walked in. In front of him lay a large room with floor-to-ceiling windows covering most of the opposite side. Through the windows he could see the North Shore and what he assumed to be Grouse Mountain. He noticed a pile of yellow material on the north side of Burrard Inlet and a tug pulling a barge towards the east.

Chapter 43 — In the City

"Mr. Wickford?" said a well-dressed young lady as she entered the reception room.

"Yes, hello! I've come to see Mr. Poulter."

"He's expecting you and will be ready in just a moment. Would you like to wait in the boardroom? May I take your coat?"

He was shown into an interior room dominated by a large oval table made of a red wood, highly polished. There were five chairs each side, none at the ends. The walls were panelled with oak. Recessed into one wall were alcoves with cupboards, also of oak. Ken walked round to the side opposite the door he had come through, placed his thin and none-too-smart briefcase on the table and looked around.

Cups and saucers of a delicate china were laid out on the counter in one of the alcoves. At one end some oak panels had been folded back to reveal a screen. At the other end was a console with numerous buttons and dials which he concluded were for controlling the lights and a projector. His situation reminded him of fables from the ancient world, Ulysses in the Cyclops's cave, the prisoner just introduced into his cell. His thoughts were interrupted when a lean young man of average height and wearing a small goatee entered the room.

"Mr. Wickford, I'm Victor Dubell. We have, of course, spoken on the phone. I'm Mr. Poulter's executive assistant."

"Good morning."

"Welcome to the office and to Vancouver. Did you come alone?"

"Yes. There did not seem any need for anyone else."

The young man paused for a moment before replying. "Let's hope so. If everyone cooperates we should be able to keep it simple. I'll be back in a minute. I want to tell our lawyer that he won't need to attend. He's on standby in case you had come with one. Coffee?"

"Please."

Victor turned to leave the room. "I'll arrange for that."

Ken, thinking that another member on his team would be very welcome just now, looked around the room again for something to occupy him while he waited. A bookshelf in one of the alcoves contained annual reports for several companies. He leafed through five, none of which meant anything to him. But he did notice that Sydney L. Poulter appeared as a director of all of the companies and as an officer of many.

The receptionist who had greeted Ken at the front door soon appeared carrying a small tray with a coffee jug, cup and saucer. At the same time, Victor returned through another door accompanied by a middle-aged man of below average height and with a slight stoop, who introduced himself as Sydney Poulter. After shaking hands, Ken returned to the chair he had staked out with his briefcase. Dubell and Poulter sat on the opposite side of the table with an empty chair between them.

"Easy trip?" asked Poulter. Then, after a few more polite enquiries: "So we are neighbours. We seem to have staked some of the same ground."

"So it seems."

Poulter's style was affable, even friendly. "Shouldn't be a problem. We're in the business of finding mines. The first step is to find the money. Then, if there is ore on your ground, we'll find it and make you very rich. Even if there is nothing there, you will still make a bit of money. I'd like to keep this as simple as possible. What do you want for your claims? I understand you didn't like what we offered."

There was a long pause until Ken replied: "The first thing we need to do is sort out the current ownership. I have a map. Shall I put it on the table?"

But Victor's response was to unroll one that had been lying on the table next to him. Victor and Ken stood up and leaned on the table to better see the map.

The first feature of the map, Ken noticed, was that all Poulter's claims were shaded in orange whether or not they overlapped those he and his helper had staked that day. All of his claims had diagonal lines through them to show they were contested. It was as if all of Chilko's claims were valid and only a small portion of his. He also noticed that the eastern crown grants, which his father had sold, were now shown as owned by Poulter.

Sydney Poulter stayed seated, his eyes focussed on the map. He had seen hundreds of such maps and little that he could be shown now would be new. He was preoccupied with the Calgary deal he was trying to put together. Then he looked at Victor who was studying the map and thought to himself, Good to have that young man on board. Seems to learn quickly. He's taking a lot of paper work off my desk. He then came back to the matter in hand with a comment that suggested his mind had never been anywhere else. "Huh! That's a lot of overlap. But we expect a bit of confusion when we get into a competitive situation. We should be able to sort it out."

This was Ken's opportunity to start on what he had planned to say. "As we all know, you and I were staking at the same time. So we have to take into account that some of your claims and some of mine lost out to other claims with an earlier completion time."

"Yes, we understand that," said Victor. "But when we've made a deal, we will all be in this together and there will be no need to sort out the details of who finished when."

Ken responded by reaching for his briefcase and pulling out a map, which he explained as he unfolded it on the table. "It might help if we have a look at a map I brought with me. On this I have used the finish times reported on the affidavits so that we have some idea of ownership."

The map was made from two sheets, each the standard size provided by the Mining Recorder and pasted together. Part of the map had been coloured by pencil crayon. Scattered red lines separated the coloured areas into fragmented patches.

Ken pointed. "The blue shows my claims, the green yours. The red line marks the boundaries between your ground and mine as indicated by the finishing times."

The three men stared at the map for the best part of a minute until Victor broke the silence. "It looks as though you staked smaller claims and finished earlier in several places."

"Yes, that's usually the way it works in competitive situations. I would have gone for larger blocks if I had had more time."

Victor's tone then became that of a schoolmaster addressing a troublesome student. "This angled line of single small claims coming right into the middle of our block, I've been puzzled by that ever since I first saw it. What were you trying to do?"

Ken was glad of an opportunity to demonstrate the complexity of the situation. "That's a technique people use in such circumstances. I put those two-posters there to get at least some of the ground I wanted, much of which was in my possession until a couple of years ago."

Victor looked directly at Ken. "But that is going to fuck up one of our big claims. That's just unacceptable. I have to tell you that we are not happy with the fact that our plans to stake were leaked. That's why you were there at the same time as us."

Ken shook his head before he responded. "That's not how I see it. I believe you initiated this staking because your geologist had seen some samples at my house. And that was after—."

Raising his voice, Victor interrupted. "Mr. Wickford, please understand, we do our own research and are quite within our rights to stake any open ground we choose."

"Yes. I realize that, but is it just a coincidence that you were staking so soon after one of your geologists had seen my samples? And does this mean that I will never be able to confide in one of your geologists again? Your geologist assured me he respected my wish not to put these claims on the market until I was ready. He said he would do no more than make a note in the file that you people should keep in touch with me because I was working on a promising property."

With his boss in the room Victor was not going to let Wickford's allegations go unchallenged. "Mr. Wickford. You are making a serious allegation. We are not used to dealing with people who accuse us of unethical conduct. If you persist in taking the discussion in this direction I see no alternative to leaving it for the lawyers to sort out. Who is your lawyer, Mr. Wickford?"

Ken was now aware he had to venture where he did not want to go. Unpleasant memories of an unnerving flight in a two-seater plane years ago flashed through his mind. The pilot had been forced to descend into cloud, into mountainous terrain, relying on instruments he was not qualified to use. While some people might have enjoyed the drama of such situations, Ken Wickford was not one of them. He did not enjoy dangerous activities or making enemies. Even less did he enjoy prodding enemies who might react in unpredictable ways. He ignored Victor's question, and faced Poulter. "And there's a another matter, also serious." His audience waited, their faces stern, impassive, and unfriendly. "I have checked the two claim posts cited in your challenge to my staking. Someone has tampered with them since I staked."

"What do you mean?" said Victor standing up and throwing back his chair.

Ken then put another card on the table. "I have well documented evidence that someone reduced the dimensions of my posts to less than the legal limit."

Victor now addressed his boss while rolling up his map. "Sydney, I don't think we need to hear any more. We should leave this with the lawyers."

Chapter 43 — In the City

But Sydney Poulter wanted his turn. "Explain yourself, Mr. Wickford."

"It's very simple. Using an axe or other sharp instrument, someone has shaved off enough wood to reduce the size of my claim posts."

Poulter's expression by now was nothing short of hostile. "And who do you suppose could have done that?"

"I have to assume it was the people who have challenged my claims."

Poulter then asked, speaking slowly and with emphasis on each word, "Do you realize who you are dealing with? Do you know how many millions I have raised? Do you know how many mines we have found? Do you know how many lawyers I employ? No one slanders Sydney Poulter and gets away with it. If you persist in this ridiculous story, it will be war between us. Take note, Mr. Wickford: when it's war I take no prisoners."

Victor, now standing and holding his papers and map, said again, "Sydney. We are wasting our time. This is for the lawyers."

Sydney Poulter stood and picked up his notebook before making a final comment. "Mr. Wickford. Consider your position and the consequences of not reaching an agreement. Get in touch with us before the end of the week. We'll hold off on talking to our lawyers until then."

And as they were leaving the room, Victor added, "The exit is the first left down the hall."

Victor followed his employer to his office and waited for the older man to take his seat behind the desk before sitting down himself. "What do you think?" he asked.

"Goddamn two-bit bush rat! Who does he think he is?" replied Sydney.

"Smart-ass. Ignore him. We've enough ground without his. Wait for a year and we'll take his ground for nothing when he runs out of cash."

"Well, I'm sure glad, Victor, that I can rely on you to handle these things. I used to enjoy dealing with the prospectors and people like that. I've never had this sort of trouble. With the oil deal taking most of my time, I don't have to put up with any son of a bitch. How did we get offside with him?"

"It started as soon as we sent in a staking party. He seemed to think we were taking his ground. I suppose he thinks he owns it all. As you know, he began staking the same day as we did. I remain suspicious as to how he found out. Anyhow, we have things under control."

"Good work." Sydney Poulter signalled he was ready to move on. "What's the next step?"

"You should vend the claims you've staked and put them in Chilko. It's all restructured and ready to go. It can pay with cheap shares. You'll get plenty."

"Okay, do it. Get that ground. Keep me posted."

Chapter 44

Claims are Vended
April

Victor Dubell's intercom flashed. He put down the pencil he was using to draft a letter to the Superintendent of Brokers ("S.O.B." in common parlance) about one of the companies in the Poulter stable and picked up his phone.

"Mr. Dubell, Mr. Poulter is calling a meeting for 11:00 this morning. Can you make it?" The caller was Marion, Sydney Poulter's long-time assistant, whose nominal job was office manager but whose roles ranged from receptionist to confidant. Her influence extended to vice president in all but name. Although long past her sexual prime, Marion retained an elegance and grace of movement that men continued to find attractive. She had been away when Victor joined and had only recently returned. In a way which continued to provide him with mild unease, she would at unpredictable moments establish her distance as if to remind him of her rank. Sometimes, as on this occasion, her technique lay in the more formal use of his name; sometimes her gentle expression of disrespect was so subtle as to leave him wondering what she really intended. Whatever her approach, Victor would have preferred someone else to be occupying that key position. He could think of no other person who so effectively took the edge off his self-assurance.

"I've got an appointment at that time," he replied. "Is the meeting urgent?"

"I think it is, Mr. Dubell. Mr. Poulter would like you there."

"Very well. I'll re-schedule. What's the topic? How long should I allow?"

"He wants to get Chilko going. He says the market is ready. And for your second question, I think you had better allow an hour."

"Thanks, Marion. You'll be there?"

"Yes, Mr. Dubell."

When Victor walked into the boardroom at 10:58, Jason Lamby, a lawyer from a local firm often used by Poulter Investments, and Leonard Marsden, Poulter's chief geologist, were already seated, as was Marion.

The boardroom table with its gleaming mahogany and curved sides could seat ten. With only six due to attend, they would sit three each side.

"Morning, Victor," said Jason. "This shouldn't take long, unless, of course, Slip has some different ideas on how to do it this time."

Before he sat down or replied to Jason, Victor moved one of the empty chairs to the head of the table. That done, he looked at Jason. "Should be straight forward. No need to make it complicated."

A minute later, Sydney Poulter walked in and sat down at the head of the table. "Hello, everyone. Thanks for making it at short notice." While everyone waited, he took a deliberate thirty seconds to arrange his papers before announcing the topic. "It's time to get Chilko moving again, Victor. She's been a shell now for two years. It is amazing what people will pay for a company without an asset. The market's ready for something to happen. Time to impregnate the old sow! So you're going to be busy, Victor."

"But, Sydney, why me?" replied Victor to chuckles round the room.

"Why? Virility, of course. And, in any case, you have the skills. That's what all that expensive education was for," answered Sydney to more chuckles.

"Marion, how many are out?"

"Five million, four hundred thousand and seventy two. About half of that is float, the rest is yours in one way or another."

"Sounds okay. Otherwise clean? I forget what was it last time?"

"Puget Resources. We rolled it back five to one in '84."

"Oh yes, I remember," said Poulter, leaning back in his chair. "We ran it up on that nickel play in the NWT in '82. Peaked at a few dollars didn't it?"

Marion replied, her face expressionless, "Yes, Mr. Poulter, and you did very well on it."

Poulter paused and, speaking very slowly, asked with a grin, "And Marion, how did you do?"

"Very well too, thank you, Mr. Poulter," she replied with a smile.

This was a phase of the junior exploration business that Sydney Poulter particularly enjoyed: a company of his now rolled back to

Chapter 44 — Claims are Vended

a small number of shares and about to issue a large number of new shares for claims he had paid to have staked and now held in one of his private companies.

The pleasantries over, Poulter reverted to business mode. "Great, now's the time to do it again. I want to put those Nisselinka claims into it. Do we still have a dispute with that turkey of a prospector? Victor, you've been dealing with that, haven't you?"

"Yes. But I haven't got anywhere. He's just a pain in the butt."

Poulter was unsympathetic: "We could make it work for us. Nothing wrong with a public scrap. If everyone wants it, there must be something there. In any case, all we need is a big enough block of claims to work with. As usual, chances are there's nothing there. We'll put in only the undisputed claims. In this market we can get a response just from announcing the acquisition. Who owns those claims, Marion?"

"They are all held by you and Victor. There's a letter agreement saying you have ninety percent and Victor has ten."

Sydney responded while flipping through the pages in front of him. "And I suppose I paid for, let me guess, one hundred percent of the staking costs?"

"Correct," said Marion with a smile.

Sydney looked up at Victor. "You got a good deal, young man. You can pay me back from your profits."

"That's fine by me."

"Okay, we'll throw in our claims. How many shares can we take for them, Marion? Or perhaps that is one for Jason?"

With Jason's years of experience applying securities law to the junior market, this was an easy question for him to answer. "If you each vend your claims separately, you should be able to get five hundred thousand between you. You might be able to get more, but I wouldn't try. The SOB will get his fingers into it and that will slow everything down."

Poulter turned to his chief geologist. "Len. Did I hear you say we've got room to work even if we ignore the disputed ground?"

"Yes, nearly a kilometre clear of other claims and fractions. Room for a program and room for an orebody."

"And you like the ground?"

"It's early stage, but it's elephant country for sure. Some nice showings on the surrounding claims and then a big patch that has never been explored. Best part about it is that we can expect to get a bit of gold with the copper. Certainly worth a try. But I can't promise anything."

Poulter replied with a chuckle and a grandstanding pose. "Leonard, the day you start promising me something is the day I get out of the business!"

Leafing through his papers again, Sydney signalled it was time to close the first part of the meeting. "Well then, everyone on side?"

When he heard no one demur, he addressed Leonard again. "What do you need, say, for everything up to and including the first ten holes?"

"Off the cuff, at least two hundred thousand, more like a quarter of a million. That would be for geochem, mapping, IP, a bit of drilling, and murphy. Everything by chopper of course, including slinging in the drill. I'll give you a firm number after lunch."

"Two twenty-five. Okay. Add seventy-five for P.R., dog and pony shows, chatting up the brokers and all that. It's going to be three hundred grand without much change," mused Sydney. "Let's start her up with a private placement. One-point-five million at twenty cents to three investors. I'll put in a hundred thousand. Victor, can you find someone for the rest? I don't suppose you're up to it yourself yet."

"Yes, Sydney, I'll find someone. And no, I'm not ready. Give me a few more months and I'll take these things all myself!" he said with a wry smile.

Poulter looked at Victor with a hint of a frown. "Be careful. It's too soon to count me out, young man. Now, back to the present. We'll be very nice and let in some others for the next three hundred grand at fifty cents. Everyone with me?"

Murmurs of assent triggered his next question. "When can you start, Len?"

"Give me a month. Just got to put the crew together. A bit of permitting. No reason to expect any problems."

Poulter gathered his papers as he rose to leave. "Goddamn permits! If it goes on like this we'll need more permits than paper for each pooped-out penny! We'll meet next week to review progress. Thanks, everyone."

A month later Chilko announced two private placements followed by mobilization of a crew on recently staked claims in the Nisselinka Range.

Chapter 45

Camp Set-up
May

"Anywhere on that grassy bench on the left," said Phil Creighton into the intercom as he pointed from the front passenger seat. In response, Grant banked the machine to the left and dropped altitude. "Right side okay?"

"Just fine." Phil, along with his brother Frank, owned Campset Incorporated, a company specializing in providing short-term camps for mineral exploration crews. In this case Campset had been engaged by Chilko Explorations to set up a camp for ten, with the possibility of expansion if a drill crew should be required. Phil knew enough about the mineral exploration business and the people who ran it to recognize that Chilko needed to drill and would almost certainly find a reason to do so. He had built into his plans the assumption that an additional three sleeping tents would be required. He had a crew of four for this job. The others were Billy, a broad-shouldered youth, riding behind him in the chopper, and his brother who was with Al, another helper, on the road twelve miles away with the lumber.

Conditions were good, no rain was expected for twenty-four hours and the bush was dry. Phil could see a few residual patches of snow in places that remained in shadow most of the day. As Grant lowered his machine onto one end of a sinuous ribbon of grass which followed a bank on the south side of a small creek, Phil was relishing the last few moments of comfort ahead of the day's work. Then intercom brought him back to the present.

"Same place for the sling loads?" asked the pilot.

Phil replied, "We'll clear a space at the other end of the bench."

The two brothers had bid the camp construction for a fixed cost to cover all labour and supplies, but they had left the helicopter cost to be billed directly to the client. They had contemplated taking a risk and including the helicopter time in the bid. The upside would have been that, if chopper time could be kept to a minimum, the job could be very profitable. On the other hand, the possibility of incurring unbudgeted time at $700 per hour was not to be contemplated.

With the aircraft now on the ground but the engine still running, Phil continued his instructions to the pilot. "Give us one hour to get some space cleared and then we will be able to take all eleven loads as fast as you can swing them in."

"That's fine. I'll have time to refuel. Does Frank have all the loads sorted out?"

"You bet! See you in sixty or so."

Phil climbed out and moved back to help Billy take equipment from the rear compartment at the back of the plane: two chain saws, two axes, and a can of fuel. They both walked past the cockpit to a place forty feet in front where Grant could see them, hunkered down and watched the machine turn around and power off. As the two men watched the departing machine, the bush returned to its usual silence.

A couple of minutes later Phil was cutting salal and willow with a machete. Using blue flagging tape, he marked out the positions to be occupied by the five tents. Four of them formed a row along the bench. Two others, including the cook tent, were to be behind the first row.

Billy needed confirmation of the task he had been assigned. "Floor logs, five tents?"

The response was equally short. "Yup. Remember the cook tent is twelve-by-thirty-two."

Billy went off, chain saw in hand. A couple of minutes later the quiet was broken again as he fired it up. He selected a jack pine, about eight inches in diameter at the base, limbed it to head height with his saw, then felled it with a clean cut. He then completed limbing the felled tree to tent-length and trimmed the trunk, now five inches wide. Within half an hour he had five similar logs. Leaving his saw on one of them, he carried a log to the grassy bench where Phil was at work.

"Easy finds?" asked Phil as Billy neared.

Billy dropped the log in the middle of one of the areas marked out for a sleeping tent before answering. "Plenty."

Chapter 45 — Camp Set-up

"Grant should be back in twenty-five. Plywood first. Then the two-by-fours. May as well set them down right on the tent sites. Propane too. You unload. Okay?"

Billy signalled his assent and went back to fetch another log.

Twenty-five minutes later, he had started back to get his last log, when he heard the returning helicopter. Moving over to a clearing between the trees he could see the dot in the sky with a just-visible smaller dot beneath it. He walked over to the southernmost of the tent sites, inspected the ground, and positioned himself back to the wind. The helicopter and its sling load, by now half a mile away and clearly visible, was turning into the wind towards Billy, who stood with both arms outstretched and pointing ahead of him to indicate the recommended approach direction. He then signalled the drop site by standing with his right hand pointing skywards. Plywood sheets and two-by-fours bundled into a net came swinging slowly towards him as the down draft from the blades tugged at his shirt and bent the vegetation around him. The bundle slowly approached the ground until the lanyard suspending it went slack. Billy, surrounded by noise and dancing bushes, walked over to the pile of lumber, grasped the point at which the four corners of the net came together with one hand, and released the clip with the other. He pointed his arm to the sky and moved his hand in a circular motion to signal the load was unhitched. The lanyard rose above him and then trailed at forty-five degrees as the helicopter picked up speed. Phil came over and together the two men opened up the net and removed the contents and stacked them nearby. They folded the net into a neat bundle, clipping three corners to the ring on the fourth corner. If the net were not ready to be picked up when Grant returned, time would be lost; delays would begin and they could be expensive.

Twelve miles away Frank and his helper had been busy unloading a one-ton pickup truck and a flat-bed. The heaviest items included a stove, a refrigerator, six propane cylinders, thirty sheets of plywood, and three bags containing the rods and brackets for the frame of the large tent. Once items had been sorted into piles of no more than twelve hundred pounds, they had to be moved a second time onto the net. The fridge and stove were easy, as they could be lifted directly off the flatbed and rocked onto a net. Frank and his helper, once they had the cargo well organized, spent most of the time waiting for a net to be returned. They then hooked up the ready load before moving the next shipment onto the returned net. When not organizing and moving the supplies, they took advantage of the comfortable seating provided by a stack of lumber.

"What they lookin' for?" said Al, who had just graduated from high school with, if his modest ambitions were any guide, a lifetime of work in the woods ahead of him.

"Dunno," said Frank as he pulled on a cigarette. "But it's probably copper with maybe moly. Possibly gold. You never know. Sometimes I wonder whether they do."

"They sure spend money."

Frank nodded. "That's right. Suits me, as long as they pay their bills."

"Who pays if they don't?"

Frank contemplated his cigarette before responding slowly. "If they don't, that gets serious. You've got to know your client. This company is run by a feller called Sydney Poulter. Some people call him 'Slip'. He seems to pay his bills. At least he always has with us. This time I'm dealing with a new man. Dubell's his name. Seems efficient."

Frank drew again on his cigarette and continued. "If someone doesn't pay a bill in Smithers you soon hear about it. So the ones you've got to watch out for are the new guys. Slip has been around for years. You may be kept waiting, but it's a pretty safe bet you'll get paid one day. He's kind'a rough but we like to do business with him."

"Rough?"

"Well, you've gotta deliver. There used to be a guy in town. Mitch someone, who did a contract with one of Slip's companies to put in some line. Twenty kilometres, I think, cut to IP standards, about three feet wide. Good contract. So Mitch asked for fifty percent up front, about $8000, and got it. Then a couple of weeks later, he sent a bill for the balance. But the company got a friend of mine to check the work. Looked pretty good at first. All six lines had been started and went for a few hundred feet, and then nothing. Slip sent in a couple of guys to get his money back. They spent a day or two in town asking for Mitch but he had skipped. Dunno what would have happened to him if he hadn't."

Al put his head to one side, listening, and got up quickly: "Here he comes!"

"Jeez. You've got good ears," said Frank, still sitting. "Can't hear a thing!"

Chapter 45 — Camp Set-up

By noon the next day, five of the tent sites had floors of plywood nailed to two-by-fours, each of which rested on at least two of Billy's logs. Two of the floors had tent frames almost complete. One was of lumber, the other of two-inch aluminium pipes connected by steel joiners.

"She's looking good," said Phil to his brother as he bit into an apple he had pulled out of one of the cardboard boxes.

"Yeah. And we were forty minutes under estimate on the chopper."

"Hey, great! That planning paid off. We were lucky with the pilot. Grant really knows his stuff."

"Sure does, 'member when he first came. Early seventies. Straight from Vietnam. Didn't talk about it much. Looked haunted. Must have seen some awful things. Said he wasn't going back. Flew as if someone was going to shoot at him whenever he landed. Never flew around before landing. Just went straight in. Set her down in one. Just like that. Used to scare me, but I got to trust him."

The four men spent the night on one of the tent floors where a tent frame had been partially completed. A large blue tarpaulin, draped over the frame, provided enough shelter. The clouds and rain stayed away. A clear sky promised a fine morning and delivered it along with a hard frost which whitened most of the underbrush and all of the grass.

By mid-afternoon all the frames were up, all but one of them covered. Frank and Al were working on the last one. Billy and Phil had finished hooking up the stove and fridge to the propane tanks and were now digging a latrine pit. The radio in the kitchen tent was hooked up and tuned to radio traffic on 4340, the frequency that handled most of the bush camps in northwest B.C.

Chapter 46

Applied Science
June

It had been over a month since Chilko had announced acquisition of the Nisselinka claims and the start of an exploration program. The market had responded with a minor uptick on the share price from thirty cents, where it had been since the number of shares had been rolled back, one new for eight old ones. The buyers were part-time speculators prepared to take a low-price bet on any of Slip Poulter's plays. The professionals were watching, but stayed on the sidelines.

On the claims themselves there was work to do. Alice, a middle-aged woman of generous girth and forceful manner, had been up before dawn. She stepped outside the cook tent, picked up a piece of rebar hanging from a pole angled against the tent and struck a triangular piece of iron with several sharp blows. Randy Hemming pulled his sleeping bag over his head in a vain attempt to shut out the sound. He had slept soundly, but climbing out of a warm bag into a cold tent was not his favourite activity. Thirty minutes left. He liked to be on time for breakfast. The alternative was Alice's wrath and a rush to get ready afterwards. As he rolled over, all the muscles in his legs and back reminded him that they had worked hard the previous day. He had carried a spool of wire on his back for over an hour before he had the satisfaction of letting it unwind as he laid it out from the generator to the first of the electrodes. Hard work but good money, that ought to keep him in the black for his last year at school. His boss expected a lot from his crew but at least he was fair. Randy rolled over again and unzipped his bag—first step of the journey out. The cold air flowed in and helped the waking process. The youth in the bed opposite had just got himself up and was staggering out, towel in hand.

Chapter 46 — *Applied Science*

At 6:30 Alice banged the gong a second time. Those already in the cookshack when Randy arrived were all coffee freaks, sitting at the table clasping their first mugs of the day. Two were about to start into the cereal and Alice was placing a large dish of scrambled eggs on the table with one hand and a dish of bacon with the other. Others entered the tent and there were soon seven hungry young men at the table. Talk was in short pulses interspersed between long periods of silence. Alice, normally a fountain of ribbing, cajoling and questionable humour, felt the mood and held her fire.

"You want me on Line 3 today?" asked Tryg, a nineteen-year-old workhorse on his first field assignment.

"Probably," answered Peter, as he helped himself to toast and jam. "But we'll meet in the office at 7:30 and I'll let you know."

The older hands preferred to keep breakfast free of shop-talk. Each had his thoughts, some of family, some of girlfriends, some of what the day would bring.

Alice was laying out the ingredients for making sandwiches—sliced meat, sliced bread, tomatoes, lettuce—together with cartons of juice and a tray of butter tarts she had made the previous evening. Twenty minutes later, people started getting up from their seats, going down to the end of the table where they could assemble a lunch for the day. As he put his together, Tryg was wondering about Alice. Interesting old duck, middle aged, friendly (most of the time), forceful, and someone who could hold a conversation on almost any topic. Why would she take a job like this, away from home, from the friends she must have? Did she have any kids? Was she ever married? Find out sometime, thought Tryg to himself. Must be a story there.

"Great looking tarts," said Peter. "We'll all be thanking you from somewhere out there in the middle of the day."

"I hope you enjoy them. Make sure you take them all or I'll have to eat them and that's not what I need."

Tryg, brown bag in hand, was about to stoop his lanky frame to fit through the door, when he turned towards the other end of the tent. "What's for supper, Alice?"

"That's not for you to know, young man," she replied.

Tryg laughed, ducked his head, and continued through the door.

At the appointed time four members of the geophysical crew were standing around a high table in the office tent. Peter was pointing to a pencil-drafted map. "So this is what we've done. Green means we've done one spacing. Thick black means all four spacings. With all the snow just melted, there's no problem with getting electrical contact but watch out for gravel beds. They could spoil it all. We seem to be seeing something below twenty metres on Line 3 but it's early yet to know whether it will mean anything. Tryg and Chris on the end of Line 4 and then onto Line 3, dragging the wire. Randy with me and doing the hook ups. Any questions?"

"Let's do it," said Randy as he turned towards the door.

Peter Scholdar had set up IPEM Surveys six years earlier. No longer young, he was now a veteran of over thirty surveys and could be counted on to get the numbers right. While Randy and Peter were carrying out their high-voltage ritual, other members of their team were laying cable, secure in the knowledge that the wire would remain without current for the rest of the day. Chris was a student in geophysics at the University of British Columbia. This was his second season in the bush. His goals were to earn enough to pay his way through the following academic year, and to gain experience in the occupation he expected to make into his career. He knew the theory on which induced polarization, usually referred to as 'IP', was based and could write and explain most of the equations that described the progress of current through the ground; but if the instrument started generating results which did not seem to fit, or if it broke down, he knew he would be in difficulty without Peter to help. He liked the outdoors, was determined not to spend his life in an office, but he was realist enough to recognize he did not want to be pulling cables for the rest of his life. Perhaps a job with a large mining company would be the answer: varied experience, different techniques, lots of travel, chance to go to conferences, perhaps to give a paper or two. His life was unfolding as it should. No, that was too general. His career was unfolding as it should. But the other important things? The girls he liked most did not seem to think the same of him and some of the girls for whom he had little time seemed attracted to him. Conclusion: a career was easier to manage than some of the other aspects of life. Oh well. This was his job for the summer, the food was great, and the money was rolling in.

Chris's helper, Sydney, predictably known as Syd, a man of twenty-two, had no ambitions to be a geophysicist. He could not have handled the instrument, and had no interest in why or how it

Chapter 46 — Applied Science

worked. This was just a job. The pay was good and, like Chris, he appreciated the good food. He looked forward to his pay cheque. Perhaps, by the end of the summer, he would be able to upgrade his Chevy beater and buy a pickup with only four or five years on it. Got to keep the job.

Lunch at about noon was an important half hour for everyone, a break from toil, time to eat and a chance to talk. Randy turned to Peter who was sitting on the same log, next to the now-silent generator.

"Remember that Candrex job we were on last year?"

Peter frowned. "You're not going to remind me about the food, I hope."

"Well sort of. Just the contrast. Isn't Alice great? Her pastries are something else. And I have to say she makes all the difference."

Peter agreed. "A lot of camp cooks can do just that, make all the difference, for good or bad."

"Any idea where she came from?"

"None at all. Seems well educated. She can talk about almost anything. We were on to the colonization of B.C. last night. She seemed to have read all about it."

"Yeah, I noticed. Did you see the car she drives? It's a Cadillac."

"So I heard," answered Peter, "but I understand it's an old one. Doesn't mean she's got money."

"No. It just seems she is something unusual for a camp cook."

"Let's do what we can to keep her," said Peter looking at his watch as he got up. "Time to get a few more readings."

Early that evening Syd was lying on his bunk flipping through a copy of Playboy, feeling hungry in more ways than one. He was anticipating the meal which he knew would be of a quality he had not experienced before working in this camp, but it was too soon to go. Supper was at 6:00 and that was not negotiable. Alice always had the cook shack to herself until everything was ready. And it was always ready on time. As soon as he heard voices outside and the sound of boots on the plywood floor of the next tent, he looked at his watch, saw it was almost time, and swung his legs over the edge of his bed. He checked the setting on the propane stove, opened the tent door, stepped down onto a platform made of split logs and then onto muddy turf. Other doors opened and within minutes the entire crew had converged on the cookhouse.

Peter was first in. "Hello, Alice. I suppose you're going to surprise us yet again with a culinary triumph."

Alice smiled. "Well, it seems to be what you all expect. So I do my best."

"We've been thinking about it all day. Nothing else to keep us going."

"Nice to be appreciated," replied Alice as she busied herself ferrying two large casseroles to the centre of the table, while those around the table helped themselves to three loaves of fresh-baked bread. Catching a moment of silence, she addressed the assembled eaters.

"Last meal like this I'll be cooking for a while. Tomorrow I expect five more, so we'll be twelve around the table."

"Who's coming?" said someone at the end of the table.

"I'm told it's the geochem crew. Anyone know anything about them? I hope they're nice and well-mannered like you guys!"

"Alice, how could you suggest anything else! Have you ever met anyone but a gentleman in a bush camp?"

"'Course not. Nothing but gentlemen, and ladies, of course. Well, come to think of it, there have been a couple of guys who didn't know the rules, at least until I put them right, that is!"

"We're all trembling, Alice. We promise to be good. And we'll make sure the geochem guys behave. Anyone know who they are?"

As usual, Peter could provide the information. "They work for an outfit called P.G. Exploration Services. There are four of them. Fellow called Jake Mowatt is in charge. Can't say I know him."

"I was told there are going to be five," said Alice.

"Oh, yes, a prospector called Daryl Sens, not part of the geochem crew. He's from Ontario and may arrive later. Supposed to really know his stuff, but I've never heard of him. He has been hired directly by Chilko. Odd that. They contract out just about everything. Didn't know they put field people on the payroll, except for their geologist. But, if he is good, that's fine by me."

At noon the next day, everyone except Alice and Chris, who had a day in camp, were out on the lines when the noise of the expected helicopter was heard. A few minutes later it set down on the pad. Chris waited for a nod from the pilot before he went to help unload. Two passengers were on board. The two remaining seats and the baggage compartment were taken up with cardboard boxes full of groceries. The pilot, still at the controls, opened his door a few

Chapter 46 — Applied Science

inches and used his boot to prevent it closing. Chris approached the machine and opened the door further to get close to the pilot so that he could be heard above the noise of the engine.

"Hi! Coffee? Lunch? Or another pickup?"

"Thanks. I'll get the others and then ferry in the goods. First trip with the guys. Then I'll put the groceries in a sling. I think it'll all go in one."

"Okay. See you when you've finished."

Back in the office tent Chris heard the engine sound change. A few seconds later the machine pulled itself into the sky and silence descended on the camp.

The geochemical crew consisted of one medical student, two first-year geology students, and a rolling stone from Newfoundland who had worked his way across the entire width of the country during the last year and a half. Jake Mowatt, the medic-to-be, had more experience of mineral exploration than the others, and was in charge. He knew what was required and worked closely with a consulting geochemist who was expected within three days to review progress and problems. He did not expect to learn anything about medicine while on the job but it was a useful way of keeping his student loan to a minimum. The geology students, Nick Benson and Mike Krutzner, were there because it was a good job and one which would help pay their dues on their way to more senior positions in the exploration business. The Newfy, Tom Mulligan, welcomed any new experience. This was his first job in mineral exploration but, as he had already been an underground miner in Quebec, a faller in Northern Ontario, and a roughneck in Alberta, he did not expect to find a job he could not handle. Although, at thirty-three, Tom was older than the others, he sought no responsibility beyond getting his job done. He wanted another experience and then he would move on. Whither, he had not decided.

By 11:00 am on the third day, two of the samplers, Nick and Tom, had reached bush thick with deadfall and salal. Progress was slow. Each fallen log had to be climbed over or crawled under. In response to the steeply sloping ground, they had to kick footholds with their boots whenever they stopped to take a sample. By now, each was carrying a load of geochemical envelopes about eight inches by three, made of heavy brown paper and filled with sand or clay. While not admitting to anything like a race, they were both aware that for the previous day, the number of samples taken by each two-man crew had been very close, and their own scores had been better than those of the other team. Now that this thick bush was holding them up, they ceased to expect another easy win. Tom liked to fan the breeze of competition, but he did not want the quality to drop. This line was beginning to look like an opportunity to slow down and start emphasizing quality, at the expense of a bit of ribbing in camp.

The trail back to camp was just under a mile of easy walking. Fallen trees had been cut so that there were none to climb under or over. Underbrush had been removed. With little energy for conversation, they walked about thirty feet apart, Nick in the lead setting a steady pace like a horse headed for home. Tom suddenly found himself closing on Nick, who had stopped and was pointing at a brown pile on the ground to his left. "See that? They're bound to be here, but that's the first I've seen at this camp. Looks like it's a big one."

Tom bent down to look at it. "Still warm! I hope he's moved away."

"Perhaps it's just ahead down the line," replied Nick with a laugh as he made a show of looking down the trail.

"Oh, yeah. I hope it's not a she with cubs."

Nick, evidently unfazed, started again along the cut-line. "We'll soon find out if anyone is worried about meeting one."

On arrival at camp, they threw their packs on the ground, where a bench made of small tree trunks had been constructed beneath a tarp draped over a ridge-pole. Each man pulled from his pack several plastic bags containing wet, brown-paper envelopes, many of them oozing muddy water. Pausing sometimes to wipe off mud so that the writing beneath could be read, they arranged the day's samples in numerical sequence. One man then read out the numbers on each bag as the other checked them off in his notebook. Above the bench, several hundred sample bags had been threaded onto wires from which they hung drying. Those already dry were in plastic buckets beneath the table.

"Last one, six hundred west, two hundred and fifty east," said Nick. "How many?"

Tom looked at his notebook, pencil in hand. "Just a moment. Ninety-six."

Nick looked disappointed. "Not as good as yesterday."

Chapter 46 — Applied Science

"But just fine," said Tom as he picked up his almost empty pack and headed for his tent. "Still on target to finish next Thursday. Time for a shower before dinner."

With backpacks slung over their shoulders, each man headed for the tent he shared with two others.

Chapter 47

Tunnel Found

June

"On your own again, Daryl?" asked Alice, as she brought another round of pancakes to the table. "Can't you find anyone to go with you?"

"That's me. Destined for a life of solitude! How about coming yourself?" replied Daryl with a grin. "Today it's the northwest corner. Nice little hike. Only three miles uphill. I could do with a strong assistant."

"Go for it, Alice!" said someone from a mouthful of toast to the accompaniment of chuckles round the table.

Alice laughed, turned her ample self towards Daryl, pancake lifter in hand. "Forget it! Must be some reason why you have to go alone. Next thing, you'll be telling me that prospectors are best working by themselves."

"Well, that's what they say. And I've just been trying all these years to be a good prospector."

Peter stood by the stove with both his hands around a mug of coffee. He looked towards Daryl. "Ever worked for Poulter before?"

"Never. I've worked for most of the Toronto promoters but few from this end. I heard that someone with my experience was needed in B.C. I was told to phone a guy called Victor Dubell. So I did. Sounded like an interesting job. So here I am."

"Well, we're very glad to have you." Peter put down his coffee mug. "And if the stories we hear are true, you'll be finding us a couple of new showings within a day or two."

Daryl evidently enjoyed the attention and the praise but kept his eyes on the table. "They tell me there are some disputed claims in the northwest. Anyone been up there?"

Chapter 47 — Tunnel Found

Silence and shaken heads around the table made the answer clear.

"Well, I may as well go and check them out. Tell you all about it this evening."

Within a few minutes everyone except Alice had left the tent after making up a lunch from the spread at the end of the dining table.

Eleven hours later, the IP crew, the geochemical samplers, and the prospector were sitting around the table. They had been joined by Grant the pilot, who had delivered a load of groceries and other supplies. After a weary day in the field, all were enjoying the opportunity to sit down, satisfy appetites, and feel the warmth in the tent. Most of them were half way into their dishes of pot roast before the conversation began to pick up.

"Bring us some papers, did you, Grant?"

"The usual bunch, *Sun, Macleans, Time*. I couldn't get *Playboy* this time. They'd run out at the news store. I'll try again on Thursday. I didn't know there was anyone here who likes to read that stuff."

"Just Alice," said a voice from the table, followed by guffaws.

Although Alice was never at a loss for a response, Nick decided to help. "No, it's Daryl. He had the last one for a week before anyone else had a chance. Right, Daryl?"

Daryl responded slowly with an air of mock pomposity. "I have to admit it is one of my favourite periodicals, but I categorically deny having kept it for a week." He paused while everyone waited for him to continue. "I have to admit that I am disappointed there is not to be a new one today, but I look forward to Thursday. And I have to tell you all that I think, after my achievements today, I deserve better treatment. In fact a reward would be appropriate."

Jake banged the table for attention. "Achievements! What did you have to carry, Daryl? Try my pack on the way home!"

"Let me guess. No, let's all guess," added Tom. "Mine is that—"

"You found the motherlode!" interjected someone from the end of the table.

Daryl cleared his throat. There was a short silence, pregnant with anticipation. "I was working my way along the base of a scree slope at the foot of that ridge which crosses the north edge of the DBL 1 claim. Light timber and an animal trail, easy walking when—"

Alice interrupted: "Better be good after this build up!"

"When I saw that that there had been a bit of a slide at the foot of a patch of outcrop. A strip of scree had moved downhill and exposed more outcrop. I thought I had better check it out. At the top of the slide the boulders had come away from the outcrop revealing an old working. Seemed like an ordinary adit, about five-and-a-half feet high. I got to wondering what happened to their spoil pile. All the spoil had to have been taken away by the creek. No wonder it wasn't there. So I started rootin' around down slope to find some evidence for what they found. Some of the weathered boulders, not really boulders, about football size, had quite a bit of chalco. The sulphide must have been on top of the scree before the latest movement. I went back up to the adit and peered in. All I had with me was my emergency flashlight. It seemed to go in at least twenty feet. Roof didn't look too good. Needs a bit of scaling so I didn't want to go in alone. I thought I could see some equipment, but I could be wrong."

"Are you sure that is on our claim?" asked Peter.

"Not much doubt about that. Any problem with that claim?"

"Yes there is," said Jake, who had earned a reputation for being well informed. "Most of that ground is disputed. When the staking was done for Poulter and his friends, there was someone else staking the same day. Both parties claim that ground, but the tunnel would have to be on the crown grant, that is not in dispute. I had been thinking that the northwest corner wasn't going to be too important. Looks like we're going to have to change that. Chilko has told us to work on any of the claims they have staked whether or not they are disputed. That leaves us a lot of ground to cover. Let's review the whole thing after it has been plotted up."

"Old workings," said Nick. "Sounds interesting. How about a treasure chest? What we really need is a skeleton!"

Mike Krutzner didn't usually say much. When he did it was usually to ask a question. "Anyone know when that tunnel might have been dug, or who did it?"

"As I understand it," replied Jake, "there are two groups of crown grants around here, the ones Daryl was telling us about on the western side of our claims, and two more on the east. They were bought by Poulter. I have been told that the mines inspector reported on both groups of crown grants in, I think, 1911 or '12, or about that time. So a tunnel over where Daryl found it makes sense."

Chapter 47 — Tunnel Found

Mike followed up his question. "Imagine what it must have been like to get up there in those days. Whoever did it didn't have Grant to give them a ride. And they had to get their equipment up too. Pack horses and donkeys, I suppose."

"Mules, not donkeys, donkey. That's how they got everything in," said a voice from the back of the tent.

"There you are, Grant. You're the mule!" said Alice.

"Thank you for that. I'll remember what sort of beast I am. Now your friendly mule has to be going as he doesn't see well in the dark. Alice, I'll be back on Thursday. I have to sling in a couple of propane tanks. Anything you need urgently?"

"No thanks, Grant. We can wait for the regular run. But, if you're coming again on Friday, could I come out with you on Thursday? I have a few errands in town I would like to get done."

She turned to Peter. "Assuming, of course, that it would be okay with you, Peter?"

"Go right ahead. You'd leave us the meal for Thursday night. I'm sure Randy will volunteer to do breakfast again. And we'll see you Friday."

"That's fine by me," said Grant.

On Friday morning, soon after everyone had assembled for breakfast, Tom addressed the others as he was walking back to the table with another helping of scrambled eggs. "Anyone seen Daryl?"

"Said he's not feeling well. He went back to his tent. Got a headache."

"That's a shame," commented Jake. "He has been on a roll. Nothing serious, I hope. He'll be alone in camp, at least until mid-afternoon when Grant comes back with Alice."

"That's probably all he needs. A few hours of peace and quiet."

Chapter 48

Tunnel Explored

June

Breakfast at the Evergreen Café on Wednesday mornings was a regular event for a select few of the citizens of Smithers. The number attending was usually five or six, but could be as many as ten, if someone brought a guest. No one had ever said that guests, either men or women, were unwelcome; they were always made to feel at home. Whether or not the participants would have so admitted, they all knew that the best occasions were those attended by only the few regulars, those who had known one another for many years. They enjoyed digging deeper into topics that had already been through the exploratory rounds of enquiry. The table reserved for these unsung pillars of the community was in the corner of an L-shaped room, away from the front entrance. In winter this part of the dining room was illuminated by a gas fire. On this cool summer day the door was open and three regulars were enjoying the strip of grass overhung by wild plum trees against a background of the Coast Mountains twenty miles away.

Ken Wickford was one of the members of this unorganized but tightly knit bunch. So was Will Herman. When Ken arrived, Will was talking to Wally Seldock and Lester Bance, preparing them for the news he was about to break.

Wally, a short man with broad shoulders on a muscular body, spoke for them all. "Morning Ken. We've just been hearing from Will about your news."

Everyone's attention turned to Ken, who evidently had the floor. "My news is pretty flat these days. Chilko are working their claims and I'm told they've strayed onto mine. But you've all known that for weeks. I've heard there is something I need to know, so I hope you guys will let me in on it. Someone has news for me?"

290

Chapter 48 — Tunnel Explored

"The story is..." began Will. "I should explain that I wondered if I should phone you or sit on it until I could tell you here. But then I heard you were coming and I wanted your friends to watch your reaction."

Ken was the enjoying the game his friends were playing. "Let me guess. They've hit gold! Can't be that. They haven't dug a single trench or drilled a single hole. And there can't be any surprises from the outcrops. I have examined just about every one of them on those claims."

Lester pointed at the man with the story. "Tell him, Will."

Will paused for effect while the others waited, sipped their coffees, and watched the expression on their friend's face. "We hear they've found an old adit. We think that it must be on one of your crown grants. Seems to have been exposed by a recent rock slide."

Ken responded slowly, showing first surprise, then delight, then concern. "No kidding! I've always thought it had to be somewhere there. I've scoured those hills, every ridge, every gully, without finding it. I figured it had to be covered by the rockslide. What's the source?"

"Can't say at this time. But reliable. I've no reason to doubt it."

"Who found it?"

"A new prospector they've got. Comes from the east. No B.C. experience. Seems to have the respect of the guys in the camp."

"So he must have been working on your ground," said Wally. "What do you think of that?"

"It's not the way to behave, but it's what you would expect from people like the Chilko gang. On the other hand it's hard to pin down boundaries when you're in the woods, and the more they find on my ground the more they will want to do a deal."

Ken, looking serious, his mind in the hills, continued talking slowly, more to himself than to his companions. "That's extraordinary, assuming it's his, of course. I mean assuming it was dug by Grandpa Wickford. It has to be on one of the crown grants, but there isn't a shred of paper to say exactly where the tunnel is. Even the government sketch doesn't help. It gets a bit complicated because we know he and his backers started a second adit about a year before he left. And it was on crown grants I don't own. They were sold by my dad."

"So this isn't a complete surprise?" asked Lester.

"No. We know he worked on two tunnels. A letter in 1911 to someone in England said they had stopped working on what he called the Raven tunnel because they had a new showing to investigate. Then there is a letter to the mining recorder in Prince George reporting that they had completed eighteen feet of tunnel during the first eight months of 1912. But we know, also from the government records, that the Raven tunnel was the same length (twenty-six feet) at the end of 1912 as it was twelve months later, so I think the eighteen feet must have been somewhere else. He wrote a letter from France in 1916 saying he was looking forward to having to decide which of the two adits he should work on first when he got back. By that time he had rounded up a bit of financing."

Will knew enough of the story to ask the right questions: "What made you think it might be at that particular place?"

"Partly elimination and partly a clue. It had to be buried by mud and scree. Most of the patches of outcrop are small and I've checked them all. The clue came in the form of a few grains of chalcopyrite in the spoil from a gopher hole. It appealed to my sense of the absurd. Here was I checking piles of dirt from holes dug by animals while I was looking for the spoil from a hole dug by my grandfather. They had been doing the same thing. But the gophers didn't have to go away and kill other gophers. So all the gophers probably got their tunnels completed. Grandpa didn't."

After a few seconds of silence, Lester spoke slowly. "I don't suppose your grandfather had to go. No draft then, no coercion. I suppose he felt he just had to. Couldn't let the side down."

Ken nodded. "I think that was the way with all of them."

"He came back, didn't he?" asked Wally.

"Yes, but terribly beat up. Shrapnel in his leg, something wrong in his abdomen—he never said what. Whiff of gas did something to his lungs. Went away as strong as an ox. Came back half the man."

"How long did he last?"

"Three years. He managed to get up to his beloved claims a couple of times. But getting there was all he could do. He went underground and tried it for a bit but he was no longer up to that sort of work. He felt he owed his backers a discovery and then he had to face the reality that he could not deliver, even if there was an orebody there. At that time his only son, my father, was only a teenager, so he couldn't pass the baton and watch his team perform. He was dead soon after his last visit to the site."

Chapter 48 — Tunnel Explored

"And the tunnel wasn't touched after that?" said Wally.

"As far as I can tell. If there had been any serious work the Inspector of Mines would almost certainly have written it up."

"So now, seventy-five years later, you might have a chance to check it out?"

"That's right. I've got to get up there quickly. I'd like to be there before anyone else, but it sounds as though I'm too late. No more details, Will?"

"I understand they didn't go in. Don't know why."

Ken was already making decisions. "Well, I have to take the opportunity. I'd better get there tomorrow. Who's coming? No chopper ride, just a nice hike."

Lester started to look ill at ease. "Nice hike! You mean ten miles uphill for a couple of thousand feet."

"I should decline for reasons we all understand," said Will with an opportunity to grandstand. "But to hell with the consequences. I'll come. I've got two days off in any case after flying six in a row."

"That's good." Ken turned to the others as if asking for volunteers for a dangerous assignment. "Who's on?"

Lester put aside his hesitations. "I'm not going to miss out, but I don't want to hold you back. No way I can keep your pace for that distance."

Ken was hardly listening. He was already planning. "We'll need flashlights, hard hats, candles, rope, pick, shovel. Mine lamps and batteries would be too heavy. In any case the tunnel is likely to be short. I think we had better take a light tent and spend the night. That means hauling food. So it's going to be lean rations for two days."

"You were saying something about not owning the claim?" asked Wally.

"No, that's the other tunnel. It's on the two crown grants to the east. I don't own them. We used to, but my dad sold it to fund work on the first tunnel."

Will was thinking less about the history of Ken's claims than the next day's expedition. "What would you say to taking Carl, you know, my nephew? He's only nineteen but as strong as a horse and he can carry a lot."

"And probably eats like a horse!" added Wally, laughing.

Ken liked the suggestion. "Good idea. He's a good kid. If he wants to come, I'd be delighted. So, that's four of us. Just right. Two in the tunnel, two outside for safety. Supper tonight at my place? We can assemble the stuff, pack and all that. Will you tell Carl?"

At 8:30 am the next morning, the four men were unloading their packs from Ken's truck at the logging landing. While they did so they were all aware of the uphill miles ahead of them, but this didn't prevent Lester getting into the spirit of the adventure. "Do you suppose those claim-jumpin' bastards are going to see us sweating up this mountain as they drift by in the helichopper?"

"Don't you worry, Lester. They're the ones who will be getting heart attacks. How many men your age could do what you are about to?" replied Ken. "I wouldn't be surprised if they come and look for us once they see the truck. I've no idea if this is one of the days they get the machine in. It must have been there a couple of days ago, if I can guess where that information came from." He looked at Will who did not rise to the bait. "But they won't see us for the first hour and a half, even if they looked. Trees are too tight. Once we get in the alpine it'll be different."

"Carl's looking worried," observed Lester as he hauled on his pack. He addressed Carl: "They are the enemy because they are trying to take Ken's claims away from him. They probably think we are looking for information to use against them, but there is nothing they can do to stop us going up there."

Carl smiled. He already had his pack on his back and was striding back and forth like the colt he was. He liked the outdoors and, having worked a couple of summers in the bush, knew his way around. He was enjoying the company and the conversation of these older men.

Ken looked into the back of the truck. "Have we forgotten anything? Okay, let's start."

Lester, as he and his companions had expected, found the going tough. At fifty-two, he was still a strong man, but years of smoking had etched away some of the lung tissue that he needed for the climb. Ken and Will were aware of Lester's difficulties and arranged to stop for a few minutes every half hour.

Like the others on these opportunities to rest, Carl sat on the ground and leaned against his pack or against a tree, but unlike the others, he managed to look like a compressed spring. When the words "Let's go!" or a similar invocation to continue the climb were heard, he unfolded and launched himself in one easy movement into his effortless stride. Lester would get up slowly, stretch,

Chapter 48 — Tunnel Explored

bend down to pick up his pack, haul it onto his back with grunt, and then take a reluctant step in pursuit of his companions.

There was no established trail. For much of the time they were heading on a compass bearing through a forest of Douglas fir and hemlock. Only after they had been climbing for an hour did the forest begin to open out. After two hours, the climb became gentle and patches of grass occupied more space than the trees, which were no more than twenty feet high and a handspan across at the base of the trunk.

With little energy to spare or opportunity for conversation, each man had plenty of time for his own thoughts. For Carl this was an adventure and an opportunity to be with a much-respected uncle. Although mining was a common topic of conversation at home and among his friends, he knew little about the industry, junior mining companies or the complexities of mineral title. Life was a breeze. Lester, a stalwart of the business community in Smithers, was there out of curiosity; he wanted to see some mine workings that had been lost because he was aware of the claim dispute, and because he was supporting his friend and the home team. Will was there because his friend might need his support and because the other side had crossed him once and he wanted an opportunity to strike a blow in response. Ken was driven by a multitude of motives: curiosity to see workings for which he had been looking for years, to get back at his opponents (how, he did not know), to re-acquire ground that had been in the family for three generations, and to do right by the grandfather he knew only through reputation.

After climbing for hours through corridors of green, where visibility was limited to a few tens of feet, they were now gazing on castles of grey, whose battlements towered above them and marched into the distance. Their path followed an animal trail running through grass, aspen and patches of small stunted trees at the base of a slope leading up to the grey cliffs. After half an hour, Ken, who had been in the lead most of the way, veered off the trail and stood at the top of a small bank that provided a good view of the cliffs ahead. When all four were assembled, he pointed towards a place about a thousand feet ahead of them where a ramp of boulders formed a base to the cliff itself. "It's got to be somewhere in that scree slope. We're looking for a place where the boulders have been disturbed. It'll probably show up as a different colour, either white or brown against the grey of the weathered rock."

"Do we spread out when we get there?" asked Carl.

"We'll see. That might be a good idea if there are parallel trails, but it would be slow going walking across those slopes. Dangerous too. Scree slopes kill more prospectors than helicopters do."

They returned to the trail and continued in single file. As they approached the scree, they could see the individual boulders forming the slope. The majority were about the size of footballs. Some were the size of cars. From its weathered appearance each boulder looked as if it had been in place for eternity. Some had indeed been there for a few tens or even thousands of years. But in geologic terms their stay was ephemeral. The entire slope was balanced in a state of near-equilibrium between the force of gravity and the resistance provided by friction and shape. All the boulders were just resting on their one-way journey downhill. The slope the men saw occupied one frame of a time-lapse sequence flickering by at twenty-four frames per century.

Carl, who had taken the lead, stepped onto a rock, raised his arm and pointed. "There's a small brown patch over there. Right below that fluffy cloud, level with that patch of dark trees. Must be about a mile."

Everyone stopped to look. Lester was squinting and evidently having trouble seeing. "I'll take your word for it, young man. I can't see a damn thing at that distance so I'm going to wait until I get there."

"Young eyes," exclaimed Ken. "We'll see how good you are at spotting the mineral."

With Ken now back in the lead, they continued along the trail. As they approached the patch of dark trees, the brown streak to which Carl had drawn attention twenty minutes ago became evident to all of them.

Despite his still-protesting lungs, Lester managed to find breath for a comment. "Looks like the kid wasn't kidding."

The brown patch could now be seen for what it was: a scar down the scree slope, exposing boulders and yellow-brown soil for a distance of about three hundred feet. The base of the scar met the headwaters of a small gully that formed an irregular channel across the low ground.

"See what happened?" said Ken. "That gully chewed a bit too much off the base of that slope. The lowest boulders had to fall,

Chapter 48 — Tunnel Explored

and then the others. Must have been quite a sight." He paused to allow himself and the others to appreciate the scale of the slide and what it would have been like to see it when it was happening, and then he turned and started up the hill. "Let's go see what we can find at the top."

They made their way slowly across the boulder field. For most of the time progress was simply a matter of putting one foot on the top of a boulder and then the other foot on a neighbouring rock. But every so often, one of the boulders moved as soon as extra weight was added. Then a bit of swift footwork was required to re-establish first balance, and then progress. Carl made it look easy. For Lester it was laboured and jerky progress. The visual concentration required for dancing across the boulder field allowed only moments for glancing ahead at their destination. When they had jumped off the last boulder they found themselves in the middle of a shallow gully floored, stones and boulders and yellow earth

Unlike the boulders in the scree slope they had just crossed, that had long since been washed clean of soil, these were packed in hardened mud. They all noticed it at once—about a hundred feet away, on the other side of the slide, was the opening of what looked like a cave. Without a word they moved across the slide. As they approached, they saw not a cave, but the top four feet of the entrance to a tunnel, the lower part partially concealed by hardened mud. Each man threw his pack onto one shoulder and then onto the ground, before climbing the slight incline to the tunnel.

"Found at last," shouted Ken.

Lester had managed to keep up with Ken, and wanted to know more. "Seventy years ago?"

"Close enough. I believe it was dug around 1913. He came back after the war but we don't think he managed to do anything more to it. So, yes. Last worked over seventy years ago. He must have used packhorses or mules to get here."

Lester, who had moved to the edge of the hole, climbed down three feet onto the low ground at the tunnel entrance. He was standing with his back to the tunnel, pointing at the mound of mud and rock a few feet ahead of him. "Look at that!"

They all moved to positions where they could look down on Lester and the object of his curiosity. What appeared to be a pipe and a piece of wheel protruded about twelve inches from the mud.

"You know what this is?" said Lester. "It is, or was, a wheelbarrow. Crushed like a matchbox!"

Ken was excited. "You know, I never expected to find any tools. But that makes sense. He always expected to return. So he would have left everything up here. We may find something else. But before we go in, let's have a snack."

Under a clear sky, their backs to a chill wind, the four men sat on flat rocks, enjoying their sandwiches while they talked about the tunnel they were about to explore.

"It must have taken your grandfather quite a while to get up here," said Carl. "Where did he start?"

"There was a trail up the Suskwa River east of Hazelton. They would have used it for a few miles, but I don't know their route after that. He would have bought his supplies in Hazelton or Prince George. Smithers came later, with the railway. He would probably have rented the packhorses or mules as well as the wrangler who owned them. I did some investigation of all that and figured it would have taken him two or three weeks to get in. Old grandpa—I never met him—would be over a hundred now. Even if he hadn't gone through that war, he wouldn't still be alive. I wonder what he would think if we had flown him in by chopper."

"He'd be hoppin' mad about losing those claims to that shyster," said Lester.

"That he would," said Ken. "And I fear he would be disappointed with his grandson for letting it happen."

Lester looked at Ken before making his comment. "Don't be so hard on yourself. You can't go through life assuming that everyone will be dishonourable. In any case, the battle's not yet over."

"Yes, I could still win. But it's a tough one. They have all the money they need. I hear Poulter can be ruthless when crossed."

"Talking about the bad guys, what's our strategy if we meet them up here? Their camp is just over those hills," said Will, pointing. "They could turn up any moment."

Ken thought for a moment and then answered slowly. "It could happen and it would certainly complicate things. But they can't object to us being on this claim. It's not theirs. It's my crown grant. But step outside it and the ground's in dispute with overlapping claims, theirs and mine. They cover the same ground and it remains to be seen who will win. In the meantime we're on ground that is mine."

Ken looked at his team. Carl had finished eating and was looking restless. Lester appeared relaxed while enjoying his first cigarette of the day. Will was leaning back on his pack, his legs

Chapter 48 — Tunnel Explored

crossed and eyes closed, enjoying the slight warmth provided by the sun.

"Carl, do you want to come in with me? We can leave Lester to finish his smoke, as for Will…"

"Ready any time," said Will without opening his eyes.

Ken donned his hard hat, picked up his flashlight and addressed his team. "Take five minutes, everyone. I'm just going to check out the first ten feet. No need for a candle. The air will be good at the entrance."

Watched by Lester and Carl, Ken jumped down into the pit where the entrance to the tunnel had been protected from falling debris by overhanging rock. In less than a minute, he emerged holding a shovel. He climbed the bank, a broad grin on his face. "You know, this must have belonged to him or to one of his partners. Bit rusty. Handle's amazing. Look at the shape. Not something you'd get in the hardware store today."

"Want to know who owned it?" asked Will joining the three.

"For someone who has just woken up, you're doing very well!" said Lester, who then turned, along with the others to see Will's finger pointing to marks burned into the wood at the base of handle. "*E.W. 1914.*"

"Wow! That is mine to keep," exclaimed Ken. He walked back to where they had lunched and gave the new-found tool a place of honour among the backpacks.

Then he made it clear that it was time to get to work. "Okay Carl. You need a hard-hat and flashlight. Been underground before?"

"No, but…"

"That's fine. Follow just a few feet behind me. Watch for loose rock. In some of these old workings you have to watch for piles of dynamite. I'm almost certain he would have used that after the war. Be careful. All set?"

Ken stepped down onto the low ground at the mouth of the tunnel, and ducked into the entrance. Directing his flashlight at the roof, then the walls, then the floor, he moved slowly forward.

Carl did likewise, but not allowing for the extra height provided by his hard hat, he bumped his head against the roof of the tunnel at the entrance. As he shone his flashlight around to see how much headroom lay ahead, he was startled by something darting across the beam of light. A moment later a bat fluttered over his shoulder. Then two more. At the same time he became aware of the pungent odour of bats, stagnant water, and damp rocks.

Ken was talking now, as he came back towards Carl, pointing his flashlight at the ceiling. "Seems they were following this vein. You see this line here, white with rusty patches? That's quartz and sulphide. Pretty skinny. Only an inch or two thick in some places. Hey! Look at this. It's widened to a foot or so. Stand back. I'm just going to chip a piece out." A few blows with the point of Ken's pick dropped a piece of rock to the ground. "See this, Carl? There's the sulphide and this gucky orange stuff is what happens to it when the air and water get to it. Mostly iron oxide." He pointed to the piece in his hand: "Can't see too well in here, but that looks like pyrite and chalcopyrite. I'll show you more when we get back outside."

They were now about twenty feet into the tunnel. Looking back they could see the entrance, a circle of light at the end of a tube. Ken stepped over a piece of rock a couple of feet across, then shone his flashlight at the ceiling. "You have to watch the ceiling at all times, especially when you see rock on the floor. You see? It fell out of here. Got to be careful. Okay, we'll go in a bit further. Take my pick and let me have the candle. I don't expect any problem. Air seems to be fresh. But you can never be sure."

They moved forward another ten feet.

"This is longer than I expected. You can see why. The vein is opening out to a good foot and a half. What's this?"

Ken pointed his light at the floor where a pile of rocks lay, then continued with his brief comments between long silences as he moved slowly deeper into the tunnel. "You see that cross fracture coming in from the right there. Where they meet, the vein gets stronger. But the rock gets weaker. Stay there and wait until I'm past. Then I'll tell you when to come on."

Carl muttered a hesitant, "Okay."

Ken moved slowly forward, his light playing from the roof of the tunnel to the floor, which was covered by a pile of rocks fallen from the roof. Once on the other side of the pile, his candle still burning brightly, Ken looked back towards his helper. "Come on now, slowly."

Carl moved forward, using his flashlight as he had seen Ken use his. His beam caught something protruding from the ceiling. Redirecting the light towards it, he said, "What's this? Looks like a rod or something."

Ken glanced up. "Looks like a piece of hand steel. Very interesting. We'll check it out on the way back. Don't touch it!"

Chapter 48 — Tunnel Explored

But Carl had already reached a hand to grab the end of the eighteen-inch protrusion.

Ken yelled "DON'T—" but had no time to complete his warning before he was forced to watch, frozen in incapacity, as he saw and heard a piece of roof give a fraction of a second's warning, crack and drop. He saw Carl knocked down. Then he saw him on the ground, covered from the waist down by a slab of rock. Dropping the candle and holding the only remaining source of light in the tunnel, he moved quickly, seized the edge of the boulder lying on the young man and heaved. It yielded not an inch.

Lester had been sitting on a pile of dried mud and rocks peering into the tunnel. He could see the two lights and sometimes the candle receding down the black tube. Occasionally he could see one of the figures silhouetted by the other's flashlight. There being no room for more than one head in the line of sight, Will was standing on the bank listening to Lester's commentary. The first intimation of disaster was a stifled yell from the tunnel, then a sudden crunching sound and the clatter of small rocks falling on other rocks. There was a slight puff of air from the mouth of the tunnel. Then silence. Lester saw a light moving quickly, then it disappeared for a second or two before reappearing.

Will was first to ask the obvious question. "What was that?"

Before Lester could answer they both heard another shout, but neither could make out what was said. Will had already picked up his flashlight and put on his hard hat by the time Lester replied. "Jeez. Let's get down there."

As they moved rapidly down the tunnel, Lester was briefly aware that they were breaking one of the rules, that there should always be someone on the outside. But there was no time to think more of that. When they were in about ten feet, they could see a light coming towards them. Ken's voice came from only a few feet away. "He's under a rock. Can't move it."

In less than half a minute all three were at the site of the rockfall. The beams of three flashlights converged on the body lying at their feet. Carl was on his back, eyes open, blood on his shirt and face. The three men heard his semi-audible mutter. "I think ... okay. Rock is not right on ... something's holding it."

Will, down on his knees shining his flashlight parallel to Carl's leg, issued instructions, his mouth within an inch of the ground. "It's held up by a rock just to the right of his knee. Could slip off any time. We need a prop ... about eight inches ... wedge shaped."

Three beams of light scanned the pile of rubble.

"How's this?" Ken picked up a rock and handed it to Will, who inserted it under the fallen slap close to Carl's knee.

"Light down his right side!" shouted Will.

Lester obliged.

Will used his right hand to push the rock to Carl's leg. "Another, about two inches, must be wedged."

Carl was moaning quietly.

A few seconds later Lester offered two small rocks.

Ken stepped back to allow Will to take the rocks.

"That's the one!"

Will pushed the rock slowly into place. "Good fit. Supported in three places. With any kind of lever we can get him out."

Lester aimed his beam at a pile of rock beyond Carl's feet. "Get that hand steel! It's just under there."

Ken stepped over and pulled on the steel, which came easily. With three paces, he handed it to Will who inserted it under the large slab and pushed down. The rock he was using as a fulcrum crumbled beneath the lever.

"I know just the one," said Ken as he moved quickly towards the portal.

Still kneeling, Will spoke into the ear of the injured man. "How ya doing, Carl?"

The reply was only partially audible and not intelligible. Will continued talking slowly to Carl.

"We've got this boulder secured so it's not going to fall anymore. Now we are going to lever it up and drag you out. Can you hear me? Carl? Carl?"

The young man did not answer.

Ken, breathing heavily from his dash to the portal and back, handed Will another rock. "I think this will fit."

"Perfect!" whispered Will as he put the new rock in place. After reinserting the steel, he pushed the end down a few inches and saw the slab move. "I can get it up about four inches. See if you can drag him out, Lester. His feet may be in the way. If so, we will prop it up and lever again. Ready?" Will pushed the end of the steel down to the ground and they all watched the slab rise by three or four inches.

"Try now!" called Will. "I can hold this…"

Chapter 48 — Tunnel Explored

Lester grasped Carl by the armpits and pulled gently at first and then harder. He slid Carl's body about six inches and then at a loud moan from the boy stopped abruptly.

"It's got to be higher," gasped Will.

"Hold it!" said Ken as he placed two more rocks under the slab, one near Carl's chest, the other near his right foot. "These will keep it up. Wait while I get another for the lever."

The second lift took the slab further up.

Hearing, "Pull now!" from Will, Lester pulled until Carl's feet were clear of the slab.

Will let the steel rise to lower the slab slowly. He leaned against the wall of the tunnel, still grasping the steel. Ken was on one knee speaking directly into Carl's left ear. Lester was breathing heavily, one hand against the tunnel wall.

Ken spoke first. "We can put together a stretcher in fifteen minutes. Who's going to stay with Carl?"

"I'll do that," said Lester.

In less than a minute, Ken and Will were out of the tunnel. Without a word, each man went to his pack and pulled out an axe, dropped its holster on the ground, and started at a pace between a walk and a run towards the coppice of small trees a hundred yards down the hill. The majority of trees had conical trunks, not the rod-shape they required. After a brief search, each man selected a tree about fifteen feet high and severed the trunk two feet from the ground. It took a few minutes to remove the closely packed limbs to reveal trunks some four inches thick at one end tapering to an inch and a half at the other. They set about trimming the thick ends to handles that could be comfortably grasped.

"Know where their camp is from here?" asked Will as he finished trimming his tree.

Ken pointed southeast. "I can get the direction from the ridge above the tunnel. Bearing's easy. Don't know about trails." He was already planning the next step. "When we've made this, I'll take off. Should be able to get the chopper in quickly. They'll have a first-aid kit at the camp but I don't know it will be any help ... except for the pain killer."

"I'll check him out as soon as we have him in the open," said Will, whose training as a pilot had included several first aid courses.

With four long poles and several short ones between them, Ken and Will headed for the tunnel, Ken with long, loping strides, Will at an irregular jog. At the entrance, Ken pulled from his pack a coil of half-inch nylon rope and a coil of string. Leaving the design of the stretcher to his friend, he lashed the short pieces to the long poles at places Will indicated. The result was four parallel poles six inches apart connected by rope and string across the central six-foot section, two rope-free handles protruding at each end.

They laid the stretcher next to Carl and were surprised to hear him acknowledge their arrival.

"I'm okay. Just my leg. Sorry, Ken."

"Don't fuss about that. Could have happened to anyone. Just lie still. We are going to slide you onto this high-tech stretcher."

They pulled and lifted him sideways. Carl let out a yelp of pain when they tried to move his left leg. They stopped and spent five minutes making a splint for the leg with the short poles before trying again. With Carl in the stretcher, Lester took the rear end, Will the front, and they started slowly towards the portal.

"Okay guys, I'm off when you're out in the open," said Ken.

As soon as the stretcher had been lowered onto the first flat place beside the trench, Will pointed. "That's the ridge above the camp. Camp is about two hundred yards south of the lowest part on a grassy bench overlooking the valley."

"I know the place well," replied Ken taking a bearing with his compass. "Ninety. Or one hundred, to be safe. But I think I could find it even in the dark."

Chapter 49

In Chilko's Camp
June

It was 4:00 pm when Ken emerged from the forest surrounding the camp. He realized he could be unwelcome, seen either as the competition, or worse, as a claim jumper acting on information he should not have had. But he had a job to do and no antagonisms, real or imagined, were going to get in his way. He looked for a radio antennae strung between a pole and a tree. There it was, with a lead down to a large tent in the middle of the camp. He knocked on the wooden door and walked right in. A large man seated on a high stool at the edge of a drafting table turned around, pencil in hand, to face him.

"My name's Ken Wickford. Sorry to intrude, but we have a man hurt up by the tunnel on my claim next to your DBL1 claim. Hit by a falling rock. Could be serious. Can you call a chopper?"

Without a word the man got up, walked to the end of the tent, picked up a microphone.

"Burns Lake base. This is Chilko camp. Do you read?"

He waited while the radio hissed and crackled.

"This is Burns. Go ahead."

"We have a medical emergency near the camp. When can we have a machine?"

"All ours are out and none within a couple of hours of you. Hold, please. I'll see what else is available."

The two men, each postponing the usual greetings and exchange of information, did nothing more than listen.

"Any station. Any station. This is Burns Base. Medical emergency at the Chilko camp, south end of Nisselinka. Need a machine. Ours are out of range."

More static. Then a response.

"This is CG Oscar Lima Golf. I could be there in twenty. Enough fuel for Smithers. Not for Prince George."

"Thanks Oscar Lima. Details in as soon as you need them."

After what seemed a long time, but was perhaps only thirty seconds, the radio indicated another transmission.

"Chilko. Please give directions and state of injured."

The man at the radio passed the mike to his guest.

Ken spoke slowly. "Injured is about two miles on bearing of two-eight-zero northeast of Chilko camp. He is with two others who are not injured. Site will be marked by orange sheets. Do you read?"

"Roger. What injury?"

"Hit by falling rock. Leg may be broken. Internal injuries suspected. He's on a makeshift stretcher. He should be left on it."

"Roger. I'll be there in about fifteen and keep you posted."

Ken handed the mike back to the man who closed the exchange. "Thanks Oscar Lima. Chilko standing by." He put down the mike and held out his hand. "I'm Peter. Peter Scholdar. What did you say your name was?"

"Ken Wickford."

"I know I've heard that name somewhere. But first things first. Not much we can do except keep this thing on. Want a coffee, or anything to eat?"

"Coffee would be great. So would something to eat."

"Someone should be near the radio. You stay. I'll see what I can find for you. Cream, sugar?"

"Both, please."

"Ken Wickford? Are you the guy disputing Chilko's claims? I knew I had heard your name!"

"That's me."

"Look, nothing personal, but I shouldn't leave you alone with our data. Cook shack's next one over. Go see what you can find. If anyone's there, say you're with me."

Ken found no one in the cook shack. He helped himself to some over-brewed coffee and found cream in the fridge. On the side table under strips of paper towels was a display of cakes and tarts. With these and a mug of coffee in hand he went back to the office tent and took the opportunity to thank his host. "I really appreciate your help. Sorry to have got off-side with you guys. Do you work directly for the company?"

Chapter 49 — In Chilko's Camp

"We're on contract. Second time we've worked for them. Seem like an okay bunch. How did you and they get into this relationship? What happened?"

"In July '86 I showed some of my other claims, miles away from here, to Bob Tranich, a geologist working for Sydney Poulter's companies. Back at my place near Smithers I was showing him some samples of a couple of prospects I have. By accident he got to see a bunch of samples from these claims here. He saw them for only half a minute or so—the time I took to realize the error and get down my ladder. He said he would be interested in seeing the property. I told him that I was not ready to market the claims yet. He said he understood how prospectors liked to prepare their claims for sale and he wouldn't ask any more questions until I was ready. I didn't tell him where the samples came from, but they were registered in my name, so a bit of detective work would have pointed in this direction. The next thing I knew, just a few days later, there was a staking crew in town. I figured that my claims were probably the target so I mobilized the next morning, but it was eight stakers and a chopper against two of us. They got most of the land to the east and there's a lot of disputed ground. Bob seemed like a nice guy. I thought I could trust him."

"I know Bob Tranich. In fact, I went to school with him. He is a good man. There's no way he would have acted like that."

"Well," replied Ken, "looked at from my experience, that doesn't seem quite true."

The crackle and hissing from the microphone went silent.

"This is Oscar Lima for Chilko camp."

Peter picked up the mike. "Chilko. Go ahead."

"I'm five minutes away. What's the landing like?"

Peter handed the mike to Ken.

"Not the best. It's a boulder field with a few bare patches. They've probably had time to put a few logs out. Will Herman is there so they know what you need. Over."

"No radio there?"

"None."

"What about the others?"

"They'll be fine. They have food and a tent and will walk out in the morning. So will I."

It was now almost five o'clock. The sun was disappearing behind some thunder clouds and Ken felt the chill as soon as he and Peter stepped outside the tent. Weary-looking young people,

The Nisselinka Claims

mostly men, two women, were returning to camp. Those who passed close to the office tent nodded to Peter and the stranger.

"With this easterly wind we should hear him any moment," said Ken.

There being no sound from a helicopter or the radio, Peter broke the silence. "That story about Bob Tranich disturbs me. Doesn't fit. Have you spoken to him since?"

Ken shook his head. "No. I tried a phone call but he was out of town. Didn't leave a message."

"He's had a long assignment in Manitoba. In fact I think he's still there."

Their conversation was terminated when they both heard the distant aircraft.

"That's him!"

Then the change in pitch. "Circling," said Ken. "Still circling. Doesn't like the landing."

Then the sound ended.

"He's on the ground," muttered Peter listening with his head tilted to catch any sound.

They waited outside anxiously for fifteen minutes, stomping their feet on the ground and slapping their arms against their sides.

Ken was first to hear it. "He's up again. Give him two minutes."

They both heard the radio and re-entered the tent, their footsteps amplified by the plywood floor.

"Chilko, this is Oscar Lima. I have your man on board. He's talking. I'm going straight to Smithers."

After a few seconds of static, the two men in the tent heard the pilot again. "Skeena base. Do you read?"

And the response from the helicopter hangar. "Skeena, go ahead."

"This is Oscar Lima. I'm going to land at Bulkley Valley Hospital. Would you alert them?"

"We've done that. Over."

"Knew you would. Please relay to them: patient is young, male. Damage seems to be to leg, that may be broken. Internal injury possible. Lacerations all over. In and out of consciousness. Tied onto stretcher. Estimate fifty minutes to Smithers."

"Roger, ..."

The rest of the conversation was drowned by the roar of the helicopter passing a hundred feet above the tent.

Chapter 49 — In Chilko's Camp

Peter laughed and threw the mike on the table. "That's his style. Just clears the trees. But he's an excellent pilot. Been with him a couple of times. Your man's in good hands. It's a bit late to join your buddies. Want a bed? You can count on our hospitality. Vancouver can sort out the problems, but please stay out of this tent, unless I'm here. I want to be able to tell them that you had no access to our data."

"Understood. And I'm very grateful."

At supper, Peter introduced Ken to the crew. "This is Ken Wickford, prospector. He's our guest for the night. But, and this is important, our head office and he have a disagreement about some claims around here. Ken has promised me he won't go in the office tent unless I'm there. Please don't let him hear anything about the project. Ken, enjoy your stay! I'm sure everyone will want to hear about the accident."

Chapter 50

First Numbers
July

Although the position did not exist in any formal way, Leonard Marsden was, in most senses, chief geologist to Slip Poulter's stable of companies. He was an officer, usually Vice President Exploration, in most of the companies, and a director of at least half of them. He had been in the office only half an hour that morning when he heard Marion on his intercom: "Chilko camp on the radio. Reception's rather broken up."

"Great! Put them through. Oh, and ... Marion?"

"Yes."

"Just stay on the line if you would—in case there is something I miss."

"Will do."

Len heard static on his line and then a voice he recognized talking to Marion. It was Derek Chanwin, Exploratek's geologist in charge of the drilling.

"Weather has been okay since the rain stopped three days ago. Nights are cold. Mosquitoes not too bad, over."

"Good luck," said Marion. "Everyone here is expecting you to find something. I'll put you through now."

"Len here. Is that you, Derek?"

"Hi Len. Everything under control. Main reason for getting in touch is to say the IP looks very encouraging. Peter and his crew left yesterday. They planned to ship you a preliminary set of results by air express last night. You should get them before midday."

Len got up and stood at the window with the telephone at his ear, its cord stretched and dragging the receiver across his desk. "Sounds good. What's it look like?" He pressed the handset closer to his ear to make out the words behind the static.

Chapter 50 — First Numbers

"Circular feature, twelve hundred metres across with readings of fifteen milliseconds on most lines, surrounded by a partial ring of twenty-five milliseconds. Looks like half of a classic doughnut. Size is all one could hope for at this stage except that it is heading for those disputed claims. There's a resistivity high as a two hundred metre patch in the centre. Can you hear me?"

"Yes, I got most of it. Sounds good. I'll spend some time on the results as soon as they come in. Would you try to reach me at home this evening at 7:00? Then I'll tell you what I think."

"I'll do that," was the reply from the field. "Any geochem results? They must be due."

Len answered, still standing with the stretched telephone cord. "I was talking to the lab yesterday. Expected here any time. One other topic: any more contact with that Wickford guy since the accident?"

"None since I arrived, at least with me. Peter heard that the kid's out of hospital. That's all I know."

"Okay. I'll try to reach you this evening."

"Chilko camp clear."

Transmissions from the camp were not scrambled, although the service had been available for a few years. Slip Poulter was in the business of encouraging people to pay attention to his exploration programs. If those in other bush camps throughout the north chose to follow his progress, that was fine with Slip.

Several people had been listening to the conversation between Leonard Marsden and Derek Chanwin.

Among them were four drillers in a camp north of Prince George.

One was Al Finney, the chief driller. "That must have been the Chilko camp. Sounds like they've got something."

Like other drillers, his helper, Ray, was familiar with the junior market and felt his advice could be useful. "Yes, but they are not drilling yet. It might be just geophysics. Don't go wasting your money on a stock that isn't even drilling."

But Al was not about to be put off. "But it's pretty cheap at twenty cents. And I've made some money on Slip Poulter's horses before. If they decide to drill, it won't hang around this level. I think I will get a few while it's cheap. Not much downside if I get in now. It's been a good month."

"Well good luck. I won't join you this time," was his helper's response.

From the other side of the tent a third man standing by the stove, cigarette in hand, joined in the conversation. "But Ray, do you have any idea how much money Al makes on the pennies?"

"Yeah. I heard he made a killing last year, but then—"

Before hearing the sentence finished, Al joined in. "Okay, I admit. I made a pile, almost a hundred grand. Then I thought I could give up standing by a noisy fucking drill for ten hours a day, so I ploughed the profits back into the market and lost most of it. So here I am. Next time I am going to keep my winnings. You see!"

A few minutes later, Al was standing by the radio, microphone in hand. "Hullo operator, can you get me 683-4848 in Vancouver."

"Standby. I will try now."

Al heard the number ring, and then a woman's voice answered, but not one he recognized.

"May I please speak to Chuck? It's Al Finney on the radiophone."

"Just a moment, I'll get him."

A few seconds later, Chuck Framly was on the line. "Morning, Al. There is only one reason for you to phone from the boonies. What's the hot tip this time?"

"Chuck, I'm sorry to phone you at home."

"Don't worry. All part of the business. In any case, you tell me things I wouldn't otherwise know."

"The stock is Chilko, on the VSE. It's been around twenty for a long time. They've got a camp somewhere in the Nisselinka Range and they seem to be getting good results, so I'd like to pick up ten thousand at twenty-two or better. I reckon there is a good chance they will go to drilling. So that should be good for forty cents."

"Ten thousand at twenty-two cents or better. I'll put that in first thing tomorrow. Anything else?"

"Nothing else just now."

"Okay Al, phone any time. Remember, I'm happy to get your calls at home."

"Night, Chuck. Finlay camp clear."

With that Al hung up the microphone but left the radio on so they could all hear a nearly continuous stream of radio traffic, mostly between mining and forestry camps and their suppliers. Much of it was a boring routine: orders for groceries or spare parts, or arranging charter flights. Some of it had all the attributes

Chapter 50 — First Numbers

of a drama as man and wife or man and mistress revealed the agonies of their relationship to the listening world.

In the office of Poulter Management that morning Marion walked over to check the fax machine. It had been busy using up paper for a couple of minutes. She pulled off eighteen pages of geochemical results and related documents. After making a copy for the file, she walked into Leonard Marsden's office, saw he wasn't there, and then checked Poulter's office. Although the two men were talking, she knew, having glanced at the tables herself, that this interruption would be welcome.

"Gentlemen, I know you were expecting the geochem results. Here they are. I believe you will like them."

Rather than hand them to either man, she walked over to the table by the window and spread them out so all of the pages could be seen at a glance. It took no more than a few seconds for them to judge the results.

Leonard was the first to comment. "Hey! That's what I like to see."

Sydney Poulter straightened his back and raised his hands, fists clenched. "About time too. It's been a dry patch since we last had sheets like these. That's what we pay good money for! And now for your opinion, Mr. Professional!"

"I need to see all this plotted. Meantime, it looks as good as I could have hoped for. Copper is over four hundred for long distances, and with patches at eight and nine hundred. Also, the gold looks promising. It seems to be very clustered. The copper-gold zone has a very sharp boundary. That's odd but nothing to worry about. Let's get it plotted."

"Time to drill?" asked his boss.

"We've got the IP coming this afternoon. If they point to the same place, you will get my recommendation to go ahead."

"Right on! Time to see some action again. Tell me as soon as you have the data."

"Okay," said Len, as he gathered up the loose sheets.

Len left the office and went straight to the drafting room. "Can you get these plotted asap?" he said to Tanya. She was one of those young women who arrive on time, and remain focussed and undistracted until the work is complete.

"Put everything else aside?" asked Tanya with a smile.

"How did you guess?"

"We all knew some results were expected. I could tell as soon as you walked into the room that you were on a mission and what you held in your hand was part of it."

"Wow! Not much chance of keeping secrets from you. I'll have to be careful."

Len spread the sheets of results on the drafting table with a flourish and raised both hands in an open-arm gesture. "Nearly four hundred samples. How long will it take? Just the copper and gold. The others can come later."

Tanya looked thoughtful. "How about noon tomorrow? Might be earlier, but I can't promise."

"That's fine. We expect the IP here this afternoon, so we will also need at least a summary map at the same scale as the geochem."

Tanya answered without looking up from the lab sheets she was thumbing through. "One to a thousand okay? Assuming the grid isn't some odd shape."

"Just fine. Go to it. I'll see you this afternoon, as soon as the IP comes in."

Tanya swivelled her drafting chair towards the table and then swung it back to address her boss as he was leaving. "Okay, Len. You know, this job is much more fun for all of us when one of the companies gets rolling."

Len turned as he was about to go through the open door. "You are absolutely right ... for all of us."

That afternoon a large map tube, some four feet long and four inches in diameter, covered with air express stickers and addressed to Leonard Marsden, arrived at the front desk. It was delivered to Marion, who opened it, searched for administrative papers such as time sheets, invoices, and expense forms. Finding none, she took the roll of maps to Len.

"Ah. Just what we have been waiting for. Have you looked at it?"

Marion shook her head and was about to leave when Leonard signalled that she should stay while he unrolled the maps and sections.

"Wait! Let's have a boo at this together," he said as he ran his finger across the displays known as "pseudo sections." On the maps labelled "Chargeability" and "Resistivity" he spent a longer time, muttering with approval. "This looks really good. Now I've

Chapter 50 — First Numbers

got to see if it fits with the geochem. I'll get a blank grid off Tanya and do my interpretation."

"It's that good?" said Marion.

"Yes. I don't remember anything quite as promising, but..."

Marion laughed. "I understand. There's always a 'but'."

Leonard then moved towards the door, waited for Marion to go ahead of him, and then headed to his boss's office.

Sydney Poulter beckoned him in and said: "So you come with the IP, I'll bet. Goddamn geopissics. They always say they've found something and then they give us a map showing what look like ripe tomatoes laid out on a plate. Then they recommend more work to be done by guess who! So what have they given us this time?"

"Looks pretty good. In fact I would have to say there is something there."

"Do you want to drill it?" asked Sydney.

"Tell you tomorrow afternoon after we've plotted the geochem and this stuff."

"That's a deal. Two o'clock and we'll make a decision. Market's ready for something to happen."

At 1:30 the following afternoon, Leonard was alone in the boardroom laying out eight maps. All covered the same area; all were the same size, with the same type of map frame. Three were labelled "Soil geochemistry," one each for "Copper," "Gold," and "Arsenic." Four were labelled "Induced Polarization," with various sub-labels. Having laid them out, Leonard removed the eighth map, "Interpretation," and rolled it up and put it in the corner. He then went to Poulter's office and, catching him in a rare moment off the phone, said: "I've laid out all the maps in the boardroom, ready for two o'clock. Is it okay if Tanya attends? I'd like her to see how all this data come together."

"Just fine. See you," looking at his watch, "in twenty minutes."

At two o'clock Sydney Poulter walked into the boardroom to find Leonard and Tanya looking at a pad of paper. Leonard, pen in hand, was explaining something. Victor sat opposite looking at a technical magazine.

Sydney Poulter was in a good mood. "After all the pre-selling you've been giving me, this had better be good. I want an excuse to drill."

There was no ambivalence in Len's reply as he pointed to the first of several maps. "Well, Slip, you're going to get my recommendation to drill, and here's why." He proceeded to delve into technical details and was onto the third map without realizing that he was losing his audience.

After a few more minutes of almost patient listening to Len's geophysical minutia, his employer took the opportunity to close off the discussion. "Looks good. So I have your recommendation to start drilling? How many holes?"

Len glanced at his notes. "I think we need a minimum of six. Two on each of these lines. I'll put that in writing by the end of the day. Do you want me to draft the news release?"

"Yes. Do that. Remember, upbeat and not too technical. I want the price up to forty cents as the drill moves in. I may have to do a bit of buying to get it there."

"Okay, Sydney. I'll draft the news release. No promises on the price."

The first, hand-written, draft of the news release prepared by Leonard Marsden read as follows:

DRAFT
19th July 1987

Mr. Sydney Poulter, President of Exploration for Chilko Resources, is pleased to announce that the recently completed exploration programs on its 100% owned Nisselinka claims have defined strong and coincident anomalies in geochemistry (copper and gold) and geophysics (Induced Polarization).

These results, together with information gained from prospecting and geological mapping are compatible with the presence of a copper-gold porphyry system.

Subject to permitting approval for which application has already been made, the company will immediately commence the construction of a 15 km access road in preparation for drilling.

Page in hand, Leonard walked over to Marion's desk. "I think this is about right. Slip will probably want to change it. What do you think?"

Marion read it and thought for a moment before answering. "Looks pretty straight forward to me. He may want more pizzazz, but I don't have any suggestions. Shall I type it up? I'll do it

Chapter 50 — First Numbers

straight away as he has to leave for an appointment the other side of town."

"If you would please."

Sydney read the typescript which Marion had put in front of him. "Too goddamn technical, but okay for now. Use Len's name and title instead of mine. I will get involved later. Did Leonard say anything about progress with the road permits? I'm not about to let the greenies persuade the bureaucrats that some special butterfly wouldn't like our road."

Marion picked up the page. "Not to me, but I'll ask him to let you know this afternoon."

The amended news release was sent to the Vancouver Stock Exchange and the news services that afternoon after the close of the market. It appeared in the press and market letters the following morning. By the end of that day, volume had risen to 120,000 shares from an average of 20,000 shares the previous week, and the price had touched forty cents but had fallen back to thirty-five.

Chapter 51

At the Club
July

In a much-frequented corner of the Engineer's Club on Pender Street there was a low table surrounded by a variable number of easy chairs. In the middle of the table was a wooden post some eighteen inches high and four inches across. The top had been sharpened to a point and the sides squared with an axe. A vestige of bark at the corners, beneath the enclosing varnish, showed that it had been cut from the trunk of a spruce or pine originally about six inches in diameter. Nailed to one side was a claim tag, a thin plate of red aluminium about four inches by three on which embossed lettering "Agent for" and "Name" were followed with hand-inscribed letters. This monument represented a claim post and stood erect to prompt anyone sitting around the table to remember the starting point for most of the wealth of their industry.

On this particular day the majority of those around the table were geologists and engineers, all involved in the mining and exploration industry. Many knew one another. One was a guest. Most had just finished ordering their drinks and their lunches when someone directed a question at a man whose grey-white hair and confident expression suggested many years in the business.

"What's new, Bob? You're always the first to know."

Accepting the last statement as usually correct, everyone listened to Bob's answer.

"Nothing dramatic, but I suppose everyone saw Slip let a horse out of his stable."

"You mean Chilko?" said Randal, a geologist employed by a large mining company.

"That's it. Could be interesting. The stock went up on just the announcement of drilling."

Chapter 51 — At the Club

"And it should go up more as drilling time approaches."

"Yeah, especially if he helps it up a bit."

After the chuckles had died down, someone asked the obvious question. "Has anyone seen the data?"

Some of those present shook their heads and someone summarized the consensus:

"I expect it's pretty genuine. Len Marsden would not have put his name to that news release if he didn't believe it."

"I did hear from the usually reliable that the geochem numbers were really impressive. As for the IP, it was done by IPEM so we can count on that part of it being genuine."

"I suppose the brokers will get a chance to go through the data very soon. They always get a head start on the rest of us," said one man to approving murmurs around the table.

Randal recognized an opportunity to bring his guest into the conversation. "Sorry Steven, unless you follow mining—and I don't suppose you do from Ottawa—this must all be a bit cryptic to you."

"Yes, I'm just a confused CA. What is this all about? I take it you are talking about a penny stock without a bean of an asset, just spending capital raised from the unsuspecting public on a long-shot bet."

"Objection!" said someone from the other side of the table. "You are partially right but mostly wrong. This—I mean the Chilko business—is how much of the wealth of this province starts. And some of it will go to people who might be your clients if you worked in this province."

"Okay, okay. Lead me through it slowly," said Steven. "There is a company called Chilko. It has a stock price of thirty-something cents. Is that what I heard? How many shares?"

"About twenty million."

"So the trading public think it's worth about seven million dollars. What did you say it has for assets?"

Each man around the table was enjoying the conversation in his own way. Some reacted to Steven's professed innocence, which seemed real but could be feigned, with sighs of exasperation, others with pleasure at the anticipation of a verbal scrap. All waited for a response from Bob, who could be counted on to be a good champion for the industry.

Bob started with the basics. "Its asset, probably the only one it has, is the mineral property they are about to drill."

The Nisselinka Claims

"Never been drilled before?" asked Steven.

Randal became guardian of the facts, such as they were. "In this particular case, I believe that is true."

"So there is no mineral deposit there?"

"That's right. And I think I know what you are going to say next," said Bob with a laugh.

"You've probably guessed," replied Steven, who was obviously enjoying himself. "I hope you don't mind me going on. I'm just an accountant who doesn't understand your business."

By this time a couple of others were standing outside the ring of chairs.

"Keep at it!" one of them joined in. "Knock us down if you can. This is important."

With a friendly glance at the last speaker, Steven continued to press his case. "So, correct me if I'm wrong. This Chilko company has no real asset? No revenue? No history? Some liabilities, I suppose. And you learned gentlemen say it's worth over a million bucks!"

"The answer is..." said Bob, pausing for effect, "that it has an acceptable chance of drilling into something worth a huge amount of money. One of those orebodies, a really good one, can be worth as much as half a billion. None of us, I believe, has seen the data or been to the property. Right?" He looked around the table. "If it's a reasonable bet, with all the right geologic signs, it probably has a chance of something like one in fifty or one in a hundred of striking it rich. Let's give it one in a hundred. On a probabilistic basis, we should value it at five million."

"So it's a steal at the current price!" said Randal.

Supportive mirth all round.

Conversation paused for the waiter, who had been hovering and looking for an opportunity to identify who had ordered the shrimp croissants.

"All right," said Steven. "I understand, or begin to understand, what happens if there is an orebody there. The price could go to several dollars, which would reflect the value of the asset just found." His summary was greeted with murmurs of assent, tinged with approval for an unbeliever about to be converted. "Now, supposing there is nothing there?" he said. "I suppose the shares go down instead of up and you've lost your investment or bet, or whatever you want to call it?"

Chapter 51 — At the Club

Unfazed, Bob supplied the answer. "That's right. The shares will go back to ten or twenty cents and the owners, if they continue to hold them, will hope that the management of the company finds another property to drill. You see, in this case there are only twenty million shares out. So there is plenty of opportunity to raise more money and roll the dice again. But once a company has issued too many shares, it has a hard time raising money and will probably be forced to roll back its shares four or five to one. You don't want to get caught in one of those."

"Hey, Bob! You call yourself an engineer? You should be in sales!" said Randal.

This was Steven's opportunity to bow out. "Yes, I'm impressed. You've just taught me something I didn't know and still don't quite understand. I think I will stick to the big miners like Inco and Falconbridge, but I will never look on the penny mining stocks in quite the same way."

"And be sure to follow Chilko!" said Randal.

Steven's smile and wave of both hands in mock surrender signalled closure of the Chilko topic. The conversation then turned to the policies of the provincial government, and the latest trade dispute with the U.S. and the way the federal government was handling it, a topic with which Steven was very familiar.

A week later, most of those who had participated in the discussion about Chilko noticed a news release announcing that Exploratek Mining Services had been engaged by Chilko to conduct a drill program on its property in the Nisselinka Range.

Chapter 52

First Drill Results
Early August

It had been a week since reports from the field had included comments on the first drill hole. Derek Chanwin, Exploratek's geologist in charge of the drilling, had reported over the radio (for this occasion, scrambled) that the first hole was mineral-bearing from a depth of twenty-two feet, where it hit bedrock under the overburden, to three hundred and fifteen feet where it had been stopped. He had been reluctant to estimate grade because the sulphide was so fine and because there was a lot of pyrite, that made it hard to see the mineral with the copper. Everyone in the business recognized the presence of such a lengthy intersection of sulphide, whatever its metal content, as an encouraging start to the drill program. Poulter had immediately instructed that the core be split with all possible haste and shipped to Vancouver for assay. He had also made it clear that any extra expense incurred to accelerate the process would be acceptable.

As in any exploration office, the prospect of first drill results on a new property charged everyone with excitement and anticipation to a level similar to that of fans in a stadium watching their favourite team. Good drill results, like a goal in hockey or soccer, contribute to a surge of adrenaline, and, if research on soccer fans is to be believed, of testosterone too. Conversely, disappointing drill results lead to a feeling of disappointment, deflation and letdown. On that day in early August everyone in the office of Poulter Management without exception was aware, not only that results from Hole 1 could arrive at any moment, but also that they were likely to be good. What was more, the interest of all those in the office went beyond supporting the home team. Everyone had a financial stake in the results. Most had benefited from options

Chapter 52 — First Drill Results

issued to employees. Many had augmented their holdings with purchases on the open market.

Burrard Geochemical, to whom the core samples had been sent, had committed to providing the first batch of results covering the top half of the hole before the close of the day's business. The results would almost certainly be delivered by fax, with Marion being the first to become aware of their arrival. Although Poulter had little interest in concealing good results, in the interests of being able to report reasonable security procedures to the regulators, he put the fax room off limits to all but her. One outcome of this slight change to procedures was that more people than usual found occasion to wander by Marion's desk and ask how things were going.

Soon after 4:00 pm the results arrived: several pages of numbers reporting metal grades for the first part of the drill hole. A glance down the numbers made Marion smile. Knowing that the sheets, once handed over, would not come her way again, she made a copy, put it in her desk and walked, papers in hand, towards Leonard Marsden's office. Her progress was well observed.

Leonard had been at his desk for several minutes trying in vain to concentrate on anything but the anticipated results. He saw Marion enter. He saw the papers in her hand. He knew the results were good from a glance at her face, but he still had to ask the question. "Am I going to enjoy these?"

"I am sure you will," was her assured reply.

In response to expectations of good grades, the samples had been done by assay rather than geochemical processes. The results were in three columns of figures headed Copper % Gold oz/ton, and Molybdenum %.

After a quick glance, Len ignored the molybdenum column and ran a finger down the other two. "Good stuff! Looks like the copper is going to average something like zero-point-eight, and the gold at zero-point-zero-two ounces could be useful. Slip seen it yet?"

"Not yet. I've got his copy here. Are you going to take it in?"

"Yes. Want to come?"

"Thank you, but I think I'll go back to my desk."

Len sat down, took out his calculator, entered the numbers and made a few notes. Then he went to see his boss, who looked up to see his geologist in the best of moods.

"So the geological team scores again?" said Sydney Poulter. "Great. Let's see." After thirty seconds spent scanning the results, he continued. "Hard to sit on this news. We don't want to release just half a hole. When are the rest due?"

"Tomorrow."

Both men knew that Marion would have told no one and shown the numbers to no one. They also knew that by now everyone else in the office would be aware, without having seen any data, that the results were good.

Sydney Poulter tipped his chair back and started thinking aloud. "This will catch attention. But we can't let it trickle out. I suggest we phone the lab and say we want checks run on the rejects of all the samples. That way we can stall it to the weekend and put it out on Monday when everyone will be paying attention."

"Then I think you should assemble everyone, tell them what's happening and make sure no one is going to do anything that might embarrass us."

A few minutes later everyone was in the boardroom waiting for confirmation and possibly details of what they already knew.

Sydney Poulter addressed the assembled company. "The Chilko results from the first half of the first hole are just what we wanted. I am not going to give you the numbers because we are asking the lab to run check samples on all of them. By tomorrow afternoon, we should have the rest of the hole. I am hoping we can get checks on all the samples and can have the results by Friday and release them on Monday. Everyone in this room knows more than the public and it's going to look bad if buying over the next couple of days is traced to someone in this room. Understand? If one of you gets caught and it leads to this office, I'll feed you to the regulators for dismemberment limb by limb. As you know, I want you all to get rich with your Chilko stock. But don't beat the gun. Questions?"

Victor raised his hand just a few inches above the table. "Of course, any leak could come from somewhere else, drillers or lab."

Poulter, looking at first if he was about to respond, said nothing, but looked at Victor for what seemed a long time. He replied with more than a hint of frustration. "Yes. That happens. But in this case even the geos on site said they couldn't estimate grade. And the lab, they run a tight ship. They have to. Len, anything to add?"

"Not now."

Chapter 52 — First Drill Results

The next day Chilko opened at fifty-two cents on the VSE, up eight cents on the previous close. By the end of the day it had gained a further ten cents to reach sixty-one. At 250,000 shares, volume was over four times that of the previous day. On Friday it dropped back to fifty-five cents on reduced volume. At 4:00 pm on Friday the laboratory delivered the initial and the check results on the entire drill hole. The two sets of results matched well. The news release on Monday, sent to the exchange and news wires late on Sunday, reported the average values for copper (0.69%) and gold (0.02 ounces per ton) for the two hundred and ninety-five feet from bedrock surface to the end of the hole. Reactions in the brokers' news letters on Monday morning ranged from cautious fence-sitting to whole-hearted endorsement. With little stock offered, the price reached eighty-five cents on relatively low volume and closed at eighty cents.

On Tuesday morning the atmosphere in the offices of Poulter Management and related companies was again charged with expectant optimism. Everyone knew the price of yesterday's close, and the volume. During the morning Marion had so many requests for the latest price that she wrote the bid, ask, and time of day on a pad of paper for all who passed her desk to see. This she updated every half hour. By the end of the day the price had touched eighty-nine cents and then fallen back to close at seventy-eight. Then word came from the field that the drill had broken down.

For an experienced promoter, bad news could be convenient.

"Drill broken? For how long?" was Poulter's first question.

Len, having talked to the drill company as soon as he heard the news, knew the answers. "Sounds quite serious. Something wrong with the chuck. They may have to get a new one. Better give it three days."

Poulter thumped the table with enthusiasm. "Great! We'll tell them the drill is down. People like to know what is happening. We like to keep everyone informed and tell them what we are doing. Marion, can you get out the first draft?"

On Wednesday morning the opening sale was at seventy-five cents and then the results of Hole 2 arrived. Marion followed the same procedure—made a copy, filed it, and walked into Leonard Marsden's office. She had not been in the office more than a minute before Tanya passed by the open door, and soon the buzz went round the office that Hole 2 was in.

Ten minutes later, Len, having studied the numbers and done his calculations, made his trek to Slip's office. Those watching concluded from the confident swagger in his stride that the numbers were good. If there had been a flicker of doubt, it was dispelled when Len, followed by his boss, went to the drafting office.

Len greeted the two occupants. "We've just got Hole 2. Now we have to figure out what it all means."

"You mean you are not going to tell us?" said Tanya.

Poulter motioned to Len that he should provide the answer.

"Just as soon as I can. You know how it is. Some regulator might ask us what precautions we took to keep the results under wraps before we put out the release. But be patient. We may need your help pretty soon."

"Standing by," said Tanya.

"So's her broker," quipped Jenny, Tanya's part-time assistant.

Poulter and Len both laughed and left for the boardroom, stopping by Victor's office to ask him to join them. With the boardroom door closed, Leonard spread out his maps on the table and pointed at one. "You see, Hole 2 tests this part of the IP. I expected it to have less sulphide and metal than the first one, but I was wrong."

Predictably, Sydney Poulter was in the best of moods. "Len, my friend, so long as you get results like these I'll pay you to be wrong all the time. Keep it up. Now tell me, these grades, are they rocket fuel?"

Len replied slowly. "So far, yes. Better than Similkameen, better than Afton. We don't have any metallurgy, of course, but I expect the recoverable value to be better even than Gibralter and Valley. It could still fool us. But you could mine these grades if there is enough of it, and the geophysics suggests there could be."

"Now, what would you expect here?" asked Sydney, pointing to an area about six hundred feet from the drill holes.

Pointing with a scale, Len traced the boundary between two shades of red on the geophysical map. "I would hope for something similar. You see it's the same chargeability level as they got where the holes were drilled. Nature might give us the same amount of sulphide and cut down on the gold or the copper. We'll never know until we drill it."

"How about here?" asked Sydney, indicating a prominent red patch near the eastern edge of the map sheet about a kilometre from where he had pointed previously.

Chapter 52 — First Drill Results

"Zip! Nothing. We expect nothing there except pyrite. In fact, I'm pretty certain on that one because we found a very small exposure in the bottom of a gully."

"Well then, we will put the next two holes just there," said Poulter emphatically.

Victor nodded and expressed his approval. "Sydney, I see what you're doing. That's cool!"

Len's discomfort was apparent. "Slip—Mr. Poulter— I think I know why you want to do that. I don't like it."

"It's got to be done."

"If you insist, then the news release has to say that these holes are designed to probe the limits to the system."

Sydney smiled and banged the table with an open hand. "That's a deal! How long to get the drill there?"

"Two days for the move. Three for the drilling. Something like that."

Victor was now showing interest in the details. "And the results about ten days after that, so two weeks in all?"

"That's about right."

"And you really don't expect any grades?" Victor looked directly at Len.

"That's correct ... I could be wrong."

Sydney put a hand on Victor's shoulder. "Victor, you're thinking along the right lines. The share price will probably drop. If it does, I don't want any buying from you. I may do that myself, but I don't want any competition."

"Understood. I won't be buying."

"That's good. This one is working well and we all understand each other. Thank you gentlemen."

By the time Victor got home, it was too late to phone his broker in the east, but he made a point of doing so early the next morning.

Chapter 53

Lunchtime Discussion
August

"Did you see the results of Slip's latest?" said Dean Renscott to his former colleague, Jim Tildey, after they had each ordered a lunchtime beer and sandwich in a downtown Vancouver pub.

The two men had worked together in an exploration camp in the Northwest Territories for three successive summers after graduating in 1958 from the University of British Columbia. They had learned to trust each other during numerous shared situations, many of which could have become dangerous. On one occasion they had both been passengers in a G4 helicopter when it landed on a patch of low shrubs, grass and rock, and the tail rotor nicked a branch of scrub willow. The spin of the machine led to one of the rotors hitting a rock and the blades beating themselves into the ground. Goaded by the smell of gasoline, they'd moved away from the machine as fast as carrying the injured pilot would allow. Dean had just said, "Here's ok" when they were knocked down by the explosion. Now, twenty-five years later, both were middle-aged. Dean was exploration manager for Purcell Mining and Jim was an independent consulting geologist specializing in porphyry deposits.

"The question," said Jim, "is whether we believe the numbers."

"And why might you not?" replied Dean.

"Because there isn't a porphyry copper in B.C. with anything like that grade. What about you? Can you take it at face value?"

Dean replied slowly. "I have to say I think it could be real, because once every couple of years we get a discovery that breaks the pattern. But I'm not about to bet any serious money on it. I also have to say I read the news release in a hurry and haven't followed the story in detail. I can't recall another first hole quite as good as that, so I'm inclined to be suspicious. It starts at bedrock

Chapter 53 — Lunchtime Discussion

under nine metres of till and continues to the end of the hole at eighty-four metres. Could you spot a hole at Valley Copper or anywhere else in B.C. and do as well as that?"

Dean respected Jim's knowledge of porphyry copper deposits. He knew Jim was familiar with all the producers in B.C., as well as many in the Southwest U.S. and some in Chile. He waited for his friend's measured response. "Perhaps, but certainly not at random. And it would be unrepresentative in any zone in any porphyry that I know in B.C. It's about twice the sort of grade you might expect. If it turns out to be representative, we'll have a new class of porphyry, and we'll see another hundred million spent on exploration next year."

"Which is why I'm not inclined to be a believer at this stage."

"So you are saying it could be salted?" asked Jim.

"No, that's unlikely. At least he's using core. I'm not a fan of R.C. holes, which seem to be common now. Handfuls of something that looks like one of those health food cereals would be easy to salt."

"But the numbers are pretty steady all the way down. If anything, they improve with depth."

"Slip may be a scoundrel, but he's a brilliant promoter. He could sell sand to the Arabs, and he can be as mean as a pit bull, but..."

"But?"

"But Sydney L. Poulter hires good technical people and his entire business—his entire stable of juniors—would go down the tube if he pulled a salting job."

Jim raised a single eyebrow. "Could an outsider do it?"

"Unlikely. That would be sophistication we haven't yet seen."

"I don't like the sound of that," said Jim. "There is much to be said for keeping the scoundrels front and centre, where we can see them. To be practical for a moment, are you enough of a believer to put Purcell into chasing the property?"

"Almost regardless of what I think, I have to take steps in that direction. Within a couple of hours of the news release I had a call from the VP in Toronto wanting to know what we were doing about it. So yes, I've pored over the mag maps, selected a few features that had a bit of promise. I've even let a staking contract. We'll ask Slip for information, tell him we would like to look at the property, and along with everyone else in town, try and acquire some moose pasture next door."

Jim reached for his drink before responding. "The old proximity game. Looks good on the maps. It keeps both the bosses and the shareholders happy, so everyone does it. Can you think of an occasion when participating in one of those staking rushes paid off?"

"Not off hand. But of course, a lot of people and companies who stake nearby do very well when they sell for a mixture of cash and shares."

Jim changed the direction again. "An interesting thing about this one is that it's right next to a showing discovered at the beginning of the century. Someone was chasing a high-grade vein. They put in a tunnel. Imagine what it took to get to a place like that."

Dean responded, "And they had to haul in all their equipment. Probably used a train of mules or packhorses. Some of those expeditions just lived off the land. I'm glad I wasn't there. Whoever dug that tunnel, if they were well financed, might have been resupplied in mid-summer, or even once a month. I haven't read the reports. I don't suppose they produced anything?"

"Just samples for assay. About three percent, if I remember correctly."

"Think of life almost a century ago. If we could tell them, whoever they were, that people would one day mine hundreds of millions of tons of just half a percent, they would laugh at the idea."

"And, if you talked about an 'open pit,' they would think you meant a glory hole fifty feet across."

"Yeah. Imagine taking one of those old timers to a modern mine, say the Highland Valley, a mile wide and half that for depth, mining incomprehensibly big tonnages."

"And not a horse in sight!" added Jim with a smile.

"And that was before the war, wasn't it?"

"Yes, off they went to the slaughter. And," Dean said, "I suppose we would have done the same."

Jim made a gesture of resignation. "Like them we wouldn't have known what we were getting ourselves into. We would have expected it to last no more than a few months. Then we could come back to this promised land and carried on where we had left off. Or so we would have thought. Some 55,000 signed up. Out of a population of 400,000 this must have been just about every male of military age in the province. If they hadn't had to abandon their orchards, mines, and farms, would this place be different now?"

"Probably not. Others came to fill the gaps."

Chapter 53 — *Lunchtime Discussion*

"But places like Walachin just disappeared. Would it be a thriving community now? Would water be flowing in that flume on the north side of Kamloops road?" asked Dean.

"Maybe, but they wouldn't have been able to keep the high-grade copper mines open with the collapse of prices at the end of the war. And then the depression came, so the farms and orchards might not have fared much better."

"So, no matter what, whoever dug that tunnel eighty years ago would have had to wait a long time to see a mine on site."

"That's if ... if this thing of Slip's is an orebody," said Jim.

On the other side of the restaurant, two men and a woman were talking about the same event.

"I missed Slip's last one, and I ain't going to do so again. So I bought a bunch at seventy cents. Now I'm getting cold feet. People seem to be saying it's too good to be true or might not be real or something. So I'm counting on you folks, who know about these things, to tell me what's going on."

The speaker, known to his companions as Brad, was a middle-aged man of substantial girth, wearing a grey suit and a colourful, slightly risqué tie. His companions, a man and women, both young, were dressed in ordinary office attire.

The woman spoke first. "The trouble with this penny stock business is that, unless you are an insider, you never really know."

The older man continued: "And, as you know, Brenda, the insiders don't talk to the outsiders."

"Hold it! Neither of you are being fair," said the young man assertively. "There are all sorts of rules and regulations in place to level the field."

"Like?"

"Like the rule preventing the insiders from buying or selling on information the public doesn't have. Like the insider trading reports. And then there are actions the stock exchange will take to force a company to reveal information. You know, if your stock starts doing something unusual. At any jump in price or volume, for instance, they will phone you up and ask you to make a news release to explain it."

Brad was in no mood to concede to the defence. "Okay, Dick, let's take those one at a time. The insider reports. They have to be filed within how many weeks of the trade? By the time they have been released to the public, the information is old. By that time it's absolutely useless."

"Not useless! An insider knows that if he buys or sells at a time when the key information is not available to the public, he can be nailed."

"Okay in theory, but all he has to do is buy through other accounts, or through friends and relations. Sometimes he will get caught, but most times he doesn't."

Brenda took an opportunity to soften the tone. "All right. Let's accept that all those good citizens are doing their thing as regulators with the Vancouver exchange and with the SOB's office. They keep the problem to manageable proportions. Every now and again they let a big one get away and everyone says the system's not working. The way I see it, there are hundreds of little companies beavering away trying to find a mine without scamming the public."

The young man almost shouted. "That's right! They channel lots of funds that people choose to invest into exploration in all sorts of crazy places. The result is that once or twice every two or three years one of them finds a biggie. Then some people get rich, which keeps the system going. New wealth is created and several hundred new jobs. Not a bad system. If the price is the occasional scam, perhaps that's not too much to pay. Be fair! There isn't a scam-free industry in the world. Even churches and charities get themselves into trouble."

"Hey, You had better sign on with a PR department. Then you could say things that those guys can't. So what about Chilko? Real or scam?"

"It has to be real. Slip Poulter has too much to lose, is too much part of the establishment. He has too much of a reputation to blow it all on false assays."

"That much we can accept," said the young woman. "And that leads us to Mother Nature. Could she be fooling us? One super hole and the next will all be duds."

"Could be," said the young man. "It wouldn't be the first time. All you need is a fault and the good stuff is all gone. The hole next door is barren. Or you get some other intrusive and you've lost the orebody again. But so far the geological description, as far as the release goes, makes it look like the real thing."

As the end of the conversation came closer, Brad's response expressed a restrained pessimism. "So, let's say I hang in with my

Chapter 53 — Lunchtime Discussion

purchase. The stock is at sixty. There are only twenty million out. That means the market thinks it's worth twelve million. And the only thing we know for sure is that twelve million is dead wrong. It will either become a couple of hundred thousand for a shell company, or a couple of hundred million for a big orebody. I guess I'll hold."

"Sell half at a buck-forty."

"Probably should. But if it gets that far I'll smell treasure and hold on."

Brenda summarized. "Ride it up and ride it down! The yo-yo man."

They all laughed.

Chapter 54

Broker Goes Fishing
August

Ben Cromer, a broker with Mantrell Securities, specialized in the junior mining market. He had moved to Vancouver in the 1960s, after the Toronto exchange had made early-stage mining finance less than welcome. A long-term client was calling on his direct line.

"Ben Cromer here."

"Morning, Ben. It's Toby."

"Good morning, Toby. What can I tell you about this morning? Or do you have information for me?"

"A bit of both, Ben. As you know, I've been watching Chilko for some time."

"Yeah, drilling more, I understand."

Ben Cromer knew that this client took pleasure in ferreting out good stories and was often well-informed. He listened carefully and, as expected, Toby had something useful to say and a request for something in return.

"Well, I think they must be on the third or fourth. No assays, of course, but I have an idea it looks pretty good. I was wondering if you had heard anything."

"Nope. But I could check. Your sources pretty good?" asked Ben, his interest piqued.

"Reliable, but not close, so they were asking me for confirmation."

"I'll see what I can do. Give me a couple of hours. If it looks good, do you want me to get any for you?"

"Yes. I'd prefer to talk about it after you've dug a bit. But if you can't get hold of me and if you think it might break out, get me 50,000."

"Okay, Toby. Talk to you later."

Ben turned his chair away from the window and his view of the mountains, flipped through a list of phone numbers and dialled. "Hullo Marion, it's Ben Cromer here for Sydney."

Chapter 54 — Broker Goes Fishing

"He's been on the phone all morning, but I'm sure he has time for you, Mr. Cromer. I'll put you through."

"Hey, Slip, it's Ben here. I have to ask. Why's Chilko moving? Anyone would think you've done it again, you old—" A moment's pause, while the speaker searched his mind for just the right term of friendly opprobrium, gave Slip the opportunity to interrupt.

"What's up, Ben? It's not like you to be limping along at the back of the pack like this. You're usually out in front! Everybody else has already phoned."

"That's harsh, Slip. You know I don't like to trouble you unless it's really important. Anyhow, old dogs drop back and stay on track. I can't follow every mad hare like I used to."

Sydney Poulter knew Ben Cromer well enough to introduce a touch of levity into a serious conversation. "Well, Ben, I'm glad you're following this one. As to your question, all I can say is that we are drilling and there are no results yet. In any case, would you really expect me to give you information I haven't released?"

"No way," replied the broker without disguising the mirth in his voice. "You wouldn't do a thing like that, and as you know, I wouldn't want any inside information. Wouldn't know what to do with it if I had it, would I? No way you would tell me grade and width or anything like that. I just wanted to know if you got some encouragement."

"Grades? No assays yet. But, as you know, Ben, I'm an optimistic kind of person and just now I'm feeling very encouraged, but that's all I can tell you. I can't say anything about the width. Might be a couple of feet for all you know," replied the promoter.

"So that's all, Slip? Keeping me in the dark, as usual. Oh well. Got to go now. I'll see it in the next news release. Good luck with the next stage." Ben Cromer put down the phone and spoke into his intercom. "Jen, can you get me Ms. Charbonneau in Prince George? I can't remember her first name."

A few minutes later he heard the intercom come alive. "Mrs. Charbonneau on the line. Her name is Marcia."

"Is that Marcia? I'm Ben Cromer with Mantrell Securities. I don't expect you remember me. We met once when Jean and you were in town."

"I remember. I'm afraid I can't get Jean for you. He's at a drill site."

"Yes, I know. I just wondered if you had heard anything from him."

"Well, he phoned last night. He said it was going well. They seem to be getting mineral all the way. He asked me if we should buy some shares. I said it was best to wait until the assays were out. Otherwise we would risk losing it all like we did last time. Don't you think that was right?"

"Absolutely. You're a wise lady, Marcia. Did he say they ended in mineralization?"

"He didn't tell me that. He just said the water was black with sulphides all the way to the bottom of the hole. I'll tell him you called. Shall I get him to phone you?"

"Great idea. I'll give you the number." Ben read out his phone number, thanked his unwitting informant, hung up, and then caught Allie's eye as she was going down the corridor in front of his office.

"Allie. Let's get 50,000 shares in Chilko for Toby's cash account. Then when we've done that, another fifty for me. What's the offer?"

"Wait - a - moment. I'll have it in a minute," responded Allie as she turned back towards her office. A minute after getting to her desk she picked up the intercom to her boss. "Here we are. There's 20,000 at fifty-five. If we take all the offers up to sixty-five, we could get 40,000. After that it is going to get expensive. Volume has picked up a lot."

"Take the twenty and wait for an hour or so. We may go higher later."

Ben watched it closely for the rest of the day, but it didn't go below sixty and Toby didn't buy any more.

The next morning when Ben Cromer watched the market open he was surprised to see a large sell order. He saw it get filled, but no sooner had that happened than it was replaced with another offer of equal size.

By the end of the following day the volume of trading in Chilko shares had exceeded any day since the shares had been rolled back. And the price was much lower. Sydney J. Poulter had phoned most of the brokers he knew to ask if they could tell him who was selling. No one provided satisfactory answers to his questions. In fact, most of the brokers appeared to be genuinely surprised.

Chapter 55

Holes 3 & 4
Early September

Derek Chanwin was enjoying his twenty-minute walk from the camp to the drill site. Drill programs were what he liked best and Exploratek had been keeping him busy since he had joined a year ago. This one was exciting. And puzzling. The first two holes of the Chilko project had produced results which could be described as spectacular. But then the office had ordered two holes on the other side of the property, in the pyrite halo of all places! He had told them that where they wanted to drill was exposed by outcrop, had been sampled, and contained nothing of importance. But despite this, they had insisted on an expensive and disruptive move of almost two kilometres to a place where no geologist in his right mind would want to drill. And he had told them there was nothing there!

But Derek had been in the industry long enough to conclude that perhaps that was the point of it all. It was bad enough working for majors. He had had his fill of their politics, changes of direction, and periodic lay-offs. Now he was seeing how the juniors worked. Plenty of enthusiasm, lots of action, but this was the first time he had seen them knowingly drilling dud holes. Perhaps the stock price was getting too high or the principals didn't have enough. What the hell! He would concentrate on the rocks. Perhaps he could get a paper out of this one: "A New Type of Alkaline Porphyry" or something like that.

After leaving the camp, he descended a couple of hundred feet as the light timber of the subalpine zone gave way to a well-wooded valley. The trail led across a meadow of hummocky grass and swamp where a couple of very muddy patches had been bridged with the trunks of pine trees cut longitudinally with a chain saw. As the scent of pine resin displaced the other smells of the forest, his peripheral vision identified a slight movement and drew his attention to a kestrel wheeling above the meadow. Then, although it had happened many times before, a spruce hen managed to startle him with its noisy take off. After a few minutes on the woodland trail, he was climbing again. He knew he was getting close but, as he heard nothing, he was beginning to fuss that the drill might be down. Then he heard it. The sound of the diesel engine had been muffled by a dense patch of trees and the slight breeze.

The drill had been moved two days earlier. Disassembling the machine after completion of the second hole and slinging it in pieces to the new location had taken all of a ten-hour day shift. It had taken most of the following morning to put the machine together and set it up to drill the next hole.

Now, after two days of wasted drilling time, Derek was looking at the re-assembled machine in action. The drill itself was surrounded by sheets of blue-painted plywood as a partial shield from wind and rain. He waited at the entrance of the drill shack, preferring to be acknowledged before walking in. No point in surprising anyone. Drills were reasonably safe, but with heavy wheels turning fast, and a noise that made conversation difficult, accidents, if they happened, could be serious. Pierre, the driller, saw him, took a glance at the spinning rods, and moved to the entrance with a cheerful grin, and shouted above the noise: "Eighty feet." He pointed over Derek's shoulder towards a makeshift table sheltered by a tarp supported on a series of poles tied to trees.

Derek nodded. He could see Brendon, a third-year geology student, stooped over the core boxes. "Back soon," he yelled to the driller, and walked over to see the core.

One glance was sufficient to confirm his expectations and his frustration. The pyrite was not only present, it was there in abundance. He took out a hand-lens and picked up one piece of core, and then another and another in search of any sign of a mineral which would carry copper. Zilch for copper, he thought. There might be some gold, but he didn't expect it.

By now Pierre had emerged from the drill shack and was waiting for Derek's comments.

"No copper?"

Derek shook his head.

Pierre countered with upturned thumbs. "I didn't think so, but it's easy drilling and good recovery."

Chapter 55 — Holes 3 & 4

"Yeah, but good recovery doesn't pay," said Derek. Then after a pause: "But maybe it does sometimes. I think this must be what they want. Well, Pierre, we should follow instructions. How long will it take you to complete two holes, each to two-fifty feet?"

"Same set up?"

"Yes. With this one minus sixty to the south, the other should be sixty degrees to the north."

"Okay. We'll be ready in four days," replied Pierre.

Derek Chanwin's discomfort with the location of the second pair of holes was accentuated by instructions from the office that the core was to be split and shipped with all possible speed. But he dutifully followed instructions and sent a batch containing all samples from the two outlying drill holes before the drill was moved back to the original location. Similar instructions for immediate processing having gone to the laboratory, the results were ready only ten days after the holes had been completed.

That afternoon, Leonard Marsden was looking through the assay report in the drafting room when he found Victor beside him, evidently expecting to be invited to share the information. He pointed to the laboratory reports. "Nothing here and nothing surprising."

Victor picked up the sheets of paper and leafed through them. "Yeah. Isn't that what you told Slip we would get?"

Len displayed his continuing discomfort with the selection of these drill sites by turning away from the table and pacing around it. "Yes, of course, what we should have done is just carry on with the real target. This was a waste of time and it's nothing we need to announce."

Victor made no attempt to conceal his irritation. "How would that help? The idea is to get the price down so the insiders are properly rewarded for a success when it happens."

The positions of the two men—standing on opposite sides of the table—signalled their opposing opinions. The geologist turned to look at his colleague. "I know that was the plan and I never liked it."

Victor's response was more a challenge than a question. "How so?"

"It's conning the public into selling their shares."

Still facing Leonard directly across the table, Victor was not about to agree. "It's Slip's company. If he needs more shares, that's

The Nisselinka Claims

fine by me. You know, you could benefit too. Just buy some when they're down."

"I wouldn't do that," and then, after a pause, "and nor should you."

His expression rich with contempt, Victor spat back: "You'll never get rich with an attitude like that."

Casting aside his habitual calm, Leonard raised his voice to reply. "What gutter have you crawled out of? Have you no principles?"

Victor, now half way to the door, fired his parting shot. "Of course I do! First principle: make money. Second principle: don't let any prick get in the way."

He slammed the door as he left.

Len, alone in the room, realized he was in no mood to do any technical work. Then he remembered that the results were only just in and his boss had yet to see them.

A few minutes later Sydney Poulter was examining the assay sheets. He did not conceal his satisfaction. "That's fine. We'll report them like good promoters, all in the interest of full disclosure, of course. The release should say something like: 'The third and fourth holes on Chilko's Nisselinka claims failed to intersect significant copper values. Drilling is continuing in the vicinity of the initial two holes.' No one could object to that."

But Len did, so the press release was modified by adding, "…testing the limits of the mineralized zone."

Chilko's announcement was set to be released early the next morning, in time for the opening of the eastern markets.

Victor went home to his apartment before lunch to make a private phone call before offices in an earlier time zone began to close. Because the person he needed to speak to was in a hurry to leave, his message was short. "The next news release will disappoint. The price will go down and it will be an opportunity to buy."

He also called a broker. "Just 100,000. That's all I can risk today."

"In the off-shore account?"

"That's right."

"I'm just going to read this back to you for confirmation."

"Go ahead."

"You're selling short 100,000 shares of Chilko Resources, CLK, at forty cents or better. And your offer is only good for the rest of today."

Chapter 55 — Holes 3 & 4

"You've got it. Thanks."

Victor then returned to the office.

Sydney Poulter had several accounts distributed among four brokerages, one in his own name and three in private companies. He began the next day by placing a sell order for small quantities of shares with his principal broker, price unspecified. By 8:00 am Pacific time, after two-and-a-half hours of trading, Chilko shares were selling for thirty, then twenty-five and twenty cents, and 150,000 of Slip's shares had sold.

"Do you want me to sell the rest at this price?" asked the broker.

"No, leave it at that for today. But I don't want it to close above twenty. Agreed? Sell more, if necessary."

At another house, Stonar Securities, the news release caught Fred, a junior broker, by surprise. "Zilch! There's fuck-all there!" he said to his neighbour in the next cubicle. "I knew there would be some holes with nothing much, but this is hard to believe. Do you believe this?"

"You must be talking about Chilko. Well, you know, Slip wouldn't be the first promoter to get greedy when he realizes he is onto a real one. We should keep an eye on the volume tomorrow."

The volume the next day was substantial. At 1:30, the close of the market, over one million shares had traded. The next day, Poulter Investments sold a few more shares and the price stayed below twenty cents, which is where Sydney wanted it to stay for at least a week.

Five trading days later, SP Investments, one of Poulter's private companies, started buying. The order was to buy 250,000 at any price below eighteen cents. This was renewed five times during the next four days. On Friday, having bought over half a million shares, Poulter was phoned by two brokers from different houses telling him that there was another big buyer in the market paying well over twenty cents. Competition at this stage was not what he expected—in fact he resented any such intrusion into his own domain.

"Big player?" he asked one broker.

"Seems so. Whoever it is has a series of bids in between nineteen and twenty-five cents. They are showing at least half a million but it looks to be more than that."

"Keep them out until you've got me what I asked for. I'll pay anything up to thirty."

"Will do, Slip. And I'll keep you posted."

Poulter walked down to his trusted confident. "Marion, as you know I'm buying."

"Yes, Mr. Poulter. I hope you're getting what you want."

"Well I seem to have competition and I have no idea where it's coming from." Then, displaying a puzzled and irritated look, he asked Marion a question. "It couldn't be Victor, could it? I told him not to."

Marion did not hesitate with her response. "I think you should ask him."

Victor was sitting at his desk and just hanging up his phone, when Slip found him. "Victor. Someone's trying to buy Chilko. It's happening just now while I want to get more myself. It's in big volumes. It's not you, is it?"

Victor's reply was indignant. "No. Of course not. You told me not to!"

"Yes. That's right. If you hear who it might be, let me know."

"Sure, Sydney, I will."

Poulter succeeded in getting most of the additional shares he needed, but he had had to pay more than he planned. Once he had acquired the position he wanted, he would have welcomed aggressive buying, but at this stage the buying suggested there were other people who had similar knowledge and the same intent.

A week later, despite the higher price he had had to pay, Sydney Poulter was ready for the next phase: promotion of Chilko Resources. After filling his coffee mug at the machine he walked slowly to Marion's desk.

"Marion, has Leonard been talking to the field recently? I've been distracted this past week and I've got to catch up and find out how it is going."

"I put through a call about half an hour ago. He should be up to date."

"Excellent. I'll see what he has to say."

Len was dictating a memo but greeted his boss without putting down the microphone. "Good morning, Sydney. I suppose you want to know what's happening?"

"How did you guess? So, yes. Bottom line first."

"I like what I heard this morning. We are half way through Hole 7 and it looks much the same as the good ones and like numbers 5 and 6."

Chapter 55 — Holes 3 & 4

Sydney turned towards a large map pinned on the wall. "Show me where we are. Seems the zone is getting bigger. That so?"

"That's a reasonable conclusion to draw," said Len, with a smile.

"So if I as a non-technical person can get that far, what about you? You should be able to take it a stage further."

Both men enjoyed the banter they played when opportunity permitted. The professional and the promoter. They each knew more about the other's business than the game let them admit.

"So have we got ... no, could we have ten million tons yet?"

"Oh, yes. That much would be easy to find with this sort of deposit, but we'll need a lot more to be economic."

"How big could it get?"

Len picked up a scale and put it on the map. "Well, if we assume that the mineralized zone is as wide as indicated by the first two holes, every hundred metres we step out in this direction could add about ten million to the tonnage. Down to one hundred metres that is."

Never inclined to use a calculator, Poulter thought for a few seconds. "So down to two hundred metres—that could be about twenty million every hundred metres?"

"Perhaps, if we're lucky."

Sydney pointed to the northwest corner of the map. "So it's all open in that direction?"

"Indeed it is. But that's where we have the disputed claims."

"Oh, yes," replied Sydney, looking irritated, "I wonder if that asshole of a prospector has been snooping on our claims again. I hear the young man is going to be okay, but Wickford must have been scared shitless."

"I'm sure he was. That reminds me, the helicopter people were asking where to send the bill. The flight was called for on our radio. I told them to send it to Wickford. That right?"

"Of course. Chilko's not a charity."

Len made it evident that he needed his boss's continued attention. "Sydney, back to drilling. There is a lot to do. I'm in the process of putting together another budget. We are going to need at least a million. I don't suppose you'll have any problem with that?"

"Don't worry. I'll get it," said Sydney as he took his leave.

At Stonar Securities, Fred had been fielding calls from worried clients all afternoon.

"I know it's down but, like you, I have quite a few shares and I'm not selling."

"Why not? Those holes have nothing in them."

"That's how it works. Not every hole hits even when you are drilling an orebody. I haven't seen a map of the holes but I expect we will see one soon. In the meantime, my understanding from the news releases is that these new holes were drilled in a different part of the property. I see no reason to worry at this stage. But I know where you are coming from. You need strong nerves for this game."

"What did they cost me? The average price."

"You got them between forty and forty-three cents, mostly at forty-one. So your average is probably about forty-one. I can phone you back in a few minutes, if you wish."

"No thanks. Just sell them when they get to forty-one. I need to sleep at night."

"Certainly. I'll do that, Joe."

Chapter 56

Drilling Back on Track
September

August had been a busy month for Chilko and September was shaping up to be the same. Things were happening in the field, lab, office and elsewhere.

In the field, Derek was pleased to see the drill back where it could be productive. He was aware that the market had responded to the disappointing holes as everyone had expected: large volumes and a lower price. He had remained uncomfortable trying to reconcile drilling outside the zone of promising mineralization and people selling their shares in response to the negative news, but he told himself that such people should not be trading in a business they did not understand. Then he reminded himself that many such people relied on the recommendations of others.

He did not know, and his discomfort would have been more acute, had he learned that an executive of Chilko had substantially increased his holding in the company as soon as the price dropped.

The drill had been on Hole 8 for a couple of hours. They had already gone through six metres of bedrock beneath three metres of overburden. Two core boxes were laid out in the open and a light rain had wet the core making its composition easier to see. A glance told him they were still in the mineralized zone and that it started just beneath the overburden. After spending a few minutes peering at pieces of core with a hand lens, he concluded that the mineralization appeared to be much the same as in Holes 5 and 6, the results for which were not yet available.

Back at camp, he went straight to the core shack where Brendon and two summer students were working on the core of Hole 7.

As he entered the tent, Brendon called, "Hi! Just back from the drill?".

"Yes. They're down over thirty feet and it seems much the same as 5 and 6."

"Which are just the same as this one here," said another student waving his hand at four boxes of core laid out on the table.

By way of response Derek gave voice to an estimate that everyone already knew. "So that adds about two hundred metres to the zone, which might be as good as holes 1 and 2. I mean the same sort of grade."

One of the principal topics of conversation in the core tent was the possible size of the mineral deposit being drilled. Brendon was as interested and curious as everyone else. "Do we have any idea how big it could be?"

Derek paced slowly up and down the tent. "It's early yet. We haven't got much feel for the width, and the trend is heading towards the disputed ground. If Chilko have any sense, they won't announce any more holes until they have tied up those claims."

In the drafting room of Chilko's office, Slip Poulter, Victor Dubell, and Leonard Marsden were looking at a claim map on which the drill holes had been plotted. Drill logs for Holes 5 and 6 lay scattered across the table. Victor summarized the situation Leonard had been describing: "So it's heading off in that direction. If it continues for another three hundred metres and we keep stepping out one hundred metres, we will be into ground that prospector thinks he owns. We could be there by the end of the month."

"It could well peter out before the border," Leonard said, "but I have to acknowledge that's not what the mag suggests."

Sydney Poulter, stepping back and looking directly at his two employees, steered the discussion away from technical issues. "The bottom line is that we have to own that ground. If we put out any more results like these, someone else is going to buy the Wickford claims and they may be even harder to deal with."

"We haven't finished with him yet," said Victor.

"What's the latest?"

Victor's response came across as confident and assertive. "Routine investigations on his credit rating and the Better Business Bureau didn't turn up anything. We've now got someone talking to the neighbours. And we'll soon be finding out what we can learn from his ex. But I don't think all that is going to work. We are going to have to get more forceful or find his weak points."

Chapter 56 — Drilling Back on Track

From the side table where he was helping himself to a cup of coffee, Poulter turned to Victor. "We, and that means you, Victor, have to get that ground. Just get it! But stay away from the dirty tricks." Then he added, "Unless you ask me first."

Victor, slightly chastened, replied with, "Okay, Mr. Poulter. I understand".

Poulter ignored the opportunity to press his advantage. "Are you both okay to meet again this afternoon? Marion tells me that Burrard should have the first results from 5 and 6."

Len and Victor murmuring assent, they all left the room.

The results for Holes 5 and 6 did indeed arrive that afternoon. The predictions from the field were proved correct; the copper grades were much the same as the first two holes. Those in Hole 5 were almost the same as Hole 2 while Hole 6 had similar copper but with more gold. The only significant difference was the greater depth of the more recent holes, two hundred metres instead of one hundred and fifty, a consequence of greater confidence now infusing the geological team. The results were duly reported to the investing public the following day. In response to Poulter's wishes, the release had an upbeat tone and did more than allude to the potential of the property. Predictably, for anyone familiar with it, the Vancouver market responded as usual to positive drill results and added nearly a hundred percent, or thirty cents, during the next three days before settling back slightly to fifty cents.

Soon after the announcement, two junior brokers were exchanging views on their way back from the coffee machine.

"What's he up to?" asked one. "Two outstanding holes and an excited market. Two duds and the price in the tank. Lots of volume. And now two more zingers. Slip's like a puppeteer with a bull hanging from one hand and a bear from the other."

His colleague picked up on the imagery. "I like that! Slip behind the curtains. No face to be seen. Just two animals doing their dance. That's him in a nutshell. Now all we have to do is figure out which is going to make him the most money."

"It's not so easy. Most of the time the bull will make him more, but it's not always like that. Sometimes the bear is his favourite."

"You getting a lot of phone calls?"

"Not so many this time as I've managed to bring in quite a few clients with experience. I don't think that this business, when you have mostly amateur investors, is worth the trouble. A lot of bitching and whining and then they pull out and watch it go up. Then I get more bitching and whining."

The two men went to their respective desks in a barn of a room holding some fifty brokers.

One floor above them in an office with a glass front door and a view of the North Shore, a partner in the securities house was leaning back in his chair, one foot on the desk and speaking into the phone. "So it looks like more of the same. Like 1 and 2, I mean. Not 3 or 4? Slip, this is one we have to take seriously. Everyone knows you're a good promoter, but this time you may have actually found something."

"And if so, I suppose you'll want me to spend some serious money, which you will raise for me at great cost?"

"And to your great benefit, I should add."

"A killer percentage, B-warrants. What else?"

The verbal sparring was part game, part deadly serious. Sydney Poulter continued: "Yes, I'm beginning to think we need two drills. Each million dollars might last a few months but not much more. So we have to get the price up or the dilution will kill us. These two holes should do it."

"I think you're right," responded the financier, "but watch out for that claim boundary. We'll feel more comfortable backing you when you've signed it up."

"We're working on it."

"Keep us posted. We'd like to help."

Just as Poulter hung up the phone, he heard Marion on the intercom tell him that a Mr. Lucas was on Line 2.

"Who's that?"

"I have no idea. He says he represents some investment fund, but I missed its name. You'd better take his call."

Slip shut down Line 1 and picked up Line 2. "Poulter here."

"Mr. Poulter. I'm Lucas Petrovic of Rarmel Investments. I like what you are doing and have just a few questions."

Sydney's "I'd be glad to answer them," lacked the bonhomie of the earlier conversation, as the caller was not someone he knew or to whom he owed favours. But any fund manager represented an opportunity to spread the word so he was glad to respond to the call.

The caller continued. "The Chilko story sounds like a real one, but can I believe it?"

Chapter 56 — Drilling Back on Track

This was not the best way to question Sydney J. Poulter, whose reply failed to conceal a defensive posture. "All our stories are real ones. What would you like to know?"

"I need to know what to believe or what to disbelieve."

Sydney put the phone on speaker, replaced it on the stand and leaned back in his chair to listen.

"Your first drill holes were most encouraging. The second round was disappointing, and now we have another batch of excellent results. So I need to know which of your announcements to believe."

As Poulter listened, he began to visualize the man he was talking to: grey-haired, distinguished, powerful, and a manager of funds who would be useful and whose respect he desired. But the questions being asked were blunt enough to rub his sensitivities the wrong way. Then he heard yet another question on the same theme. "I need to separate fact from fiction."

Poulter did not answer immediately. He needed a moment to think. He knew his fuse used to be short, but it hadn't caused problems for a long time. He didn't expect it to melt this time. But melt it did as he shouted his response into the phone. "I stand by my drill results. Facts or ficts I don't give a..."

But his string of alliteration came to an abrupt halt, terminated by his more rational other self. Before he could articulate a measured response, he heard a click as the line went dead.

Poulter slammed down the phone.

It became one of those afternoons when staff in the office learned that it was best to avoid their boss. After talking quietly in twos and threes about what could have triggered such a mood, some went home. Those who remained worked with their office doors closed.

On Monday morning of the following week Sydney Poulter dropped himself into the chair in front of Leonard's desk with a quick, "Morning, Len. Would four million keep you going for a year?"

Leonard thought for a moment before responding. "I'll have to sharpen my pencil for that. It would certainly do for a few months. A year? I'm not so sure. If we get up to three drills, it won't be enough. We'll be going through about a million a month. Then, if it continues to hang together, we'll be forced to spend something on metallurgy, talking to the local people and all that other stuff.

And, of course, we really need Wickford's ground and that may cost a bit."

As he pushed himself out of his chair, Poulter closed off the conversation. "Let me have your numbers month by month. There's a group in the east who seem keen to do it."

Leonard, well aware that little could be achieved without the money, spent most of the afternoon estimating costs for the next six months. He presented them to his boss the same day.

The next morning at 6:00 am, as offices were opening in the East, Poulter was on the phone. Two hours later he called Leonard and Victor and asked them to meet in his office. "I think we have a deal. For the financing I mean. We should have the term sheet from them tomorrow."

Always driven by high energy, Sydney Poulter was now being further stimulated by the Chilko project. News from field and lab was exciting, brokers were phoning him, his team was working well, and now a major fund was offering money.

The following week the price of the shares, having reached a high of eighty cents, was on a steady decline. Sydney was on the phone to broker after broker. "Who's selling? Where is it coming from?"

Among the answers he heard were: "Haven't a clue," "Beats me," and "Thought you would know." But a broker well known to him was more useful. "Slip, it's your company. You and I know where most of the shares are. Just about the only source for volumes like we've been seeing is you, yourself. Unless, of course, they don't possess—"

But Poulter did not let him finish. "Yeah. I'd reached the same conclusion. They have to be short."

The broker carried on with the same logic. "And who would do that, in these volumes, in the middle of a promising drill program? You must have been talking to some financiers and, as you know…"

Sydney Poulter had been burnt before by signing with financiers who agreed to raise a certain sum of money "at market." Such deals looked good until, when the deal was about to close, the share price was pushed down by the financiers selling shares they did not possess, but which they knew they could replace with cheap shares after closing.

"You're right again. You know the game too well. You're forcing me to conclusions I was trying to avoid. They're doing a

Chapter 56 — Drilling Back on Track

push-down. But, you know, they've gotten ahead of themselves. We haven't signed yet. I'll show them what happens when they try to screw me. Just watch. Hey, you want to do lunch tomorrow?"

"You're on. See you at the club. After the market, 1:15."

Sydney put down the phone and went to see Leonard in the drafting room.

Leonard was standing against a table, leaning on his elbows, and peering at a map.

"Ah! There you are! Where are we drilling now and where next?"

Leonard went to a map on the wall on the other side of a large drafting table. Once there he explained the drilling. "Here, you can see we're at the end of Line 19 where the copper is getting weaker."

Poulter came right to his point. "Well, I need some really good holes. This selling has to be by the shorts, and I think I know who it is. I'm gonna hit 'em where it hurts."

Leonard nodded. "I wondered whether that was happening." Then he reached down to the table for a drafting scale and pointed it at the map. "We could move the two drills to here, to the middle of Line 20. Not quite where I was planning, but an easy change."

"And you could rush the results?"

"We could do that. An easy move. We'll get the hole down in three shifts and we'll air-freight the core."

"And good numbers?"

Leonard laughed. "You know, Slip. No guarantees. But, yes, I would be very surprised if that area doesn't treat us well."

Within the hour, instructions had gone to the field to start the next line in the middle instead of at the west end and to drill and deliver with all possible speed. Four days later the core was driven to Prince George and shipped by air express.

The next morning, as he did from time to time, Sydney invited Victor to review progress over lunch at his club. As usual, after drinks had appeared on their table, Slip summarized his perception of the current situation. "Most of our ventures are going well and this means there is a lot to do, lots of balls in the air at once. I'm sure glad you're here to help out."

"It's a pleasure. I'm learning a lot."

"As you've noticed, until we started getting good results, I didn't do much with the Nisselinka project, but you've been on top of it. Now I'm going to join you and we're going to have a lot of fun."

"Yes. The upside is certainly there. We're still working on that prospector. If he has a weak spot—and everyone does—we'll find it."

After Sydney had paused to exchange a quick greeting with a passing club member, he realized that Victor wanted to introduce another topic. "I should mention that I've tightened up some of the routine procedures."

"Can't believe they would be interesting, but tell me anyhow."

"The drivers taking samples to Vancouver have been doing it without a break. The last thing we want is an accident."

"Agreed."

"And now that the press and public are taking an interest in us, I've arranged for the trucks with the samples to be locked."

"Playing safe is playing soft, but it makes sense this time. Keep it up. Now I want to introduce you to one of the tricks in this industry that they may not have told you about in business school."

Victor looked particularly attentive. "Sounds very interesting!"

Slip continued, his tone confidential. "I've been talking to some people in the east who want to finance us. We agreed on terms and all that. Then, as you noticed, the price started going down. I'm sure it was them shorting. It'd give them a better price and more profit. At our expense, of course."

"You're right. They didn't teach us that. Are we committed?"

"That's the point. They sent the contract which they've already signed. All they need is my signature. But they've played their cards too soon." Sydney was smiling with satisfaction. "We have them on a string and we're going to make them dance. We're going to put out some good holes and make them cover."

"Buy back the shares they never had. That's neat! What can I do to help?"

"Nothing. Just watch."

The assays came available in the middle of the following week and were everything Leonard had expected and Poulter had hoped for. They were announced the following day and the reaction of the market was predictable: a one-day jump of twenty cents and a similar move the next day. With the price flirting with a dollar, the Northern Miner newspaper requested a site visit. Two of the local finance houses offered private placements at only a few cents below the new price. Poulter's' plans for vengeance were falling into place.

Chapter 57

Connections Off-Stage
September

The investment community was keeping track as best it could of what was happening in the world of Chilko Resources, but it could not know everything. Over three thousand miles away, on the other side of the continent, two men and a woman sat in a small meeting room on the twenty-fifth floor of one of the older and smaller buildings in the vicinity. The senior of the two men, a stocky individual with close-cropped hair and a loosened tie, broke the silence.

"This is getting serious. Rick phoned twenty minutes ago. Mad as hell and asking what we were going to do about it."

"We should never have invited him in," said the other man.

"That's easy to say now. We were doing him a favour. You know, that's the sort of thing important clients expect."

"Did he know the risk?"

"Of course he did. Anyone in his position knows the downside of taking a short position."

"What's he got into it?"

"He's exposed to just over a million if the price goes back to its previous high. Peanuts, of course, to him, but that's not the point. We could lose him as a client."

"Or worse," said the woman. "He's known to be vindictive."

The trio lapsed into another silence, each trying to think of a way out of the situation none of them expected to find themselves in.

"All we need is a break. Some negative news. Then we could bring the price down enough for him to get out."

"What are you hearing from the young man in Vancouver?"

"He has kept me informed of what's happening until now. He just dropped the ball on this one. He said there was no way of knowing that it would bounce back so quickly. I was speaking to him two days ago. I told him that one of our clients was badly exposed by this run-up in price. He assured me that we would have another opportunity to get out and that it would be easy to arrange another price drop. He said that if I gave him the go-ahead, it would probably take about a month to fix. I said to him, 'Just do it, and quick.'"

"Does he know what happens to people who let us down like that?"

"I'm sure he does."

In a part of British Columbia near to neither the drill site nor the office, a heavy-duty mechanic, Douglas Barrett, and his wife Marlene, operated a small, run-down motel and restaurant. After years in Mackenzie, where Douglas worked at the pulp mill, they had chosen to settle in Williams Lake. The bank manager had been pleased to lend them the required capital, secured against the house they had just bought with the proceeds from the previous house and their savings. Before they signed, the manager had been honest enough to tell them that eighty percent of new restaurants went bankrupt within two years. Despite the warning, they decided to go ahead, confident in their abilities. As they had expected, the first six months had been slow. Midway through the second six months business became even slower and they were doubting their decision. Customers were few, expenses exceeded revenues, and the couple's relationship became tense. Then things improved. Crew cabs full of young men and a steady stream of pickup trucks carrying supplies of all types kept them busy. Exploration crews were prominent. Chilko, one of the companies which opened credit accounts, was particularly active in August.

Whenever possible Douglas and his wife did their best to learn about their clients and their likes and dislikes. Marlene was good at chatting up the crews. "Jeff! You back again! Anyone would think you spend your life driving up and down the highway."

"That's exactly what we do. Sometimes it's twice a week up and twice a week down," replied Jeff, a heavy man in his late twenties who, having spent a few years driving the big rigs on transcontinental routes, had set up his own business with three small trucks.

"Well, we're sure glad to see you, and we hope you keep on doing it."

"Don't worry. We've got a lot to do before we're finished."

Chapter 57 — Connections Off-Stage

"From Vancouver, I suppose?"

"Yup," said Jeff.

"To Prince George?"

"No, we go beyond Vanderhoof to a helicopter base. We take up supplies, groceries, equipment, anything they need. And on the backhaul it's mostly samples: boxes of drill core, geochemical samples, rock samples. Today it's nearly all geochem bags on their way to the lab."

"Through the winter?"

"If it doesn't get too cold, I think they'll keep at it. A really cold snap would put it on hold. They've got a lot to do and, from what I hear, they're getting good results."

Marlene was pleased. "That's what we like to hear. Another year like this and we'll be able to pay off the bank loan. What would you like? There's liver and onions today, as well as the usual."

"Just what I need. I parked at the back like last time. That okay?"

"That's right. We're thinking about getting security lights out there. But we've never had any trouble."

"Don't worry. Truck's locked. A big coffee first, please."

Some seven hours later the same truck was at the laboratory of Burrard Geochemical, at that time busy enough to be running two shifts a day. As part of a now familiar routine, Jeff backed the truck to the loading bay and went into the office to report arrival, accept a cup of coffee, and hand over the keys so that unloading could begin.

A couple of minutes later a lab worker, still in his white coat, returned holding up the keys. "Jeff, do you have another key for the padlock? This one doesn't work."

"That's the right one. I've used it a gazillion times. Let me show you." Jeff put down his coffee and strode out to the truck, jumped onto the ramp, lifted the padlock, and pushed in the key. But it wouldn't go in all the way.

After two minutes of frustration he shouted. "Goddamn lock! It's the right key. I've used it since May and I locked it myself. Must be something broken inside. Do you have a bolt cutter?"

Five minutes later the back was open and several hundred pounds of large plastic bags were transferred into the lab's receiving room. Each bag contained about fifty brown geochemical envelopes, each containing about half a pound of soil in various shades of yellow-brown.

The Nisselinka Claims

Ten days later Sydney Poulter was looking for Len, when he found him pouring over geochemical results from two weeks ago. "You see the numbers at the end of those two lines?" said Len pointing to the map. "That's mostly underlain by recent basalt. I'm surprised to see anything there. They're much stronger than I expected, patchy too."

Sydney's question came out as a statement. "But it still extends the mineral."

Len nodded. "Probably. In a general way it does. But we'll need to check it. It's odd to see strong results in that place."

"But we should keep the investing public properly informed."

"No, Sydney. No. This is of no real significance. It's not what the lawyers would call 'material.' The drill results are where the action is. The geochem is no longer important."

"Maybe so. But we need to get it out. I'll do the first draft."

Which is exactly what Poulter did; and after some softening of the language by Len, it was released.

Predictably, the market shrugged.

Chapter 58

Meeting At Cuprick
September

Cuprick Metals & Mining Company was one of a limited number of international mining companies with a head office in Vancouver. Its large and well-regarded exploration staff conducted exploration programs in many countries, but an additional and important activity for the team was to keep track of junior companies, many of whose finds had become significant orebodies.

"Thank you all for being on time," said Ted Bridgeman to the group of people assembled in the boardroom. Present were members of his exploration team, the VP finance, the in-house counsel. "As you are about to hear, we—I mean those of us in exploration—have reached the conclusion that this deposit Chilko is now drilling on their Nisselinka claims is for real, and that Cuprick should consider getting involved."

"And, Ted, will you put up with a sceptic in your audience?" asked Brent Atterson, with one eyebrow raised, a steady gaze, and the merest flicker of a smile.

Everyone knew that Brent and Ted had fallen out on more than one occasion. Both were in middle management and both aspired to lead the Corporate Acquisition unit which had been proposed and was likely to be formed within the year. Ted had spent his entire career in exploration. Brent had trained as a mining engineer, worked on one mine before taking an MBA, and since then had been employed in the corporate development side of various mining companies.

"Absolutely, Brent. Most of us who have been following this one have been sceptics at one stage or another. We have no party line. You are going to hear from several different perspectives."

"I'm looking forward to it," replied Brent without looking up from his notes.

The Nisselinka Claims

"The plan is to begin with the undisputed facts: location, claims, access, number of shares out, etcetera. Then when we have assimilated those, we will grapple with the drilling, geophysics, geology and what we think they all mean. Before I go any further, I should say that Chris Henderman said he might attend. That seems unlikely to me, but his intention gives you an idea of how important this project may be."

The people in Bridgeman's audience looked at one another. Some appeared puzzled, some amused and others merely interested that the president and CEO of a large international mining company should concern himself with an early-stage exploration project. But those who knew him were not surprised. Henderman had been known to take a personal interest in several exploration projects long before they had a measurable value.

"Ron," said Ted addressing his draughtsman, "all yours. I'll work the projector."

Ron got up rather diffidently and started with a map of British Columbia showing the location of the property. This was followed by a map showing Smithers, Burns Lake, roads and railway, then a claim map. "As you see, access is not ideal, but once the road has been put in, the claims will be within an hour of the main highway."

Several other maps followed on the screen, each showing a smaller and smaller part of the property. These were followed by slides, some taken on the ground, others from the air. It was a good-enough delivery. It could have been provided more economically by Ted himself, but Ted's style was to involve his people as much as possible. He liked them to present the work for which they had been responsible. For this and other reasons, he was generally reckoned to be a good boss.

He introduced the next speaker. "Share structure and all that are being handled by Ellie."

Ellie Landon, a young woman who worked in Corporate Finance and whom everyone respected, began in her self-deprecating style. "I don't have any fancy shots like you've just seen. This is the boring stuff. The essentials are here on this single sheet. Most of the items—number of shares, for instance—are put out by Chilko itself. Some of the others, such as the size of the float and the principal employees, are the result of our data collection."

"Snooping?" asked someone, prompting a few laughs.

Chapter 58 — Meeting At Cuprick

"Not exactly. Most of this information is out on the street. For the rest, it's just a matter of finding the right person to talk to. You all know that Chilko is run by Sydney J. Poulter. He—"

"I'll interrupt, if I may," said Brent. "Sydney J. Poulter. That brings me to my first question, why are we getting involved with someone like that?"

Bridgeman replied firmly: "The answer is very simple. It doesn't matter who we are dealing with, as long as we can make a deal that brings us an orebody."

"And are we going to believe what he says?" asked Brent. "Have you heard the rumours that it is all a scam?"

Bridgeman replied without attempting to disguise the irritation in his voice. "Yes, of course. We know a lot of people don't trust him. As for: 'are we going to believe him?' Why would we even think of going down that road? We don't have to. We will generate our own facts. Those are the only ones we will believe. We should let Ellie finish."

Putting her next transparency on the overhead projector, Ellie pointed to a line and continued her review. "As you see, they have a full tank of unexercised options. The brokers have nearly a million B warrants outstanding. So, fully diluted, there are almost twenty-three million shares out."

Someone asked, "Did anyone notice the number of shorts?" but before the question could be answered, Atterson jumped in with another. "All of which is irrelevant unless there is something there," he said, raising his voice half an octave. "Can we get on to the important stuff?"

"We're coming to the technicals," replied Bridgeman. "But I want us to stick to the agenda. Any more questions on the shares? No? Then, I'd like to make a comment on the number of shorts. Just in case anyone doesn't know about the practice, I'll explain. A lot of money can be made by selling shares you don't have and buying them later at a reduced price. Evidently—"

"And you can lose a lot if they go up instead. I know someone who got caught like that."

"Thank you, Phil, for that. As I was saying, evidently some people think that there is nothing worthwhile on the Nisselinka claims and the price is going to dive. We recognize they may know something we don't, but—"

"Exactly, Ted, you hit it on the head." Atterson was not going to let his opportunity pass. "This is why we have to be so very careful. Short selling is for pros and pros usually take the trouble to dig out at least some of the facts."

But Bridgeman had the chair. "Let's move on. Next is Peter Scholdar, who carried out the IP for Chilko and is here with their permission. He'll tell us about the results."

Peter had done enough presentations to groups like this to avoid boring the non-technical people with the intricacies of reading electrical potential in the ground. His maps were hand-coloured black-line prints that he pinned on the wall. "Red means high changeability, orange not so high, and blue is low. So, generally speaking, we expect a significant amount of sulphide where there is orange, and plenty of it where we show red."

Brent Atterson indicated that he had another question. "Peter, let me please take a moment to confirm my ignorance."

"Any time," replied Peter entering into the game with a smile.

"I understand you are measuring sulphide, both the good stuff and pyrite?"

"That's right."

"So both the red and the orange could be all pyrite, which is no good to anyone?"

"As far as our instruments go, you're quite right. But in this case we—sorry, I—understand there are two holes, one into the red, the other into the orange. I was pleased to see that both holes produced the amount of sulphide we expected. And I understand they both produced significant amounts of chalcopyrite. And, as you know, the grades are pretty good. So at least some of this area," Peter pointed to the map, "is more than just pyrite."

"If you believe the grades," responded Brent with emphasis.

"That's right, I'm assuming that we can believe what they report."

"Thank you, Peter," said Ted. "To summarize, the evidence of Peter's company—a third party contractor we can trust—is that there's lots of sulphide, but we have to rely on the junior's data to believe there is any copper." He thanked Peter again for being available.

Once Peter had left the room, he called on Judy Rielle to explain the geochemistry. "I think a lot of people have been waiting to hear your story first hand, Judy."

"Oh, well, I'll do my best to explain what I found." Holding a sheaf of transparencies, Judy walked over to the projector, placed the first on the glass, and looked over her shoulder at the screen

Chapter 58 — Meeting At Cuprick

before starting. She was a knowledgeable and organized geochemist who expected, and usually obtained, the attention of the people to whom she was speaking. Aware that her figure was something of a distraction to most men, she met the gaze of her audience one person at a time to keep their attention focussed on the topic. In this she was not altogether successful.

She put the first transparency on the projector. "This is the geochemical map for copper. It was provided by Chilko when Chuck and I visited their camp. What caught my eye was that two of the Chilko lines had very high copper values, but values in the adjacent lines were much lower. It looked so odd and there was no obvious feature to explain it, so I borrowed a shovel and dug a few pits to check on the high value lines, twenty samples in all. When we got the results, imagine my surprise when I didn't get any of the high values seen on Chilko's map. So Ted asked Mr. Poulter if we could re-run some of his samples—a routine procedure to check why there was a difference between their samples and ours. Getting slightly different numbers from their samples was, I suppose, to be expected, but I wasn't expecting to find my check sample lines so different from Chilko's. Mine had low copper, like the other Chilko lines."

Judy would have fielded questions, but Bridgeman pre-empted her. "Thank you, Judy. That was a good bit of sleuthing. It is going to be very interesting to get the lab report. Now it's Chuck's turn to tell us about the drill holes. I understand they look pretty genuine."

By this time Chuck, a young man who appeared to those who knew him out of place in a suit and tie, was at the screen. "That's it. The core has plenty of chalco. I'm never happy with visual estimates but, for what it is worth, the assays seemed to match what I saw. I took some samples by quartering the core and they matched well. I saw some of the drilling, watched core being removed, and saw that it looked much the same as the core that had been sampled. Here are some pictures."

Chuck's presentation was interrupted by the door opening.

Ted turned towards the entrance with exasperation, only to see the President of Cuprick enter the room. Chris Henderman closed the door. "Good morning Ted, Brent. Good morning everyone. Ted, I am sorry to be late, but I hope you won't mind if I sit in on this. I figure I will have to bring myself up to speed sooner or later and this seemed a real opportunity."

"I'm glad you came," said Ted. "Your timing is perfect. You won't have to listen to my introduction. We're already deep into the facts."

Chris Henderman laughed, sat down. "I always like it when I get the timing right. Go right ahead."

"You have met everyone here, I believe."

"That's right. I think I can put a name to all of you."

Chuck returned to his slides to complete his presentation. The meeting then turned to discussion and continued for another half hour.

The next morning the Chilko office was humming with calls from the field, from brokers and shareholders when Marion put through yet another call to her boss. "Slip?"

"Speaking."

"It's Ted Bridgeman on the line."

"Hi Ted! How's it going?"

"Not so well. I hate to be the bearer of bad news, but you're not going to like what I have to tell you."

"Go ahead. I've had my share of crap and corruption to handle."

"That's not it. Remember when you kindly let two of our people have a look at your Nisselinka property and review the results? You had some geochem numbers that looked spectacular. At the same time the IP was emerging with a strong chargeability. On the strength of those you decided to commit to drilling."

"Yup. Seems like it was a good decision."

"Our geochemist took some check samples, mainly as a way of comparing our results with yours and to see how the metals were coming through the till. The bottom line is that your sample results and ours don't agree. That was why I gave you a call last week to ask for access to some of your sample remainders."

"Go on."

"Well, your very strong geochemical anomaly is questionable. We get a bit of copper in some samples but nothing like the high numbers from your survey."

"What d'you mean? Our numbers are excellent."

Ted Bridgeman then spoke more slowly, with greater emphasis. "Yes, Slip. But on the basis of comparing your samples and ours, yours appear to be false. We may learn more from the lab, but in the meantime you've got to recognize that your samples may be salted."

Chapter 58 — Meeting At Cuprick

After a short silence, Poulter almost shouted: "I've never heard of such nonsense. Someone might salt core, but soil samples? You've got to be kidding!"

"Slip. I am not kidding. I am deadly serious. Do you want to come over?"

"I'll see you in five at your place."

Slip Poulter grabbed his jacket from behind the door, sped down the corridor with a quick, "Back in half an hour," to Marion.

Three minutes and two jay walks later, he was in the foyer of Cuprick Mining & Smelting.

"Mr. Poulter, Mr. Bridgeman is expecting you," said the receptionist. "I'll show you in."

When Sydney Poulter walked in, Ted Bridgeman rose and offered his hand. "Unless the lab comes up with some explanation, this is going to be a miserable story that will do none of us any good."

"Let's hear it."

Ted Bridgeman pointed towards a small table with a sheet of paper on it. After they were both seated, Bridgeman drew a deep breath as if to emphasize the gravity of what he was about to say. "As soon as we had your permission, we sent one hundred of the samples that your people collected to be reanalysed. This note, which came by fax this morning, is from the lab manager."

Poulter glanced at the hand-written note. It was very clear. The reported numbers were false and the samples had been salted. He stood up and paced the room, deep in thought.

Bridgeman, still sitting, suggested that they do nothing until the lab report was available. "That could be any time soon."

Sydney Poulter took his leave and walked slowly back to his office. As he passed Marion's desk, she said. "Sydney, Henry Chong phoned from the lab. Wants you to call him."

Poulter sat in his office and picked up the phone. He listened to Henry's accented English with a deepening feeling of foreboding.

"You see, Mr. Poulter, we went back to the garbage bin and found the geochemical bags from that batch. We cleaned about twenty bags, removed all the sand and soil from them. We tested the bags for copper. Mr. Poulter, the paper bags alone have high values. That copper could not come from the soil. I think someone put a copper solution in the bags before they came to our lab."

Sydney Poulter lunched alone at the club. Several men greeted him. Two of them asked if he would join their group. He declined. After his meal he went to the smoking room, where he helped himself to a coffee he did not drink and to a newspaper he did not read. He returned to his office at 2:30 and phoned his housekeeper to say he would not be home for dinner. He had an emergency to deal with. He drove home in the early hours and let himself into his house. The house was quiet. He left most of the lights turned off. Pouring himself a glass of cognac, he stood for a long time staring at the city spread out below him. He thought of his early days as a jobber in the Montreal exchange and how proud he had been when he became a junior broker; he remembered the times when he was desperately short of cash and how it had started to arrive. He remembered the pleasure of his first car, a Volkswagen beetle with many miles and minimal comfort. Such a pleasure, that first extravagance on an automobile. He thought of his achievements within the mining industry, and forced himself to recognize that someone was trying to take success from him. Then he shocked himself by realising that, whoever it was, might just succeed.

He went to bed and to sleep, but it was fitful, and what sleep he did get put him back into yet another occurrence of a dream with which he was all too familiar. He dreamed he was walking through a city of tall buildings, but none of them taller than him. He saw no windows in the buildings, but perhaps that was because they were too far away. Then, as he trudged through the city like some Gulliver, the cladding on the buildings started to slough off. And as the cladding came off, the contents of the buildings flowed out, and the buildings, while remaining vertical, subsided from their bases and collapsed slowly onto the ground. As he passed beyond the city of collapsing buildings, he began to wade through deeper and deeper water. On the other side of the water was another city, which he recognized. He would go to his office. When he arrived, he realized that the office was not there. Then he awoke, turned over, tried to get back to sleep, and then decided to get up. It was 4:30 am.

Chapter 59

Digging In
October

With very little traffic at that early hour, Poulter's commute to the office was quick. He sat at his desk with the door shut, continuing to feel his world collapsing around him. He stared at document after document, put each aside, and then realized he had done no more than look at them and had registered nothing. After an hour, he took himself to a nearby café offering cut-price breakfasts. He had a coffee and doughnut before setting off on foot for Stanley Park. He walked, deep in thought, along the Seawall to Brockton Point before turning back. As he walked, and for reasons beyond his understanding, his mood of despondency began to subside. His ambling pace gave way to a brisk and purposeful stride as a plan began to form. Back in the office he worked alone for another hour before hearing the first voices. A few minutes after 8:30, Marion came in to announce her arrival.

"Good morning, Sydney. I hope you weren't here all night."

"Not quite. I'm sure glad to see you. I'll let you know in an hour or so, but I think we are going to need a staff meeting today. Possibly as soon as eleven o'clock."

"Just let me know," Marion replied before leaving the room.

Sydney Poulter now turned to the task he knew he had to complete. It would be difficult and unpleasant. He had to announce to the world, over his own name, that some of the excellent results already released were false. He also had to say that they were the product of salting. Phrases came to mind: *...regrets to announce ... product of salting by persons unknown ... Chilko management pursuing the culprits vigorously ... assistance of the RCMP requested.* They all hurt. He was living the ultimate nightmare for any promoter.

Which, of course, it was. But after twenty minutes with his door closed he had a draft, the essentials of which were: *Sydney*

J. Poulter, President of the company, deeply regrets to report that at least one hundred and twenty of the anomalous geochemical soil samples reported in the news release dated 15th July 1987 were deliberately contaminated by persons unknown. Although Chilko's management has no reason to suspect that the drill samples have been subjected to the same contamination, stringent precautions are now being put in place. An independent consultant will be engaged to supervise re-drilling of some of the holes with good intercepts and to retain custody of the samples until they are delivered to the laboratory.

Slip then picked up the phone to call Compliance at the Vancouver Stock Exchange and was put through to a someone he knew by name but had never met.

"I'm Sydney Poulter, President of Chilko Resources. We are in the middle of a drill program near Smithers and we have a very serious situation on our hands. The only way to handle this is to halt the goddamn stock."

The response was much as Poulter expected. "As you know, that is not a step we take lightly. There are always investors who are disadvantaged by a halt in trading. You had better describe it to me now and then again in a letter applying for the halt. If you fax the letter over to me, I will get back to you within the hour."

Before the hour was up, arrangements had been made to stop trading in Chilko shares.

The people assembled in the boardroom were apprehensive. Conversation was stilted and attempts at humour, though appreciated, did not succeed. Everyone was casually dressed, the men tieless and the women in typical fall attire, except that none of them wore pants because Sydney was known to dislike them on women.

"Everyone here?" asked Poulter, addressing no one in particular.

"Marion went out. She will be back in less than a minute," said Len from the other side of the table.

Poulter waited for her return, then made sure he had everyone's attention. Speaking very slowly, he began, "I know you are wondering what this is all about. Well, here's the situation. It's very serious. The bottom line is that someone is trying to destroy us. Your jobs are at stake, and so is just about every venture we run out of this office. So's my reputation." He paused and stared over the top of his spectacles at the attentive faces looking at him. "Someone has salted the geochemical samples from the Nisselinka

Chapter 59 — Digging In

job." In response to the puzzled expressions around the table, he explained: "I know it sounds absurd, but it makes sense for the scumbags who did it. As most of you know, Chilko has an enormous short position, about fifteen percent of the float. Whoever did the salting almost certainly owns most of that position. And now those scoundrels are forcing Chilko to tell the world that its geochemical results are not to be believed."

"Sydney," said Victor from the other end of the table. "You've no idea who might be behind this?"

Without even a glance at the questioner, Poulter replied, "I have no idea who. I may have some enemies, but I know no one who hates me enough to risk going to jail for it. And that's where they're going to rot." He paused and then continued. "As I said, we have to tell the world that we have this problem. After we have done that, nobody will believe any of our numbers, including the drill results. The price will plunge. Then the shorts will be able to cover. We're in deep shit, but we have to wade through it."

He glanced at a notepad in front of him. "The lab is preparing a report. Until I can see it, I can't tell you all the details, but I can tell you this. It was our Batch 13 which was hit. Henry Chong of Burrard Geochem tells me that the geochemical bags appear to have been treated with a liquid in which copper had been dissolved. He said it was blatant and unsophisticated. It will, of course, be a matter for the police to investigate. He says it could have been done in the field or during transport. He thinks transport was more likely because some of the bags are totally saturated, as if they had been at the bottom of the plastic bags used for shipping."

Poulter looked up at the faces of his audience. "I have already requested a halt in trading to take effect immediately. In fact it may already be in place. Then we are going to put out a news release. That's going to take a few hours because it will need to be reviewed by the lawyers, some directors too, but they'll do what I say. It should be out by the close of market this afternoon. We will announce the salting of one batch of geochemical samples, that we are now checking all samples, and that we have no reason to suspect the drill results. We will also announce that we are going to engage an independent consultant to review all our data, the drill holes in particular."

Not a word was spoken until, after thanking his team for their support, Poulter had left the room.

The following day, Dr. Geoffrey Praine, Ph.D, P.Eng, was sitting at his desk in downtown Toronto reviewing a final draft of a complex technical report. It had been commissioned two months earlier by a midsize junior in negotiations to acquire a copper property in Mexico. This client wanted to be made aware of all the negative features of the mining property for sale. The company had completed its own study and already possessed a good understanding of the merits and defects of the property. But not only would Dr. Praine's report provide evidence of due diligence, it might also provide a few levers for improving the price. Dr. Praine provided a valuable service, but because of the combination of his name and his speciality he was apt to be labelled "Dr. Pain" or "The Pain." Moreover, as the good doctor was known to be of a dour demeanour, these appellations were sometimes combined, as in "The dour doctor Pain". None of this subtracted from his reputation as a knowledgeable professional with a fastidious and effective dedication to his work.

Dr. Praine took the call from Sydney Poulter. After listening for a few minutes and asking several questions, he said, "Yes, Mr. Poulter, we could do it. You realize, your entire crew would have to leave the camp; we would have to replace the drill crew with one of our choosing and then drill at least two holes, perhaps three, close to some of yours? This will not be cheap, and could take as much as three weeks."

"I understand."

"And, of course, the report we prepare for you might say things you don't want to hear. For instance, we might have to say that the drill results you have reported cannot be corroborated."

"That's a risk I am prepared to take."

"Very well then. I will send you a letter of understanding for your review. If that is acceptable to you, we will begin work within five days of receipt of your cheque for a hundred and fifty percent of the estimated cost of the investigation. The balance, if any, will, of course, be refunded to you when the project is complete."

"May I expect your letter before the weekend?"

"Yes, indeed. By courier tomorrow or the next day. Thank you, Mr. Poulter."

"Thank you, Doctor Praine."

Chapter 60

Pub Rumours

October

In a corner of a downtown pub that was dark enough to make a spelunker feel at home, Reg Merasko and his friend and colleague, Tom Franman, had each been served a pint provided by one of the emerging micro breweries. Tom was an accountant, and Reg a geologist who worked for a locally-based, mid-size mining company. Both men were preoccupied with the menus open in front of them, when a stocky young man with a smile as broad as his shoulders pulled up a chair. "Okay if I join you? Or is this confidential stuff?"

The newcomer was warmly welcomed. "Good to see you, Tuck. We'll let you in on it. The big question is what type of hamburger. So, what's your news?"

Tuck, whose real name was Kevin Lefriar, worked in the Vancouver office of Queensland Mining. All three men had the same topic in mind, but first they had to order their lunches or conversation would be interrupted by the waiter.

Kevin turned to Reg as soon as the menus had been folded. "You saw Slip's latest?"

"Yeah, at two-fifty feet of point-five-five with a few dollars in gold. Should get things moving. I hear the choppers have been busy up there."

"Believe it?" said Kevin.

"The results? Yes, Tuck, I do," said Reg slowly. "I think so ... mainly because Slip's a pro and is not about to do anything silly with his drill holes."

Kevin, the cheerful sceptic, liked to explore any divergence in understanding. "But you've heard the rumours about the geochem?"

"Yes, I've heard something about them not being reproducible. But I prefer to believe the reported results until I've got something tangible against them."

"I think I can arrange that," said Kevin with a grin. He got up slowly and walked across to the bar where several people were waiting for a table. He approached a man and a woman talking, glasses in hand. "Want to come and join us? We're just discussing the Chilko hole."

"Hullo, Tuck. Sure, who's there?" asked Judy, statuesque as usual. She was known to the rest of the group as Cuprick's geochemist. Also known was that Cuprick had a policy of staying close to the promoters, Sydney Poulter in particular. Her companion, Angus, was a broker with one of the smaller houses.

"Just Reg and Tom," said Kevin.

After greetings had been exchanged and two more chairs acquired, Kevin continued, addressing Judy. "Reg still believes Slip's geochem was okay. I've got a feeling you know something he doesn't."

Judy threw back her hair and laughed. "Yes, Tuck, I suppose I can tell now." She looked at her watch. "I trust no one is going to leave the table in the next five minutes, before the market closes." She had everyone's attention. "Slip is going to put out a news release this afternoon saying that the geochemical results are questionable and are being investigated."

"Oh shit!" said Tom glancing at the clock on the wall. It was 12:56, four minutes before the market closed. "Go on!"

"We re-did some of the geochem lines and our results did not match what had been reported. A bit of gold and copper but nothing like as much as they had reported. We informed Slip four days ago. To his credit, he told the lab to re-run the samples and check for anything that would explain the discrepancy. Then yesterday afternoon he told us that the lab had just informed him that the dirt bags Chilko submitted had been doctored. I suppose "salting" is the right word. We advised him to make it public immediately and just an hour ago he sent us the news release he's putting out this afternoon."

"How did you get involved?" asked Reg with a tone of incredulity and disappointment.

"Chuck and I went there for a routine property examination. No outcrop where Chilko was working, but Chuck liked what he

Chapter 60 — Pub Rumours

saw on the higher ground to the west. I looked at the geochem and the sites they had sampled. Numbers didn't make sense."

"Evidence?"

"First, the map made me suspicious. The anomaly was from samples on two lines. All samples forming the anomaly were over much higher than the neighbouring lines and there were very few intermediate values. So I took my own samples, right next to some of the high ones. All the samples were on glacial till or close to basalt. It didn't look right."

"How do you explain the hole they've just released? It was right in the middle of the geochem," said Tom in a failing attempt to dismiss the bad news.

"Haven't a clue. But I'm not going to buy Chilko just now," said Judy.

Chapter 61

A Broker in Trouble
October

Angus McKay, a broker who prided himself on balancing risk, had a large clientele within the mining community. He had also introduced a number of non-mining clients to the rewards of mining stocks. While his clients often had occasion to tell him he had got them out too soon, Angus was usually able to point to the fall he had avoided for them. His technique was to get in early and sell soon after the enthusiasm had started. He had participated in the financing of Chilko at twenty cents and had bought a lot for his clients during the slow period before drilling was announced. His own and his clients' holdings amounted to about one and a half million shares. It was, by most standards, not a huge quantity, but it represented a lot of optimism for many of his clients. The stock had been rising well. It had been over fifty cents for two weeks. With only six holes of an eight- or ten-hole program completed, there would be plenty of time to get out.

But now Angus was reading a news release the likes of which he never expected from one of Sydney Poulter's companies. He had tried to phone Poulter himself but the man, whom he did not know well, was unavailable. Selling now was no longer an option. The price would open at around twenty cents, if that. The story would prompt headlines in the business press and probably hit the front page of the Northern Miner next week. There was no point in checking the price. The stock had been halted. This was one of those bleak situations, he told himself, when the best he could hope for was new information which just might change things. He needed to talk to his friend and client, Kevin LeFriar, whose jovial and carefree manner concealed a shrewd and well-informed mind. They had known each other for four years. Each provided the other with information on the mining market from a

Chapter 61 — A Broker in Trouble

different perspective. Even more important, they shared a sense of humour that managed to find absurdities in the most unpromising situations.

His call was connected quickly.

"Morning, Tuck. Do you have time to meet after work today? I want to talk about Chilko."

"I'd like to talk about that one too. It's not an easy one to call. I'm working on some ideas, but I hope you know more than I do."

"How about the Georgia at four?"

"That's fine. You'll be at leisure after work, and I will still be toiling. Sounds about right."

"But you didn't get to work at six-fifteen this morning," replied Angus.

"Okay. See you at four," said Tuck.

Both men enjoyed these late afternoon meetings. Angus, talking towards a large glass of beer held in both hands, revealed his thoughts: "If Slip pulled this one—I mean, if he was responsible for salting those samples—that'll be the end of him. Recovery impossible."

"I wouldn't bet on it. Collapse the price. Buy it all up. Put it back on track. He's done it before."

"Believe that?"

Kevin laughed. "No! Not by salting his own project. He doesn't need to go to that length to get himself more stock. Too risky. Bad for his reputation. Whatever he might have done as a younger man, now that he has made his pile, what he wants is respect. D'you know him?"

"I met him once when he was pitching a property to us and at a reception, but I don't pretend to know him. What about you?"

Tuck answered slowly. "I've been on a couple of field trips with him. He comes across as very focused. You might say driven. He likes the money, but he wants something more. Heaven knows what. Adrenalin, for all I know. He likes it when people are waiting, poised, for his next comment."

"And his comments can be colourful," added Angus.

"Used to be. And off-colour. Vivid, entertaining. All that sort of stuff. But he's not like that any more. He's toned it down."

Angus could not stop himself visualizing the faces of his clients who owned the stock. He continued to ask about the man who was the source of his troubles. "Now that he's cashed up and, as you say, chasing respectability, how do we explain his current predicament?"

"Someone took a run at him."

"Manipulating the stock from outside the company?"

Kevin spoke with the confidence of a man who understood the situation. "Sure. That's much the safest place to do it. No insider reports to make. Off-stage. Almost complete anonymity. Have you seen the short position?"

"I certainly have."

"First I tried to convince myself it was just an outcome of the cynical market and negative sentiment. Then when this news broke it all began to fall together. But it took me a while to believe what was staring me in the face."

Neither man said anything for a while, each engaged in his own thoughts. Kevin broke the silence. "I suppose you have your entire list of clients into it?" Then he played another card. "So it's time to tell them about the opportunity."

"Tell me first," said Angus.

"Well, it all depends on whether the results of the first two holes are real."

"You think they might be?"

"If the salting was done by an outsider, it could be because that person wanted to buy more stock before it went up. If so, he must have been sure the drill results were genuine."

"Go on," said Angus.

"Or, with the stock at fifty-five cents and about to go higher with good results, someone had some shorts to cover."

"If that's it, the salting wasn't to make the property look good?"

"Exactly. It was to make it look bad."

"And if the results are for real, covering those shorts is going to send the price through the roof!"

Both men had seen it before: a short seller caught in a rising market having to buy back the shares he didn't have and, in so doing, increasing the price he was going to have to pay.

"Which is why I would like you to buy me some more shares when it opens."

"Tuck! What makes you think the results are genuine?"

"I have a friend who saw the core at the drill. He said, and I quote: 'It would have been very difficult to have faked them.'"

Angus leaned back in his chair, with the look of someone who has just had his death sentence revoked. Slowly and methodically,

Chapter 61 — A Broker in Trouble

as if enjoying every moment, he lit a cigarette. After the second draw, he said, "So how many shares do you want?"

"I'll take $5,000 worth, assuming they are less than 20 cents."

"So that is 25,000, or more, if the price is down further." Angus had pulled out a notebook and was writing.

Tuck pointed to his friend's notebook. "Actually, I think it will open lower, so I hope for more. Me first, please, then your other clients."

"Of course. But I am not sure many of them will want to play this game. And even if they do, I would not want them in unless they really understand what is happening."

"Yes. The risk is real."

"Risk in junior mining?" said the broker with a laugh. "You've got to be kidding!"

"It's been known to happen," said Tuck, looking forever innocent, and then more seriously. "But I am concerned about what the guy who holds the shorts may do when he starts to lose. If he hasn't covered, he could get rough."

"But you still want those shares?"

"Sure do, because if those drill numbers are correct, we know which side to bet on."

Angus closed the conversation relieved and relaxed. "Okay, that's enough business for the day. Time to go home! I'll give you a call tomorrow and tell you what happened."

Chapter 62

Old Documents
October

Ken Wickford glanced at the bundle of envelopes and fliers he had taken out of his mailbox earlier in the day and left on a table in the kitchen. Mostly junk, he thought to himself, but I have to go through it. A page-size white envelope caught his attention. It was thick enough to hold numerous pages and had been sent airmail from England at considerable expense. It was addressed to "Kenneth Wickford Esq.". His first reaction was, What B.S.! I thought they'd given up on that ages ago. The return address, "Smith, Glenham & Wright, Lawyers," provided adequate explanation for the honorific, but increased the mystery. Intrigued, he took care to find a letter opener to use on the expensive envelope. The covering letter was on thick textured paper. He ran his thumb over the embossed letterhead, puzzled and curious.

```
                          Smith, Glenham & Wright
                               Merton High St,
                              South Wimbledon,
                                London, SW20
                              5th October, 1987
```

Dear Mr. Wickford,

We represent the estate of Mrs. Amanda Benson who died on 19th September, 1986. Among the papers found by the executors are the documents listed below and included herewith. We have been instructed to send the documents to you because they appear to relate to a mining claim in Canada, which used to be owned by your grandfather, Edward J. Wickford, in the early

Chapter 62 — Old Documents

part of the century. These documents are now your property. With the possible exception of the agreement (Item 4), which has almost certainly lapsed, neither we nor the executors believe these papers to have any monetary value. But they may nevertheless be of some interest to you.

Yours faithfully,
Steven Wright, LLB

Ken put the letter to one side and turned over the enclosed pages one by one: two letters from his grandfather, both written on a typewriter. These he would read later, slowly and with great interest. Three old pages that appeared to have been removed from the British Columbia Minister of Mines Annual reports for 1914, 1915, 1916. No interest. Seen those many times. A letter to his grandfather from someone called Mabel congratulating him on his discovery. That would be interesting. So would three pages of typescript signed by both Edward Wickford and Albert Sanders and headed "Right to Purchase". Although there were more pages to examine, Ken immediately focused on the agreement. At first glance it appeared to be an ordinary option agreement but with some turns of phrase from a more formal age. Then he realized that the two crown grants to which the agreement referred were ones he had never owned. His disappointment lasted some three seconds before he realized they were the crown grants acquired by his grandfather, sold by his father, and now possessed by Chilko. An option on Chilko's ground! Unlikely. But what if? That would change the game. But an agreement now over seventy years old? Impossible! It would have to go in the "interesting but useless" category. He then turned his attention to the remaining documents. Most were letters between Edward and Albert Sanders about progress on the crown grants and how to obtain financing. He put the papers back in their envelope and began the process of cooking himself an evening meal. As he was to eat alone, the food and its preparation would be simple.

The next day Ken phoned Bill Grange, the Prince George lawyer he had known for years and consulted from time to time.
"Morning, Bill."
"Hello, Ken. Still wrestling with that Poulter guy?"
"He's still a problem, but today's question is not directly about him. It's a very long shot so don't spend too much time on it."

"Sounds interesting," said the lawyer.

"I've been sent some papers, mostly letters, left to a person I never knew—someone in England who financed my grandfather's exploration. Among the papers is an option, although they didn't call it that, drawn up in England, on two 1890s crown grants now owned by Chilko. The claims used to belong to my grandfather, but my dad sold them in the thirties. Is there any chance the option could be valid?"

"Zilch. Not a chance." Then, after a pause, "No, let me change that to 'highly improbable.' Drawn up in England, did you say? To mean anything someone would have had to register it, I mean the option, against the title to the claim, and that would be in B.C. And if the encumbrance were registered, why would Chilko, or the previous owner, have bought it? What was the option for? All of it or just part?"

"It mentions 75 percent but it's more complicated than that."

"I don't like to disappoint you, but…"

"Okay, I understand."

"Tell you what," said Bill. "Give me the legal names of the crown grants. I'll have a title search done. No charge unless something comes out of it."

"I'm going to be in P.G. next Thursday."

"Good. Bring the agreement. I have a professional curiosity in any mining agreement that old. Come by on Thursday afternoon. How about 2:00 pm?"

"That would work well," answered Ken. "See you then."

As he drove to Prince George the following Thursday, Ken was looking forward to the meeting. He had been a client of Bill's for years and the two of them had developed a good working relationship. A lot of their conversations, even those in the law office, remained unbilled. By tacit understanding, Bill's invoices were less in Ken's lean years and greater when he prospered.

Ken was shown into a meeting room as soon as he arrived and Bill joined him a moment later.

"Good to see you, Ken. Easy drive? Coffee?"

"Yes and yes," replied Ken sinking into one of the chairs.

"I'm glad to be able to tell you that the option you told me about may not be as dead as I expected."

"No kidding! How so?"

Chapter 62 — Old Documents

"Well, there is nothing certain yet, but here's the situation. A search at the Land Titles Office in Smithers turned up an agreement that is, I assume, the one you are talking about. It was a right-to-purchase signed in 1914 and it lapsed in 1926. There were no other encumbrances on either of those two crown granted mineral claims. This fits with the two separate title searches not finding anything. The first would have been when your father sold those crown grants and the second when they were purchased recently by Poulter Investments. But the story gets a bit more complicated."

Bill Grange continued: "The way it works, or the way it used to work, is that wherever a land title document was filed, there would be copies in both Victoria and the regional office. You see, in those days, when your grandfather registered that agreement, copying was by hand. In effect, the government had two originals. One of them was for Victoria, the other one for the regional office."

"With back-up like that, there can't be much room for mistakes."

"That's true—most of the time. Fortunately it's rare, but sometimes the system breaks down. Every now and again, a document gets lost in transit. Only a few years ago, there was a plane crash in Terrace that destroyed some land title documents."

"I remember that plane crash but didn't know about the documents. So, it can happen, even now?"

"Exactly. So I acted on the hunch that a duplicate or some other document had never reached the branch office."

"You mean there's another agreement?"

"There is. Same parties. In effect it's a replacement of the one we see in Smithers. So we have agreement number one in Smithers and Victoria, and agreement number two only in Victoria."

Ken looked puzzled. "Two?"

The lawyer took his time before explaining. "I was as surprised as you. They sent you a copy of the second agreement between your grandfather and Albert Sanders."

Ken Wickford stood up and started pacing around the room. "So that explains how a search in the branch office could have missed the second agreement in the 1930s and again recently when Poulter bought the claims. I suppose it's not common practice to search in both places."

"That's true. It's hardly ever necessary."

"Does this mean there is a separate option agreement?"

"Yes. Sort of. It's a follow-on from the first agreement, but with a wrinkle. It confirms exercise of the option in the first agreement, Sanders having spent the required amount of money to acquire seventy-five percent, but then it goes on. It says that, if both Sanders and his heir were to die before any production took place on the claims, then the property could be claimed back by your grandfather or his descendants. It's called a 'covenant to reconvey.' It's not common. In fact I've never had to deal with one before. I believe the last in B.C. was in the forestry business in 1944."

Bill Grange walked to the sideboard and returned with the coffee. Ken Wickford, now sitting again, followed the trail with more questions. "So this second agreement, could it still be valid?"

The lawyer looked at his client. "I have to tell you in passing that I wish all the files I work on were as fascinating as this."

"You should become a prospector! It's always interesting."

"One day, perhaps. That's for my retirement. Just now I'm hot on the trail of an agreement drawn up over sixty years ago on a couple of crown grants a century old. As I see it, the reason it may still be valid is that there was no termination date for the reconvey clause."

"So I can apply to have the claims returned, given, surrendered to me?"

"Not so fast. That's a possibility, which is why it's worth pursuing. But we're not there yet."

"Anything I can do?"

"No. I've got to dig deeper. My current opinion, and it may change, is that if anyone doing a title search on these claims could have found evidence of this document, then the option would still be valid."

Ken was waiting for more when Bill Grange summarized the situation. "Leave it with me for a week. I'll get back to you by phone. At that stage you may want a written opinion from me, or you may have enough to run with it yourself."

"That sounds like a sleepless week, but this happy client will be waiting for your call."

The two men parted with a firm handshake and Ken Wickford left for the long drive home.

Chapter 63

Greenies in Town
October

Lunch at the Skeena Room of the Taku Hotel in Smithers was a favourite for business people, both local and visiting. Civil servants of all types favoured the place and were usually well represented. Sadly, the quality of the salad bar, acknowledged by the locals to be the best in town, was not matched by the beer. The hotel's inventory was limited to the high-distribution brands, or "chemical beer" as Lester Bance called it.

Lester and Wally Seldock, who had shared several business deals since Lester became a resident eight years ago, had arranged to meet to discuss purchasing a commercial lot at the south end of town.

"It's a bet on the town's economy," said Lester.

"And that," replied Wally, thoughtfully stirring his coffee, "is a bet on the economy of the north."

Lester nodded. "We'll have our ups and downs, but people are going to need our lumber and our minerals." Then he added, keeping a straight face, "They might even want some of your cows".

Wally, well accustomed to being ribbed about his cows, responded with a serious answer and a question. "You know, I don't lose money on them. Not much at any rate. You know what worries me?"

"Knowing you, probably lots, but I'll guess it's politicians you have in mind."

"Not exactly. It's those damn greenies. I was visiting my brother in Vancouver recently. His wife's a teacher and she was telling us about how most of them—the other teachers, I mean—are constantly slagging logging and mining. You know, if that should become mainstream, like it has in California, they could almost shut down a town like this."

"I know what you mean, but I think you're going too far. All we've got is a few weirdos chaining themselves to trees, blocking logging roads and things like that."

Without looking round, Wally pointed over his shoulder. "See those two at the buffet counter? The woman with long red hair and the guy with her?"

Lester adjusted his glasses and peered towards the buffet table. "Don't know them. Tourists?"

"Not quite, but they *are* from out of town. They have been here for a month or so. Greenies. No idea where they are staying."

"Do they matter?" asked Lester. "I thought we were going to talk about purchasing this lot. I told the owner—the bank, that is—that we we're interested."

"Yes, we have to discuss that, I know, but bear with me for a few minutes. Those people are part of what I'm talking about. They both work for Greenpeace and have set up an office in town. They haven't done much yet except, I am told, given a couple of talks at the elementary school."

Lester's reply revealed a touch of irritation at the hijacking of his agenda. "Are you telling me that we should take a couple of new-age hippies into account before we spend a couple of hundred grand on some commercial real estate?"

"Just a straw in the wind, best not ignored," said Wally. "Look, the line up has gone. Let's get our lunch."

Their selections made, they walked back to their table, plates in hand, passing the couple they had been talking about. Wally responded to the man's glance with a nod of his head and a, "Hi, there," before re-joining his friend, who was already seated. For a while they said nothing as each man enjoyed his food.

"I don't know how they do it," said Wally between mouthfuls, "but we never have salads like this at home."

"I'll bet you haven't said that to Marge."

"Wrong. I did just that about a month ago."

"And?"

"Haven't had any salads of any kind since," answered Wally, laughing.

"Sounds like you blew it."

Chapter 63 — Greenies in Town

"Don't think so. I think that we'll soon be having top-of-the-line salads. Marge will find out all about it and then do it better than anyone. Then you and Betty had better come and sample it."

"We will look forward to that."

"Lester, I have an idea."

"You usually do, but I don't commit to going along with it. What is it?"

"That Greenpeace couple." Wally looked straight at Lester. "Want to talk to them?"

"I'm not sure I would have anything useful to say. I'm on one planet and they're on another."

"But," said Wally, "you would not object if I asked them to join us?"

Lester acquiesced. "Go ahead, but let me finish my hamburger first."

A few minutes later, Wally pulled himself out of his chair and walked over to the Greenpeace table.

The young man with the angular face and a pony-tail and the young women with the red hair looked up.

"Hi, my name is Wally. I believe you both work for Greenpeace?"

"That's right. Do you want to sign up?" replied the girl, with an open smile and a hint of laughter.

"We were wondering if you would care to join us," said Wally, looking at the man.

"My buddy and I were talking about Greenpeace and we realized we needed to know more."

The young man looked at his companion, as if for instruction.

"Sure, let's do it," she said. "I am going to get my dessert, then we'll come over."

A couple of minutes later, the two men watched the couple leave the buffet table and come towards them. They paid particular attention to the woman. She was wearing jeans and a loose blouse matching her red hair, and leading the way. If they had communicated their thoughts they would have agreed that she was probably in her mid-thirties and unusually attractive.

"Now I know why you wanted to talk to them," said Lester without looking at his friend. "Next, you'll be telling me this all relates to the business decision we have to make."

Wally had no time to reply before the couple arrived. Soon after the introductions, Lester and Wally learned that Helen was from Toronto and had spent three years full time with Greenpeace in Vancouver. Prior to coming west she had taken a degree in geography and anthropology from the University of Toronto. Her companion, Wim, a tall young man with long hair, was from Amsterdam where he had worked with an environmental organization nipping at the heels of the chemical industry.

"What made you come to Canada?" asked Lester.

"Since I was a kid, I used to read about Canada. Then I learned about cutting rainforest so I was joining another environmental society in my home town. Last year at one of the meetings I saw an advertisement for this job in British Columbia. The society at home wants us to come and see what is happening here." Wim's English was serviceable but noticeably accented, and occasionally displayed the sentence structure of his native tongue. Having said his piece, he evidently expected approval and encouragement.

"And he is seeing plenty," interjected Helen. "We had him on Vancouver Island, blocking a logging road. Then he was in the Kootenays, picketing at a new mine site."

"So you must find Smithers kind of boring," said Lester. "Nothing much happening here."

"Not just now," replied Helen. "But this town is close to a lot of wilderness—mountains, forests, wild animals, and wild streams."

"That's part of the reason Wally and I are here. We were both brought up in northern B.C. We love the outdoors. I used to do a lot of hiking. I still go fly fishing in places that hardly anyone else ever gets to."

"That's good," said Rudy. "We want to keep it for activities like that. We have to stop logging and mining."

Lester and Wally were both about to say something, but Helen got in first.

"You see, most of us are aware of what has happened in other parts of this continent—the loss of the great redwood forests of California, for example. When did you last see a herd of buffalo? B.C. has one of the largest temperate forests left in the world. Some people here—I don't know what your line of business is— are in the process of destroying it. Our job is to stop the process before it is too late."

"All right, I think I see where you are coming from," said Lester. "But I should tell you that I am a businessman. I used to be a logging contractor. I don't do that any more, but I do buy and sell timber rights. And my friend here spends a lot of his time selling

Chapter 63 — Greenies in Town

equipment to the mining business. So you couldn't find two nicer guys to talk to!"

"Wow! Glad to meet you," said Helen. "But I'm a realist. Chances of converting either of you are zip. You belong to the older generation. You did it your way. But that is going to change, whether you like it or not. But if you do decide to see the future, we would of course be delighted." Her tone changed from gentle mocking to forceful advocacy with little room for a middle ground, but she was evidently enjoying the situation and the opportunity for a serious debate.

"What's wrong with logging?" asked Wally.

Rudy moved forward in his chair, signalling his wish to respond. "This is one of the last places in the world where at least some of the temperate rain forest is still intact. We have to keep it like that."

Helen added, "There is nothing wrong with logging, if it is done with the environment in mind. But clear-cutting huge tracts of forest is wasteful, ugly and damages the ecosystem."

Lester's response was delivered without a hint of emotion. "But if we stop logging, the price of lumber will rise. Then you'll have to pay more for your houses."

Rudy addressed Lester with feeling. "Building houses of wood is wasteful. Bricks or stone are better. Also, most of the wood in this province gets sold to other countries."

With a gesture of his hands Lester showed a hint of irritation. "And the other countries pay us money. That allows us to pay our workers and suppliers, so the people of this town can afford decent lives. If you shut it down, we will have to go somewhere else."

"That's one of the difficult parts of what we are trying to do," said Helen. "On the one hand we would rather not harm anyone's job. On the other hand, we have to stop the clear-cutting and the mining before this wonderful land is ruined forever."

With Wally preferring to listen and hold his fire, Lester was left to stall the advance.

"Ruined for ever? The trees grow again. It's a renewable resource. People need the lumber. Our people get paid for supplying it. Why spoil a good thing? I do admit we haven't always done things in an environmentally friendly way. We now do it better because the whole of society has changed its attitude."

Wim replied with an earnest intensity that admitted no compromise. "People like to see the forests, to hike in the hills. There are fewer and fewer places in the world where this can be done."

Lester responded, "That's part of the problem. Europe has cut its forests and built over its wilderness. So there's not much left. Now you people want us to preserve this wilderness for yourselves, and if that means we have to find other ways to earn a living, too bad! Do you expect us to go along with that?"

Wally interjected: "I hesitate to ask about mining, but let's hear what you have to say."

Helen signalled to Wim that she would handle this one. "Mining makes an awful mess. A huge hole in the ground, devastation all round, acid drainage into the streams."

"Do you people drive cars?" asked Wally.

"Yes, we could not get around without one. And now you are going to ask where the metals come from. There needs to be mining somewhere. Yes, you're right. But it has to be done in an environmentally friendly way, and there are some places where it shouldn't be done at all. This wilderness in northern B.C. that we are trying to save is one of those places."

Wally continued his defence of mining. "So you rich folks are going to mine in someone else's back yard so you can leave ours in a pristine state? Export the disturbance to some poor country. Is that fair?"

Helen adjusted her seating position and looked directly at Wally. "You're going too far! It depends where the mining is done. It can't be done where it damages the environment, whether in this country or in the developing world."

Lester took his turn. "You've been in this town long enough to realize that lots of folks here are trying to find an orebody. Some of them are professionals, others are part-timers. If one of them succeeds, the mine will make a bit of a mess over a tiny area, but there will be lots of new jobs, say five hundred, perhaps even a thousand. And each of those jobs will create several more. Think of what that would do for the people in this town. Then, when the orebody is mined out, the forest will grow back."

"That's just a vicious circle," replied Helen. "You find a mine. You have boom time. Lots of jobs. People come from all over to fill the jobs. Then there is a bit of a downturn, that creates a call for more industry. Perhaps another mine, perhaps a factory. So more people come. Soon you have the whole place paved over."

Chapter 63 — Greenies in Town

"Whoa!" said Wally. "That's BS!" Lester protested.

"I expect you to protest. But look at California again as just one example."

"Or my country, or most of Europe," said Wim.

"Do you two realize," said Lester, slowing his words until he had everyone's attention, "that you could fit most of Europe, say France, Germany, Belgium and Holland into B.C.? How many hundred million people are there in Europe? And B.C. now has about two million."

"Yes, we do realize that. And we hope there will never be a hundred and fifty million in B.C. In fact we're doing our best to keep it the way it is."

"So all the miles and miles of forest, scrub, tundra, alpine country and grassland will stay like it is, mostly unused?"

"That's what some people in the environmental movement would like. Others—"

"Hold it!" said Lester raising his hand. "Let's stop there a moment. You say some people in your organization want to lock it up forever? And they think they will make the world a better place?" He was making no attempt to disguise his disdain for a point of view he could not begin to agree with. "People in this town will have to sell their houses, leave family and friends, and move to other places in search of work? Do you realize what they think of what you are trying to do?"

At this point, the Dutchman wanted the floor. "Let me please speak for this. For Canadians who now are living in Smithers, it is most important to have work. With new jobs the town will grow and people will be happy to have work. But Canadians who live in the future will want to have the forests and the mountains and the salmon and the bears. We are looking to the future."

Wally, watching his friend, realized that this was becoming one of those rare occasions when Lester's easy going, roll-with-the-punches, laugh-about-it style was being displaced by irritation.

"So you people," Lester began, "have the presumption—no that's the wrong word, try 'cheek'—to tell us, the people of Smithers and other towns like this, that in the interests of our children and the children of other Canadians, we have to put up with a reduced economy, a lower standard of living, lessened dreams, and that we may even have to move out of our homes, while the resources around us go unused."

"You didn't let me finish," said Helen. "There are others, like me, who want a sensible compromise. We say no to unrestricted clear-cuts and to mining wherever something is found. But we don't want to close down all logging or all mining."

She was looking serious and focused now. "But, to answer your question, some of the trees that could be logged at a profit and some of the metal which could be mined will, if we have our way, remain unused. And there is nothing so unusual about that. If the Americans found the richest orebody in the world in Yellowstone Park, or the Germans in the Black Forest, or the English in one of their best-loved patches of country, do you think it would be mined? In each of those cases, more value is put on the other uses of the land. So we have to make choices."

Lester adjusted his position on the low chair, and started to speak. His words came slowly and deliberately as if to suppress any hint of strong feeling, a technique he used with effect in the council chamber. "On this much, we agree. Now let's consider some claims owned by a mutual friend of ours that are now being explored. He's in town right now and just might drop by. His claims are over a hundred kilometres from here. They're up in the mountains at almost five thousand feet. There is some good timber, never been logged. Some scrub timber, some open ground above the tree line. Some beautiful scenery and some I never need to see again. No one lives within fifty kilometres. If they find enough copper to make a mine, what will you people say?"

"I shouldn't speak for Wim, but I believe he would say all development must be stopped. For myself, it should be reviewed and, if it passes rigorous environmental tests, I would let it go ahead."

Lester looked at his watch and glanced at Wally. "This is getting to be a long lunch hour, but I told Ken we would be here until two. That's another fifteen minutes. After that I have to go." He turned to Helen and her companion. "I hope we can meet again. Perhaps one of you would like to come to one of our Chamber of Commerce meetings. We have one every month."

The conversation continued in a less intense way. They learned that Helen had been raised on a farm in the Kootenays, had travelled around the world in her early twenties and had started participating in environmental causes when she got back to Canada. Then, in the midst of the conversation, Wally stood up and raised his hand. "There's Ken. Okay. He's seen us."

Chapter 63 — Greenies in Town

When Ken Wickford arrived at the table, Wally had no difficulty putting the introduction in context with their conversation. "This is the young man we were telling you about, the one with the mineral property he'd like to make into a mine."

He turned to Ken. "Ken, we'd like you to meet Helen and Wim. They are with Greenpeace. They are charming people, but they don't like forestry or mining."

Ken exchanged a firm handshake with Wim and then extended a hand to Helen, who had her hand half way towards him when she paused, raised both her hands, gasped, "Ken!" and fell into his embrace.

After a few awkward seconds, the reaction of the three others was summarized by Lester. "Not your first meeting, I think."

Ken, beaming, answered. "Yes, in Australia, the Gold Coast, many years ago."

Another chair was dragged to the small table and they all sat down, but the conversation was broken and unfocused until Wally took his leave. "My time's up."

"And that's my cue too," added Lester. "I think you two must have a lot to talk about." He handed his card to Helen.

"Do you have one?"

"Yes, I do." said Helen as she handed one to each of the businessmen. "Wim doesn't. We didn't expect him to be here long enough."

Lester combined his leave-taking with an invitation. "It's been good talking to both of you. Always interesting to meet people with a different point of view. And remember the Chamber of Commerce meetings."

The two older men left. Neither said much until they reached parking lot where, standing by his car, Lester voiced what both had been thinking about.

"Interesting, eh? Young Ken's life is going to be even more exciting."

"And wouldn't we like to be young again!" answered Wally as he turned towards his own car.

Chapter 64

Trump Card ?
October

Lester Bance and Wally Seldock were at the back of the Evergreen Restaurant when Ken arrived.

Wally opened with, "Nice girl you used to know!".

Ken laughed happily and dropped himself into one of the easy chairs. "Yes, we haven't seen each other since Australia. That was years ago. Just a few letters for a while. Nothing since."

Wally had to ask, "Did you tell her about your mining work?"

"You guys told her!" said Ken, and then added: "And, no. We had other things to talk about!"

Lester and Wally's enquiry into their friend's past adventures came to an end when Will Herman arrived with his nephew, Carl, who glided in on crutches and became the centre of attention. A cascade of questions prompted a grin from him.

"I'm doing fine."

"The break healing well?"

"They say it was a simple fracture and they don't expect any problems with it."

"And inside the rest of you?"

"Just bruising. Seems to be clearing up. Still got sore places, but it's better every day."

"Hey, I see they're advertising for underground miners at Erikson. You now have experience," said Wally.

Carl's laugh was answer enough.

"Well, welcome to our club," said Wally. "No dues, no membership, just good talking."

Lester added, "And something to drink. So we'll start by drinking to your full recovery. Here's to you, Carl."

After Will and Carl were seated, Lester opened the next topic with, "You know, Ken. When this saga of yours is over, we won't

Chapter 64 — Trump Card ?

have much to talk about. All our other topics will pale in comparison. How could anything compete with a mining accident, a medivac, discovery of an old tunnel, a staking rush, and even some scoundrels?"

"I look forward to less drama. You guys have ring-side seats, but I'm in the arena with the lions. Anyone want to trade places?"

"Don't believe it," said Wally. "You have the upside. You wouldn't give that up."

"Well, that's what I want to discuss. Maybe you, or some of you, would provide advice. Then I think I am going to be looking for someone to share the risk and possible reward."

"Sounds interesting. So you are going to send us down to get rid of Mr. Poulter?"

"Victor Dubell first, please. But you have to hear my news. And I want your wisdom."

Ken took his time. He began with enough family history so that everyone would understand the situation, then said: "A couple of weeks ago I got a registered letter from a law firm in England enclosing some documents. They'd been left to a remote cousin, someone I'd never even heard of, and were passed on to me because they had belonged to my grandfather. Some were publications I had already read, most of them pages from the annual report of the B.C. Minister of Mines. But three of the documents were really interesting. One was a 1912 letter from my grandfather to the man who would later finance the first work on the claim. The other two were agreements." He paused to pick up his glass of beer, and then carried on. "One agreement was a short handwritten note assigning a ten-percent carried interest in the first group of claims to a native Indian called Charley Raven. It was payment for finding the copper showing."

"He might still be alive!" said Wally. "And if he is, and if you make any money on this, will you feel you owe him something?"

"I don't know about the legals, but I know what my grandfather would have wanted. I never met him, but my dad used to talk about him. Things like duty and honesty were big with him."

"Not so unusual in that generation."

"And it makes sense to me, so that's what I will have to do."

Lester was nodding approval. "I like that in anyone I'm doing business with. Eh, Wally?"

"Yes, of course, but there will be no money for anyone if Chilko finds nothing or hits an orebody and leaves Ken out."

"And the other agreement?" Lester asked.

"I'm coming to that. The person my grandfather knew, who must have been something of a mining man as well as a financier, bought an option on the Raven claims and two Eastern crown grants in 1914. He thought there was a future in copper, but he particularly liked gold which had already made money for him."

"Just before the war," said Wally. "The agreement didn't lapse?"

"No. My grandfather was in France for three years. The two men must have met, talked about the agreement (called a 'Right to Purchase' in those days) and then revised it in 1917 when he was convalescing in England after being wounded. From what I can figure, the outcome of the later meeting was an amendment to the original agreement."

Ken sipped his drink. No one spoke.

"By this time the eastern claims were more interesting to the financier because of the gold. He also had time to think about the chances of Edward being killed. The revised agreement took this into account and gave special treatment to the eastern claims. They were, if you remember, the ones my dad sold in the fifties and that are now in the middle of Chilko's ground. I tried to buy them back several times, but the price was always too high. Chilko's purchase was very recent. They paid much more than I could have even thought about."

"Have you shown this agreement to a lawyer?" asked Wally.

"I certainly have."

"This is getting interesting. So you have his opinion?"

"His first comment was to tell me there was absolutely no way an option agreement as old as that could be valid. And, of course, the claims would not have changed hands if there had been an outstanding agreement. Then—and I'm leaving out some details here—the lawyer found the other, revised, agreement, but it existed only in the Land Titles office in Victoria, registered in B.C. in 1919. No mention in the Smithers records."

Lester was sceptical. "Sounds improbable."

"Yes. Apparently it hardly ever happens, but every so often there is a glitch and a document goes missing. The second agreement is an option, but an unusual one. The investor had put up some money under the first agreement and had acquired a seventy-five percent interest. But the second agreement goes on to say that, if both he and his heir die before there is any production, the property gets returned to my grandfather or his heirs."

Chapter 64 — Trump Card ?

"And that would include you?"

"So it seems."

Wally posed the question that any businessman would ask, "And there's no termination date on the get-it-back clause?"

"Correct."

"And you could acquire the claims?"

"Possibly."

"Price?"

"Just a token amount. If certain things happened, they were to be returned to my family. And those things—death of the financier and his heir and the lack of production—have happened."

"So you could take the core out of Poulter's play?" asked Wally.

"Maybe, but there are some legal questions to sort out."

Two voices responded at exactly the same time "Like?" "Exactly what?"

"Well, as I understand it, it all depends on whether the buyer of the crown grants could have been expected to find out that this second option existed. I think of it as an option, but the lawyer has another name for it—a 'covenant to reconvey.' Chilko may say that there was no way anyone could have known of the existence of this option."

"I have to think they would be right," was Lester's thoughtful comment.

"That was exactly the lawyer's first reaction. His opinion just now is that sufficient due diligence would have found this document."

"No trace of it in Smithers?"

"None he could find. Its absence in the regional office explains why it was missed twice: when my dad sold in the thirties and when Poulter bought it recently. I'm told that sort of snafu is very rare but does happen, usually when a document is lost in transit. Hard to believe, but…"

Lester raised a hand. "In some ways it doesn't really matter. Whatever the merits of your case, if this becomes public it's going to spook a lot of investors. It would be a cloud on the title right in the middle of what might be an orebody."

Everyone waited for Ken to say how he planned to play the hand he had been dealt.

He did not disappoint. "So here's a draft letter I want to show you. It was prepared by Pinfold Grange."

"They're a good law shop. Who are you dealing with?" was Lester's question.

"Bill Grange."

"I've never met him but I've heard he's diligent. Go on."

Ken had two copies of the draft letter for Chilko, which he passed around.

```
Draft letter to Chilko Resources Inc.
```

We write on behalf of our client, Mr. Kenneth Wickford, who is in possession of an agreement which entitles him to acquire ownership of certain crown-granted mineral claims in British Columbia.

The agreement was among a package of documents mentioned in the will of Mrs. Amanda Benson, a remote cousin of our client.

By this will Mr. Kenneth Wickford became aware of an option agreement, drawn up in 1914 and amended in 1917, which includes a covenant to reconvey. This document confers on Mr. Wickford the right to acquire full title to two crown-granted mineral claims in British Columbia by making a payment of $100 (one hundred dollars). The agreement was prepared by Park and Wilderby in London, England and was registered there in 1918 and British Columbia in 1919. An original of this agreement is filed with the records of these two crown grants in the British Columbia Land Titles Office in Victoria.

Please consider this letter as notice to Chilko Resources ("Chilko") of Mr. Wickford's wish to exercise his option to take ownership of the claims, the consideration for which is enclosed in the form of a banker's note for the sum of one hundred dollars.

We also act for Mr. Wickford in his dispute with Chilko on certain of his mineral claims staked in the Nisselinka Range. In this context we wish to inform you that we regard the existence of this option as a matter of material consequence to Chilko. Accordingly, we expect to see this disclosed by

Chapter 64 — Trump Card ?

```
Chilko and to be filed as part of its public record.
In the absence of public declaration by Chilko of
the change of ownership of the crown grant, we will
advise Mr. Wickford to issue a news release to make
this information public himself.

Copies of Mrs. Amanda Benson's will and the option
agreement are enclosed for your records.
```

Not a word was spoken as the five people around the coffee table read and reread the letter. All but Carl, who would have been uncomfortable doing so, settled back in their chairs, deep in thought.

Wally was the first to break the silence. "That's like rolling a hand grenade into their office!"

Ken responded with feeling: "But how else do you treat people like that? I've told Will, but not the rest of you, that they've been talking to Jill. She said someone offering an insurance scheme for university education for the kids got in touch. It seemed all he was really interested in was getting the dirt on me—at least that's her take on it. Last year they threatened to get Will fired. They don't negotiate. All they do is use bully tactics. My claims are unsalable because they have challenged my staking. What am I expected to do? Play dead?"

Lester was the next to comment. "Well, Ken, that's a very strong card you have. So is their attempt to invalidate your claims. If you do nothing you will probably lose your claims, and you could lose a fortune. If I were in your shoes, I would go after the bastards with everything you've got. And about your invitation to join you: as you know, doing business with friends is not usually a good idea, but this is just plain exciting. It's my ticket into the arena where all the action is. So, if you have a few shares for sale, I'll take them."

Wally was not going to be left out: "I'm in, if that's what you want. But, you know, here's my advice whether you go it alone or invite us in: first report the threats to the police, give them a bit of time to put a file around it, and then send the letter about the crown grant. If that doesn't force them to negotiate, then crank it up one step and make it all public to the investment community."

Lester, evidently enjoying himself, said, "That's right. Now you know you're not alone with the lions and tigers and whatever else they put you up against. I have another suggestion. All those dirty tricks that Chilko has been up to don't really make sense. Poulter has a reputation as a promoter of penny stocks, most of which lead nowhere, but he's been in the business for years and has made a lot of money. I wouldn't trust him an inch, but those cheap and nasty moves don't fit. We don't know how his organization works. Maybe he doesn't know about everything that happens within it. So, here's my suggestion."

Lester shifted in his chair, before starting on what was on his mind. "I have a friend, Bob Strang. You know him, Wally. He's going to be in Vancouver for a couple of days later this week. He's a municipal councillor in Prince George and could almost certainly get to see Poulter. Would you have any objection, Ken, if I were to ask him to spend a few minutes with your antagonist?"

"That's fine by me. Nothing to lose, and we might learn something."

Chapter 65

Hubris & Nemesis
October

Vancouver was looking its best as Sydney J. Poulter drove his BMW M6 south across the Lions Gate Bridge at 6:45 in the morning in late October. A strong west wind was plucking white caps out of the sea. Visibility was unlimited and the sky was almost cloudless. He liked to drive this car when he felt unpressured, and preferred to leave it in the garage when rain was expected. Life, he decided, was treating him well. He had, he admitted, made some enemies, but that was something no successful promoter could avoid. He had channelled several hundred million into exploration for orebodies. Some of his shareholders had benefited to the point of becoming rich. While having no mine to his credit, he claimed responsibility for several discoveries that might eventually see production. And now Chilko was beginning to look like a major discovery.

Dr. Praine, the independent consultant, had phoned the previous day to say that the three holes they had drilled had corroborated the Chilko holes and that he would be sending a report for arrival today. He had also said that he would enclose written permission to Chilko to publish the report, provided it was released in its entirety. In all, he didn't think Mr. Poulter would have any difficulty with the report, as it was unequivocal in its confirmation of the Chilko drilling. Sydney was thinking that he had played this one well. He had confronted those who'd tried to destroy both his company and his reputation and he had come out on top. This morning's news release was going to be a pleasure to write. The company was well structured and he owned a sufficiently high proportion of the stock. If it reached three dollars, which was a reasonable goal, he would benefit by over twenty million dollars— before tax of course, but he had ways of keeping that down. This

The Nisselinka Claims

discovery of gold and copper in northern B.C. would do wonders for his status *and* the economy. Jobs all round. Could be as many as five hundred. In Smithers and Prince George they would think of him as a benefactor. Keys to the city? Do they do that? Well, there was a ways to go before he was there. But, meantime, he was having fun. By now he had driven through most of the park and was approaching Lost Lagoon. He didn't even try to suppress a smile. Life was indeed treating him well.

But when he returned through the park some thirty-six hours later, life would not seem so kind.

Poulter's first task that morning was to make a draft of the news release to announce Dr. Praine's conclusions. Courier packages from Toronto were guaranteed to arrive by 10:00 am. He had a couple of hours to wait. In the meantime a few phrases or sentences could be penned: These included: "unqualified confirmation" ... "all doubts about the Chilko drilling having been laid to rest" ... "the sinister attempt to sully Chilko's reputation can now be left for the police to handle."

Shortly before 10:00 am a courier package was delivered, but to Marion's surprise it was not from Toronto. It came from a law firm, Pinfold Grange, in Prince George. The letter referred to two crown grants which Marion remembered the company buying when they first became interested in the Nisselinka Range. She remembered thinking at the time that the price had been rather high for the small area they covered. She walked quickly to the drafting room to look at the claim map on the wall. The claims owned by Chilko and undisputed were coloured in blue. Near the middle of the blue claims lay the two crown grants. She went to a neighbouring map to see the locations of the drill holes. It was obvious to her, as it would have been to anyone familiar with open pit deposits, that any mining operation covering those four drill holes would require the crown grants. She went back to her desk where she noticed another courier package, probably the one they were expecting. She would deal with that in a moment. She took a deep breath and walked to Slip's office.

Mr. Poulter was in a good mood. Pacing up and down, pencil in hand, he beamed as she came in. "I've got some good words for the news release to try on you, Marion. Any sign of that report?"

"I think it's just come in, but we received another one ten minutes ago and I've been dealing with that."

Chapter 65 — Hubris & Nemesis

"Topic?"

"It's a lawyer's letter enclosing a money order. They say their client, Mr. Wickford, wishes to exercise an option on those crown grants we bought in May."

Sydney Poulter stopped pacing, stood still, and said nothing for a few seconds. Then he exploded. "What bloody cheek. Insolent son-of-a-bitch!" Then he smiled and said, "Just tell him to get lost ... no, tell him I don't have time to slap mosquitoes today."

"You had better read it. They enclose an option agreement dating from 1917!"

"Lemme see it!"

He read the letter standing up and handed it back. "Never heard such nonsense. Get in touch with Jason. Ask him to get back to me as soon as he has seen it. I'll see the other package as soon as you've dealt with it."

Dr Praine's letter was everything Poulter could have hoped for. The letter made it quite clear that they had looked only at the drill holes and could say nothing about the geochemistry or any other observations or measurements. But the letter also made it clear that the three drill holes they had drilled confirmed the Chilko grades and widths in the adjacent holes. He looked at his notes. Then he got up, pencil still in hand, and stared out of the window. Now, he thought, he could get on with the news release.

Or could he? It soon became obvious to him that all the good expected from a release that removed doubt about the drilling would be negated by a challenge to title. Work and creativity on the news release ground to a halt.

Marion's voice on the intercom broke up a cascade of contradictory and disturbing thoughts. The news release today? Forced to announce a challenge to title tomorrow? Next week? Start litigation against Wickford? He could see the headline: "Prominent promoter sues prospector."

He picked up the phone. "Yes, Marion."

There is a Mr. Strang on the phone. He wants to speak to you. Says it's important."

"Never heard of him. Who is he?"

"He said he would identify himself, if you insisted, but would prefer to explain that himself."

"Okay, put him through.... Poulter here."

"Mr. Poulter, I'm Bob Strang from Prince George, where I have the honour to sit on the municipal council. I'm passing through Vancouver and am looking for ten minutes with you."

"Normally I'd be glad to meet you as we have a crew operating in the north country, but not today. I've some urgent things I have to deal with."

"Mr. Poulter, I'm only in town for one day. I can be very brief. The basic information I want you to have will take less then five minutes. We can leave any discussion for the phone."

"Very well. I can see you today at 11:00 or at 3:00."

"I appreciate that. It's almost 10:30. I'll be at your office in thirty minutes."

"You know where to come?"

"I do indeed."

Poulter put down the phone, puzzled, and spoke into the intercom to ask Marion to come in.

"You know who that was? That was someone from Prince George. He says he sits on council there and has something to tell me. Any idea what it could be about?"

"No. Unless some of Chilko's crew have been painting the town red."

"I don't think he would come and see me about that. Well, we'll know in a few minutes. Did we get those bills of sale from Sundial Oil in Calgary?"

"Yes, they came in late yesterday. I have your copy here; another is with Jason to look over."

"Let's see it. You should know that the Praine report gives us an all clear, but I can't concentrate on the news release."

Poulter asked her to stay and review documentation on several of his companies, most of them juniors in the mining exploration business, but he found it hard to focus.

Bob Strang, middle-aged with greying hair and wearing a suit, arrived at 10:59 am.

"Yes Mr. Strang, Mr. Poulter is expecting you. I'll show you into the boardroom." Marion led the way and before leaving asked the guest if he would like coffee, but the offer was politely declined.

A few minutes later, Sydney Poulter entered the room. The two men introduced themselves.

"As I explained on the phone, I'm from Prince George. As you might expect, I have several friends in Smithers. One of them, knowing I would be in Vancouver, asked me to come and see you

Chapter 65 — Hubris & Nemesis

about a problem you and he share, so I'm taking this opportunity to see if you can help us with what I hope is a solution."

"I'll do what I can."

"I expect you know of Mr. Wickford, resident of Smithers?"

"Kenneth Wickford. Yes I do. We were competing for the same ground during a staking rush. Met him just once."

"He has been telling my friend of a series of incidents, almost trivial in themselves, but which could amount to an attempt to intimidate. He has been advised to compile a file and submit it to the RCMP, but I offered to meet with you to see if the temperature could be lowered before things get out of hand."

"Incidents like?"

"There was a case of two strangers sitting down, uninvited, at his table in a restaurant. They told him that contesting claims belonging to you or one of your companies could be dangerous."

"Not my style. Go on."

"On another occasion two men—not the same ones—came to his house and told him not to contest your ground."

"And?"

"Mr. Wickford keeps a couple of horses. They are always in the stables at night. One morning Mr. Wickford found one of them had been taken to the other side of a nearby field and tied to a fence post. No harm had been done, but there was a note attached to the horse saying 'Contesting claims is dangerous for horses and their owners.'"

Poulter gave voice to an indignant statement of defence. "I've done hundreds of mining deals and dealt with dozens of prospectors and claim owners. I think that only once in twenty-five years have I heard of that sort of thing. I would certainly never get involved in that way myself."

"What about those who work for you?"

Poulter paused. "We certainly hire a lot of people of all types. I suppose some smart ass could be taking a line on his own. But I find it hard to believe."

"Will you give the matter some thought?"

"I will. But tell me, where did you get this information? From Wickford? I assume there are witnesses?"

"A friend of mine, a citizen of Smithers, heard I was coming to Vancouver and asked me to get in touch with you. He and Mr. Wickford are friends, but he is well known in Smithers and his word has to be taken seriously."

Sydney Poulter looked at his visitor with a penetrating gaze and nodded to signify he understood.

Meeting the gaze, Strang prepared to take his leave. "Before I go I have to tell you that I and, I'm sure, all my fellow councillors recognize the value of mineral exploration and mining to our community. We welcome you people for the jobs and wealth you create. I wish you well in solving this problem."

"I assure you it has my urgent attention."

"I appreciate you giving me the time when you are so busy. Goodbye, Mr. Poulter."

"Goodbye. I'll show you out."

With that the two men left the room.

Sydney Poulter lunched alone, returned to his office at 2:30, then read and reread the Praine report. The news release did not go out that day.

In the office everyone soon became aware that their boss was in another of his dangerous moods. Marion, who had worked for Poulter for eight years, had seen him down and seen him angry, but never quite like this. By 4:30 he had made four trips to the coffee machine, and had covered the table in his office with file folders. He had asked for anything related to Chilko: project files, all correspondence, internal and external, dealings with government agencies, accounting records, and resumes of everyone who had worked on the property. To Marion's consternation, as even she could not recall where they had been filed, Sydney asked for the records of long-distance phone calls. Towards 4:30 people started picking up their newspapers or briefcases and leaving. They left quietly, knowing that something was up. Only Marion stopped by to wish him good night.

At 5:00 pm Poulter flipped through the Yellow Pages, made an arbitrary pick, and ordered pizza to be delivered before the main doors to the office building closed at 5:30. Around 6:00 he took a small telephone address book from his top desk drawer and dialled one of two numbers written against the word: "Sam."

"Can you put me through to Sam, please."

"I'll check for you, sir, but I believe he is off shift," said the woman's voice at the other end. After a pause. "I am sorry, sir, but he's off until noon tomorrow."

Slip dialled another number. "Sam?"

"Yes."

Chapter 65 — Hubris & Nemesis

"It's Sydney here. I'm sorry to call you at home."

"Don't worry, Mr. Poulter. Any time. What can I do for you?"

"I know it's short notice, but could you make arrangements for me tonight?"

"Absolutely. Usual room? I'm reasonably certain it will be free."

"Good man! And…"

"I was going to ask. Who would you like? Unless of course you wanted to be absolutely alone."

"Would Sanny be available?"

"Let me have your number and I will phone you back within the hour. Is this for you or someone we don't know?"

"Just me. I'll be here when you phone."

Half an hour later the phone rang. Slip picked it up and heard Sam say:

"That's fine, Sydney. Room 2022. Available from now. You'll be alone until 10:00."

Chapter 66

Reversing the Tide
November

The next day, being an early first into the office, Sydney Poulter had a quiet hour to himself. In his neat pencil handwriting, he wrote a note to Marion, asking her to get a temporary receptionist from one of the agencies so that she, Marion, would be able to help him all day. He put it on her desk. A few minutes later he wrote another note saying the long distance records he wanted were for the months of May to July in 1986. At 8:20, he heard people coming into the office. A few minutes later, Marion came in to acknowledge the notes.

"Good morning, Sydney. I hope you were not here all night again."

"Not quite. I'm sure glad to see you. Today, we're going to separate the raisins from the rat shit."

With characteristic calm in a storm, Marion replied. "We'll have a temp here by 9:00. Shall I start on the telephone records?"

"Not yet. First, could you get me a chronological record of our hiring and leaving. Not just this office. Field crews too."

"I certainly can. That's easier than the telephone records that are buried in the archives."

Two hours later Sydney J. Poulter was staring at a memorandum. Even though it was only five pages, he had already read it three times. On the top right hand corner of the first page was "Page 1 of 5" and initialled "RT." It was dated July 19 of the previous year. The message on the fifth page was unmistakable: that the writer could not recommend the Lynx claims for the reasons given, but that Poulter Management should stay in touch with this prospector, Ken Wickford, because he had a property that could become interesting. Meantime, do nothing because that would involve breaking a confidence.

Chapter 66 — Reversing the Tide

Speaking into the handset instead of the hands-free intercom, Sydney said, "Marion, who worked for us last year and signed himself 'RT'? Was that Tranich?"

"Probably. If you let me see the document, I will be able to recognize the signature."

"Come and see it."

Marion confirmed that the note was written by Robert Tranich. "We should check the day-by-day folder. Sometimes there's something there that didn't get into the property files, or have you already looked?"

"No, this is the only one I've seen. Where's Tranich now? He didn't stay very long did he?"

"Only six months or so and then he got a good offer from a company in Flin Flon. I liked him and was sorry to see him go."

"Can you get hold of him?"

"I'll see what I can do."

That afternoon Marion announced that Mr. Tranich was on the line.

Sydney picked up his handset. "Is that Bob Tranich?"

"It is indeed. What can I do for you?"

"First, thank you for phoning back so promptly. I have just a few questions and absolutely no complaints. I do need a bit of help on some things that happened here last year."

"Go ahead."

"You met a Mr. Wickford somewhere up by Smithers?"

"Yes. I examined a property of his. Likeable fellow. Good prospector."

"No kidding! I've heard him described as just about everything else. A scrappy bush rat, a legalistic son of a bitch. Are we talking about the same guy?"

"Doesn't sound like it. Mind you, he and I met for only a couple of days. But when you spend time with someone in the bush, you usually get a pretty good feel."

"So what property did you examine? Was it the Nisselinka?"

"I don't recognize that name. The claims I saw were called Lynx. They were interesting enough, but for the reasons I put in the file, I could not recommend them."

"So you wrote him to say thanks but no thanks?"

"Correct."

"He's been mad at us for some time. He says we staked his ground."

The Nisselinka Claims

"Which ground?"

"We call ours the DBL claims. I'm told he referred to his as the Raven claims, after some old crown grants that he owns. I can give you the location details, if you need them. It's all public information. In fact we are drilling now. I was prompted to call you when I saw your memo advising us to keep in touch because he had a promising property. I understand he didn't want to deal it then because it was only partially staked."

"You mean you or your company staked the property that he told me about in confidence?"

"Bob. I don't know what happened. I am trying to find out."

"Well, it wouldn't have taken much research to put two and two together. Old crown grants belonging to a K. Wickford, copper and gold, Smithers area. That's disgraceful! And what about my name? It must be mud!"

"Listen, Bob. We are in this together. I've got to get to the bottom of this to clear my name, yours and Chilko's."

Bob Tranich's silence at the other end of the phone prompted Poulter to make a request. "May I get back to you if I have more questions?"

"Yes, but you have to keep me informed. This is serious."

"Bob, thank you for your help. I will be in touch."

After putting down the phone, Sydney picked up the day-by-day folder that Marion had brought him. All its pages were copies of original documents filed elsewhere. He looked yet again at the copy of Tranich's report. But there were only four pages. Page five was missing and so was the instruction to remain in touch with K. Wickford.

The following day, Marion succeeded in reaching Ken Wickford on the phone and persuading him to accept a call from Mr. Poulter.

"Mr. Wickford?"

"Yes, who's speaking?"

"I'm Sydney Poulter of Chilko Resources. Believe it or not, I'm not phoning about the letter your lawyer sent. I'm phoning about how we came to be in a staking contest with you. Something has gone wrong with Chilko's involvement with you and it may well be our fault. I would like to meet you in person."

Ken Wickford took a long time to reply. "Why the sudden change?"

"That's one of the things I want to explain, but face to face."

Chapter 66 — Reversing the Tide

"You want me to come to Vancouver?"

"I suggest we meet in Prince George."

"Who would be coming?"

"Just you and me. No assistants, no lawyers. Just you and me trying to put things back on track."

"If that's what you're promising me, I can be in Prince George at any time."

"Tomorrow evening? How about we meet for dinner at 7:00 pm at the restaurant in the Great North Hotel."

"I'll be there at 6:30 tomorrow evening. If my flight is delayed I'll leave a message for you at the hotel."

Ken Wickford had been in his study when the phone rang. He had remained on his feet for all of the short conversation with Sydney Poulter. When it was over he replaced the phone, slumped onto the chesterfield at the end of the room, and stared into space. Poulter himself had phoned. The devil himself had asked to meet. What did this mean? A trap? Or had the "hand grenade" forced him to negotiate. What more could go wrong in the relationship? Could there be any downside left? But Poulter had sounded conciliatory. Something might come of meeting him. It was worth a try.

The following afternoon Sydney J Poulter was on his way north. Prince George, a town of some fifty thousand people, close to the centre of the province, straddled the Fraser River and lay at the intersection of the major transportation routes. It had been a hub for logging, mining and farming since the railway arrived early in the century. The airport was on a plateau three hundred feet above the river. As the twin engine wide-bodied jet was about to touch down, Sydney, staring out of the window at the approaching ground, felt the relief of being able to act in the face of adversity. Although he still felt beleaguered and embattled, he gained satisfaction from knowing the period of inaction was over. Whatever his failings and whatever his other strengths, he thought of himself as a man of action, not only of the pre-emptive strike and the strategic move, but also of dogged, grinding defence. And that was what he was doing now and almost, but not quite, enjoying himself.

As the taxi took him down the hill, he thought of the troublemaker he was about to meet. After checking himself into the hotel, he'd have almost two hours to spare. Mr. Wickford had been represented to him as the source of so many problems. They'd met once in Vancouver and parted under strained circumstances. The absurd challenge to Chilko's title on the crown grants purchased recently only reinforced the impression that Wickford was going to be difficult to deal with.

He took a quick shower, then sat in a comfortable chair and read through the various reports and letters concerning Ken Wickford. Five minutes before the meeting, he took the elevator to the ground floor and walked into the Branding Iron, a bar attached to the dining room. As his eyes adapted to the low light, he recognized Ken Wickford coming towards him.

They shook hands with no more than a "Glad you're here" and "Good to see you" before Ken led the way to a table in a corner. Any problems they might have had about how to open the conversation were pre-empted by the waiter asking what he could get them. Sydney ordered a Martini, Ken a scotch and soda.

Ken opened. "I don't suppose you make a special trip to see a prospector very often. I'm impressed."

"You're absolutely correct. I don't—at least I haven't for fifteen years. Now I leave others to meet the prospectors and I am beginning to believe that in this case it has led to a shitload of trouble."

"And not just for Chilko," said Ken with no change of expression.

"I know. I know you haven't had much reason to enjoy this relationship. That is one of the reasons I am here."

Ken waited for Poulter to continue the conversation.

"I have only a vague idea as to how we—I mean Chilko and you—got offside. Did it start with the staking?"

"That was the start of the trouble. But I suppose you know that I had dealings with you people earlier?"

"A property examination?"

"Yes. I had, and still have, some claims called Lynx. Your man Bob Tranich..." Ken sat back in his chair as the waiter, interrupting as only waiters can, delivered two drinks. "Bob Tranich, geologist, senior type, examined my Lynx claims. I spent a whole day with him and enjoyed talking to him. Seemed to know his stuff. I learned quite a bit from him. I thought I could trust him but I was wrong. I suppose he's your head geologist by now?"

"No. He doesn't work for us any more. Someone in Flin Flon offered him a job he couldn't refuse. We were sorry to lose him. So what changed your mind about trusting him?"

Ken kept his response short. "He didn't keep his word."

Chapter 66 — Reversing the Tide

"Go on."

"The day after Tranich and I looked at the Lynx claims I showed him some samples from the Lynx and other properties. You see, I have most of a barn just for keeping rocks. By mistake I passed him a box with some samples from claims I had only partially staked. He hadn't had them for more than twenty seconds before I realized my mistake and asked for them back. You see I was up a ladder and he was at the bench below. So he handed them back. But that still gave him time to see what I had. He said he really liked what he saw. He said the samples looked like they came from a copper-gold porphyry."

"Did you tell him where they came from?"

"No, I didn't. But I did mention I had held them a very long time."

"That wasn't giving away much."

"Not so. All you have to do is find out from the mining recorder what I own. Then you can see when each claim was acquired or transferred. These ones, mainly because of the crown grants, that have been in my family for three generations, would stand out like a sore thumb."

"So these claims—the ones we are talking about—are the claims on the Nisselinka that you and we are fighting over?"

"That's it. You people staked them soon after Tranich saw my samples."

"But he gave in his notice about a week after visiting you and was gone within the month."

"He must have made some recommendations about my properties before leaving."

"He did. He wrote a memo to turn down the Lynx claims, and in the same memo he recommended we keep in touch with you about the claims you were not ready to deal."

"Can I get you another drink?" asked the waiter. Both men, intent on their conversation, declined the waiter's offer.

Ken leaned forward. "So the memo said it needed to be researched and located so Chilko or one of your other companies could grab it!"

"Wrong. It said we should keep in touch so that we could have a chance to examine the property when you had it ready."

"So how come you fielded a staking crew so soon after that memo?"

"That's exactly what I have to find out. This may be hard for you, after all that has gone on, but I ask you to please listen to me. I don't believe in screwing prospectors. Even if I did believe in cheating people out of their claims, it wouldn't happen because we would soon go out of business. We need you people just as much as you need us."

"Then someone in your company must have a completely different approach to yours."

"And I have to find out who that is. But before we get onto other parts of the problem, I want you to read this page from Tranich's memo. It seems to have been the last he wrote on this project."

Ken took the single sheet and read it slowly. The message was clear: keep in touch but don't do anything. Without glancing up he was aware of Poulter's penetrating stare. Finally looking up and straight at the man who had been his opponent for many painful months, he said, "It looks good, but how do I know he did not recommend something else without writing it down? This could be just to lay a false trail."

"Goddamnit, man! What do you think we are? Have you ever asked around to find out how we do our business?"

"I'm sorry to upset you. But see it from my point of view. A company grabs some ground of mine using information they were not supposed to have. They threaten me—"

"What do you mean threaten?"

"The worst one was when your people—"

"Who?"

"Victor Dubell."

"Threatened you?"

"Yes. He told me on the phone that unless I was more cooperative, my friend Will Herman might lose his job. He threatened Herman personally and told him and me that all he had to do was complain to the owner of the helicopter company about a leak of confidential information."

"Details. I want details."

Ken recounted the several phone conversations he had had with Victor.

Slip looked at him impassively, and then pulled out a small notebook and started to write.

Ken asked, "Another drink?"

"No, thanks. Are you hungry?"

"Yes, let's eat."

Chapter 66 — Reversing the Tide

As they were heading for the restaurant on the other side of the bar, a young man who had been sitting at a table by himself, stood up, spoke to a waitress carrying a tray with a drink, and followed her to the restaurant.

Ken Wickford and Sydney Poulter were silent while each examined the menu and then closed it. Neither man regarded this as an opportunity to socialize. For Poulter it was a step towards resolving a dispute. Even more important, it might become a means of finding out about the rot at the core of his organization. For Wickford the meeting was justified only because it might lead to a deal he could accept.

Slip Poulter had met many prospectors, most of whom he liked and most of whom he would have no trouble trusting. The man in front of him was in many ways typical: a loner, knowledgeable about geology and prospecting, and the owner of a dream. Yet in some ways he was different. Poulter could not put his finger on that difference.

Ken Wickford had dealt with promoters before and had learned to be careful. He had experienced or heard of most of the tricks and was aware that he had more to learn. He was on his guard, with every antenna tuned to spot the catch when it came. He decided to open up a new front. "I have to ask you. What is it you want? Why have you gone to the trouble of meeting me?"

"Because I'm up to my ass in alligators, and the barracuda are snapping at my nuts. And you are one of the few people who can help me."

Ken, who was beginning to enjoy the banter, suppressed a comment on aquatic biology and Poulter continued. "I'm not kidding. First, I don't like getting offside with people like you. Second, I need to find out how it happened and who did it. Third, I think that if we can work together on this, we will both benefit. Can you believe all that?"

"Believe *you*? That's a lot to ask," replied Ken with a smile. "But let's try again. What do you want from me?"

"You've already given me a lot. I now know that one of our people threatened you and I know who it was. I suspect someone used confidential information against you and I have an idea on that one too."

"Okay so far. But what are you proposing?"

"We have to solve a number of problems. My first priority is to find out where we went wrong. You have to stop that absurd

The Nisselinka Claims

challenge to our crown grants. Also, of course, your line of small claims at the centre of ours."

"Yes, I realize those two-post claims escalated the conflict, but I'm sure you know, in a scrap we have to use what weapons we have."

"That I do. And once the ground situation is tidied up, I can announce it and attribute those difficulties, as well as the salting, to the same patch of rot that let it happen."

"So you would be mixing good news with the bad news," mused Ken.

"Not quite. I would be admitting the problems at the same time as announcing the steps we have taken to clean them up."

"All right. So you need from me the terms I would have asked if I'd had time to complete the staking without competition from you."

"That's right. When do you think you could have that done?"

"Within a week probably."

"Great. I'll be back in the office. Please fax it as soon as you can."

"Yes. It will be just a two-pager. No frills."

"That's just fine. Now the next subject. I need to know more about the threats against you. Could you send that information, too?"

"So after a year or so of believing you were the master organizer behind all those dirty tricks, I now have to believe you don't know anything about them? That will take some adjustment, but I am going to try."

"That's what I'm asking. I realize that until we have identified and removed the culprit, it may be difficult for you to cooperate with us."

"There were several incidents. Two strangers in the Taku bar in Smithers, threats to a friend, a note on a horse, someone phoned my ex-wife..."

Their talk continued. They skipped dessert but not coffee. Ken was only vaguely aware of the other diners. There was a couple at a table against the wall on his left. If he had been in a more observant frame of mind, he might have wondered whether they had spouses elsewhere. Insofar as the decibels were any guide, the foursome behind him were enjoying the evening. He cast a glance at a lone diner at the other side of the room and thought that he had perhaps seen him before. Poulter paid the bill. They

Chapter 66 — Reversing the Tide

both thanked the waiter as they passed him on their way out. As they entered the lobby, Ken suddenly realized where he had seen the lone diner before— again dining alone, reading a magazine, in the restaurant of the Taku Hotel, when the two strangers had come and sat at his table.

In an instant, all feelings of trust that he had been developing towards Poulter evaporated. He turned towards his dinner companion and said with a change of tone that must have caught Poulter by surprise:

"I thought you said you would come alone?"

"I did indeed. We could not have got as far as we did, if I had brought anyone."

"What about your bodyguard?"

"What do you mean?"

Slip's look of puzzlement seemed so genuine that Ken almost forgot his anger. "While we were dining and talking, we were being watched by the same guy who watched those two goons accost me at the Taku."

Slip Poulter turned pale. His convivial, confident demeanour was instantly replaced by a look of concern, even fear. "Listen, you have to believe me. I did not arrange for anyone to intimidate you in Smithers. I did not arrange for anyone to come tonight."

They were both silent for a moment while the implications became apparent to both of them.

Poulter broke the silence. "We've both got to be careful. Don't tell me where you are staying tonight, but please be careful. I look forward to hearing from you. Goodnight."

They shook hands and Poulter turned towards the elevator.

Chapter 67

Negotiation
November

Ken returned from his meeting with Sydney Poulter in Prince George with the good news of a possible rapprochement and the disturbing story of the unknown observer. The three friends discussed at length the situation and the choices available to them and concluded that there was little they could do about an unknown third party, if he existed. Their objective had to be to get a satisfactory deal with Chilko. They talked at length about what might lie under their claims and on how to handle Poulter and his organization.

Lester Bance and Wally Seldock each invested $10,000 for five percent of Ken's mining claims, thereby putting a notional value of $200,000 for all of it. Ken told them they were paying too much, but their insistence won the discussion. All three knew that their investment could turn out to be a bust. They also knew that its value could be a multiple of what they had invested.

"Of course," said Lester, "that much cash won't cover any serious litigation, but it should be enough for you to play the next round. They've behaved like bandits, but I don't think we'd have a chance in a legal challenge to their staking. Let's start from scratch. Ken, what terms would you have asked for if they'd come to you when you were ready to deal it?"

"Oh, I suppose, after all we've gone through, something more than the usual typical terms."

"All of which wouldn't amount to a hill of beans. Eh? Unless there's a mine, of course," replied Lester.

"Unless there's a mine, that's true. But, if there isn't, I can't expect to make a fortune."

Lester wanted Ken and Wally to follow his train of thought. "Some things about this case don't fit. On the one hand we have

Chapter 67 — Negotiation

that fiasco with the salting. On the other we see Poulter, who has other horses in his stable, taking Chilko very seriously. I have to conclude that he may think he has a mine. Just in case that's right, the deal we make has to treat us well."

Then Wally, the other half of the tag team, picked up where his friend had stopped. "If it's a mine, it won't be financed by Poulter, or the shareholders of Chilko. What we have to do is link our value to Poulter's. Whatever currency he is going to benefit from, we want the same."

"In that case," said Lester, "Let's put our property into a private company. Then we merge it with Chilko. Whatever happens to Chilko, we and Poulter will share the benefit." Then, with half a smile, he added, "Or fate".

Wally nodded approval. "That's good. As they say, 'stay close to your enemies.'"

"You know," said Lester addressing Ken, "you each have a knife at the other's throat. Neither of you can do anything alone. You cannot—sorry, 'we' cannot—sell our claims. Nor can Chilko, unless Poulter can get rid of that option or covenant or whatever it's called."

"So Poulter is waiting for you to suggest terms?" asked Wally.

"That's what he said," replied Ken. "It's been three days since we met. I think I have at least a week. In some ways time is more on my side than his."

Wally was known for digging slowly through the facts before being forceful with his opinions. "Ken, correct me if this is wrong. The current situation is that Chilko has about half the ground and so do we. They are paying for the exploration, that has cost you, us, nothing. So we could argue that we should have somewhere around fifty percent, less whatever the exploration so far has cost."

Ken got up to pace the room. "Well, we each have about half of the staked ground. They claim more than half, but I don't think some of it has a chance with the claims inspector, or in court, if it comes to that. But all the drill holes are on their claims. The trend is towards our ground, but we don't have any holes yet. The other thing, of course, is that they have put up all the money and will have to continue doing so. Whatever the other terms, we need a free ride."

"So," said Wally, "taking Poulter's side for a moment, they have made the properties (theirs and yours) more valuable. They have taken all the risk and will go on doing so. Perhaps they should have seventy-five percent."

But Ken wasn't about to forget the history of his claims. "Yes, that's okay if you look at only the current situation. It doesn't take into account the information they stole from me. If we had all the ground I was going to stake—if they hadn't cheated—we would have the whole thing under option to someone." Then, after a pause, he added, "But, I have to admit that if I had signed an option without having a single hole into the property, I wouldn't get thirty percent."

"Okay," said Lester, leaning back in his chair, "here's a plan. Tell him you want to merge the two companies, Chilko and ours. We get Chilko shares and Chilko gets the whole property. That should make him happy. But tell him it should be fifty-fifty, with recognition for the work they have already done. He won't like that. Then tell him you want to negotiate in the presence of a mediator, if necessary. As he owes you something, you never know what he might agree to."

"So we tell Poulter we are prepared to merge as equals?" asked Ken. "We won't get that, but it would be a place to start."

Wally thumped the table with both hands. "I like it! Prodding the dragon again. Let's do it."

"Do we want to get close and personal with the dragon in his cave?" asked Lester who, getting no answer, continued. "I think that's worth trying, but we have to remember the man may have an ego. In fact he probably has a big one, and that can make negotiation much more complicated."

To which Ken added, "He needs some good news. Sorting out the claim problem and doubling the area he controls would give him a hell of a lift."

The conversation continued for a while until Ken, feeling that what they had discussed should be turned into action, said: "One step at a time. I will get the ownership in a new company. Named or just a number?"

"Just a number," responded Wally "Looks less personal and suggests we might be able to play his kind of game."

"Then I'll respond to Poulter's request for terms by proposing fifty-fifty ownership," said Ken.

"He won't like it," said Wally. "You might even be introduced to a new expression. I've heard he comes up with a new one every so often."

Chapter 67 — Negotiation

"I don't know the man," said Lester, "but I've heard he's not what he used to be. Less bluster and banging, more respectability. But put aside who you're dealing with and remember you have some very strong cards: the attempts to intimidate, the doctoring of the claim posts, and the killer option on his crown grants."

"Okay. I'll confront the dragon and get back to both of you."

After he had made arrangements to transfer ownership of the Nisselinka claims to a private company, Ken Wickford phoned the office of Chilko Resources. He didn't recognize the voice answering the phone but assumed it was one of the women he had met when visiting the office in the early spring. He asked to speak to Mr. Poulter.

"Mr. Wickford, yes, I'll put you through right away. I know he's been waiting for your call."

The next voice on the phone was no longer strange to Ken.

"Ken Wickford? I'm glad you phoned. How are you doing?"

"I'm fine, Mr. Poulter. You asked me to get back in touch with you and tell you my terms for an option."

"That's just what I said and just what I need. What you need, too, I believe."

"All my Nisselinka claims are now in a private company."

"Nothing wrong with that. Sometimes makes it easier. Are you the sole owner?"

"No. I'm the principal owner. There are two others. What I suggest, Mr. Poulter, is to merge our private company with Chilko so we get Chilko shares."

"That's good too. And we'll see what we can do to make those shares, yours and mine, really valuable. Should be possible. Seems we're onto something. Next step is to agree on the number of shares you guys are going to have. Do you have any ideas on that?"

"We're working on it. It's something we need to discuss. Could you and I meet somewhere?"

After a pause, Poulter replied, "We could do that. Where would you suggest?"

"How about Prince George again?" said Ken, wondering how Poulter would react.

"Okay. I'll make arrangements. Next week okay?"

"Any day would be fine for me."

"Tell you what. I will bring a lawyer. He won't negotiate, but will be there to tell us what we can or can't do. Will you bring one too?"

"I'll bring someone. Probably not a lawyer."

"Good. And no spooks this time. No one following us around!" said Poulter in a tone that could have been taken as good humour.

Ken laughed. They agreed that Poulter would arrange the venue and time and get back.

The meeting room chosen by Sydney Poulter was on the fourth story of the River Inn, one of the less prominent hotels in the town. A row of windows on one wall overlooked the Fraser River, at that time of year a sinuous line of deep green water flanked by snow-dusted banks. Poulter and his lawyer, Jason, were already in the room when Ken and Lester arrived. After the greetings and enquiries about one another's journeys, all four men slipped comfortably into discussing professional hockey, the Canucks in particular, until it became time to accept that with formalities done and the ice broken, they could start discussing the topic they had assembled to address.

Not knowing what Poulter's strategy would be, and believing they had a strong hand, Ken and Lester had agreed that they would play a defensive game. They waited for Poulter to make the first move, which he proceeded to do in a disarming way.

"Gentlemen, let me start by apologizing for the way we have treated you, Ken. The information about your property was extracted from the files and used against you despite Mr. Tranich making it quite clear that all we should do is keep in touch. We owe Bob Tranich an apology, too. One of my employees, you know his name, acted in an unconscionable way. I was quite unaware of what he was doing." He paused and provided an opening for a question.

Ken took the opportunity. "Does he still work for you?"

Poulter replied with hint of discomfort. "Yes. I have not had a chance to talk to him. He's been away on a vacation that was agreed to long ago and we've been unable to get in touch with him."

Lester asked: "So you had no idea what he was up to?"

"None, none at all. He came to us with qualifications up the yin-yang. Good references, too. He's smart and works hard. I gave him lots of rope because I thought he could take a load off me. I'm the first to admit I screwed up, big time."

Chapter 67 — Negotiation

Lester played a statesman card. "I think I'm right in saying that, despite all the regrettable things that have happened, there should be immense value for all of us in the two sides reaching an agreement."

"Amen to that," replied Poulter. "I owe you one, Ken." Then after a pause, he added: "But you have to understand that I'm not about to give away the shop. I have shareholders in a public company to look after."

"And we can assume you're a shareholder?" asked Ken with a touch of irony.

"Damn right I am," replied Poulter.

"So, if we become shareholders, we'll all be on the same team."

The four men in the room shared a comfortable chuckle.

Ken continued with his questions. "So, as I understand the objective, if we can reach agreement, then all the claims, Chilko's, ours, and the disputed ones, will all come under one owner. Is that right?"

Murmurs of assent provided Poulter with an opportunity to retain the lead. "That's exactly it. One owner, one objective, shared wealth."

"Then all we need to do is agree on the number of Chilko shares to come to Ken's company," said Lester.

"That shouldn't be too difficult," answered the promoter. "We can afford to be generous. How about 100,000 shares for the first three years. Then another 200,000 for Chilko to exercise. That makes half a million shares. You guys could also take a one percent royalty, that we could buy for some large sum."

"Half a million shares," responded Ken. "You've got, what is it, ten million out now? So we would get five percent of the company?"

"That's about right. Standard sort of deal."

"We were thinking we should get a lot more than that."

"That would be unusual. You bring us the property and sit back. We take the risk, raise the money, get everything done."

Lester said, "Until the drilling started, all the work on the property had been by Ken and his family. Let's forget for moment how you came by the information. The present situation is that Chilko's and Ken's land holdings are about equal. Except for Chilko getting credit for the money spent, the ownership should be about equal."

Poulter's posture stiffened as his amiability dropped away. "In that case, we are a long way apart. You're not being realistic. I've never heard of a deal where the prospector ends up with anything like fifty percent of a company. Even twenty percent would be rare. Jason, what about you? Have you ever heard of anything like what they are asking for?"

"Not that I can remember. It would certainly be most unusual."

At this particular stage in the negotiations, Ken felt it was time for him to be forceful. "We've both got to be realistic. One of the realities is that Chilko's ground has a hole right in the middle. Those old crown grants. No major is going to take on that ground until that is sorted out."

While Poulter was considering his response, Lester raised the stakes. "There are also some other realities. I know, Sydney, they were not of your doing, but they were done by your company, in your name..."

"Hold it! Hold it!" said Poulter, raising his voice and looking directly at Lester. "What are you suggesting?"

Lester's answer was slow and emphatic. "We may as well put them on the table, because they are facts that will not go away. I'm referring to the attempts to intimidate. That's serious. I'm referring to the poorly thought-out attempt to discredit Ken's staking. It's all documented and photographed."

"Damn it, man! I came all the way here expecting to negotiate a reasonable deal with reasonable people and, and now you try, and..." Poulter paused for breath, "...and try to blackmail me."

Ken was not going to let Poulter's response carry any weight. "This is not blackmail. We are not threatening to report these things. We mention them again because they form part of our cost. Your company put me through hell. As a consequence of what has happened, both sides in this dispute have unworkable claims. The terms cannot be what they might have been if I had completed the staking."

Lester attempted to smooth the troubled waters: "I think we should break for lunch. Ken and I need to talk. Perhaps you two need the same. How about we meet here at 2:00 pm?"

Poulter's remark as he picked up his notebook was an abrupt, "Let's go, Jason."

After the door had shut Lester looked at Ken. "I hope you didn't mind that. I thought we needed to get those facts on the table. Otherwise we'll be just wasting time."

"I think that's right. He's not going to be a pushover. And I'm in no mood to give it all away."

Chapter 67 — Negotiation

"D'you think they will be back at 2:00?"

"I was wondering that. They may just piss off back to Vancouver."

"I doubt it. They need a deal. He has too much at stake. He's not going to throw away the opportunity."

"Where do we go for lunch? Know anywhere good?"

Sydney Poulter and Jason were engrossed in conversation while their lunches remained untouched. Jason had been counsel and confidant long enough to know his client's foibles and frailties as well as his strengths. Together they had survived several crises and emerged each time strong enough to create the next one.

"What the hell's he want?" exclaimed Sydney. "I can't place him. He's like a lot of prospectors in some ways. Most of them are not too bad to deal with. But I can't figure him out. And this side-kick of his? Who's he?"

"Lester Bance is a prominent member of the business community in central B.C. He's in commercial real estate, but he ran for mayor in P.G. once. Didn't get in, but he's well respected."

"D'you think we can deal with them? Any point?" asked Poulter.

"That really prompts two other questions. Will they deal with us? The answer is almost certainly yes, but at a stiff price. The other question is do you want to pay the price?"

After a pause, Poulter said: "Go on."

"I seem to remember you telling me that the airborne geophysics showed the trend continuing onto Wickford's ground."

Poulter's reply came with a touch of irritation at an off-topic answer. "It does."

"Have you told him?"

"No way," was the dismissive response.

Jason replied in the avuncular manner that Poulter had come to tolerate, even appreciate. "We need to be careful there. Negotiating without revealing information we have over his ground could get us into trouble. But let's put that aside for a moment. The point to make is that, if his ground is as good as ours, then we want to make a deal. If his is better, we *must* have a deal. And if your ground is as good as you say it is, then double that is really valuable. If you become the principal owner of the whole play you would have something with a lot of upside. What if he does get almost as much out of it as you? Yours is the name that gets attached to the whole."

Poulter's initial irritation yielded to his colleague's argument. "There you go again: solid and sensible. Keeping me on track and out of trouble. Is that what I need?"

Jason laughed. "Any idea what it might be worth?"

"Len was doing a few estimates. I had to squeeze them out of him. I think it was something like seventy million of contained value for every hundred metres along the length of the thing. About six hundred metres on our side and there could well be a thousand metres on his. So, add it all up and the value contained comes to something over a billion. So Chilko's market cap could be a couple of hundred million. With the shares we have out, fully diluted, we might get to ten dollars."

"We'd better stop counting these chickens or it will ruin our ability to negotiate."

Sydney Poulter leaned back in his chair and spoke towards the ceiling: "This could be it, what I've been scrapping and scratching for all my life. All that shit and abuse I've put up with may have been worth it. Right?"

Jason, opening the door for his client, replied, "You're almost there, Slip."

As they emerged from the elevator, Ken said to Lester, "How long will we wait for them before we abort the mission? One hour, two?"

Lester pushed open the boardroom door. "If they're not here within the first hour, it'll be a fair bet that they've gone home."

They were both surprised to find Poulter and Jason already sitting at the table. No one said anything until Lester and Ken had taken their seats. Then, after a protracted silence, Poulter said, "Okay. It's time for you guys to tell us what you want. But it has to be something I can sell to my shareholders."

Having already discussed with Lester how they would respond to this inevitable question, Ken was ready with a response. "Assuming you and we have about equal areas covered, ignoring for the moment the gaps in your claims, but allowing for the money you have spent and are going to spend, we think you should have sixty percent of a combined company to our forty percent."

Poulter responded quickly. "And what if there is an orebody and it's all on our ground?"

"Perhaps your percentage should be higher. And, if that's how we do it, would we get more if we have more of the orebody?"

Chapter 67 — Negotiation

Poulter, his face a stony stare, was about to say something, but Lester got in first. "The point we want to make is that, if the ownership of an orebody is roughly equal, then we would not want less than the percentage we are talking about."

Poulter pushed his papers away from him and his chair back. "Then try this for a structure. Without numbers. We take an option on your ground. We pay for the first year with shares, and the second with more shares. Then, if we want to continue beyond the end of the second year, we have to exercise the option by merging the two companies."

Both Ken and Lester murmured approval. Ken said, "Sounds like a good start. That would give you a chance to value what the whole thing looks like."

To which Lester added: "Another advantage is that the investment community would recognize that you have all the important ground tied up."

"So far okay. How about the numbers. A hundred thousand shares the first year and two hundred the second should be generous enough to interest you."

Lester jumped in before Ken could say anything. "I always believe in seeing the whole thing before agreeing to parts of it."

Ken laughed. "You know, I was going to say almost the same. I got screwed once by agreeing to terms bit by bit."

Jason, who had said little, but had been all the while making notes, looked up. "I suggest that Sydney and I have a chance to confer. That okay, Slip?"

"Makes sense. We'll be back in twenty minutes."

Ken and Lester had the room to themselves. Ken remained seated; Lester went to look out of the window. Neither spoke for a long time. Then Lester turned to face his friend.

"We need to set it at a level he would feel he had to pay if there is a big orebody with a significant part on our ground." He came back to the table and sat down. "If the price is too much for the quantity on our ground, he can always try to renegotiate."

Ken nodded. "In other words, a price that he will find steep today."

"Exactly. My guess is that he will probably offer us twenty percent. I don't think we need to accept less than forty. But it's up to you. There's a risk he will walk, and then you're back to square one. You've all that history in the property and some commitments."

"Yes. Those alimony payments mount up, but they would be small change if this works. And I have to do something about my grandfather's promise to Charley Raven, the Indian band member. The other thing is my family's ownership for three generations. It's not something the textbooks would take into account, but it does influence my decisions."

"Remember the advice 'Don't get mad. Get even.'"

"I know. I know. So let's make it forty or fight. Has a good ring to it. Echoes of a war long ago."

Jason and Sydney returned only ten minutes after they had left. As soon as he sat down, Sydney came right to the point. "Your move. We need your numbers."

Ken obliged. "To execute your option to merge we have to have forty-five percent."

Poulter looked horrified. "How, the fuck, can you justify that!"

Ken's reply was calm, almost matter-of-fact in its tone. "Our current ownership of half the ground, the gaps in yours, and the history of our relationship."

Poulter made no attempt to conceal his feelings. "Damn it! Damn you! Do you want to kill the deal?"

Ken delivered his reply without emotion. "No, we would much rather reach an agreement. Remember, you don't have to exercise. You will only do so if there is a lot of orebody on our ground. And in that case, you will be glad to acquire it. We don't want this attempt to fail. Nor do you. As a public company you don't have a land package acceptable to a major. And sooner or later you will need a major to take on the heavy lifting."

Poulter's response lacked the earlier bluster. "Look, I can't go to our shareholders and tell them we have signed to give forty-five percent to a prospector with not a single drill hole on his property. Take thirty-nine and I think I can sell it."

The response came from Lester. "I don't think that would be acceptable, but it's time for us to retreat. We'll be back in a few minutes."

With that he and Ken left the room. Once the elevator doors had closed, the two men glanced at each other and each realized they shared satisfaction with the progress so far. Lester's comment was

Chapter 67 — Negotiation

first. "We're almost there. Now we counter. What do you want: forty two? Forty three?"

By this time they were in the foyer of the hotel.

"Round the block?" asked Ken.

Lester nodded.

Once outside, the chilly air encouraged a brisk pace.

Ken picked up the thread. "Forty-two. If it continues onto our ground he'll be able to sell it. I suppose we should insist on a couple of board seats."

Lester, amused at first and then serious, replied. "I'm not sure I would sit on one of Poulter's boards, but I agree that we should have the right to appoint. What about cash in the first two years?"

"That would be useful. Make the cash fifty the first year, then a hundred, forty-two percent of fully diluted on exercise, no cash calls on us of course. All subject to full agreement."

"Good. They should draw it up, but it's going to cost us quite a bit to have our lawyers dicker over the details."

"Let's do it."

They returned to the boardroom where, after some sputtering by Poulter, the atmosphere became focused towards reaching agreement. Half an hour later, they had agreed on a draft. The parting was respectful, just short of amicable.

"Time for a drink," suggested Lester as soon as they were alone.

"Yes," replied Ken, "and there are a few things to talk about."

In a less occupied and less noisy part of the bar, they found two comfortable chairs fronting a gas fireplace.

"I think that went about as well as we could have hoped," said Ken.

"Agreed. We'll soon see if he means what he said," replied the older man.

Ken pulled his chair closer to the table. "I have a lingering concern. Nothing we discussed. D'you remember the man I told you about who seemed to be spying on Poulter and me in Prince George?"

"I remember. You know, it could have been just coincidence."

"Yes, I've thought about that, but I am still haunted, if that's not too strong, by the look on Poulter's face when I told him I thought we had been followed. It was something approaching fear."

Lester, sipping his drink, thought for a while before responding. "We have to recognize that people like Poulter can have dealings with very nasty characters. At one level he is boss of his own little empire. But he may have someone yanking his chain when he steps out of line." And after more thought: "There is not much we can do about it, except to keep our noses clean, and have all the legals covered. Pending more evidence, I still think coincidence is the most likely explanation."

Neither having to drive anywhere that night, these two-thirds of the shareholders of 54924 B.C. Inc talked through dinner, and in the bar until it closed.

Chapter 68

All Clear
November

Sydney J. Poulter took a lot of satisfaction from sending out Dr. Praine's all-clear on the news wires. He had held it back while he was negotiating with Ken Wickford in Prince George and during the subsequent week while the preliminary agreement was being prepared. He now had two events to announce. Each warranted its own release. The two, in close sequence, would be particularly effective. Sydney was aware he would face criticism for the generous terms of his deal with Wickford, but his response would be that he had doubled Chilko's holdings. His company now held rights to acquire one hundred percent of claims covering some three kilometres along the apparent trend of the mineralization. Only if drilling indicated an orebody extending onto Wickford's ground would Chilko have to hand out all those shares. He felt no obligation to mention the old agreement that Wickford had produced as a threat to the core of Chilko's claims. He felt no animosity towards the prospector because he, Sydney J. Poulter, respected the use of all weapons in a hard fight. So now he could work on announcing the agreement. The timing looked good. The market was primed. The naysayers would have to retreat. He would show them.

That Tuesday Angus McKay was among the first to see the Chilko news release and among the many to follow the share price. Having put several of his clients into it after the salting scandal had first emerged, he relished the news of Dr. Praine's approval. It was both expected and welcome. With no need to buy or sell the stock, he could enjoy the moment.

This he did by phoning his friend Kevin. "Tuck, I owe you one."

Kevin laughed. "Yes. I guess you do. A lunch would be good. You see, all you have to do to make money in your line of business is to listen to a geologist!"

"Not so fast! You were right on target, but you were not using any geological know-how. Psychology would be closer. You understand Poulter. What's the trick?"

"Yeah. That helps. I doubt that he has any principles beyond his own best interests. But he's smart, so, as investors, we have to know where those interests lie. When push becomes shove, he won't bother about collateral damage. So we have to bet on him. And be alert enough to recognize a mistake, if he makes one."

"And you think he has a live one now? I mean is the deposit there?"

"I've been thinking that for some time. I think it is, but like any geologist, I always leave room for doubt."

"You take comfort from the report?"

"Oh, yes. The good Doctor Pain has made his pronouncement. That's major."

"You'll be asking me for more shares soon!"

Kevin chuckled. "I just might, but I'll wait for the excitement to subside."

"Got to go, Tuck. Someone else on the line. Has to be about Chilko."

"Okay, Angus."

The incoming call was indeed about Chilko.

On Wednesday morning, after the Chilko release, the price of its shares gapped from eighty cents to a dollar forty. The volume was heavy, and not just on the market. The phone lines were buzzing. At mid-morning, Angus McKay, who like most brokers had been at his desk since 6:00 am, was walking down Granville Street for a cup of coffee, thinking about his son's hockey practice that evening. Anyone in the mining business walking in the vicinity of Pender and Howe at that time of day could expect to see or meet someone else in the business. That's what happened as Angus was waiting to cross the street.

"Morning, Angus."

He turned to see Ted Bridgeman of Cuprick M & M. Ted was not a client, but the mining fraternity in Vancouver was small enough for any member to know most of the others. Knowing the network of who did what was one of the keys to success. In this

Chapter 68 — All Clear

case the two men were well acquainted. As they crossed the road together, Bridgeman opened what each hoped would be a useful exchange. "I trust you've got your clients well positioned with Poulter's latest?"

"Yes, indeed."

After reaching the sidewalk they stepped out of the stream of other pedestrians and continued their search for a few grains of truth that might add to each man's understanding of the Chilko story.

Angus restarted the conversation. "I was fortunate enough to bet on Poulter."

"At the beginning?"

"No, but after Slip hired Dr. Praine I knew that he would do so only if it was in his own interest. In other words, he knew something that I could only guess at."

"That was smart. Your clients were too. Smart enough to take on a real risk."

"That's right, but I was careful about who I got into it. They had to understand the game or I would steer them in another direction. I suppose Cuprick's following it closely."

"Oh, yes. Like any of the large miners, we have to follow a hot story like this one."

"And I suppose a big copper-gold in B.C. is just what you guys would like."

Bridgeman smiled. "That's a well-informed guess, Angus, but you wouldn't expect me to tell you just what we are looking for, would you?"

"You know, Ted, I just might. I know Cuprick keeps its ear to the ground and you never know when someone like me could have just that bit of information you need."

Ted Bridgeman looked at his watch and closed the conversation. "Okay, Angus. Give me a call when you've got the next one."

"That's a deal, Ted," was the response as the two men turned their separate ways.

The three shareholders of the numbered company were also following the market. They had convened Thursday morning at Lester's office to discuss the situation.

"Not bad for a one-day gain," commented Wally.

"Surprised?" asked Lester, looking at Ken.

"Not really. I've been all round that country. There are patches of mineral everywhere. I suppose the drill holes didn't have to hit but, if Poulter was concealing anything at that first meeting in Prince George, he would have to have been a good actor. I'm relieved, not surprised."

Wally voiced the important conclusion. "So if Chilko exercises the option and shares continue to be worth this much, we'll be rich!"

"And you, Ken," said Lester, "will be extremely rich."

Wally quantified: "Tens of millions!"

"And you'll be in serious danger!" said Lester, feigning a look of serious concern.

Ken threw a puzzled glance at Lester who continued. "Rich and single. They'll all be after you!"

"And he won't know if it's him or his money they love," added Wally, laughing. "What will you do if you don't have to work, Ken?"

"I have lots of interests, books and travel among them. But first I have to close that file on my grandpa's obligation."

Lester nodded slowly, Wally looked puzzled.

Ken continued. "You know. The percentage for the Indian who found it. I didn't even know his full name until I got that package from London, but I've always known the Raven claim was named after someone."

"You really feel you've got to do that?" said Wally. A second later, he added, "He can't be alive any more."

Ken took time to respond, feeling his way as he spoke. "Yes, I do. It's a sort of debt. It can't be ignored. You see, my grandfather had an obligation that I'm sure he would have honoured if he'd been able. I have benefited from his claims, and I am now able to fix what my grandfather couldn't. My grandfather owed something. I owe my grandfather. Therefore I owe Raven or his family something. I want to close the circle."

No one said anything until Ken, a lighter expression on his face, said, "Don't worry, Wally, you don't have to contribute."

But Lester wanted to know more. "How will you do it?"

"I'll try to find his name and whether he is still alive, but I don't expect that will lead anywhere. But I should be able to find out where most of the native people who worked on the Bulkley Valley farms came from. Raven must have come from a reserve or his interest could have been registered. Finding where that was

Chapter 68 — All Clear

or is shouldn't be too hard. Then some sort of scholarship fund is probably the way to go."

"I'm with you on all that," said Lester, "but don't ask Poulter to join you. He wouldn't understand."

His commitment explained, Ken was feeling more relaxed than he'd felt in a while. "You know, I'm not sure you're right on that one. He just might. But his assistant—he's the one who wouldn't begin to understand." Then he added, "As for the rest of the money, I really don't know what to do with it yet. But there's plenty of time. I might even find that Jill would put up with me again if I won't have to work so hard."

Wally and Lester murmured approval but Ken's mind was taken over for a moment by the image of Helen, vivacious, attractive, and ... until it was quickly pushed off the screen by Wally's voice.

"You know, Marge was saying just a week ago that she thought that it was a real possibility."

Ken put his hands in the air and rolled his eyes. "I give up. What's a guy to do when the women start predicting his future!"

Chapter 69
─────────

Missing

November

When he arrived at his office ten days after returning from Prince George, Sydney Poulter's first words to Marion had touch of urgency, "Any news of Victor?"

"Nothing."

"He was due back the day I left for Prince George. That was a week ago last Monday. Now it's Wednesday. Where is he?"

"We just don't know. I phoned his home again yesterday and got no reply."

Sydney looked angry and then puzzled. "That's odd. For all his faults, that's out of character."

Marion nodded. "I agree. The only contact I have is his mother somewhere in Ontario, but I thought it too soon to start alarming her."

"All right. Put that on the agenda for early tomorrow."

Along with many others' in the industry, Slip's optimism about the market's reaction was well justified. On the day after the second release, the stock rose to a dollar ninety.

After checking the price mid-morning, Marion called to her boss as he passed through her office, "Seems you called it right in making that agreement with Wickford."

"Thanks, Marion. It does indeed." Then, after taking a few more steps towards his own office, he stopped and, facing Marion, added, "You know, I've a hunch that there was never enough volume when the price really went low for the shorts to buy back. Those that didn't could really get hurt."

Marion replied in her usual, calm manner. "That could be bad for us."

Chapter 69 — Missing

"Yes, Marion. It could get rough."

That afternoon Marion's voice came through Sydney's intercom. "Call is for you. It's Sergeant Trevelyan of the RCMP."

Poulter picked up the phone and, after listening for a while without comment, said, "Oh! When was that?" Then, "Yes. We can do that. Everyone. 3:30 pm. I'll make the arrangements."

Two hours later, all Chilko personnel not in the field were assembled in the boardroom. Mr. Poulter introduced the Sergeant, who began by saying, "Thank you all for being here at such short notice. As you have may have concluded, it concerns your missing colleague, Mr. Victor Dubell." The policeman paused to look around at his hushed audience. "I regret to have to tell you that he may have been involved in a serious accident. He has not been found, but we have located his car. It was in the Similkameen River. It must have left the road at considerable speed. We believe it happened sometime on Sunday night. The car was mostly submerged. The doors were shut but there was no person or body in the car. "

Tanya, who had a habit of saying what she was thinking when others would have held back, raised her hand. "I saw him just before he went on vacation. He looked stressed to the limit. I have never seen anyone in quite that state."

The sergeant's next words took everyone by surprise. "I have to tell you, all of you, that it was not an accident. The tires were shot out."

It was some thirty seconds before anyone said anything. Len broke the silence and asked the question for everyone. "Foul play?"

The policeman gave his answer with a dispassionate, neutral expression. "We don't know. We're keeping all possibilities open at this stage in the investigation."

A murmur rippled through the room as everyone adjusted to his or her understanding of the situation.

Poulter asked, "Is all this public knowledge?"

The policeman looked at his watch. "In just under ten minutes, it will be made public. We informed next of kin this morning. I now have a request. I am sure you will all understand why. I would like to spend some time with each of you, one on one. I have only a few questions. I don't think it will take more than five minutes each. You are under no obligation to be interviewed, but I ask for your help in the belief that what you tell me could help our investigation. I should also say that we have no reason to believe that any of you is in danger."

No one declined to be interviewed. Each person left after the interview was complete. By 5:00 pm the office was empty.

Chapter 70

Later

1988

A few months after the option to acquire all of the Wickford claims had been signed, Chilko announced that drilling had shown that the copper-gold mineralization extended onto the Wickford ground. This was followed by a merging of Chilko with the private company and a private placement for two million dollars at twenty cents above what had been the market price for almost a month. The stock increased in price by a further twenty cents for a few days before settling back to a dollar eighty-five, five cents below its former price. Within a month, Chilko had engaged a second drill to work the optioned claims. When four of the first five holes to be drilled on the optioned property delivered similar grades and intercept lengths to those on the Chilko ground, the market indicated that it recognized the significance, and the stock rose another fifty cents. In early summer, Chilko announced an impressive tonnage at grades significantly higher than any open pits being mined in the province. By this time the stock, benefiting from the attention of a different class of shareholder, was now above three dollars, a price that made both Sydney Poulter and Ken Wickford wealthy men. It became inevitable that Chilko would be taken over by an operating company capable of raising the capital required to bring such an orebody to production.

1989

Ken Wickford was one of many shareholders who tendered their shares to Cuprick Mining & Smelting's offer of four dollars and ten cents. In the early summer of 1989, soon after the Cuprick takeover, Ken accepted an invitation from Ted Bridgeman of Cuprick Mining & Smelting to see what was happening on the claims that used to be his. Getting there was easier than it used to be. He sat in the front of the helicopter, next to the pilot, with Ted, now Cuprick's vice president of exploration, sitting behind him. Moments after taking off from the base, the machine headed south to gain altitude before approaching the mountainous country to the north. A few minutes later the pilot nosed the plane north towards the hills. As they flew just above the pine forest, Ken thought of the many times he had trudged up the same hills. They climbed, the forest thinned out, and the remaining trees became smaller. At the upper elevations most of the trees were concentrated in gullies and on north-facing slopes. At around 5,000 feet the trees, except for a few stunted and windswept pines, yielded to grass, scree slopes and craggy cliffs. In less than ten minutes they had covered a distance which used to take him most of a day on foot. He thought of his grandfather having to journey for three weeks to reach the same ground.

Then he heard Ted on the intercom. "You will recognize that we are now over the ground you staked. We know the mineralization continues to where that dozer is and that the pit will be almost a mile in length and half a mile wide. Hard to believe, isn't it?"

A minute later he continued: "We'll land on that ridge and walk down to the drill, if that is okay with you. Probably take us about half an hour, but there are some things I want to show you."

"That's fine," said Ken, enjoying the comfort of the helicopter and the majesty of the view beneath him. "I'd like that."

But his thoughts were on the future pit that was now emerging in the minds of Ted and his colleagues. Ken was in silent conversation with himself: A pit that large? Here? Although no stranger to open pit mines and their size, it was hard to comprehend one covering so much of this ground, ground with which he was so familiar. As the landscape he knew well flowed beneath him, he imagined how it was going to be transformed. Gone would be the patches of timber, grassy knolls and outcrops he'd often hiked through. Spoil all this? But that's what I—no, we—have been working towards. That estimate in the paper, what were the numbers? They said hundreds of millions into the B.C. economy. All those people, drillers, miners, shopkeepers, truckers, even the government. Oh, yes, shareholders too. What to do with my shares?

His thoughts flashed back and forth from the past, to the future and back, to days spent alone in the hills, dump trucks spiralling their way round a huge hole in the ground, his grandfather

Chapter 70 — Later

arranging expeditions, wealth beyond his dreams, mule trains, a tunnel driven with black powder.

Then he heard Ted ask the pilot to swing to the left and head west. Once on this path, with the afternoon sun ahead, Ken had a fine view of a grader working on a road. Looking beyond it, he recognized the place where he and Will had had their encounter with the bear. Farther to his left he could just make out the spoil from the tunnel where Carl had been hurt and could so easily have been killed.

His thoughts then turned to being a wealthy man—yachts? No. Cars? No. Would his children benefit? Probably, but there were hazards ahead. He and Jill would steer them clear of those. Now that he had returned to family life, he realized how much he had missed it. His reverie was broken by the voice in his headset. It was the pilot asking where to land.

Ted knew exactly where he wanted to go. "That ridge right ahead and just above us. Could you pick us up at the pad?"

"Can do," replied the pilot. "How long will you be?"

"Give us an hour."

"That's fine. I'll have time to get some fuel."

Ken went back to his thoughts. Life, always a challenge, was becoming more complicated.

The machine landed on a grassy ridge flanked by some scrubby pine. Ken had said he would welcome the short walk with Ted, but just now he would have preferred to be alone with his thoughts.

Some four miles north of the Nisselinka claims a sow bear and two yearling cubs were exploring new territory. Because of noises to which they were not accustomed, they were leaving the only land any of them had ever known, land that the sow had always occupied and defended when necessary. The cubs would stay with their mother for another year, perhaps two. Then they would have to look after themselves. On a grassy slope a mile to the west of the migrants a seven hundred pound male bear, a silver-tip grizzly, raised his head to sniff the wind from the east. Whatever he smelt prompted him to start down the hill with evident purpose. Every few yards he stopped to sniff the wind again. Then he continued in the same direction. This was, after all, his territory.

Helen had followed the progress of Chilko in the newspapers. The possibility of a mine in the remote wilderness of central British Columbia, something she had been concerned about for years, was becoming real. Headlines such as "Drilling Continues at Nisselinka" filled her with foreboding. When she had learned of the Cuprick take-over, she realized the mine site was almost certain to become an open pit and that there was no more she or the organization she worked for could do to stop it. The most disturbing news had been that the mine was going to be large. She visualized the removal of timber covering square kilometres, the destruction of habitat for animals and birds, a huge hole in the ground, roads, tailing dams, dump trucks, noises and fumes.

On several occasions she had picked up the phone to the Greenpeace office in Vancouver and discussed whether the mine could be stopped and what measures they could take. Blocking roads had worked on Vancouver Island. They agreed that they were unlikely to get support in the local communities of Smithers or Prince George and that their best chances lay with the citizens of Vancouver, Toronto, and perhaps Europe.

But the chance meeting in the Smithers restaurant had taken the edge off her drive to stop this destruction. Since then, she and Ken had met a few times. It had been seventeen years since they had parted, but she had never quite forgotten their time together. Nor, it seemed, had he.

Doug and Marlene Barrett were enjoying a meal they did not have to cook. They had gone to one of the better restaurants in the neighbouring town, 100 Mile House, to celebrate a big event. Having put nearly all their savings in starting a motel and restaurant and having looked bankruptcy in the face a year ago, they had now paid back most of the bank loan. "It picked up just like that. I still can't understand it," said Marlene.

"Well, that's mining for you. It comes and goes. They came in time for us," replied Doug.

"Cheers!"

Less than a year after the accident and his passive participation in the medivac, Carl announced his intention to become a pilot. He and his uncle were back in the office of Nisselinka Helicopters, which Will had founded with the proceeds of his mining investment. In addition to his interest in flying, Carl had become curious about his ancestry and his relatives in Europe. Hanging out with his uncle gave him the opportunity to get more information. His uncle was glad to provide it. Carl knew that his grandfather on his mother's side had served in the First World War in a German

Chapter 70 — Later

infantry regiment, and that he had survived. But now he learned that two of Grandfather's brothers had not survived the war and that their names were inscribed on a memorial somewhere, but Will did not know where. "I'd like to go there sometime, meet my cousins, and see the memorial," Carl said.

Will Herman nodded his head slowly. "And so would I. Ken was talking about doing the same at the Canadian memorials. Let's talk about combining our trips to that part of the world."

When the stock price reached four dollars Sydney Poulter had appeared to his employees to be more relaxed. He ceased to be the first into the office every day and would frequently leave early. Although accustomed to a comfortable income, he took great pleasure and substantial satisfaction from his newfound wealth. But this period of contentment was shaken by the consequences of a routine medical examination. His doctor arranged for tests. This led to more tests and then to an appointment with a specialist who told him that the results confirmed the cancer his doctor had suspected.

Sydney took the news with equanimity. He asked about the treatment and the chances of success. He learned that the treatment would be unpleasant, that he would have to take two or three months off work, and that the chances of success were no more than sixty percent. The oncologist recommended starting radiation as soon as possible, but Sydney said that he had some things he had to do first.

Anyone following Sydney Poulter on his first day in Hamburg would have wondered what the man was looking at or looking for. After the first five days in the German city he had walked along several streets, some of them many times. He stopped only twice, once at a café and the other time at a dingy restaurant. He'd proceeded at a slow pace, looking around as he walked. At other times he'd gazed at the buildings. Often he would turn around, apparently to see the street and its buildings from another direction.

He recognized nothing. Nor did he expect to. It had been most of a lifetime since he had seen it and it had been very different then.

After ten days in Hamburg, and still travelling alone, Sydney Poulter took the daytime flight across the Atlantic to Montreal. He didn't like flying, but going first class lessened the tension.

The next day, after a leisurely breakfast in a comfortable hotel, he climbed into the cab that the hotel bell hop had whistled up. Leaning forward he handed the driver a piece of paper on which he had written an address. Two blocks beyond a stretch of mid-market, residential housing, the taxi stopped. They were at the entrance to a building whose function was almost as evident as its Victorian age. He went through a small door set into one of a pair of large metal gates. On the left was a door labelled "Bureau de Reception". In response to a greeting in French from a young Quebecoise sitting behind an oak desk, he gave his name and said that he had come to see Madame Tremblay. After consulting some notes on her desk, the young lady confirmed that he was indeed expected. Within a few minutes a grey-haired woman entered the room. Sydney could tell from her demeanour that she occupied a position of authority.

"Monsieur Poulter?"

"C'est moi," replied Sydney.

"Bienvenue. Je m'appelle Monique Tremblay. Vous parlez Francais, or would you prefer English?"

"It's over thirty years since I spoke French. I have forgotten most of it. English would be preferable."

"Very well. Like most of us in this town, I am comfortable in both languages."

"Thank you," replied Sydney.

"I was, of course, very pleased to get your letter," said Madame Tremblay. "We have some funding from the government, but the gifts we get make a great difference. Would you like me to show you around?"

"I'd just like to see the dormitories and the dining room," replied Sydney.

After half an hour of touring the facilities, and after seeing perhaps a hundred uniformed boys in the hallways going from one room to another, he and Madame Tremblay took seats at a small round table, one of a few items of inexpensive furniture, in her office.

"Mr. Poulter, when someone says they want to make a donation, we look for their name on the list of those who used to attend this institution. I could not find your name anywhere."

Sydney smiled and replied: "You were correct to assume that I used to be here, but I changed my name shortly after leaving."

"Ah, that explains it," said the lady.

Chapter 70 — Later

"I wanted something that sounded more Canadian."

"Others have done that too. We try to keep our records up to date. Would you care to tell me your former name?"

Sydney replied, looking beyond Madame Tremblay as if she were part of an audience he was addressing. "Maybe ... eventually ... but not just now. But I would like to make a donation, as I mentioned in my letter."

"That would, indeed, be very welcome."

Sydney pulled an envelope from the breast pocket of his jacket. It was an unmarked white envelope with the flap tucked in, not sealed. He handed it across the table.

"Thank you, Mr. Poulter. Would you like me to open it now or later?"

"I would take some satisfaction from knowing how you will use the money. In fact I would appreciate an opportunity to influence how it will be spent."

Madame Tremblay opened the envelope and looked at the only content—a cheque. She stared at it for a long time as if pondering how to respond before saying, "Mr. Poulter. This is very, very generous." Then, after a pause, she continued, "We are not accustomed to gifts of this magnitude and just how we will use it will require much discussion."

Sydney replied: "I am sure you will make good use of it." Then he said: "I have to be going now, as I have a plane to catch this evening."

"Back to Vancouver? I hope you have a good flight."

"Thank you."

"Let me phone a taxi. May I put you on the list to receive our monthly newsletter?"

"Thank you, but not this year."

About the Author

ROBERT LONGE, an avid reader with an interest in history, has worked in mineral exploration for many years as a geologist, consultant, and chief executive of a junior public company. His own experiences searching for mineral deposits in many parts of the world convinced him that the industry, much of it based in Vancouver, provides enough excitement, unique characters and engrossing situations for an entire genre of novels.

The Nisselinka Claims is his contribution.

CPSIA information can be obtained at www.ICGtesting.com
Printed in the USA
LVOW07s1040030615
440980LV00002B/21/P